I0819108

Praise for Camilla Bruce's previous novels

AT THE BOTTOM OF THE GARDEN

"All the elegance and all the venom, like one of E. Nesbit's supernatural stories served with a side of arsenic."

—Grady Hendrix, *New York Times* bestselling author of *Witchcraft for Wayward Girls*

"The combination of creepy folk-horror notes and tense, gory, and haunting scenes conjures plenty of scares. Readers will want to sleep with the lights on."

—*Publishers Weekly*

"Camilla Bruce tills the macabre for all of its Edward Gorey glory, cultivating one gorgeously morbid gothic novel that's just as gleeful as it is gashlycrumb. At the bottom of this particular garden you will find a wicked sense of humor that harkens back to the best of Roald Dahl's *Tales of the Unexpected,* with all its vicious thorns intact."

—Clay McLeod Chapman, author of *What Kind of Mother* and *Ghost Eaters*

"A classic example of gothic horror . . . Never manipulative but genuinely cathartic, *At the Bottom of the Garden* is a story of two children coping with the dissolution of their entire world, and discovering a new one in the process."

—*BookPage*

"Camilla Bruce writes dark fantasy like no one else out there. A gothic masterpiece, *At the Bottom of the Garden* is a propulsive novel with gorgeous prose and incredible characters you won't soon forget. You'll never look at the wicked stepmothers of fairy tales quite the same way again. Put this book at the top of your TBR pile immediately; you won't regret it."

—Gwendolyn Kiste, Bram Stoker Award–winning author of *Reluctant Immortals* and *The Haunting of Velkwood*

"The audience will crow to watch the deliciously awful Clara get her comeuppance, as her not-so-friendly ghosts do everything they can to make her even more miserable than she already is. . . . Mystery and thriller fans will find a lot to love in this romp through the ectoplasm."

—*Kirkus Reviews*

"Wonderful spooky, rich in intrigue and full of surprise, *At the Bottom of the Garden* is the excellent Camilla Bruce at her absolute best."

—Laird Hunt, author of *In the House in the Dark of the Woods*

"At once supernatural, paranormal, and homicidal, its surly vibe will have mood-readers in a ghastly state in no time."

—*Fangoria*

"Bruce's unique cast of characters is both charming and terrifying. A young synesthetic musician, an even younger sensitive, a murderous aunt, and a houseful of furious ghosts—it's all here! A delightful read."

—Louisa Morgan, author of *A Secret History of Witches*

YOU LET ME IN

"Creepy, pagan, detailed, entrancing . . . I loved it."

—Joanne Harris, author of *Chocolat* and *The Strawberry Thief*

"A bewitching, beguiling, and deeply unsettling tale . . . It will ensnare you from page one and keep you riveted until the end."

—Caitlin Starling, author of *The Luminous Dead*

"Haunting and harrowing, the kind of fairy tale that keeps you up at night because the monsters are real . . . I couldn't look away."

—Alix E. Harrow, *New York Times* bestselling author of *Starling House*

"A relentless, heartbreaking exploration of isolation, grooming, and the cycles of abuse that pursue the vulnerable."

—Sarah Gailey, author of *Magic for Liars*

"An enthralling story, a genre-blender that perplexes . . . superb."

—*Booklist* (starred review)

IN THE GARDEN OF SPITE

"An amazing book—riveting and heartbreaking . . . I couldn't put it down."

—Karen Kilgariff and Georgia Hardstark, #1 *New York Times* bestselling authors of *Stay Sexy & Don't Get Murdered*

"A chilling, pitch-perfect novel that should finally make Belle Gunness a household name . . . a superb and unforgettable read."

—Deanna Raybourn, *New York Times* bestselling author of *A Murderous Relation*

"Mesmerizing . . . Fans of fictionalized treatments of notorious murderers will be fascinated."

—*Publishers Weekly* (starred review)

"Extraordinary . . . Bruce does a marvelous job of reimagining this real-life murderer, without excusing her crimes."

—*The Times* (London)

THE WITCH IN THE WELL

"A startling and original plot is woven around a cast of gleefully unpleasant characters—I was gripped from the very first page."

—Lucie McKnight Hardy, author of *Water Shall Refuse Them*

"A compelling, creepy story of angst, obsessions and lost friendship."

—*BookPage*

"Bruce masterfully plays with perceptions of reality, truth, and magic. It's a uniquely told and riveting read."

—*BuzzFeed*

"[This is] a superb folk horror tale that delivers an imaginative feminist take on the historical persecution of witches through the conflicting viewpoints of three complex and at times believably unlikeable female protagonists."

—*Toronto Star*

ALL THE BLOOD WE SHARE

"Chilling, terrifying, utterly addictive . . . a beautifully written, spellbinding read."

—Karen Coles, author of *The Asylum*

"A horrifyingly realistic view into the minds of a serial killing family that really tormented the old West."

—*BuzzFeed*

"A riveting portrait of the dark side of the American dream."

—*Publishers Weekly* (starred review)

BY CAMILLA BRUCE

You Let Me In

In the Garden of Spite

The Witch in the Well

All the Blood We Share

At the Bottom of the Garden

The Temptation of Charlotte North

the temptation of charlotte north

the temptation of charlotte north

CAMILLA BRUCE

new york

Del Rey
An imprint of Random House
A division of Penguin Random House LLC
1745 Broadway, New York, NY 10019
randomhousebooks.com
penguinrandomhouse.com

A Del Rey Trade Paperback Original

ISBN 978-0-593-72497-2
Ebook ISBN 978-0-593-72498-9

Printed in the United States of America

1st Printing

BOOK TEAM: Production editor: Christa Guild • Managing editor: Paul Gilbert • Production manager: Ali Wagner • Copy editor: Martha Schwartz • Proofreaders: Megha Jain, Lara Kennedy

The authorized representative in the EU for product safety and compliance is Penguin Random House Ireland, Morrison Chambers, 32 Nassau Street, Dublin D02 YH68, Ireland. https://eu-contact.penguin.ie

For the girls

the temptation of charlotte north

THE ISLAND OF MARGARET'S KEEP, 1910

·1·

charlotte

The shed is a terrible place to be—a rectangular box of dirty gray wood where I have spent far too many of my days. Mother locks me in here for any perceived infraction—of which there are many. Especially of late, now that I am seventeen and no longer a child. Now that I desire things that go against her wishes.

My mother has a will of steel, but sadly for her, so do I.

At least the boards are set far enough apart that some daylight spills inside, painting a golden cage on the floor. There are shelves on the walls loaded with things that will not fit anywhere else, like a bucket of grease, wool shears, three coils of rope, and a tin box heaped with rusty nails. From hooks on the walls hang several dusty overalls, and a pair of boots with holes in them resides on the floor underneath. There are no lamps and no candles—no light at all save for the bars on the floor and what little sneaks inside through the single window set high up on the wall, though it is laced with spider-webs and covered in grime and salt. The walls, too, are coated in the taste and smell of the sea. Even the air is saturated with brine; and if I listen, I can hear it, too: the rise and fall of the waves. Not even the clucking of the chickens in the barn next door can compete with the wash against the stones. I am used to it, though; we all are. Margaret's Keep is not a large island—only five miles across at its widest point and three hundred and fifty souls year-round. We barely even notice the sea. It is only in here, in the shed, that it comes rising from the back of my head to the front of my mind, and I can hear every breath it takes clearly.

I try to match its rhythm with my exhales.

The door to the shed is a flimsy thing; hastily thrown together from thin boards and hinged. Looking at it, you would think it would be easy to break through—just a well-aimed kick and it would splinter. I am sad to say that it is not so. I have tried it many times before. It is sturdier than it looks, and the padlock on the outside is vicious and heavy, hanging proudly like a medal on an officer's chest. Only Mother has the key to open it, and she keeps it safely tucked away.

When I was younger, I would often cry and bang uselessly on the door whenever Mother locked me up. I would beg on my knees to be let out, threatening Mother with all sorts of damage if she did not immediately open the door. I no longer beg or threaten. I have long since learned that such is fruitless. But I am far too old now to be punished in this way. I suppose that is why a new set of feelings has entered my rage: shame and humiliation at being treated in this way, and for no good reason at all. I can see it in my sisters' eyes, in our housekeeper's, and even in Father's, when I am finally let back inside. They all know that the shed is no longer a suitable punishment.

Their disapproval will not change Mother's mind, though. She will do as she pleases, and then blame *me* for it happening in the first place: *If only you hadn't . . . If only you were . . . If only you could . . .*

But clearly I can *not,* or else I would not find myself here, over and over again, locked in this terrible ramshackle shed with nothing but flies—and the sea—for company. The shed even haunts my sleep. For as long as I can remember, I have had horrible dreams about being trapped—staggering around like a bear in a cage, bellowing for my release.

The cage never relents, though. Its salt-crusted walls stand firm.

It takes seven steps to cross the length of the floor: *one, two, three, four* . . . After seven I knock on the wall three times before turning back again. It serves no purpose, but I have done this ever since I was a child, to pass the time and numb my mind.

One, two, three, four, five, six, seven . . . knock, knock, knock.

One, two, three, four, five, six, seven . . . knock, knock, knock.

When I was a little girl, they kept coal in the shed, and I would use it to draw on the walls: human figures and mazes mostly—I was taken with the latter as a child. Perhaps in my young mind I needed to believe that there was always a way out, no matter where I was trapped. My hands were black with filth when I was done. I can still see my artwork some places in here: faint outlines etched deep into the wood. Mother caught me doing it once and made me wipe off the coal using a wet rag. It did not truly work and you could still see misty ghosts of my figures, which only enraged her further. They did not keep coal in the shed after that.

Back in my drawing days, "mischief" had been what got me in trouble—or that was what Mother called it anyway. I cannot recall much of it, except for Mother's anger when we passed by the graveyard, which was often enough. When I was very young, I thought I used to see people in there: wispy souls drifting between the graves. They appeared so real to me that I would sometimes wave or even talk to them. I remember once following the misty specter of an old woman between the withered stones. Though she looked as if she was eighty years old, she ran like a colt in spring with the young me hot on her heels. I remember the lady looking back, laughing—and I was laughing, too. But then the happy chase was interrupted by Mother, grabbing my neck in a steel grip and yanking me out of my fantasy. I recall drawing the old woman when I got home, right here on this wall. As I grew older, I stopped seeing them, so maybe Mother was right, and it was only a quirk of my youthful mind. Still, it seemed a harsh punishment just for having a lively imagination. I suppose it is a fear of the irrational that makes parents behave in such a way.

Later, it was other infractions that landed me in the shed, like when I threw my new dress into the fire in Father's study because I did not want to attend a dinner, or when I stole Mother's watercolors and threw them in the sea to punish her for speaking harshly to me. Another time, it was because I cut off my braids so that I could be a boy and not have to do any needlework. I do admit those were acts of mischief.

More recently, it has been a man that has put me in here—one that I have grown to love, though I am told I should not. The first time I saw him, he came to dinner with his pretty wife. It was just a few days after they had arrived on Margaret's Keep, and we were all on our best behavior. Back then, I had found the new reverend to be handsome but dreadfully boring—a man of no consequence to me. He and Father had spoken of the island as we ate our fish and glazed pears, while Mother tried to entertain Mrs. Hill—though the latter barely said a word all through the meal. I had mostly thought of other things and waited for the dinner to be over.

For three years after that, I thought very little of Jasper Hill, although I could not help but notice how our new clergy—young and energetic—seemed determined to breathe fresh life into our small church. Among his efforts was the children's choir, set to practice every Monday, and he needed a volunteer to help him lead it. It did not even occur to me to offer. I am as musical as a bay horse and find most psalms tiresome, but Mother was present for the announcement as well and—tired of seeing me around the house now that my schooling was done—she figured it was a *splendid* idea for me to have something noble to do with my time. I agreed only reluctantly, and only out of boredom. I sat through my last lessons in the schoolhouse at fifteen, and when the question of the children's choir came up, I had already turned sixteen, so a change was admittedly in order.

The choir was small, with only seven children, and one of them was my youngest sister, Sophie. The fact that Jasper Hill was at the rehearsals, too, accompanying the songs on the piano, was of no importance to me. I dutifully did as I had been instructed and taught the children how to perform in such a way that it did not hurt the ear. Whatever he and I said to each other had only to do with music.

I suppose it was a slow thing, like bread dough rising. After six months, by the time the choir was ready to give its first Sunday performance, the reverend and I were laughing together, and quite often stayed behind after practice to exchange frank opinions on the day's work. We spoke of other things, too, like ourselves and the island. To my surprise, I found him to be amusing—*funny* even.

He said that we had become friends—that he was *happy* to be my friend—but it did not feel like a friendship to me. Rather it felt like something warmer and sweeter—something that grew bigger every day, until it had become this unwieldy thing that I could not keep contained. It was something about how our eyes met and held whenever we spoke. How neither of us wanted to look away. How his hand would gently land on mine when we sat next to each other in a pew, listening to the children—or rest on my shoulder when we rifled through sheets of music together.

I sensed that he wanted to be close to me—and I wanted to be close to him, too. I felt like he truly listened when I spoke, and that my opinion was valuable to him. We understood each other so well and laughed together often. I do not laugh much normally; it is not entirely approved of in my mother's house. But with Jasper Hill, I did. We laughed about little things mostly—like how Lillian Fisher sounded like a squeaking mouse when trying to reach the high notes. Other times we laughed for no reason at all, but only because it felt good. Jasper Hill said that laughing was celebrating life, and I *felt* that, too, when I laughed with him.

Soon, I thought of Jasper Hill all the time: when I walked on the beach, when I embroidered a flower, when I lay in bed at night . . .

Especially when I lay in bed at night, and was certain that my sister had fallen asleep on the other side of the room. Then I would think of Jasper Hill as my hands dipped under the covers, and I touched myself where I felt it the most. I imagined that he, in his bed at the clergy house, touched himself in the same way, thinking of me, too. Sometimes I did not stop before the sweetness overflowed, and left me shattered in a million pieces.

It felt like I was *with* him then, in the darkness of my room.

I started leaving him small gifts in the vestry after practice. It was nothing much—just a few caramels or fresh cookies from the kitchen, wrapped in cloth and tied with a bow, or a posy of flowers, gleaned from the greenhouse. Violets, mostly. All innocent gifts—no more than that anyone else with a heartfelt appreciation for our reverend might do. Mrs. Hill, though, must have the nose of a bloodhound sniffing out foxes in her chicken coop, because she *knew*. As soon as she stumbled upon those foil-wrapped caramels, she *knew*. I learned later—through our housekeeper, Mary Boden, whose aunt Noreen is employed at the clergy house—that the Hills had a terrible argument after those caramels were found. One that had lasted long into the night.

"I am so sorry, Charlotte," Jasper Hill had said on the following Monday. "I have to ask you to retire from the children's choir. It certainly is a shame, since you have done good work here over the past year, but the gifts you have given me . . . they are not *seemly*." I could tell that he did not believe his own words, that another person had put them in his mouth. After all, how could one find fault in simple caramels or fresh flowers?

Mrs. Hill must have spoken to Mother, too, because the latter was *furious* with me, and the Hills never came to dinner again. I had made things awkward.

I did not appreciate being blamed, though, for something not entirely my fault. So instead of quelling my feelings, the dismissal only added indignation to the mix, which made the brew even stronger than before. It has been three months now, and I still love Jasper Hill. And from the expression in his eyes when he looks at me, I know he is not indifferent either.

"You are utterly shameless," Mother accused me today as we made our way home from church in the chilly spring air. She, my sisters, and I had walked the dusty road like a murder of crows, all dressed in black, as is the island's Sunday custom. Sophie, the youngest, had a black ribbon in her cornsilk hair and walked two steps ahead of the rest of us. Adelaide had been crying because there was a spot on her nose that made it turn bright red. She soothed herself by sucking on one of her blond braids—a habit Mother intensely abhorred. My older sister, Evelyn, walked with her back ramrod straight and her dark hair hidden under one of Mother's hats, set with flowers and berries of wax, trying to look grown-up now that she is engaged to be wed. Seen from behind, she and Mother look almost the same these days, which is certainly fitting, since Evelyn has always taken care of us other three. Of all of my sisters, Evelyn is the one that looks the most like me, with the same curly, nearly black hair. I am shorter than her, though, and fuller of figure. My sisters have all inherited Mother's slim build, while I received mine from someone unknown. I do not mind, though, since it makes me appear more like a woman, which Mother in turn finds bothersome.

"How can you behave like that? *Preening* in front of him," she hissed at me today. It felt utterly unfair. All I had done was look at him, and you *should* look at the priest when in church. The wind had caught the fat, black plumes of Mother's hat, and made them flicker like the wings of a dying cormorant. We walked the same path as we always did, snaking along the cliff. Below us, the sea roared, foamed, and danced. On the other side of us, sheep grazed blissfully. We lifted our heavy skirts to keep them off the dust, and as we passed Margaret's Tower, we all averted our eyes. The weathered stone walls had nothing to teach us but shame and misery, Mother always said. Local legend held that a woman—Margaret—had once been imprisoned there, as the sole resident of the island. Some of the locals claimed it was because she was a witch, but my family told a different tale: that it was her punishment for committing adultery. As big a sin as any in my mother's eyes, and doubtlessly the reason she was so upset with me, for drawing the attention of a married man.

Not that marriage appears to make him happy. The reverend always seems quiet and wary around his tepid wife. And not that marriage makes Mother happy either: I have never seen her content, and she and Father frequently argue. So, either marriage is not as wonderful as its reputation, or people wed the wrong person. Perhaps marriage should not be the only path, but I suppose God had his reasons for making it so.

I wonder if the reverend ever laments its existence.

"We should have taken the carriage," Adelaide complained on the road, when the wind threw dust in her eyes and made her cry again.

"Father wanted to ride," Evelyn replied. I figured he was already home by then, smoking by the fire, a topped-up glass in his hand, both his feet well rested, enjoying the time free of my mother. The scent of roast from the kitchen was surely tickling his broad, red nose.

"Making *eyes* at the reverend is *not* how a young lady behaves," Mother continued, refusing to be derailed.

"Not here," Evelyn hissed. "People can see." I knew that she only said it to save me. It is a particular skill of hers to always find the right thing to say to dissolve Mother's fury—or at least temper it some—and this time was no exception. Mother, who abhors a spectacle, would certainly not risk being the cause of one. She started walking again and said no more, though her eyes were still narrowed with fury, and her cheeks had turned quite red, so I knew already then that I was headed for the shed.

It is certainly not the first time Jasper Hill has landed me in here, so the ritual has become familiar. Over the years, I have found ways to occupy myself, and know all the best places for spying on my surroundings.

If I look out between the boards of the back wall, I see windswept fields of grass all the way to the sea. Sometimes a sheep or two veers into my vision. If I crane my neck, I can see Margaret's Tower rising like a rotten finger, reaching toward the sky. If I crane my neck even farther and squint, I can see the church spire, too: a black spear rising just as high as the tower. Even farther out, on an islet of its own, stands the lighthouse, but I cannot see that far from the shed.

When I look out on the other side, by the door, I can see the stables and the carriage shed on the opposite side of the yard—low buildings constructed of rock and wood, like most houses on the island. To my right is our home: two stories high and the largest on Margaret's Keep, made entirely of precious wood. It is supposed to be white, and Father has it repainted every summer, but by the time spring arrives, it is always shedding. The wind and the salt take their toll. Only the red front door seems to always survive the winter, gleaming like a ripe sweet berry. Perhaps we should have painted the whole house red.

Next to the shed is the barn, and below our house sits the island's only store, which Father owns, and the small harbor where the fishing trawlers come in to unload, which Father also owns. Next to it is the red-painted building where the fish are taken in, gutted, and salted in barrels to be sold on the mainland. Father owns that as well. Father owns most of the island, and most of the trawlers, too. Almost everyone on Margaret's Keep owes their livelihood to Father. Even if they do not work for him, they still depend on him in one way or the other. Some have even borrowed money from him to buy their own boats or more sheep. He says he has brought prosperity to Margaret's Keep, but that prosperity is mostly for us—though we often pretend it is not so. As does the rest of the island.

Mother would trade most of it to be able to go back to the mainland and live in a town house like her sister, Anne, but she knows it is not to be. She says she counts her blessings: among the souls who call this place their home, we are by far the richest. Still, the wind gives her headaches and the sea makes her sick. But perhaps that is because she was not born here. *I* was, though, and the wind never bothered me. Maybe it is different if the island is all you know—when its soil is in your blood, traveling your veins.

When I am done with looking out at nothing, I go to my corner. This is the most comfortable spot in the shed, with a small, three-legged stool to sit on, and a ragged old coat to pull over my knees on chilly days. The stool was even more comfortable before, when I was a smaller being, but it can still hold my weight so I will not complain. The corner is where I end up when I am done pacing like a restless dog and am resigned to my fate. The walls there are crowded with the ghosts of my childish drawings: plenty of faint mazes and graveyard people. There is something else hidden in the boards as well: tears—lots of them, soaked into the grain. I must have wept gallons over the years, sitting in this corner.

As I pull the coat up over my thighs, I think about Mother and Reverend Hill. I think about *Mrs. Hill,* too, and the sad fate of those caramels, treated as evidence of foul play. And suddenly it is as if something in me rips in half, and I feel like screaming, cursing, and tearing the shed apart—but I do not. I just sit there while something inside me breaks. I do scream, but it is silent. I do curse, but that is quiet, too; and I rage as I weep, but the rage has nowhere to go but deeper inside me, then through me, and out, like a mighty exhale. It slips through the walls like a wind, sweeps like a gale across the island, and a blinding headache shoots through my skull, turning the world bright white for a second.

I sense that something answers, even before the ground beneath me shakes. The stool beneath me topples, and I am thrown back against the wall hard enough to hurt. An animal fear takes hold of my heart and squeezes, even before the rumble reaches my ears and the box of nails on the shelf falls over to shower the floor in sharp splinters.

I scramble on the floor, feeling the tremors reverberate in my bones. The tattered coat has tangled with my legs and I kick it away so I can rise to my feet, precarious as that is with the world itself tossing like a ship on rocky sea. I throw myself against the wall in front of me and cling to the rough boards as I press my face to a crack to look outside.

The first sight to greet me in the blinding light is Margaret's Tower coming down, its stones hurtling fast toward the waves below, in a cloud of dust and sea spray.

·2·

ruth

Tea with the Hills is awkward. The reverend and his wife are as polite as always, but there is something between them—just below the surface—that makes me ill at ease. It had been just as tense the previous Sunday as well. The two of them had barely looked at each other, and I had halfway decided to make an excuse if the Hills ever invited me again. But once the question had slipped from Mrs. Hill's lips after church today, I just could not find it in myself to refuse. I suppose it is an unfortunate consequence of being a well brought up woman: one cannot bring oneself to offend.

Yet I cannot for the life of me figure out why the Hills insist on having me Sunday after Sunday. It seems to me that the two of them need some time together to resolve whatever lies so heavily between them. I would never suggest such a thing, of course. I would never meddle or breach etiquette. No, I will just sit here on their sofa, drink my tea, and express my deep gratitude for being invited—like a proper lady should.

"How are things at the schoolhouse? Do the children behave?" Mrs. Hill lowers the teacup back onto the dainty plate. The china is thin and fragile, painted with blue roses and rimmed with gold, and clatters loudly in Mrs. Hill's hands. She sits next to me on the plum-colored sofa. Her back is very straight, and the white lace at her throat moves when she talks, the jet and silver brooch bobbing up and down. She is horribly thin, just skin and bones. Her color is pale and her blond curls have no bounce. I think Mrs. Hill is unwell.

"Everything is fine," I assure her, adding a bright smile to the statement. The smell of the lukewarm tea in my hand makes me feel faintly sick: too much sugar and too much milk. Mrs. Hill prepared it for me herself. "The children are a rowdy bunch, but nothing out of the ordinary. I shall make little scholars of them yet." I laugh, but it falls horribly flat. Outside the windows, the seagulls cry as they battle the ever-present wind.

"That sounds wonderful, Miss Russel." The reverend's voice holds genuine admiration. He is known for having a soft spot for children, and the islanders often lament that he has none of his own. He certainly appears to have the energy for it. The reverend is a handsome man with clear brown eyes, and a shocking mane of shoulder-length hair the color of roasted chestnuts that is sure to raise some eyebrows on the mainland. His movements are energetic and his skin holds a healthy glow. Today, he seems just as disappointed by the tea as I am, and has drunk very little. Instead, he serves himself dainty cookies, studded with raisins and drizzled with sugar, from the silver tray. Crumbs rain down on his white shirt and into the chair's upholstery whenever he takes a bite. The couple do not look at each other. In fact, they make an effort not to let their gazes cross. Whenever the reverend speaks, Mrs. Hill's nose twitches up with something like disgust. A hard and heavy silence frequently falls between us.

"Mrs. North wore an uncommonly fetching hat today," I offer, hoping to oil the stagnant wheels of our conversation. Hats and other attire are so blessedly easy to talk about. When in doubt, I often turn to feathers and satin bows, though I do not own any myself. Mrs. Hill does not take the bait, however. Instead, her face grows even colder and more unreadable than before. Could Mrs. North have slighted her? It is, to be fair, a bit odd that the most prominent family on the island has *not* been invited to Sunday tea with the reverend. In fact, it should have been Mrs. North—not I, a working spinster—seated next to Mrs. Hill right now. I cannot say why this fact has not occurred to me before. Perhaps my mind is so full of arithmetic and chalk dust that there is simply no room for such speculations.

Reverend Hill must have seen my confusion, because he comes to my rescue. "Mrs. North's hats are indeed legendary." He beams at me across the table, his smile just slightly strained. "It's a new surprise every Sunday."

I latch on like a hungry puppy, grateful for the lightness of his tone. "Evelyn, too, seems to have developed a taste for couture," I say. "Before you know it, all the four daughters will be sporting hats to rival their mother's." I try to keep up the lightheartedness, but neither Hill laughs. The reverend's face even closes up to match his wife's somberness.

"It's disgraceful, isn't it?" Mrs. Hill snaps, startling me. The spoon clatters wildly as she slams the fragile china cup and saucer down on the polished table.

"Antonia—" the reverend says in a warning voice.

"The hat?" I ask, confused. I always thought Mrs. North looked most elegant.

"The *girl*." Mrs. Hill sets her eyes on me. The blue orbs burn with anger.

"Antonia," the reverend says again, and now he is halfway off the chair. The cookie crumbs tumble down his legs, headed for the floor.

I gently place my cup back on the table, then look between the two of them, utterly confused. "Perhaps I should leave—" I begin, but Mrs. Hill has placed a bony hand on my shoulder and squeezes it just hard enough to make me feel uncomfortable.

"Don't tell me you didn't see her." Her gaze bores into mine. "Don't tell me you did not see that *snake* making *eyes* at my husband from the pew." Her face suddenly shifts from anger to devastation. "Miss Russel, you must *know,*" she insists. "You, of all people, must *know*! Didn't you teach the little devil in school?"

"Who?" I ask, mesmerized by the wildness of her gaze.

"*Charlotte,*" she snaps. "Who else?"

"Antonia, that's enough!" The reverend's voice thunders from the other side of the table. When I glance up at his face, it looks utterly pained. "This has nothing to do with poor Miss Russel," he adds more softly—with which I wholeheartedly agree.

"I never taught Charlotte," I answer in a voice meant to be soothing, which nevertheless quivers from the shock of Mrs. Hill's behavior. I had not noticed anything untoward in Charlotte's behavior today. But all the North girls radiate a certain entitled privilege due to their exalted position on the island, and Charlotte—with her shining black curls and laughing dark eyes—is the most striking of the lot. So perhaps a natural target for jealousy?

I gently pry Mrs. Hill's fingers off my shoulder. Thankfully, she relents without a fuss, and her bony hand drops away. I am suddenly grateful for the countless times I have broken up skirmishes—big and small—in the schoolroom. You learn quite a lot about calming heated minds as a teacher. "The two eldest North girls were already gone from the schoolroom by the time I arrived here two years ago," I explain, happy to still have her attention. "And I believe the two of them had private tutors for some of their education, anyway." That said, I cannot help but add, "All the North girls seem very well-behaved to me."

"Oh, she may have the rest of you fooled, but she cannot fool *me*." Mrs. Hill's face takes on an expression of loathing. "That girl is rotten to the core—"

"Antonia!" Now the reverend comes around the table, and had I not been there, I think he might have slapped her, judging by the look on his face. Instead, he checks himself just in time and stops right next to the sofa, fidgeting and clenching his fists. A sheen of perspiration covers his brow. "You must forgive my wife, Miss Russel," he says in a stilted voice. "She has not been well."

I am just about to open my mouth and assure him that I understand when Mrs. Hill speaks up again, her gaze now firmly fixed on her husband. "And my illness gives you the right to *devour* that girl with your eyes?" She rises from the sofa and stands before her husband. "And in church, Jasper—*in church*!" Her voice has risen considerably, and I can hear their elderly housekeeper, Noreen, fussing outside the door, no doubt summoned by the heated voices.

The reverend stretches out his hands in an effort to placate his furious bride. "No, my dear. I only meant that your sickness makes you see things that simply aren't there!"

I squirm on the plush seat. This is all so terribly uncomfortable.

I abruptly rise. "I should go."

Neither of them seems to hear me, though. Mrs. Hill laughs—a hard, shrill sound, better suited for a fishwife, and it almost makes me smile to think how, under the veneer, we are all much the same. My amusement is short-lived, however.

"I was never sick in *my mind,* Jasper," Mrs. Hill shouts, seeming not to care at all that I am still in the room. "You cannot blame your lustful thoughts on *me*!"

"Stop it!" Reverend Hill's fist hits the table. China, silver, and milky tea jump. Even the cookies on the tray make a startled bid for escape before falling back down on the lace-edged liner. "I cannot believe that you would make such a spectacle of yourself in front of poor Miss Russel." He makes a sweeping gesture in my direction; I am still standing, poised to flee. "I'm so terribly sorry," he says to me. Red roses ride high on his cheeks. "This has nothing to do with you—or even Charlotte North." He shakes his head, looking in that moment like an utterly broken man. "Please, try to forget that any of this ever happened."

"Certainly," I say, my voice a touch clipped from all the excitement. I want nothing more than to be out of here. To forget.

The china clatters again, but this time it is not due to our disastrous party. The sugar spoon leaves its nest, and Mrs. Hill's teacup leaps off the table to crash against the floor. On the wall behind us, a heavy gilded mirror lifts, then crashes back against the painted boards.

"Goodness!" Mrs. Hill shrieks and flees, with me right behind her. Under my feet, the floorboards shake, and all the windows in the room give a tinkling sound. The lace curtains all shiver on their rods, and a petunia in a windowsill topples over, drizzling the floor with black dirt.

I realize, within a fraction of a second, that we are in the middle of an earthquake.

·3·

charlotte

No one remembers me, locked in the shed, when the ground shakes and the tower crumbles; showering the sea with salt-crusted stones. It takes a little while before anything happens, and I even start to wonder, from my place behind the wall, if something terrible has happened inside. If Mother has been hit in the head by one of the large pans that hang from hooks in the kitchen ceiling, or if Father has been struck by one of the elk heads mounted on the wall of his office—or if something has happened to one of my sisters. Sophie, perhaps, tumbling down the stairs, or Adelaide being flung from the bed, where she has doubtlessly been crying, to strike her head against the floorboards. None of those options are good.

Since it is Sunday, the yard is vacant, and so is the driveway across the fields. I scurry to the other side of the shed to take in the sight of the tower once more—or what *used* to be the tower. Now it is just a square of stones, jagged and sharp, like broken teeth. All around the base, fallen stones lie scattered in the winter-yellow grass. The wind licks their rough faces, eats their mortar, and turns it to dust. When I look down over the cliff's edge, I see the sea below gorging itself on the stones that fell, swallowing them into its wet salty belly. Even now, a rock or two drops from the ruin and into the busy waves. *Thump, thump, splash,* it says, as a rock hits against the cliff before finally landing in the water. The horizon is forever changed. The sight I have been used to since childhood is gone. Margaret's Tower is no more.

I go back to the other wall to watch the house and the yard. Distressed lowing can be heard from the barn, where we keep chickens and dairy cows. The former are strangely silent, and I imagine the birds sitting tightly together upon their perch, waiting for the danger to pass. The horses, however, are restless in the stable, and I can hear at least one of them kicking the wall.

After twenty minutes or so, the red door to the house finally opens. Mary, our housekeeper, peeks outside, scenting the air like a cat. As soon as she has deemed it is safe, the rest of her follows her nose outside, and she stands at the top of the stairs, tall and wiry, her graying hair hidden by a brown-checked headscarf. She places her hands on her hips as she surveys the yard, and it does not take long before the rest of the household come scurrying out as well, squinting at the daylight like little mice. Adelaide, Evelyn, and Sophie—all still dressed in Sunday black—take cautious steps out on the dirt and shade their eyes with their hands as they gaze at the jagged ruin of the tower. Mother looks pale and worried when she comes to stand next to Mary, wringing her hands in front of her. The women part like the sea in the Bible when Father makes his presence known, his bulk filling the width of the stairs. His steel-gray mustache quivers when he breathes. He has no hat on, which is rare outside the house, and his balding head glistens in the sunlight. Through the open door, the scent of roast pork comes seeping out and reaches all the way to the shed, slipping in between the boards.

My stomach rumbles loudly.

I could have called out to them, but I do not. I want them to remember me by themselves; but so far, none of them seem to notice my absence or worry about my well-being, even though I am locked in a ramshackle shed with all sorts of dangers on the shelves above my head. As my sisters move around in the yard, looking down the driveway or across the landscape to Margaret's Tower, I find I regret being worried for *them*. While I had imagined them meeting all sorts of misfortune, they have not given their locked-up sister as much as a thought!

Father steps inside again, and then reemerges with his hat and coat. He is no doubt headed for the harbor below, to make sure that there is no damage. I wonder if he will brave the spooked horses, but likely he will decide to walk; it really is not far. Even before he has left the yard, I can hear another man's voice in the air and I think it is Father's foreman come to fetch him, so maybe there *is* damage. I idly wish that is so, since it does not seem fair to me that Margaret's Tower should be the only casualty of whatever it is that has befallen our island.

As soon as Father has left, my sisters find their voices.

"Nothing else seems to be damaged." Evelyn's gaze scans all the buildings in the yard. Even from a distance, I notice the pearl engagement ring glimmering on her finger. It is brand-new and the metal has yet to turn dull.

"It might be worse on the other side of the island," Mary says with worry. Though she resides with us, the rest of her family lives there.

"What if it happens again!" Sophie sounds distressed. She has twined her arms around Evelyn's waist, clinging to her for dear life.

"What if it happens again, and it's worse!" Adelaide does nothing to soothe her younger sister. She bites her lower lip nervously.

"I cannot believe it is gone." Evelyn looks at the tower's remains with astonishment written on her face.

"We're lucky it was just that wicked old pile," Mary says with a grunt. "We're lucky *this* house is sturdy."

"What do you think it was?" Sophie asks her. She has unwound her arms from Evelyn's waist and looks up at the housekeeper, who is still standing at the top of the stairs, next to Mother.

"An earthquake, I reckon," Evelyn answers.

"We never had one before." Mother sounds surprised.

"Well, something must have changed. The earth must have moved."

"What does that even mean?" Mother is utterly puzzled.

"Oh, I don't want it to happen again." Sophie clings to Evelyn once more, but sounds more excited than afraid now. Perhaps her fear never ran deep.

"Maybe we should go back to the church," Adelaide suggests. "Isn't that what we're supposed to do if something awful happens?" My heart sets up its pace when I hear the words. I, for one, would not mind going back—the reverend is sure to be there. It will not do me any good, though. Even if they decide to go, if no one remembers I am here.

This, too, would have been a wonderful time to speak up and remind them that I am locked in the shed, but again my annoyance from having been forgotten makes me choke on the words. How can I be a "bad influence" on my sisters if none of them even notices my absence?

Mother seems to think on it before she replies. "We won't go anywhere before your father returns. *He* can decide what to do."

"What about the tower?" Evelyn stares at the new horizon. "Do you think it's safe to go there? Not all the way, but closer." I can hear a hint of adventure in her voice.

"Why do you want to go to that ungodly place?" Mother asks.

"Well, it's gone now, isn't it? Maybe God took it down himself." Evelyn knows well how Mother would like to think so.

"There could still be stones falling," Mary warns her.

"Oh, but there's barely anything left." My older sister dances on the spot like a colt. "And we wouldn't go too close."

Mother snorts. "What would your future husband say if he heard you being so foolhardy?"

"I do hope James would have accompanied me."

"It doesn't *feel* safe." Adelaide sides with Mother. "Even if the stones have stopped falling, what if it happens again, and we are thrown into the sea?"

Now it is Evelyn who snorts. "You have too much imagination, Adelaide."

"*I* am not afraid," Sophie chirps. "I'll go with you, Evelyn."

"No, you will not," Mother snaps from the stairs. "None of you will go *anywhere* before your father comes back." With those final words she turns her back and marches into the house. Her black skirts brush the threshold as she slips inside. Mary reaches a hand out to Sophie, signaling that it is time for her to come inside as well. My little sister only reluctantly lets go of Evelyn's waist and frowns as she saunters to the stairs, but she would never dare to oppose our mother.

One by one, they slip inside, and I have all but given up on any of them remembering me when Adelaide pauses on the stairs, then quickly turns back and approaches the shed. As she crosses the yard, she keeps looking back at the house, terrified that Mother will catch her in the act.

"Charlotte," she whispers against the door and I rush to meet her on the other side. "Are you unharmed?" Her voice brims with worry, which soothes my lonesome heart.

"I'm fine," I whisper back, although I did consider—if only for a moment—to pretend to be hurt in some way. "Why didn't you come to get me?"

"Mother." Adelaide groans. "She said it made no difference to her if the sky was falling down. You still deserved to be punished."

"I suppose she would rejoice if I perished in here." I do not even bother to hide my anger. "Nothing would please her more, I think, than if the roof of this shed came down to crush me. She would call it *just*. She would say it was God who wanted it so."

"Charlotte!" My sister gasps. "You shouldn't say such things, even if you imagine them." Adelaide thinks that saying things aloud can make them happen.

"She should at least have checked on me."

"Perhaps," Adelaide agrees through the door. "You shouldn't have made her so mad, though. You know how she hates it when you stare at Reverend Hill like that—"

"Stare at him *how*?" I know what she means, but feel the need to punish her for making me feel so utterly forgotten.

"You *know* how." She sounds so scandalized that I cannot help but smile. It is not that I bat my eyelashes at him or anything of the sort. It is just that as soon as the reverend and I lock gazes, the rest of the world falls away. There is a burning there in the air between us that is palpable enough that other people notice. It cannot be helped. It is just how it is.

"I'm not afraid of Mother," I say, and mean it. It has been years now since she managed to rouse any fear in me—and *she* knows it, too. Why else this frequent urge to lock me in the shed?

"Well, you are braver than I am." A thud against the door tells me she is leaving, and when I look between the boards, I can see her rushing back across the yard, headed for the front door of our once-white house.

The shed feels even smaller—emptier—after my sisters disappeared again. Boredom threatens like bad weather, a dust-gray cloud hanging over my head, but I cannot give in and let it torment me. I know from before how it will only cause more misery. I have to keep my mind occupied. Idleness is my greatest adversary. I can no longer draw with coal on the walls, but I can still walk the length of the shed.

One, two, three, four, five, six, seven . . . knock, knock, knock.

One, two, three, four, five, six, seven . . . knock, knock, knock.

It is on my third turn that I notice how the earthquake—if that is what it was—has shaken some of the old boards loose from the wall. When I knock on them, they flap like wings, sending a fresh surge of air inside. I can tell it will not take much to pry them far enough from the wall that I can slip outside. It is a hazardous plan as Mother might come to release me soon, but the chill air and the freedom is too great a temptation, and before I even know I have made up my mind, I crouch down to the floor and make my way outside, splinters and debris in my hair be damned.

I slip out quickly, like a rat from a trap.

When I reenter the world, the afternoon is quiet; only the sea and the gulls break the silence. Even the wind has ceased for a moment. I fill my lungs with the crisp fresh air and stretch my back, while my gaze scans the horizon.

Then I set off—not toward the house but toward what is left of Margaret's Tower.

·4·

jasper

The earthquake is over as soon as it began. One second, the world rattles, then the next it is perfectly still again. Only the broken china, the quivering curtains, and the dancing chandelier testify that something out of the ordinary has happened.

For a long, breathless moment, the three of us do nothing but stare at one another, open-mouthed and shocked. Not surprisingly, Miss Russel regains her bearings first.

"Good God," she utters, smoothing her beige tweed skirt. "I think the island just shifted!" A smile plays upon her lips.

Antonia rushes to one of the windows, presses her hands to the windowsill, and stretches her neck to survey in all directions. "The tower is gone," she says, amazed. "There is almost nothing left."

"What?" Both Miss Russel and I crowd beside her, staring out at the cliff, where the tower, indeed, has vanished. The tall, jutting structure that has filled the islanders with such trepidation and talk of witches has simply tumbled into the water below.

"It's so strange," Antonia mutters. "The sky seems so naked . . ."

"It must have been a very unsound structure," Miss Russel says in her sensible voice. The woman is so short that she must stand on her toes to get a proper look above the potted plants. "Perhaps it's a good thing that it fell like that, so suddenly and completely."

"I certainly hope no one was walking on the path," I say, imagining the tragedy in my mind.

"It fell *away* from the path," my wife reminds me, in a voice that has regained some of its hardness. Clearly, our argument is not forgotten. Inwardly I sigh as the shame comes rushing back. It is true; my gaze had snagged on Charlotte North today more than probably was warranted. But then, she is so beautiful and vibrantly alive that she draws the eye, reminding me of what life was like when hope still lived among us.

I know Charlotte thinks she is in love with me, and that I should not encourage such sentiments, but she is young and her fancy will alight on a more eligible target soon enough. I will never let this thing between us go further than it has, but I must admit that it makes me feel alive again, to be the object of a young girl's desire when my own wife holds me in such profound contempt. When the loss we experienced together only widens the chasm between us instead of drawing us closer.

It is nice to know I can make *someone's* blood run faster.

Still, I feel utterly mortified when I glance at poor Miss Russel. The earthquake has, in fact, been a blessing—something to cool my wife's madness before it got any worse.

"You must be pleased, Reverend," Miss Russel says. "A source of superstition and fear is suddenly gone without you having to do a thing."

She is right, of course. Though I am not pleased to see a monument from the past—painstakingly built—fall into the sea, I will not mourn the outlandish beliefs that hopefully will vanish along with it. I had not been more than a week on the island before my inherited housekeeper, Noreen, informed me of the ghost light that sometimes could be seen in the tower's single window, beckoning sailors to shore. Many members of the church have feared to even walk past the weathered structure, and have adhered to pagan rituals to feel safe. The legend of the tower's origins is horrible as well: A woman imprisoned by her cuckolded husband to live out her life in solitude. It seems such a cruel and heartless fate that it is no wonder my congregation—and their ancestors—let their imaginations run wild.

I do wish it had been God's light and reason that had chased the darkness from the tower, and restored the islanders' peace of mind, but I will take an earthquake. And who knows what might be behind it—the Lord's ways are, as I well know, mysterious.

The grounded Miss Russel no doubt shares my sentiments about the tower's fate. She seems quite excited, and I suppose that to an inquiring mind like hers, an earthquake must be a delightful occurrence.

"I never heard of anything of this nature happening here before," I note.

"And I hope it won't again," Antonia says with a shudder.

"If you ask the older generation of islanders, they may have stories of other earthquakes," Miss Russel says. "I always think of them as my very best resource when it comes to local history."

"Good riddance!" Antonia steps away from the window and wipes her hands on her black skirt. "Let there be no more whispers of witches and ghosts."

"Let's just hope there is no damage to people's property," I say, thinking of some of the older farms on the other side of the island. Most structures on Margaret's Keep are built of sturdy stone, but mortar can crumble and roof beams can rot.

"You could ring the church bells, Reverend," Miss Russel suggests. "They will all come, and we can tally up the damage."

"No," Antonia snaps. "I have had quite enough of the islanders today."

A painful knot instantly erupts in my belly and my body tenses up, desperately afraid that her madness will be ignited again. But then, I *am* the reverend and this *is* my calling. "You can stay home," I say, knowing that I sound curt, but unable to help it. "Miss Russel is right. It is my responsibility to offer comfort in times of crisis."

"It's just the one tower—" she begins.

"We cannot know that for sure," I say. "And what if there are more shivers on the way? The church is by far the safest structure—" I interrupt myself when a new surge of shame comes rushing in. I should have thought of ringing the bell myself. Miss Russel should not have had to remind me. I blame Antonia and the soured afternoon. The painfully awkward tea party.

"Noreen will take care of you, I'm sure." Miss Russel places a hand on my wife's thin, silk-clad arm. Emotions cross Antonia's face as quickly as bursts of lightning: annoyance at Miss Russel, distaste at the thought of church.

"The North girls likely won't come," I say quietly. "At best, they will send their man to figure out what is going on." People like the Norths can comfort themselves well enough, and have no desire to be confronted with simpler people's woes.

"Miss Russel will go with you, though." Antonia places her own hand upon Miss Russel's. "You won't go there alone."

I sigh and think of how fragile she has become—she who once thought she could command the whole world. I miss the old Antonia keenly. I open my mouth to reply, but Miss Russel is quicker.

"Of course I will," she says warmly.

And so, it is Miss Russel and I who prepare to walk the short distance to the church. I find my black coat in the hall and pull my hat down as far as it will go, to keep the constant wind from blowing hair into my eyes. Noreen, always alert, comes drifting from the kitchen to help Miss Russel with her own sensible coat, and place the sturdy umbrella she favors in her hand. The two women chatter behind me.

"I would have known by now if something had happened to any of mine," Noreen says. "Our boys are fast runners," she adds, meaning that her family is vast and plentiful and has an excellent network of children to bring messages between their households.

"But wouldn't you like to come to the church with us?" Miss Russel asks her.

"I'll take care of Mrs. Hill," Noreen replies with firmness. It is certainly not the first time she has been burdened with this task, for which I am eternally grateful. The elderly housekeeper has a patience with my wife that even the angels must envy. And she also knows just how much laudanum to give her in order to ensure a long and peaceful sleep.

I close the door to the clergy house behind us, and we start down the road toward the small stone church, built with boulders from the beach. Our feet are uncertain for the first few yards, unsure if the ground beneath our feet will hold our weight or throw us off like an unruly horse. My heart pounds a little faster than usual, and all my muscles are tense, as if I am walking on slippery ice. I hold out my arm to Miss Russel, who grabs hold with a look of gratitude. She must feel the same uncertainty as I do, although the island looks much the same as it did this morning. It is just our trust in it that has weakened. I imagine other, stronger earthquakes to come, and shudder.

As I scan the weather-beaten landscape, I despair, once again, at the lack of trees or vegetation of note to rest my eyes upon. I always thought that this island, consisting mostly of rock, had to be safe from the elements, but clearly I was wrong. Perhaps it is a blessing that there are no trees to be thrown down when the winter storms howl, or the ground shakes. There are sheep, though—and lots of them, seeing as how they are one of the few species to thrive in this harsh environment. These are not the sleek sheep of the mainland, though, dressed in neat, white coats, but larger, gray ones, whose rams are fearsome beasts with horns that can rival the devil himself. There is a smattering of sheepdogs, cattle, and horses strewn across the island, too, but mostly the grassy fields belong to the sheep, and there are no fences to keep them in. They plague my garden frequently, and I have often found them grazing among the gravestones. The only place they will not go, according to Noreen, is by Margaret's Tower. I have seldom had reason to seek the place out, though, so I have not witnessed this myself.

Once, an animal found its way into church during the sermon. Thankfully, the local farmers took swift action and promptly chased the ewe back outside. To my horror, the creature was renamed Mary Magdalene following the incident. Allegedly, she gave birth to conjoined twins the following spring, which the locals seemed to think was a punishment for interrupting my sermon.

Sometimes, I do find it hard to reconcile *my* God with the capricious deity worshipped by the islanders, even if we share the same Bible.

Today, the sheep are meek and tightly clustered together, savoring the comfort of their kin—not unlike what we are about to do in the church. I catch the gaze of a ragged ewe, and see a stark terror there. The animals' bodies all shiver, and even the seagulls above are unusually quiet, tentatively assessing the suddenly treacherous landscape below.

None of us trust Margaret's Keep today.

Miss Russel, too, is quiet beside me. She has pulled her shapeless felt hat far down to help with the wind, and holds my arm in a firm grip. Despite her modest stature the schoolteacher looms large on the island and is a fixture at every event, always wearing her sensible shoes and carrying an umbrella, just in case. Her nose is a little too long for her face, and whenever I see her, I think that she resembles a bird, like a finch. I have always held a particular fondness for Miss Russel—likely because we are both newcomers here, and two of the very few souls who cannot claim generations of ancestors calling Margaret's Keep home. I also appreciate her calm demeanor and clear head, which is why I—foolishly—asked Antonia to include her in our Sunday tea. I squirm inside again just from thinking of the disaster that had unfolded before the earthquake came and saved us.

I suppose I should thank the Lord for that mercy.

"You must think us utterly uncouth," I say to Miss Russel, adding a laugh that is meant to be light, but which sounds weak and nervous to my own ears. "It was a disgrace, I know." I feel red stains of shame burn in my cheeks.

"I'm not one to judge." She is staring straight ahead, clearly uncomfortable with the conversation.

"I don't mean to add to my own embarrassment—or to make you feel any worse," I say, in a clumsy attempt to put her at ease. Antonia has never before lost her bearings in front of other people, and I am simply not sure how to handle it. "I just want to offer my deepest apology," I say at last. "And tell you that I wish it hadn't happened."

"So do I." A hint of humor colors her voice and I take this as a good sign. "I will not speak of it to anyone, Reverend, if that is what worries you," she adds, and just as she says it—and to my own great shame—I realize that, yes, I *had* been worried that she would spread word about the reverend's mad wife around the island, even if this would have been highly uncharacteristic of the staid Miss Russel.

"I appreciate your discretion," I admit, "but my apology is heartfelt. Antonia has not . . . been herself for a while."

We are nearly by the church now, and I can only see the top of Miss Russel's head as she strides beside me. The umbrella in her free hand swings back and forth with her movements. When she does not reply to my latest apology, I cannot help but prattle on, utterly unable to stop myself—even though I know she would have preferred if I kept quiet. I suppose it is nerves getting the better of me, making me ignore her silent wishes.

"We came here so she would get better," I say. "Her doctor on the mainland thought the fresh air would do her good, but it doesn't seem to help." I want Miss Russel to *understand,* for reasons I cannot quite determine. "She was different, before. Before . . . we lost our son. It quite ruined her, you see. Body and mind. There will be no more children," I admit, as we approach the church's large, wooden doors.

"I am so sorry to hear that," Miss Russel says, while I fumble with the iron key. "Sadly, losing a child is a fate all too common. Not all women handle the grief well, and there's certainly no shame in it."

"It has made her insecure," I admit as the double doors open. "She worries that I long for a wife that is . . . intact." I swallow hard as we step into the church, still unaired from the morning's sermon. The vaulted room smells of hot wax, brine, and a plethora of unwashed bodies.

"But why Charlotte North?" The question shoots from Miss Russel's lips with such force that I realize it is this, more than anything else, that has been on her mind since the terrible tea. "How did Mrs. Hill get that idea into her head?"

"Oh, it is a long and silly story," I say, as I lead the way toward the bell tower. The sounds of our footsteps on the flagstones reverberate between the tall walls. "Charlotte used to help me with the children's choir."

"Oh, yes. I remember that now." Miss Russel sounds relieved to discover that there is a shred of sense in my wife's madness.

"She took a shine to me," I admit, with another hot flush of blood to my cheeks. "It was utterly innocent, but Antonia didn't handle it with grace." I look back just in time to see Miss Russel offer me a pained smile.

"Perhaps you should consult her mainland doctor again," she suggests as we start climbing, and I can hardly fault her for the advice. She has certainly earned the privilege.

"Perhaps," I reply, as we make it to the first landing. "But I fear it will do no good. The emptiness of her womb cannot be cured." I say it quite without thinking, not considering who I am talking to.

"Not all women need children to thrive, Reverend," Miss Russel replies. "In fact, I think most of us can do just as well without."

I do not know what to answer to that, and so, feeling somewhat chastised, I finally fall quiet. Miss Russel is grateful, I'm sure. Yet it is not until we are in the small, square chamber below the giant bell that I realize how this tower, too, might be unsafe if the ground should shake again, and that Miss Russel should probably not be there with me. It seems as though my mind has utterly fled since the interrupted tea.

Miss Russel herself seems unconcerned. She gazes out from the small, arched windows set into the thick stone wall, walking by them one by one. The glass in the windows is old and thick; the island wavers as if submerged in water, but the landscape and the buildings can still be made out, as can the restless sea surrounding Margaret's Keep.

"It is a beautiful view from up here," Miss Russel muses. "But Mrs. Hill is right: the sky does seem naked without the old tower."

As I pull the rope and the bell above me lets out its first, booming peal, I let my gaze wander, too, taking in the sheep farms and the trawlers lining the harbor.

I make it a point not to look at the North house.

No good can come of that.

·5·

ruth

When I step out of the white-painted schoolhouse the next morning, the world seems normal again, as if the earthquake had never happened. There is a cold wind blowing, but the day is otherwise lovely, and I even spot a pale slice of sun through the window while pulling on my gloves and buttoning my coat. My trusty felt hat is already in place.

The two hours we all spent together in church the day before, sharing stories of where we were when the earthquake struck and eating ungodly amounts of fruitcake, has already taken on a haziness, as if it was all a dream. As it turned out, the only real casualties had been Margaret's Tower and some birds' nests loaded with eggs that had met a cruel fate in the sea. The people were rattled, but not quite afraid. Some of them even called the earthquake a godsend, seeing as how it had ridden the island of the "wicked" tower—a comment that had left the good reverend looking slightly exasperated, but then it had already been a trying day for him.

Living with the rough sea as your neighbor makes for sturdy people, I suppose. What is a minor shift in the dirt compared to winter storms and raging waves? My students had seemed almost giddy when they arrived at the church, which in turn had inspired today's foray.

My charges mill around me in the grassy field surrounding the schoolhouse, performing their usual wild ballet. It is not too often that my students are brought out on excursions. What is there to see on Margaret's Keep that they have not seen a hundred times before? Unlike me, they were all born here and are quite jaded when it comes to the wonders of the island. The earthquake was a blessing in that regard, seeing as how no one and nothing was harmed. Finally, something new and extraordinary had happened right outside our doors—something worthy of a lesson under the open sky. I feel happy and optimistic as I start down the dirt road with the children in tow.

They have been taught to walk in an orderly fashion, filing behind me in pairs, but of course that is not what they do. We have not walked for long before a knot of braids and cotton dresses has formed behind me, and the sound of excited chatter reaches my ears. A few of the boys have entered the windswept field that runs along the road and are passing me by at speed, skipping across ditches and rocks, shouting and laughing. There are only twenty of them, though, so I do allow them some freedom. I often find that they are better at focusing on their letters and numbers if they have burned through some energy first. My colleagues on the mainland would certainly not have approved of my approach—and the men in particular would have been aghast at what they would deem my laxness—but none of them are here on Margaret's Keep, so I will do as I please.

I pause and turn back to see the girls scatter like chickens, haphazardly forming unlikely pairs. Their mouths curl into secretive smiles. They know they have broken formation, but also know they are safe from punishment. The boys in the field are too far away to make their mischief a secret.

Adelaide North walks right behind me, though, and it is her I have turned to talk to. "Did you and your sisters go to the tower yesterday?" I ask. Living so close by, it would only have made sense if the Norths wanted to assess the damage.

"No." The girl looks up at me with pretty blue eyes. She clutches one of her thick blond braids in her hand. "We wanted to, but Father forbade it. I suppose he thought the earth might shake again." Insecurity flickers across her features. At thirteen, she is a most curious child, with a demeanor better suited to a girl of ten. All the North girls are like that: hothouse flowers suffering from an acute lack of experience with the world. They have none of the rugged sturdiness of their island peers, and despite their wealth, I pity them. I know from experience how excess does not always equal happiness.

"Yes?" I urge her. There is clearly more that she wants to say.

"Charlotte might have gone." She lowers her voice. "Though if she did, she wasn't allowed to."

I suppress a smile. If only my students' guardians knew just how many secrets were revealed in the schoolroom. "Well, I suppose she was curious," I say.

Though she never was a student of mine, I have picked up enough to know that Charlotte can be willful—though I have trouble believing the girl is as bad as Mrs. Hill had suggested the day before.

Just thinking about that disastrous tea makes me feel ill at ease. I feel sorry for the Hills, but for Charlotte, too, who must carry the brunt of Mrs. Hill's ire, which appears to be considerable. Young girls do foolish things when their hearts are snagged; it is a story as old as time, and deserves compassion rather than loathing. Yet Mrs. Hill seems to be beyond such considerations—beyond reason, even. My heart aches for her, and for the reverend, too—and for poor Charlotte North and her young, inconvenient infatuation.

"Did your sister say anything of what she saw?" I ask Adelaide, as it would be helpful to know beforehand what condition the ruins are in.

Adelaide shakes her head. "She just came into the house and went to our room, but where else could she have been?"

"Lots of places, I reckon," Annabeth Ferryman pipes up. She is a coarsely built, red-haired girl from one of the sheep farms, and I have often wondered about the friendship between her and Adelaide North, since they seem so little alike. I suppose the island's scarcity of suitable playmates is to blame for the pairing, but the girls seem to like each other well enough, so who am I to question their bond? The world will tear them apart soon enough.

"She was not where she was *supposed* to be," Adelaide replies in an impatient voice, glaring at her friend.

"And where was that?" I ask idly. Not from any particular curiosity, but because it seems to suit the conversation. I had figured Adelaide meant her sister ought to have been in her room or some such, doing her correspondence or reading a book, which is why I am at a loss when the girl goes silent. The hush is sudden and deafening, and for some reason the air feels thick enough to cut. Adelaide squirms before me and tightens her grip on the braid. Somehow—although I do not know how—I seem to have made a blunder.

"The shed," a clear voice declares from the back of the little group. Sophie North smiles up at me with the sunny confidence of an eight-year-old. "She was supposed to be in the shed."

"No, she was not." Adelaide immediately spins around. Now it is her sister who is the subject of her glare. "Why do you lie like that?"

Sophie's face instantly falls.

"Oh, never mind that," I chirp, intent on ending this conversation, which clearly has nothing to do with the earthquake. "Let's move along, children, or we won't reach the tower before nightfall." And so on we walk as if nothing has happened, although it does take some time for the chatter behind me to start up again.

I cannot help but think about it, as I lead the group down the road, passing the occasional farm and herds of grazing sheep. What on earth did I say to make Adelaide act in such a manner? And what shed did Sophie speak of? It is all a mystery to me. Though I always do my best not to pry into other people's business, my mind keeps dwelling on the exchange. Even though they are a vital part of Margaret's Keep, the Norths are nevertheless set apart from the rest, and very few people are privy to their private doings. I suppose the divide is unavoidable with George North being such a powerful man. I had been surprised to learn, upon my arrival, that I would teach his youngest daughters, since I had assumed that they all went to boarding school on the mainland, and I still don't know why this is not the case.

According to my predecessor, the Norths had often hired tutors when Evelyn and Charlotte were still in school. The arrangements had rarely lasted, though—I suppose the island's remoteness was to blame—and when the tutors eventually left, the girls had been sent back to the island's own school. Somewhere along the way, the Norths must have given up on tutors altogether—perhaps the bother of finding and hiring simply became too much—because in the two years I have been on the island, Adelaide and Sophie have always been in my classroom.

I remember how I found there to be something *right* and *just* in that fact when I first arrived—that the children who so greatly benefited from the others' toil and trouble sat next to them to learn their letters and shared their bread at lunch. I had found it liberating, in a way, that the scarceness of people and resources on Margaret's Keep had made the difference between those who had and those who had not less discernible.

In time, though, I had come to learn that the difference was still there, only—perhaps—more subtle.

We climb a small hill, and suddenly it is there before us: the edge of our tiny world, the cliffs and the tower—or what little is left of the latter. Behind it lies the glittering sea, dotted with tiny fishing trawlers, and below us to the left we can hear men shouting to each other at the harbor. They are probably loading George North's pride, a steam-powered cargo ship aptly named the *Seagull,* to bring the fish to the mainland. The vessel is vital to the island, ferrying goods and people alike. For people like me, with no boat of my own, it is the only option. The airborne seagulls are rife around the pier, screaming like harpies above our heads. When I first came here, they had frightened me—their aggression and their size—but I have gotten quite used to them now. Last year, I even joined some of the women as they scaled the cliffs to hunt for eggs, though I still prefer the chicken variety.

The boys who ran ahead of us are already in the ruin, and play among the rubble. They have found some sticks of driftwood and brandish them like swords, as befits the ancient surroundings. I shepherd the girls across the grass quickly. It will not do if a boy loses an eye on my watch, and their playing can be rambunctious. I let out a deep breath of relief when we have reached the tower and I have secured all the sword sticks in my hands. The boys sulk, but I have no compassion. I tell them all to look closely at the ruin, because they are to write a report on it when we have returned to the schoolhouse.

The children are happy enough with the task, and begin to slowly move around—some of them in groups, the others in pairs. I join them, too, but mostly from fear that the remains of the tower may still not be safe. The inside of the tower was in better shape, I realize, than the sides that have faced the wind and rain. The erosion is less pronounced, though wear is visible here as well, manifesting in shallow grooves that run across the stone. There is barely anything left to examine, though. The walls that rose so high the day before have utterly come down. What is left is a jagged square that is hardly any higher than a fence. I am, however, flummoxed to discover a regular mountain of beach pebbles right where I remember the entrance used to be. It is an uneven heap—likely stirred by the earthquake—but at its peak, it easily reaches my hips. I sidestep it as I move around and notice that the children do the same.

Before it fell, the structure had felt menacing to me: perhaps due to its sheer height, or because of the doorway—long since robbed of an actual door—that had gaped toward the fields like a screaming mouth. Perhaps it was because I had known the story of Margaret's imprisonment, and could clearly see how far you would have had to climb in order to reach the tower's only window. It had been centuries since it was possible, though. The wooden stairs that had led to the heart of the tower had long since rotted away.

Good riddance to all of it, I think as I walk among the fallen stones, echoing Mrs. Hill's sentiment the day before. Suddenly I regret this whole excursion, realizing far too late that Margaret's story is perhaps too sad, and troubling, to be the center of a pleasant outing. We are already here, though, so there is that.

Nothing to do now but see the day through.

When the students have walked around for half an hour, inspecting every piece of rubble there is, I shepherd them into the remaining square of the tower and have them sit down on the jagged edges of the fallen walls. I am not happy to have them perching there like chickens. I would much rather have them sitting on the ground, but the grass is both cold and damp, so I do not have a choice. I do, however, forbid them from sitting on the side facing the sea, where the cliff's edge is merely three feet away.

I start my lesson, hoping to chase the gloom with words. "Do any of you know when the tower was built?"

Simon Fisher, clever and bright, raises his hand in the air.

"A hundred years ago," he says, and all the children laugh. They know the island well enough to know it is far older.

"*Two* hundred years ago," Molly Boyden says next, and the children all laugh again. The sound of their laughter is soothing to me, like a sunny tonic for dark thoughts.

"It was built in the sixteenth century," I tell them, and gingerly take a place on the crumbling stone myself. "So about *four* hundred years is reasonable to assume. Do you know who built it?"

The children all shake their heads.

"No wonder." I smile. "*Nobody* knows the name of the man who built the tower, though they say that he was rich, and maybe even noble." I have managed to get their attention now; they look at me with rapt expressions. They have doubtlessly heard the story before—flimsy and unsubstantiated as it is—but as with any good legend, it cannot be repeated often enough.

"Do you know the name of the builder's wife?" I ask, and all their hands shoot up in the air, followed by giggles and smiles. I point to Sophie North.

"Margaret," she exclaims. It was an easy one, though. They all knew that.

"Why do you think the tower—and this island—is named after her?" I ask, and something secretive creeps into their little faces, but none of them seem inclined to answer. Perhaps I should not have asked. This is a story better suited for whispering by the fire on a dark, stormy night. But perhaps I can put their minds at ease.

"The truth is that nobody knows for sure," I tell them. "This happened so long ago that no one else lived on this island, and when a story is that old, it has inevitably changed so many times over the years that no one knows what the truth was in the first place. I suppose you have all heard of how Margaret was imprisoned here for being a witch?" I look around to see a few of them nodding. "The story goes that Margaret had dark powers, and had to be kept in the tower so that she wouldn't hurt anyone, but that is unlikely to be true, don't you think?" I look around at my students again, but now there is no nodding. Rather, they view me with an ounce of suspicion, as that is the prevailing view among the islanders.

"Margaret could just as well have been ill," I continue unperturbed. "Perhaps she had to be kept away so she wouldn't infect anyone else. If you look at it this way, the tower might have been a *good* place for her to be in her final days—a comfortable home, if a little lonely . . . Do you know why there was a window up on the wall?"

Now they all spring back to life, and a forest of hands rise up in the air. I decide to let Annabeth speak.

"She would signal to boats if she needed food," she says.

"That is right." I straighten up. "According to legend, if Margaret needed something from the mainland, she would put a lit candle in the tower's only window. The fishermen that passed by would see it and let her husband know." Even if I speak in a lighthearted voice, the story remains utterly grim.

"Why would anyone say that the tower is a bad place if Margaret wasn't a witch?" John Newell asks, so eager that he forgets to raise his hand.

"Perhaps, as time passed and the story changed, people began scaring each other with stories about the witch—we do like to do that, don't we? But as you can see, there is nothing to be afraid of here. We are sitting in what used to be the tower right now, and except for there being little grass on the ground where the high walls have kept the sun away, it is just like any other place on Margaret's Keep." A violent shiver runs down my back as I say the words.

"Do you think she is buried here?" Sophie North sounds worried, and I can clearly see why; the Norths live very close to the ruins.

"Even if she is, nothing has changed since yesterday," I assure her. "Bones are just bones, and the dead cannot hurt you, Sophie. They have gone home to God."

With that, I deem the lecture complete, and I cannot help but feel relieved when I rise from the ruin, my backside aching from the hard, jagged stone.

But as I gather up the children and start the walk back across the field, accompanied by the seagulls as before, I suddenly have the strange sensation that we are being watched. I tell myself it can be anyone—a curious farmer or a worker at the pier—and force myself not to look. Nevertheless, we are barely halfway across the field when I turn my head and glance back. What I see makes me feel inexplicably uncomfortable, although I cannot say why. Perhaps it is just that she must have moved so very quickly to get in there so very fast.

In the midst of the square structure—where we were all sitting just a few minutes ago—stands a young woman dressed all in white. Her dark hair is loose and hangs over her shoulders. It is a miracle, really, that the wind does not make a mess of it.

Without ever smiling, or greeting me in any way, Charlotte North stares at me from the ruins of Margaret's Tower.

·6·

charlotte

The meat swims in a gravy so nice and thick that it makes me want to drink it straight from the pitcher, while the potatoes lie like pale and naked newborns at the bottom of the serving bowl. There is cabbage, too, the cut leaves blackened around the edges, and gray-green peas from a can. I eat the meat but nothing else; I just cannot stomach vegetables today. The beef, though—luscious cubes laced with onions—*that* I can eat, and it slips down my throat with ease.

Mother and Father each sit at their end of the table. Adelaide and Evelyn are opposite me, and Sophie sits beside me on her chair, eating her peas one by one. The usual dinner sounds bother me today, though they are nothing out of the ordinary. The clinking of cutlery against the fine china, the chewing and shifting upon the seats. Even the rustling of Mother's skirts, or the sound of Adelaide swallowing bothers me, although I do not have a headache. Behind me, on the other side of the window, I can feel the sea moving relentlessly.

It has been two days since the tower fell.

"I have written to the university and asked for a geologist to be sent here." Father wipes his mustache and folds the linen napkin before putting it down next to his gravy-stained plate. "We need to know if the earthquake was one of a kind, or if it might happen again—or, God forbid, if it did any damage we haven't seen yet. Fissures in the cliffs or some such." He picks up his fork and spears his remaining slice of potato.

"I will not have you girls walking down on the beach," Mother adds. "A boulder could have been dislocated and might fall down on your heads." She looks at us all in turn, her pale eyes peering down her long, slim nose. Her hair is piled high on her head: half-gray, half-black. The shift happens somewhere just below her shoulders, and I have wondered many times why she does not cut off the black, because her youth is never coming back again. The pearls in her ears have aged poorly, too. They look dull and dead, like beach pebbles.

"Where are we to take our afternoon walks if not there?" Evelyn reaches for the silver salt shaker. "The roads are dusty and the fields are wet."

"Perhaps you ought to stay inside," says Mother.

Father disagrees. "Nonsense. They need the air, or they will wither like flowers." He tends to gain a flair for the poetic when he has downed enough wine.

"What is the geologist going to do?" Sophie is still short enough that her toes dangle a few inches above the floor. Her blond hair is adorned with a crisp, white bow. My youngest sister is always curious and eager to learn. At eight, she is already brighter than half the adults surrounding her. Not that it will do her much good. She will not be able to use it for anything, shackled to a man in a town house on the mainland. Rather than being proud of her mind, Mother praises her sunny disposition and eagerness to please, which enrages me at times. Anyone can be pleasing; not everyone can be bright.

"He is to survey," Father answers her question. "Search for fault lines, that sort of thing. I am a tradesman myself, so I cannot tell the specifics, but I am sure he will be of use."

"Maybe he will knock on the cliffs with one of those little hammers," Adelaide suggests. Her eyes light up when she thinks about it. There is a lot Adelaide would do if she could, but almost everything she knows is from books. Out of all of my sisters, Adelaide is by far the least composed. Her mind flutters like a butterfly, unable to settle down for long. She is easily distracted, but everything she does is infused with enthusiasm and abandon. She is awkward, though—unsure of herself. Mother hates that about her. At least her skin has cleared up now, so her nose is not red, but white and blemish free.

"I suppose the geologist will have to stay here with us." Mother raises her wineglass, and my stomach ties into a knot. I dislike having houseguests and always having to be on my best behavior.

"I suppose." Father shrugs, and his big bulk quivers. "He is an educated man and must be housed accordingly. I can hardly put him up in the store." Besides the grocer's small quarters, the store contains a guest room where visitors to the island sometimes stay—repairmen and such, mostly. The building also houses Father's office: a cramped room with a large oak desk that I rarely have reason to visit.

"Perhaps the reverend will have him?" Evelyn seems to have forgotten that we no longer speak of Reverend Hill—hard as that might be, with him being almost as important as Father. Mother coughs loudly, choking on her wine, while Adelaide sniggers. Evelyn herself turns a shade paler when she realizes her blunder. My elder sister is always concerned with setting a good example for the rest of us—a task that has been drilled into her since childhood. Mother never needed any help in the nursery because she always had Evelyn, a perfect helpmeet cast in Mother's image, though far more reasonable and even-tempered. Common sense is what Evelyn clings to—often a scarce commodity in our household. Evelyn is our rock in furious waters, and I hate to think of how it will be when she leaves to marry on the mainland.

Father seems oblivious to the disruption around the table. "Hill is not like the old reverend," he muses. "He might welcome a scientist into his home. I have heard him say that he admires them. It is how the world is now. God and science must walk hand in hand."

"*I* certainly miss Reverend Jones," Mother huffs. Her lips have become a tight line, tainted dark from the wine. "*He* was a true reverend, never any nonsense—and he knew how to put the fear in people."

I snort at this but keep my peace. I, too, remember the old reverend: as gray of hair as he was of skin, looking rather emaciated. His bodily weakness had done nothing to deter the fiery passion of his faith, however, and he gleefully delivered his tongue-lashings every single Sunday. I never liked being told what to do or how to behave, so he and I never got along. Who was Reverend Jones to tell me how to conduct myself? I know he was supposed to be close to God, but all I ever saw was a self-important man who rejoiced in making others feel bad about themselves.

Back when I imagined seeing people in the graveyard, I had spent many grueling hours in Reverend Jones's office at the clergy house, sitting next to Mother on terrible, straight-backed chairs, while he spoke of "the devil's delusions." He said that I had to turn to God to fortify my weak mind and make it less susceptible to evil. I never felt evil, though, never felt weak—and all his talk ever did was make me feel angry.

No, I, for one, do not miss Reverend Jones, and perhaps that is one of the reasons why it took me a while to realize just how different Reverend Hill is—how very modern in his ways.

I do not mind God at all when presented through his lips.

"You merely miss *Mrs. Jones,*" Evelyn says to Mother, speaking in a tender voice. Ever since she became engaged, my sister has shown Mother more understanding. It is as if she can allow herself compassion now that she is about to leave. Her fiancé, James Eckhardt, is set to visit Margaret's Keep this summer, and Evelyn spent most of the winter on the mainland with our aunt, just so she could be close to him. They will get married this fall, unless something awful should happen to derail their plans.

“Mrs. Jones was a wonderful friend.” Mother sighs and toys with her fork. “She knew the value of a woman’s solitude. So does Mrs. Hill, of course, though for different reasons.” She drops the fork with another deep sigh and casts a dark look in my direction.

“She is sick, isn’t she?” Sophie slips another pea between her lips.

“That is what they say,” Mother replies cryptically. No one knows for sure what ails Antonia Hill besides the fact that she has no children. She seems awfully spry to me, though, when glaring at me in church. The fact that she considers me a rival gives me an illicit thrill. She would not have been so worried if her husband was indifferent.

“Mrs. Hill merely has a nervous disposition,” Father says. “It’s quite common among well-bred women.”

At this, we all roll our eyes. What does *he* know of female ailments?

“She should go somewhere,” I say, “to rest.” I suck the delicious gravy from my fork. Mother shoots me a look of disgust, and Adelaide sniggers again. I smile around the tines.

“Careful, Charlotte,” Evelyn says. “Mother might put you in the shed again.” She grins while she says it, making of it the mockery that it is, but the truth is that we all feel safer when Father is with us to soothe and temper his wife.

“As if that helps,” Mother huffs. “She was quite the weasel last time.” She gives me another dark look. Apparently, she had been very surprised not to find me in there when she went to let me out.

“The earthquake shook the boards loose,” I remind her. “I didn’t make it happen.”

“Well, you should have stayed anyway.” Mother’s nostrils flare. “I locked you up for a reason.” Her lips have become tight and bloodless.

“And the island let me out,” I say, lifting my chin just a little.

“The earthquake *scared* her, Hester,” Father says to placate Mother. “I would have slipped out, too, if it had been me.” His sharp gaze measures her across the table. Adelaide and Sophie look to each other, silently communicating worry. Might this be the beginning of another domestic storm? My younger sisters do not handle them well.

"Then why did she go *there*?" Mother asks. "If Charlotte was so afraid, why didn't she run into the house?" They speak as if I am not there, as if they are having a private conversation. I chew my meat and pretend not to care.

"She has already explained that she was scared of being sent back into the shed." Father sighs and drinks more wine. "You should stop this nonsense, Hester. The girl is almost eighteen."

"Seems to me that she is running straight *toward* danger rather than trying to avoid it." Mother sniffs, pretending not to have heard Father's disapproval. It was an unhappy coincidence that Mr. Norris had seen me running to the tower after the earthquake. Exactly why I went, I cannot say; I barely even remember it happening. I suppose I just wanted to see it for myself: the tower reduced to rubble, its belly split open to reveal the inside.

By the time I had regained my senses, it had started raining, and I stood there by the cliff's edge, drenched through and freezing. The sky was bleeding dark by then, and the church bell was no longer chiming. I cannot say how long I stood there. Mary thinks I had a shock, and gave me tea with rum to warm me up when I got home. They had been searching for me, she said, but clearly no one had thought me mad enough to go to the fallen tower by myself.

Had it not been for Mr. Norris, it would have remained a secret as well.

"Perhaps you should go to Aunt Anne again, Charlotte," Mother says when a moment has passed. "It would be good for you to see something other than this godforsaken island. Perhaps this time you will even make an effort to expand your circle of friends." Her face looks very stiff when she says it, so she is doubtlessly thinking of Reverend Hill again, and what had happened in church. But I do not want to go to Aunt Anne. The sole reason for me going there is to meet a man—a rich, spoiled man with a dull and polished mind, but I do not want a man like that. I do not want a life that is bordered by rules I find utterly boring and pointless. I want to feel alive! I want to feel passion and lose myself in feelings. And I know I will never find that fire amid the china and silver in Aunt Anne's dining room. My spirit will die there—perish in the chilled soup—and I will never have the life that I want, where every day is an adventure.

"I would rather not," I say calmly, and fill my plate anew. I am famished, it seems—I cannot get enough. The meat from Mrs. Norris's stove has never tasted better.

"You should look to Evelyn for guidance," Mother continues nevertheless. "*She* certainly made the most of her time on the mainland." Her voice brims with pride, and a pair of hectic roses appears in her sallow cheeks.

"Catching a boy's eye is not hard," I say, trying to make light of it, though I do not wish to offend my sister. Evelyn has done well for herself—or so they claim.

But Evelyn *is* offended. "James is hardly a *boy,*" she declares. "And if it's not hard, why haven't you yet?" What she does not say lies thickly between us. She thinks my infatuation with the reverend is repulsive; she thinks I am acting like a child, nurturing ridiculous notions. She thinks I ought to put my silly desires to the side and set about securing my future, like she has.

She will never understand how Jasper Hill speaks to my passion. When I look into his beautiful eyes, it is almost as if I can see myself in there: the same desperate need for escape. I know that he feels it, too: how the world that we have created for ourselves is so small that we barely experience life at all—and if we were not meant to live life fully, why does the desire for it burn so bright? I want to be the reverend's knight in shining armor, freeing him from the dullness of his life, as he can free me from mine. Together, we will travel and see the world—not from the safety of a carriage, no, but on our feet, walking dusty foreign roads.

I cannot say any of this aloud, as Evelyn will not understand, but I am unable to keep entirely quiet. "Marriage is not everything," I remark, which earns me a raised eyebrow from my father.

"It is for you," Mother snaps. "We cannot feed you and clothe you forever—"

"Perhaps you can be a teacher." Sophie looks at me with her innocent eyes. "Like Miss Russel at school. She feeds and clothes herself," she reports, full of admiration.

"Only because she doesn't have a husband," Mother says, as if that should be obvious to everyone. "Spinsterhood is not a worthy goal," she tells her youngest, but Sophie is still smiling dreamily. Still adores Miss Russel.

"*I* could go to Aunt Anne," Adelaide says. "I wouldn't mind 'expanding my circle of friends.'"

"You are too young." Mother sounds annoyed all of a sudden. It happens with bothersome frequency, her mood changing for no good reason. "It is *Charlotte* who is the problem," she says, and her voice grows louder by the second. "*Charlotte* is the one we must unload—"

"There now," Father interrupts, but Mother opts to ignore him. Suddenly, she has risen and stands with her whitening knuckles pressed against the tablecloth.

"It is *Charlotte* who must go!" she exclaims while her breathing turns labored; her chest strains against the white silk of her shirt. "We must send her to Anne before she does something—"

"There, there." Father is up as well. Within seconds, one of his hands is on Mother's narrow back, soothing her with gentle strokes. "We will take care of Charlotte; don't you worry yourself."

Mother's face twitches as if she is in pain; she bites her lip and closes her eyes, then groans and gasps for air. Beside me, Sophie has started weeping. This time, though, Mother manages to vanquish her demon. Her face smooths out, her shoulders slump, and she sinks back down in the chair.

"Shall we have cake?" she asks in a voice that is far too happy, looking around the table with eyes that are too bright. I give Sophie my napkin to wipe her tears.

"Cake sounds delicious." Father sits back down as well.

"Is it with berries?" Adelaide asks. Her voice, too, is far too cheerful.

"And whipped cream," Mother replies, smiling with all her crooked teeth.

·7·

charlotte

After dinner, my sisters and I gather in the front room to sew. It is a handsome room with blue-painted walls hung with framed photographs, and a forest of houseplants crowding the windowsills. It also holds the piano—which Evelyn plays the most—and paints and charcoals for Adelaide. The latter does not paint today but repairs a pair of stockings. Evelyn embroiders a pillowcase with her future monogram: hers and James's initials woven tightly together and imprisoned within a wreath of roses. Sophie is still in training and works on a sampler of simple flowers, though she groans all the time and makes sloppy stitches and is unlikely to ever become a passionate seamstress.

I am meant to hem a skirt, but like Sophie, I keep getting it wrong. My mind is such a beehive, I cannot concentrate at all. My mouth still tastes of meat and gravy, and—despite the copious amount I ate—my belly still rumbles when I think about dinner. The only thing that can distract me is to think of Jasper Hill, which honestly ignites an entirely different type of hunger. I have this fantasy where I am awfully distraught because Mother wants to marry me to a middle-aged widower with a potbelly, and Father has for some reason agreed to it. In my hour of crisis, I have nowhere to turn but to my trusty reverend, and I slip away and hide in the vestry after his Sunday sermon. My family looks for me, but in all the wrong places, and far away from church. In my fantasy, Mrs. Hill is ill that day and has not even been present.

When the reverend finds me and I tearfully tell him what has transpired, he takes me into his strong arms and presses me to his broad, hard chest. I can feel his heat through his clothes.

"You cannot go," he speaks into my ear. His voice is ragged with emotion. "You belong to me, Charlotte. No other man can have you!" Then his lips are on mine and we share a wet kiss, and his hand lands on my breast, and—

"When I am married, you can come and stay with me on the mainland." Evelyn does not look up from her stitches; all I can see is the dark crown of her head. I assume it is me she is talking to, though. "Perhaps you will find that more to your liking than staying with Aunt Anne."

"Why do I *have* to go to the mainland?" I ask. "Why can I not stay here?"

"Why would you?" Adelaide sits next to Evelyn on the smooth, cream-colored sofa. Between them in a basket rests an array of sharp implements: scissors, pins, and needles, as well as several twists of colored threads. "Why do you want to be here when you could be somewhere else?" She sounds breathless. "I would love to go to the mainland if Mother would let me."

"I suppose you would," I say, and I am not mocking her. Adelaide is different from me; she would like nothing more than to leave Margaret's Keep for a lawyer and a town house. She does not have anything holding her here, like I do. I will not abandon Jasper Hill to live out his life in dull misery. When I leave, it will be with him by my side. "There is nothing for *me* on the mainland," I say, "but that doesn't mean there's nothing for you."

"It will be your turn soon enough," Evelyn soothes her. "You are already thirteen. A few more years and you can come and stay with me, and then I will introduce you to everyone I know."

"Can Annabeth come, too?" Adelaide still sounds breathless.

Evelyn looks uncomfortable; she shifts on the seat and puts down her sewing. "I don't think Annabeth would thrive on the mainland."

"Why not?" Adelaide is instantly stung, indignant on Annabeth's behalf.

"You know why." Evelyn picks up the pillowcase again and trains her eyes on the flower wreath. Her blue skirt falls around her legs like waves.

"She is a sheep farmer's daughter," I say, in case Adelaide needs a reminder. "It doesn't much matter out here, but it will over there. She would never be accepted among Evelyn's new friends."

Adelaide's lower lip juts out, so she is definitely sulking. "Why does it matter what your father does?" she asks the air. "The rules are unfair. Annabeth has as much right to go to the mainland and find a good husband as I do."

"Annabeth will find a good husband here," Evelyn says calmly, having regained her composure.

"Why does *anyone* have to go to the mainland?" Sophie says from the chair next to mine, her voice brimming with sorrow. She is deeply dreading the day when Evelyn will leave us for good. Parenthood had long since lost its luster for Mother by the time she was born, so Evelyn has been her whole world.

The latter puts down the pillowcase again and looks at our youngest sister with compassion. "You know how it is, Sophie. The mainland is where opportunity lies for girls like us. There's not much of a future for any one of us on Margaret's Keep, lest we should marry a farmer." Her lips curl up at the edges. The mere idea is ridiculous.

"Then why doesn't Charlotte want to go?" Sophie asks. The half-finished daisy in her lap is all forgotten.

"Charlotte is just misguided." Evelyn gives me a dark look. She has Mother's nose and eyes, but none of her anger—which I suppose is a good thing, especially for James.

"Charlotte is *not* misguided," I say. "Charlotte just wants to stay here."

"Charlotte is *in love.*" Adelaide sniggers. "She just wants to be close to the church and—"

"Because she loves *God.*" Evelyn's eyes shoot daggers at Adelaide, then shift to worry when she moves her gaze to Sophie. "Charlotte will come to her senses, though." Evelyn's voice brims with feigned optimism. "She will come to see reason in time."

I choose to ignore the remark, even if I know that it is tailored to provoke me. What does Evelyn know anyway about the way love can work on body and mind? The heady intoxication it can bring. I am quite certain that she marries James only because it is the right thing to do, and not because she feels any passion. Not like the one I have for Jasper Hill.

When she was younger, Evelyn would often lose herself in romance novels, and requested them from the mainland all the time. Her favorites were books about highwaymen and noble ladies, but since she had found a husband of her own, her reading of such stories fell by the wayside. Perhaps she no longer remembers what love is supposed to feel like. The only books I see her with now are on housekeeping and entertaining, and pamphlets on how to raise infants and keep a husband happy. The only good thing about this is that her collection of romance novels is now free for me to peruse—which I do, frequently and shamelessly. While Evelyn always read her novels in bed at night, I take delight in reading them openly in the front room, to Mother's great chagrin. She can hardly deny me the pleasure, though, since she never forbade Evelyn from reading them, and now it is too late.

I am so preoccupied by my musings that I do not pay attention, and suddenly a sharp pain has me yelping in my seat. A wave of sickness comes rolling in when I see that I have buried the sharp sewing needle deep into the pad of my left ring finger. My sisters are on their feet in seconds, and crowd around me to inspect the damage.

We all close our eyes when Evelyn pulls the needle out.

"Find bandages," she commands Sophie, who runs from the room at once—relieved, I suppose, to be away from the blood that blooms upon my finger and threatens to drip down on the skirt I am hemming. Adelaide quickly moves it out of the way.

"Perhaps that was a warning," Evelyn says quietly.

I pretend not to understand. "A warning of what?"

"A warning not to set your sights on a man already married."

• • •

My ring finger still thumps with pain when we make our way upstairs to bed. Evelyn and Adelaide carry candles to light our way on the steps. Mother and Father are still downstairs, and we can hear her complaining voice in his study. Doubtlessly, it is I who has once again caused her dismay. The kitchen is all quiet, though. Mary is always in bed by eight, seeing as how her day starts so early. She will have had her dinner with Mr. and Mrs. Norris, a middle-aged couple who live in a cottage behind the stables and serve as our barn manager and cook. Doubtlessly, the servants' meal in the kitchen has been far more pleasant than the one we shared in the dining room.

When we reach the landing, we say good night. Sophie and Evelyn go to their rooms, and Adelaide and I enter ours. Before, I used to share with Evelyn, but after she got engaged, Mother thought it more suitable if she had a room of her own, and sacrificed a guest room for the purpose. It would only be temporary, after all. Sophie now resides alone in the room she used to share with Adelaide—something she rather strongly dislikes. I myself would certainly have preferred to have a room of my own, but even I can see that an eight-year-old and a thirteen-year-old might not thrive together, and so I did not complain when Adelaide moved in.

The room is simple: two walnut beds mirror each other across the floor, while a writing desk resides under the white-curtained window. There is a sizable dresser and a wall closet, and in a corner dwells a small coal stove, rife with swirling ornaments. The walls are painted a dusty blue and hung with things we have made ourselves: stitched verses and painted flowers, mostly. A maze that I stitched from imagination when I was about ten has a place of honor above my bed. The cold, gray-painted floor is covered by a woven rug in blue hues.

Adelaide and I stand with our backs to each other as we change out of our day dresses and into our nightgowns, both made of white cotton and hemmed with Irish lace. The candle stands on the writing desk; its flickering flame is mirrored in the dark windowpane. The night outside is quiet; the seagulls are finally resting. Only the sea is there, rolling softly.

Adelaide sits on the room's single chair, facing me while brushing her hair exactly one hundred times. When not braided, it falls around her shoulders like a cloak of pale moonlight. I sit down on my bed and start on the great work of freeing my own tangled tresses. I idly wish that I, too, had inherited father's straight, plain hair in place of Mother's coarse curls.

"What did you see at the tower on Sunday?" Adelaide suddenly asks.

"The same as you all did from the yard," I answer. "It must have become crooked over time, because almost all of it had fallen into the sea, and there was nothing left but some pieces of wall, and a pile of pebbles." My hands are deeply buried in my hair, working on the hard knot of a ribbon, which is difficult to do with a bandaged finger.

"You must have been the first one to see it after it fell," Adelaide muses. The brush makes no sound as it passes through her hair. When she is done, she will braid it anew, to rest upon her pillow like a silken rope.

"There was nothing much to see," I repeat, though a sudden pain has taken hold in my gut. "Just rocks." My gaze shifts to the window. "It's so strange that it is gone."

"The boys at school say that the witch is let loose." Adelaide shudders on the chair.

"Then they are fools," I say, though a shiver travels down my spine, and the bellyache does not let up.

"Maybe," Adelaide agrees, "but nothing save the tower fell down." She says it as if it is evidence of something sinister going on.

"Nothing else on this island is that old," I remind her. "The stones were barely held together anymore. It was too old to withstand—and it was lucky that it happened when no one was around. We walked past it just the same day."

"I know," she says, and then, after a pause, "Do you think it is still a wicked place now that the tower is gone?"

"I never thought it was wicked in the first place," I answer.

Adelaide's lips split in a smile. "Neither does Miss Russel. She brought us there on Monday—all of us." Her smile widens as she considers the transgression. "Annabeth and I talked about it later, and figured that Miss Russel didn't know any better, seeing as how she is new to Margaret's Keep." Though she has been here for a couple of years, Miss Russel will be seen as "new" for at least a decade yet.

A sudden sympathy for Miss Russel blooms in my chest. "The islanders will not stand for it."

"That's what Annabeth and I thought, too. But if the place isn't wicked anymore, maybe it doesn't matter that we went."

"Best of luck to Miss Russel," I say. "The ire of Margaret's Keep is sure to come down on her now."

Adelaide smiles. "Perhaps she can fight them off with her umbrella."

"What did *you* see, though, when you were at the tower?" The knot in my stomach tightens.

"The same as you did." Adelaide shrugs. "Just stones—and seagulls."

"Exactly." I finally get the ribbon loose and let it pool down on the bed.

When we have finished braiding our hair, blown out the candle, and slipped in under the covers, Adelaide asks, "Do you really not want to leave Margaret's Keep because of Reverend Hill?"

"What is it to you?" I fire back.

"It only seems like such a poor reason." Adelaide can be annoyingly candid. "He is married—and a reverend. He doesn't seem such a grand prize to me."

I twist under the covers, suddenly craving meat again. "At least he is someone I *want,*" I say, "unlike Aunt Anne's terrible suggestions."

"But you know you can never have him?" My little sister sounds serious.

"You cannot know that for sure," I huff, although of course I know that the obstacles are great. Antonia Hill being the greatest. But then, if Antonia is ill, there might be hope for me yet. A widower could look where he liked.

"Mother and Evelyn say that you are making a fool of yourself—and of all of us. Mother says you have too little to keep you occupied after leaving school. Maybe you should find something to do, Charlotte?"

"On the mainland?" I roll my eyes in the dark. I will *never* give Mother what she wants. I will remain a spinster rather than live like her, bound to a man I do not like, and burdened with daughters I despise. Why does she even want us to repeat a cycle she has thoroughly proven does *not* lead to happiness?

"Why do you do it, though?" Adelaide's voice has dropped a notch. "Why do you make such a *spectacle* of it? Maybe if it wasn't so *obvious* that you like him—"

"*Love* him," I correct her.

"Well, maybe if it wasn't so *obvious* that you love him, Mother wouldn't be so mad."

"I am not afraid of Mother," I say, then let out a breath of relief when Adelaide does not reply.

I lie awake for a while after that, just thinking of Jasper Hill. I recall the time we brought the children's choir down to the sea and told them to sing louder than the waves, to make sure that the words of praise reached heaven. Our singers, especially the younger ones, took the assignment to heart, and sang as loudly as they possibly could, their little faces turning quite red. Sophie, too, had abandoned all caution, and roared her song into the wind.

Jasper Hill and I stood a few steps behind them, looking out on the crashing waves. We were so close that our fingers nearly touched. From time to time, he would turn his head and smile at me with pure joy. Mary had made cookies for the choir, which I carried with me in a basket, and the air around Jasper and I smelled of cardamom and brown sugar.

"Angels born from salt and rocks," he leaned in to say quietly in my ear.

I laughed. "Smelling of sheep and with feathers in their hair."

"Should we join them?" he asked, and did take my hand then, as we stepped up to stand next to the children. Our voices joined theirs as we, too, sang to the sky and the water, with kelp licking the toes of our shoes.

His hand remained in mine, quite warm, and I was suddenly overwhelmed by a torrent of feelings so strong that it nearly made me cry. There was the sensation of his skin against mine, which was pleasurable in itself, but also the bond made by our linked hands. I could not help but notice how *right* it felt—how *good*. As if it was always meant to be this way: me and Jasper Hill together, singing into the wind. Two souls destined to stand side by side.

I wish those days back again as I lie there, tossing and turning on the pillow. I wish Mrs. Hill had never found the caramels, or that I had not been foolish enough to give them to him in the first place.

My heart is dark with frustration when I finally drift off to sleep.

• • •

I have a nightmare in which I am back in the shed, sitting on the stool in my corner. It is windy outside—the walls around me rattle, though

I barely notice because I am preoccupied with prying a ring off my finger. It looks like Evelyn's engagement ring, though it is far larger, and in place of pearls, there are large black seeds embedded in the silvery metal. It holds my ring finger in a vise, and I wake up to a hot and throbbing pain in that same finger. Though it had stung when I first pierced it with the needle, that pain was nothing compared to the one I feel now. There is no wonder the ache seeped into my dream.

I gingerly touch the bandage and can feel heat through the layers of cloth. It is as if the whole finger is burning. I pinch it very lightly and moan from the pain. Who would have thought that a tiny wound like this could fester? I have pierced myself with the needle many times, but I have never had this happen before. I consider lighting the candle to have a look at the wound, but then I figure there is little to be done in the dead of night and decide to try to find sleep again.

I do not succeed.

I twist and turn, but the bedclothes feel too hot now, even if the air in the room is chilly enough. I smell my damaged finger through the bandage, and catch the unmistakable scent of pus.

I think about Jasper Hill again to distract myself—of his tall frame and strong fingers, his dark brown eyes and thick mane of hair. I think of kissing his lips, and of lying naked beneath him, feeling his sweat-slick body on mine.

When that does not work, I think of Margaret's Tower, and the sight of it tumbling from the cliff. I wonder if it truly once housed a witch, or if there is another reason why the islanders call it a "wicked place." Though I am an islander myself, we Norths are not privy to their secrets.

I wonder what I did there on Sunday.

I am finally about to drift off again when I hear it: something is moving above me. It sounds as though someone is up in the attic, pulling something heavy across the floorboards. I think of rats, then of seagulls. Perhaps one has built a nest up there? But the sound is somehow too orderly. What could a bird be doing to make a sound like that?

I glance across to Adelaide's bed in the darkness, but she seems to still be sleeping. I can hear her even breathing in the air. The noise in the attic continues: something is being dragged back and forth across the floor.

I barely feel my finger anymore; all I can think of is the noise. Fear comes creeping as I lie there, listening. Has someone gotten inside—and if so, who, and what do they want from us? Then I wonder how Adelaide can still be sleeping. No one should be able to sleep through such noise. I try to remember what is up there, what could be moved around: a chest of drawers, the old dining room chairs, crates of paintings, trunks of china . . .

Get up, I think. *I must get up!* I have to tell Father that someone is in the attic. But my body has stopped listening to me, and I am moored on the sweaty sheets, unable to command as much as a muscle. The air around me reeks of meat, cooked and dripping with gravy.

I must get up! I must get up! Something is very wrong.

Then the knocking in the walls begins.

·8·

charlotte

At first, I hear it from the wall behind my bed as a series of sharp raps: knock . . . knock, knock, knock, knock . . . It sounds as if someone is knocking on a front door, wanting to be let inside.

Then the sound moves, and suddenly it comes from under the window, just behind the writing desk—but there is noise still coming from the attic, too. The thing up there has quickened its pace and rushes across the floor like a sled on snow.

Every time a new sound erupts, it feels as though my heart stops in my chest, and I renew my efforts to move, to *get up,* but my body will not respond. Only my eyes, quite useless in the dark, seem not to have fallen under the spell, but move rapidly around, taking in the night-dark room, searching for *something* to tell me what is happening. I try to make a sound to wake up Adelaide, and a few muffled sounds escape my lips, but none of them are loud enough to rouse my sister.

The knocking moves on to the floor between our beds, below the woven rug. Knock . . . knock, knock. The thing in the attic rushes across the uneven boards; it sounds very heavy. Perhaps it is the chest of drawers. My muscles ache from trying and failing to move on the sheets. My skin is so wet that the cotton of my nightgown is glued to my body. The parts of me that escaped the covers when I tossed and turned earlier have chilled in the night air and now feel painfully cold.

My damaged finger, however, is as hot as a piece of smoldering coal.

The knocking is in the wall above my bed again. It shifts idly around over my head, skipping between the blue-painted boards. I want the noises to cease, and for my body to *listen to me*. I dread every knock, and even think that the shed is *nothing* compared to this: being trapped in my own bed.

Then, suddenly, it is morning.

The sunlight floods inside between the white curtains, Adelaide yawns and stretches in her bed. From downstairs, I can hear Mrs. Norris in the kitchen—the sizzling of fat, and the shouts as she chases the barn cat off the table. A faint scent of fresh bread has found its way up the stairs. Outside the window, the seagulls scream, just as they do every morning, and I can hear Sophie out there, too, speaking to Mr. Norris.

There is no knocking in the walls, and no sounds from the attic.

I sit up with a gasp that startles my sister and can smell myself in an instant: sour perspiration and pus from the wound. My hair hangs in tendrils around my face, so my braid must have come undone sometime during the night.

"Goodness, Charlotte, you are as white as a sheet." Adelaide's eyes go wide. She scrambles out of bed to cross the floor and press a damp hand to my brow. "Do you feel like you have a fever?" she asks with concern. "You don't look well at all."

"I'm fine," I croak, though, clearly I am not. I fight Adelaide off so I can finally *get up* and escape the cocoon of cotton sheets that has held me so cruelly captive. A surge of relief passes through me when my naked feet hit the cold floor, though I avoid stepping on the rug, remembering only too clearly the knocking that sounded underneath it.

"Let me get Mary." Adelaide is out of the door before I can stop her, the nightgown billowing around her ankles. More than anything else, I just want to stand there and breathe, reacquaint myself with this world of sounds that belong to daylight and not the night.

Whatever it was, it has passed, and I do feel quite myself again.

Mary comes thumping up the stairs and enters the room with her skirt held high, showing a glimpse of her knitted stockings. "Are you unwell, Charlotte?" she asks, and pushes me to sit down on the dratted bed. She squints at me with worried eyes.

"I slept poorly," I say. "I am drenched in sweat."

Another cool hand touches my brow. "I think you have a fever," she says.

I hold up my finger and wave it in the air. "It might be infected," I say.

"That tiny little wound?" She tuts and catches the swollen appendage between her own. I hiss when she starts unpacking it from the bandage. My finger is quite red and much bigger than the others. The wound itself is just a pinprick, though it weeps a reeking liquid when Mary gently pinches it. "The needle must've been filthy," she says, and takes my other hand to guide me downstairs, treating me as though I am an invalid and not just a clumsy seamstress. "We should rinse it out—maybe open it," Mary threatens as we make our way down the steps. "Mrs. Norris can make a poultice."

"I'm hungry," I say. I am *starving,* in fact. "Could you ask Mrs. Norris to fry some ham?"

"Certainly." She sounds puzzled, but looks pleased, too. "It's good that you have an appetite." She brings me into the kitchen, where I patiently sit below the array of copper pans, while Mary and Mrs. Norris tut and groan in equal measure as they inspect my swollen finger. Mrs. Norris cleans the skin, first with brown liquor, and then with boiled water. Mary winds a fresh bandage around the ugly thing, hiding the damage from view.

"It sits *inside* the finger," Mrs. Norris warns me. "If the swelling doesn't go down on its own, you might need to go to the mainland."

"Oh, I don't think it will come to that," I say, mostly to reassure myself. It is such a tiny wound after all. How serious can it be?

"I'll make you a tea for the fever," says Mrs. Norris. "And I'll make ham, too, if that's still what you want."

I nod my head with vigor. That is most certainly still what I want.

I go back upstairs to dress—clumsy and slow with my throbbing finger—then I join my sisters in the dining room for breakfast. Mother, thankfully, breaks her fast with Father at dawn, and is nowhere to be seen. She is probably up in her private room, painting, as has been her habit for as long as I can remember. She wields the brush while smoking cigarettes and drinking glass upon glass of port. She always paints the same thing, though: houses, large and small. Some of them are on a city street, others in the countryside, seated among sheaves of golden wheat. There are no people in her paintings, only houses. I sometimes wonder if she pictures herself in them, or if she imagines other people living there. Perhaps it is her way of leaving the island.

Her way of escaping us all.

I sit down in my seat at the table, where a plate of delicious, pink ham is waiting, and meet three pairs of worried eyes: two of them blue, one brown, like mine. I sigh inwardly, though I do not let it show. I feel awful from the night's ordeal and am not ready to face the barrage of remarks that I know must be waiting.

Nevertheless, they arrive.

"I never thought a prick of the needle could turn so serious," says Evelyn. Her own unblemished fingers are daintily curled around a piece of half-eaten toast.

"Mary said you have a fever," Adelaide informs me. "I did say that you looked terrible," she adds, not without some smugness. I refrain from letting her know that she has crumbs clinging to her cheek.

"It cannot be all that bad." Evelyn's brow furrows. "You're sitting here, after all, eating rich meat—"

"Is it very painful?"

Sophie is the only one I deign to answer at the moment. "Not terribly so right now," I say, although it throbs and aches. "Perhaps Mary and Mrs. Norris's administrations helped." I pick up my knife and fork and start cutting. When Adelaide offers me a piece of toast, I decline. She is dressed in a sensible brown day dress, while Sophie has donned a red-checked skirt under her pristine white shirt. They are both attending school after breakfast. Evelyn and I wear day dresses, too, but we are not to do anything but lounge about the house.

The meat hits my tongue, salty and pink. It is the best thing I have ever eaten.

"Let's hope you won't need to see a doctor." Evelyn gives my bandaged finger another worried glance. "At least you won't have to sew again for a while." She knows how much I hate it.

"Unless Mother decides it will be a good lesson for me," I reply. It would be just like her to make me suffer through a grueling chore despite a painful wound.

"If you can abstain from angering her, she might not." Evelyn's eyebrows rise just a fraction. "You do look quite haggard, though."

"I couldn't sleep at all," I admit. "I heard the strangest noises in the attic, and then inside the wall—I thought somebody was in the house . . . Someone who wasn't supposed to be." I look between my sisters as the memories of the terrible night come washing over me again.

"In the attic?" Adelaide offers me an incredulous look. "How could someone even get up there without anyone noticing?"

"I don't know." I spear another piece of meat.

"It was just the fever, don't you think?" Evelyn sips her tea. "Wild dreams are often associated with a high temperature—"

"But what if it was not?" I look between Evelyn and Adelaide. "We cannot be sure before we look."

"Who would want to break into the attic?" Evelyn's voice is the very epitome of calm and reason. "There's nothing of value up there—"

"Maybe it's a vagrant," Adelaide suggests.

"When did you last see a vagrant on Margaret's Keep?" Evelyn's lips twitch. "Father would know if any strangers arrived—"

"Perhaps he was a stowaway on the *Seagull,*" Sophie says.

Evelyn fastens her gaze on mine. "What exactly did you hear?"

"Something heavy being pulled—or dragged—across the floor." I notice how my mouth has gone dry, just as my heart starts pounding in my chest.

"Like one of the chests?" Adelaide asks. "Like the one with children's clothes in it?"

"I don't know." I reach for the tea Mary has poured for me in an effort to moisten my parched tongue. "It kept going back and forth up there, as if it was being pushed around. I wanted to get Father, but then—"

"What?" Evelyn's pale gaze pierces me.

"Then I heard knocking in the wall," I say.

"*In* the wall?" Sophie's eyes have gone wide. "You mean *outside* the wall?"

"I—I don't know." I feel confused.

"No one can knock from *inside* the wall." Sophie gives a satisfied smile and shakes her head. She wipes her little hands with a linen napkin.

"Could it have been a bird?" Adelaide asks.

"No," I say, "I don't think so." I will never, ever tell them of how I could not move. They would just roll their eyes at me and secretly be worried.

"What about a rat?" asks Sophie.

"It had to have been an awfully big one." And one that could use its little paws to knock just like a person.

"You should have woken Father," Adelaide scolds me. "If nothing else, he could have put your mind at ease—or you could have gone to Mary, so she could have looked at your finger sooner."

"Yes, I suppose I should have," I say, then drop my gaze to my plate and attack another slice of ham with my knife. I have eaten half of the sizable portion already, but still feel famished.

"You are unusually meek today." Evelyn's eyebrows have traveled even farther up on her brow. "Perhaps that finger serves a purpose, keeping you in check."

"Perhaps." I try to smile, but then, just as I shift the ham around in the grease, I catch sight of something glinting on the china. I spear the meat with my fork to lift it away—and feel sick with shock when I see what it was hiding.

On my plate, swimming in juices, lies one single, vicious sewing needle.

My sisters and I stare at each other across the breakfast table. Wide eyes meet and cross like swords. I hold the sewing needle in the air between us. It is such a tiny thing: shiny and new from the look of it. The sharp end points up to the crystal chandelier.

My heart races in my chest.

"Oh, Charlotte," Adelaide breathes.

"What game is this?" Evelyn sounds angry. "What are you up to, Charlotte?"

"*I* didn't put it there," I bark at her. "Why would I do such a foolish thing? I'm not a *child,* Evelyn!"

"Oh, please," she says, but despite her bravado, I can tell that she is shaken.

"Maybe it was just a mistake," Adelaide suggests in a brittle voice. "Perhaps it fell out of Mrs. Norris's basket in the kitchen—"

"Maybe it was stuck on your bandage." Evelyn invents an explanation of her own.

"Oh, just think of what could have happened if you had swallowed that!" Sophie looks sick.

"What if it was placed there on purpose," I dare suggest, eyeing them all in turn. "Maybe someone didn't much appreciate the attention the needle prick brought me—"

"Charlotte, no!" Adelaide is up from her chair at once, shocked by the suggestion. "None of us would ever do anything like that!"

"The only person in this room known for craving attention is *you,*" Evelyn snaps from her chair.

"Who then?" I ask, still holding the needle in front of me. "I cannot imagine Mary or Mrs. Norris doing it."

"Yet they are the only ones who *could,*" says Adelaide. "They were the ones handling your food—"

"But it stood unguarded in here before I came down," I argue. "Any one of you could have done it."

"But *none* of us was alone with your plate," Adelaide keeps protesting. "We were already seated when Mary brought it in."

"So maybe it was *all* of you, then." My hand that holds the needle shakes.

"*Of course* not!" Evelyn sounds outraged. She slams her palm against the table; china and silver spoons clatter and jump. "Get ahold of yourself, Charlotte! None of your sisters would do anything to hurt you." Her eyes are dark with anger.

The ruckus has summoned Mary, who comes bursting in with worry on her face. She blanches when she sees the needle and is served the sorry tale.

"I cannot believe it," she exclaims. "The ham went straight from the pan to the plate, and I brought it in here myself. Mrs. Norris will be devastated!"

"Could the needle have been stuck on Charlotte's bandage?" Evelyn's face is stiff with anger.

"Maybe." Mary sounds unsure. "But don't you think I would have felt it when I put it on her finger?"

"The needle was *under* the ham," I point out. "How could it have fallen *under* the ham?"

"Did anyone else come into the kitchen while Mrs. Norris made the food?" Evelyn asks Mary.

The housekeeper shrugs. "Only Mrs. North. She came to advise on dinner."

As if summoned by the mention, Mother appears in the doorway. She looks slightly disheveled. Her hair is hastily braided but not pinned up, and her ruffled shirtwaist is unevenly buttoned.

"What is this noise?" she complains. "Why must you be so *loud*?"

"It seems that Charlotte found a needle in her food." Mary's gaze is on the floor. "We cannot figure out where it came from."

"A needle, huh?" Mother approaches the table and squints at the tiny weapon pinched between my fingertips. Then her gaze fastens on my bandage. "Didn't you hurt yourself with one of those?"

I nod but do not answer. Despite myself, I feel a pang of anger that my mother is not more concerned. I certainly should not let it bother me. I am not a child, and my mother is entirely without compassion. I know that well already.

"Perhaps it serves you right for being such a klutz." A smile tugs at her lips. "Perhaps it is a warning to mind your needle—"

"She thinks that *we* did it." Sophie's lips quiver. "But we did not! No one did *anything* to her food."

"Of course not," Mother scoffs. "Why would you do something so silly?"

"I assure you," Mary shoots in, "that none of us in the kitchen—"

"Of course not," Mother says again. "That would have been absurdly foolish of you, and I know you all appreciate your positions."

"Then who?" I say, looking between them all, feeling more tired by the second. My bandaged finger throbs.

"Yes, who indeed?" Mother's eyes meet mine. She still has that little half smile on her lips.

"Not me!" I cry, but Mother just snorts and turns her back, then sails smoothly back out the door like a warship.

"I will get you a new plate," Mary says, while whisking the first one away.

"Don't bother," I tell her, dropping the needle in my tea. "I have quite lost my hankering for ham."

·9·

charlotte

When Adelaide and Sophie have left for school, Mary, Mr. Norris, Evelyn, and I go up into the attic. We are well armed with a lantern, fireplace pokers, and scissors, and Mr. Norris has brought along some rat traps, too, convinced that rodents are the culprits. I am the only one who feels this search is urgent, but the needle on my plate has bought me some leverage, so no one protests when I insist on an inspection.

Mr. Norris has brought up a stepladder to wedge into the trapdoor in the ceiling outside our bedrooms. He goes up first, lantern held high, and the flickering flame colors his gray beard yellow. Mary follows next, then me, and lastly Evelyn. The latter is in a foul mood. She thinks it is highly unlikely that someone has broken into our home to sneak a needle onto my plate. I think so, too—but what happened in the night still haunts me, and I know I will not rest soundly in my bed again unless I am assured that it is safe. My fever seems to have broken already, but that is by no means enough to convince me that all will be well come nightfall.

I *must* know what is up there, or I shall never sleep again.

The cramped space of the attic spreads out before us, heaped with things we no longer need. The scent carries traces of sun-heated roof tiles, dust, and salt from the sea. What I do *not* smell, however, is the unmistakable stench of rodents' nests or the reek of seagull droppings. My nerves are on edge, and I cannot help it. I should feel safe in this moment. There are people, light, and pokers all around me, but nevertheless I feel scared.

Mr. Norris carefully makes his way across the most cluttered portion of the attic while the rest of us huddle by the trapdoor, already longing for the order and daylight below. The glow from his lantern reveals only what we have expected to find: the trunks and the chairs, the chest of drawers, and crate upon crate of Mother's paintings. The surprises are few and not terribly important: I see a dollhouse, all forgotten and empty, which I faintly remember from early childhood, and a rocking horse that Father bought for my brother, George, when he was born. Sadly, the child did not live for long, and no one has ever played with the toy, yet the paint has cracked and its mane has tangled. Everything is covered in a veil of dust.

Mr. Norris walks slowly farther into the cavern, to where the knickknacks grow sparser and the floor opens up—over where my room is located on the floor below.

"I cannot see anything out of the ordinary," Mr. Norris says in his gruff voice, though his hand is still brandishing the poker, ready to strike if he has to.

Mary climbs in after him, traversing trunks and hatboxes. "The dust seems undisturbed," she says, scanning the floor with her eyes. "I cannot see any signs of animals either." Mr. Norris lifts the lantern higher in the air to make sure she gets a good look.

Beside me, Evelyn turns the other way, squints into the darkness of the other half of the attic. "We ought to search it all, shouldn't we? In case someone is hiding."

Mr. Norris and Mary move back toward us. When we turn our attention to the left side of the room, I notice how my body is stiff and crowded with minor aches, telling me that I must have been very tense while they searched. We move some chairs around and push Mother's crates away to make a clear path. I watch again with bated breath as Mary and Mr. Norris move into the darkness, just to find that half, too, empty and undisturbed.

"There is nothing up here," Mary says at last, and Evelyn shoots me a hot look of triumph. "Perhaps you ought to go talk to the reverend if the nightmares persist," the housekeeper suggests, and my heart leaps at the suggestion.

Evelyn snorts. "Surely, the reverend has better things to do than listening to Charlotte's fantasies."

"One never knows." Mary shrugs. "Sometimes talking to someone about matters of the soul can be a great comfort."

Evelyn rolls her eyes, but says nothing.

"But what were the noises if there's no intruder?" I ask.

"The earthquake could have shaken something loose," Mr. Norris speculates. "Perhaps there is a board knocking against the wall. I will have a look around."

"Thank you," I say, but feel discouraged. Perhaps Evelyn was right and it was all in my mind. Perhaps it truly *was* the fever?

But that does not explain the needle under the ham.

• • •

I barely eat anything before dinner, although my stomach growls and I strongly crave beef. I ask Mrs. Norris for broth for lunch, but keep turning the spoon over in the bowl, worried that a needle will poke its eye above the surface like the fin of an insidious shark.

I am not much better at dinner, even if Mrs. Norris has made parsley soup and salmon, which I normally enjoy. I cannot shake the feeling that the food is tainted—*foul*—and I keep pushing the fish meat around on my plate. I inspect every bite before chewing, but still feel reluctant to swallow. Nobody remarks upon it. Perhaps they think my poor appetite is due to the fever or the pain in my finger, though the first is gone and the latter reduced to a dull ache. Mother looks at me with the eyes of a snake; her contempt is an almost tangible thing, writhing in the air between us.

"No more pins in your soup?" she asks me when the meal is almost at an end.

I shake my head but do not answer. I cannot spar with her today.

"It probably fell out of her bandage," Evelyn says.

"Of course," Mother replies, but she does not look as if she believes it.

I dread the night that is closing in.

Yet everything feels so utterly normal when Adelaide and I retire. We take our turns at the washbasin before changing into our nightgowns. Adelaide brushes her hair like always; her jaw moves while she silently counts. I free my finger from the bandage, and smile with satisfaction to see that the swelling has shrunk.

The fear comes creeping back, though, when Adelaide blows out the candle. I would like to ask her to keep it lit, but Mother does not like waste, and my sister is obedient.

We both crawl into our beds. I ought to be exhausted from the trying day, but find that I am not. In fact, I am wide awake—alert—under the chilly covers. It is my body, I presume, that does not much like to be back in the place where it was held captive the night before. While Adelaide already snores softly, my ears strain, searching for noises out of the ordinary. I stare up at the black ceiling, as if daring the sounds to come back.

Nothing happens.

I force myself to relax—lure myself into believing that maybe the others were right, and it was indeed bad dreams and fever that had caused the disturbance the night before. Perhaps the needle in my food *did* fall out of the bandage. Then, just as I roll over and close my eyes, I feel a sharp jab in my ankle.

I cry out and sit up, heaving for breath. Adelaide is on her feet at once, rushing across the room.

"What is it, Charlotte? What is going on?"

"I don't know," I cry. "Something bit me!"

While Adelaide fumbles with the matches and lights the candle, I throw the cover aside and look down on my foot. A sphere of blood forms on the surface of my skin, before it bursts and trickles downward as a bright red rivulet.

"Oh, Charlotte, you're bleeding!" Adelaide looks pale and anxious. She reaches out a hand as if to touch the damage, before quickly pulling it back again. "What did that? What bit you?"

"I don't know," I reply as the blood hits the white sheet and blooms on the fabric.

"A mouse?" she asks, eyes wide.

"I don't know," I say again, hissing from the pain. "Find me something to stop the blood."

While Adelaide searches for a handkerchief, I frenetically pat the area around my foot with my hands, desperate to find an answer that makes sense.

I find it in the end. A sewing needle is embedded under the sheet, its sharp point barely visible as it peeks out through the cotton.

"Oh, Charlotte," Adelaide gasps. "How did this happen?"

I press the handkerchief to my ankle with tears rising in my eyes. I think, but do not say, that maybe it is Mother who does all this to punish me—for being clumsy, yes, but also just for being a nuisance. Perhaps she is still angry about what happened in church, even if I did nothing more than look at the reverend. Perhaps this is her way of making my life so miserable that I will have no time to think of Jasper Hill.

Perhaps she tries to chase me to the mainland.

"Maybe there are more." Adelaide sounds terrified and presses a hand to her mouth. "Get out of the bed, Charlotte!"

I do as she says and come to stand next to her. I have tied the handkerchief around my ankle, but the blood is seeping through.

"Maybe we should get someone?" Adelaide frets. "Mary, perhaps—or Evelyn?" She does not suggest Mother.

I shake my head, thinking how they will likely suspect me of doing it to myself. "We'll search the bed," I say, "and then we'll see."

Adelaide finds a second needle hidden inside the pillowcase, and when I strip the sheet off the bed, another three drop to the floor. We search every inch of the mattress with our hands, and feel around for sharp metal in the creases and folds of the bedclothes.

By the time we are done searching, we have found ten needles—not counting the one that stabbed me in the leg.

·10·

ruth

Never had I thought that my excursion to Margaret's Tower would cause such a fuss, but I suppose that is the curse of the newcomer: you cannot gauge just how deep superstitions and beliefs run in an established community. I considered it, of course, but the much-feared tower was no longer *there,* so what better time to teach the children that the place was void of ghosts? Their guardians disagreed, however, and two of the mothers paid me a visit the very next day, just as school ended, to make sure that I knew their feelings.

"It's not just the tower," Mrs. Newell said, standing inside the schoolroom, which still smelled of the children's labor: sweat, graphite, and buttered bread. Her hips were nearly wide enough to touch the desks on either side, and I wished that I had such a presence; no one could ignore me then. "The dirt itself is foul," she continued, placing her rough, broad hands upon those ample hips. The ends of the gray headscarf tied under her chin quivered with the power of her fury.

"It's cursed, that place." Mrs. Fisher picked up the thread, shaking her head violently. "It's been a place to fear ever since Margaret herself lived there."

"But how do you *know* that?" I asked. "Have any of you ever seen anything—?"

"No." Mrs. Newell cut me off. "Because none of us are stupid enough to go there." She shook her head and rolled her eyes, implying that I was the exception.

"Then how do you—" I paused to change tactics. "Have you ever known *anyone* who has experienced *anything* around the tower?"

Neither of them replied. Mrs. Fisher wet her lips with the tip of her tongue. Her bony hands curled into fists by her side. Clouds came drifting on the sky outside the window, blotting out the sun, and the waning light matched the gloom of our discussion.

"Do any of you know just what terrible thing might happen if one goes to the tower?" I asked them next, foolishly thinking I had made a little headway.

"We aren't to speak of it." Mrs. Fisher's jowls quivered. "Don't you know that speaking of such things might call them?"

"Call who?" I pried.

"That we can't say," she snapped.

"But I was there myself. I saw nothing out of the ordinary—just a ruin."

"And you brought *our* children there with you." There was genuine fear in Mrs. Fisher's eyes. "I don't expect much from newcomers," she chided, "but I do ask for a little respect. You *must* have known, Miss Russel, that we don't go to that place—"

"But why? It's hard to fear a place that does not immediately seem like a danger unless someone has done the courtesy of telling you *why* it is feared."

"You *must* have heard the stories!" Mrs. Newell fixed her gaze on me. "You *must* have heard of Margaret and the devilry she was up to."

"*Allegedly* up to," I corrected her. I *had* heard about the light in the window, of course: a flickering candle signaling to the fishermen to lure them to shore. The tale said nothing of what the ghost of Margaret wanted with the weather-beaten fishermen, though, which I considered a narrative flaw. "According to my predecessor, those stories are rumors only. He also told me that Margaret might have been nothing more than an unhappy wife with a wandering eye, locked up by her husband to save his reputation." I was starting to feel irate myself. Surely, nothing I had done warranted such a scolding.

"Perhaps she was both," Mrs. Newell challenged me. "Bad apples might contain many flavors, and if you have broken *one* of God's laws, why not another?"

"But you don't *know* that," I tried again, exasperated. "And even if she *did* dip her toe into the 'dark arts,' who can blame her? It must have been terribly lonely, living in that tower all by herself."

That had certainly been the wrong thing to say.

"Is that what you teach our daughters, Miss Russel? That a bit of loneliness excuses a dance with the devil?" Mrs. Fisher's lips twisted up with disgust.

"You are to teach our children good moral values, aren't you? What moral is there in excusing an adulterous witch?"

"Compassion," I croaked. "Compassion and understanding—"

"We don't reward wickedness on Margaret's Keep," Mrs. Newell interrupted.

"If only you could tell me what you think is—or was—in the tower—"

"We don't speak of it," Mrs. Fisher stated again. "And neither should you go poking about. It's none of your concern."

"You *knew* we didn't want our children to go there," Mrs. Newell persisted, "yet you took it upon yourself to bring them there anyway."

"Just because you don't know any better, it doesn't give you the right," Mrs. Fisher concluded. "We keep them away for a reason, and you should have trusted that our judgment is sound."

Mrs. Newell delivered a final blow. "We speak for all the parents. Some of them want you to leave, but I don't know. We'll see."

With that, they turned their backs, left the schoolroom and me behind. They did not say goodbye or even look back, but just left me standing there like a punished child, vaguely ashamed and utterly confused, wondering—with some ire—if they would have dared speak to me in that manner if I had been *Mr.* Russel, and sported a fine mustache.

• • •

Days later, I am still quite shaken, and wary of what might happen on Sunday in church. If my visitors are to be believed, the whole island is upset by my so-called transgression. Surely they will not confront me there? Or will they? Am I in for a mob—torches and all?

As I tie my boots and fetch my umbrella, preparing to visit the island's lone store, I think that if they do, I will have no choice but to die on the pyre.

To me, Margaret's Tower—or its ruin—is still just a pile of old rocks.

·11·

jasper

Antonia is by the window again, the breakfast tea cooling in her hand. She has stood like that every morning since the earthquake, and her nights have been restless, filled with evil dreams. Her gaze is trained on what is not there: the tower with its jagged crown reaching toward the sky. She never paid much attention to it while it was still standing, but perhaps that is just it, I think, as I butter my toast at the dining room table. Perhaps the thing that has her so utterly bewitched is that something that seemed so robust has fallen. Perhaps it reminds her of her own cruel fate.

But I shall not ask, so I will never know.

"Try to eat something," I say instead. "A little dry toast, if nothing else."

"I cannot stomach it, Jasper," she replies, still with her back turned to me. Her slender form is framed by blinding sunlight and wisps of lace curtains. Her frizzy curls ignite like a halo. With her blue day dress on, she brings to mind depictions of the Madonna—though I cannot say that aloud either. Even if I mean well, she is sure to take offense, due to what is *not* in her arms: a baby, wholesome and holy. Antonia holds only tea.

"Perhaps we should see a doctor," I say, thinking of the arrangements that have to be made: book places on the *Seagull*, find a physician willing to see us, and then catch the *Seagull* to go back again. We must stay on the mainland for at least one night.

Antonia still refuses to look at me. "Doctors never did me any good. But you should send for more laudanum. I'm almost out."

I want to say that perhaps her dreams would not be as wicked if she did not partake so generously of the medicine, but I know better than to taunt the bear, and so I keep my peace. "I will see to it," I say instead, and am secretly happy for it, too, since it will provide me with an opportunity to step outside and enjoy the crisp and chilly spring air. Being at home can be stifling sometimes—especially when Antonia is unwell. I wish I was the kind of man who could patiently hold his wife's hand through her sickness and never feel a pull to leave her side, but I am not. "I would feel better if you ate something," I tell her. "Perhaps one of those?" I point with my butter knife to the bowl of hard-boiled eggs on the table, sandwiched between a butter dish and the toast rack, and all of it engulfed in the scent of hot tea. "Did you dream again last night?" I ask, when my wife does not respond to my plea.

"Uh-huh." Her head bobs up and down upon her slender neck. "I dreamt of seagulls circling the tower. They screamed as though their feathers were on fire."

"What then?" I ask, oddly intrigued.

"Then the tower was gone, just the ruin remained, and the birds spiraled downward into its center, where they were swallowed up by the earth."

"That sounds awfully dramatic," I say. "Why was it so frightening to you?"

"Because the birds didn't want to go there," she replies. "They didn't want to be swallowed up, but they had to. They were compelled."

"Why would the earth swallow them up?" I taste my tea; it is awfully bitter.

"Perhaps there is something down there." Antonia finally turns her head to cast a frightened look over her shoulder. Her pallor does not look good and her eyes are burning as with fever, though I placed my hand on her brow this morning and found it cool to the touch.

"Might it not be that the old story about the witch has wormed its way into your mind, my dear? I know some islanders say she is buried where the tower stands—stood."

"Perhaps." She sounds indifferent. "She was not a witch, though. Not the way Noreen tells it. According to her, Margaret was an unfaithful wife who cuckolded her husband. Twice. After the last transgression, her spouse had her imprisoned on the island as a punishment, denying her company for the rest of her life. The tower was the price for the insult to his dignity."

"Aren't witches and unfaithful wives the same?" I ask, in an attempt to be playful. My wife will not have it, though.

"No, Jasper. One story is a fairy tale, while the other might well be true." She adds a loud, overbearing sigh to the statement.

I pretend not to sense her impatience with me. "No matter who or what she was, I don't see why Margaret would want to swallow all those birds."

"Maybe she just wanted to live," Antonia says cryptically, still with her gaze glued to the ruin—and again I cannot shake the feeling that it is herself she is speaking of.

• • •

After breakfast, I find my black coat and ready myself to step outside. As I start down the road, I cannot help but once again despair that *I*—not Antonia—am the one to be taking the air. The plan when we moved here was for her to get better. Her doctor and I had decided that the city was too much for her and that she ought to recuperate in more peaceful surroundings. Her recovery had been the entire purpose of accepting this post so far away from everything we knew. But Antonia has only gotten worse.

Instead of embracing the island, as I had hoped she would, she prefers to stay inside and barely speaks to a single soul aside from Noreen, who—as proven by this morning's discussion—might not be the best conversational partner for my delicate wife. Though the housekeeper is a kind and competent woman who has served in the clergy house since long before we arrived, she is in every way a child of Margaret's Keep: simple and prone to gossip. It is not what Antonia needs at this time, and I wish she would find better company for herself, but there are few suitable options, and I fear that last Sunday's disastrous tea has scared poor Miss Russel from our door. This truly is a shame, as Antonia could have benefited from the teacher's common sense. Other than Miss Russel, there is only the Norths, whom my wife utterly despises since the whole Charlotte debacle.

Just as the thought of them passes through my mind, I see their home rise before me, stark against the horizon, seated on top of a sloping hill and overlooking the sea. My heart gives a painful twinge when I see it, and I instantly avert my gaze. I will not think about Charlotte. Why would I think about her? She is young and foolish, that is all—infatuated with me because there are no others. Soon enough, she will find herself a spouse on the mainland, just like her sister did . . . and yet my gaze scans the rows of windows and ogles the red-painted front door, which beckons to me like a flame. There is no one in the yard but old Norris, pushing a wheelbarrow across the hard-packed dirt. Smoke streams from both the house's chimneys, or at least it attempts to, before the harsh wind that is this island's curse quickly blows it away.

I avert my gaze. The North residence is not where I am headed.

Instead, I follow the road past the hill and down toward the harbor, where the seagulls are plentiful and fishing vessels bob on the water, their masts rising naked toward the sky. Alongside the pier runs the red-painted building where the catch is taken in and prepared for transport. From my vantage point, coming from above, I can see men moving around down there, stacking barrels. On each side of the harbor, steep cliffs rise out of the water to form solid walls tufted with green. Directly to my right is the spot where the tower should have been, balancing on the edge of the cliff, but now there is nothing at all.

It is not the harbor that is my destination, though, but the brown-painted building sitting right above it, which serves as the island's grocery and post office. The store belongs to Mr. North, of course. Everything here belongs to him—though a kind, elderly man, Mr. Samuelson, runs it with his wife. As I open the door and hear the little bell jingle, I wonder what it must be like to be the daughter of George North—a king, in a sense, if ruling only a very small patch of land jutting out of the sea.

Mr. Samuelson himself is behind the wooden counter today, peddling coffee and sugar in brown paper bags. His register covers one-third of the counter's surface. It is a monstrous thing, rife with keys and ornamental swirls. Whenever Mr. Samuelson operates the handle on the side, the monster chimes as the drawer leaps open.

Mr. North spared no expense when outfitting his store.

I line up with the other customers to perform my errand. Two people are before me: a farmer called Overton, who is at the counter, and—lo and behold—Miss Russel. Her cheeks are ruddy from the wind, and her bun threatens to come loose at the neck. She carries her black umbrella under her arm. Just the sight of her makes me shrink inside. Though she had handled the disaster with grace, I fear that I will never be able to interact with her again without feeling the painful shadow of Antonia's spectacle. I wonder where her students are, but perhaps it is still too early for lessons.

"Reverend," she says when she sees me, adding a tiny smile. "I trust that you have recovered?" I get flustered at once, and she must have noticed, because she quickly adds, "Since the earthquake."

"Oh, yes," I reply, relieved. "We are lucky that nothing was lost."

"Except the tower," she reminds me.

"Oh, yes. That." I try to smile, but the awkwardness I feel prevents it from fully forming on my lips.

"I think people appreciated coming to church to talk things through," she says next. "It's good to check in with your neighbors after a dramatic incident."

"I never thanked you for your assistance," I say. "It was good of you to help out—and to prevent the children from running wild."

"One cannot fault them for being excited." She smiles. "Earthquakes are apparently unheard of on Margaret's Keep. I asked around, and no one has ever reported such a thing." Her smile suddenly falters, and her gaze turns distant, as if she just remembered something. "There is something, though, Reverend . . . something you can help me with, if you truly want to thank me." An expression like pain crosses her features.

"Yes, of course. Anything," I say at once, eager to make amends.

She lowers her voice and lifts her eyes to mine. "I seem to have made a blunder."

"Is that so?" I ask, slightly baffled. I cannot imagine Miss Russel doing anything wrong.

Her voice drops another notch, and she glances at the shopkeeper, busy with wrapping a parcel. "I brought the children to the ruins of Margaret's Tower," she explains in a voice that is barely a whisper. "And now the whole island thinks me *insane*."

I stifle the laughter that threatens to spill out of me, since I know—despite its ridiculousness—that this is indeed a serious matter for most of the island's population. Miss Russel, too, smiles, and our gazes meet as we exchange a silent understanding.

"Are they still whispering about the 'wickedness'?" I ask, and Miss

Russel nods, with another fearful look in Mr. Samuelson's direction. "Let us talk outside, after we have made our purchases?"

When Overton has left with his parcel, Miss Russel has bought her tea and eggs, and I have ordered the laudanum for my wife, the teacher and I meet again outside the store. We are close enough to the harbor now that I can clearly hear the shouted orders the fishermen exchange, mingled with the rush of the sea and the seagulls' ever-present cries. I can even spot Mr. North down there, his bulk unmistakable as he saunters along the pier, inspecting the wooden trawlers and the larger *Seagull,* whose daily journeys to the mainland make life bearable out here, loaded as it is with letters and parcels, in addition to people and countless barrels of fish. Miss Russel sees him, too, and her face instantly turns fearful.

"Did Mr. North voice concerns?" I ask her.

"No, not yet. Perhaps he is above such superstitions. Besides, he takes little interest in his daughters' education. Perhaps he is above that, too."

"You worry, though," I note.

"Oh, yes. The Norths' displeasure is the last thing I need. Mrs. North's ire is legendary."

"Is it? I had not heard." I am genuinely puzzled, and my thoughts go to Charlotte again; I simply cannot help it.

"They say that she has a gruesome temper." Miss Russel rolls her eyes. "But so far it's just the farmwives that have knocked on my door, wanting to let me know what a horrid mistake I have made. I only wanted the children to explore the site, Reverend." She looks utterly crestfallen. "I merely wanted to teach them about earthquakes and legends—let the children know that there doesn't have to be much truth to them." Her gaze fastens on a harried seagull and follows it to sea.

"Do you want me to mention it in church this Sunday? I can certainly spare a few minutes to soothe their minds." And work off my debt to Miss Russel, too.

"Oh, thank you, Reverend, that would be wonderful!" Her whole demeanor becomes suddenly lighter, and it warms my heart to see it.

"We cannot have our children miseducated due to old, silly superstitions," I say.

"Certainly not." She laughs.

"And the Norths *are* educated people, so I doubt that you will have any trouble there," I add, as the two of us head up the road, side by side.

"I certainly hope not." She sighs. "Both Adelaide and Sophie were there with me that day—but I saw Charlotte there, too, after, so perhaps they truly don't mind."

A dizzying surge passes through me at the mention of her name, though I do my very best to suppress it. Yet I cannot help but look at the house again when we pass it and wonder if she is in there. When a dark silhouette briefly appears in one of the upstairs windows, my heart skips a beat in my chest, and I almost miss my step.

"Are you all right, Reverend?" Miss Russel looks at me with concern.

"Certainly." I straighten, and give Miss Russel a shivering smile. "I merely tripped; perhaps a stone in the road." I feel like a schoolboy caught in a lie.

The Norths' red front door snags my eye once more and will not easily let go.

Even after it is gone from view, I can feel it like an eye, burning on my back.

·12·

charlotte

For the next two days, I am hounded by needles. I find them in my shoes, in my clothes, in my food, and in my teacup. I tell no one and swear Adelaide to secrecy, since I have no time for my family's distrust. If someone besides Adelaide happens to be nearby when a sharp point pierces my skin, I pretend that it is my finger that ails me, and do not mention how the first tiny pinprick has gained several siblings of late.

Luckily only the first wound has festered, though the infection is hard to shake. Whenever I think that it has gone away, it turns out that it was only dormant, and my poor finger swells up once more. So far, I have managed to hide the extent of the damage from Mother, fearing that she will send me to the mainland and add a visit to Aunt Anne while I am there. But I know I cannot hide it forever if it does not pass on its own.

Every night, I sleep in Adelaide's bed, worrying what might be hidden in the covers of my own. My sister is gracious in sharing her bed, though she frets and worries every night, wondering where the needles come from. I wonder, too, as the store in the sewing basket has not diminished, and none of the staff have reported a theft of needles. Such tools are not hard to come by, though; they can easily be bought at the store. Yet, I cannot fathom how someone would go to such lengths—unless it is Mother, of course. And just because it *could* well be, I am even more adamant not to cause a stir. She clearly means to make a spectacle of me, just to give her cause to send me to Aunt Anne. Even Father will insist if she tells him I do it to myself, and therefore engage in "irrational behavior." But I will not give her the satisfaction.

"We can set a trap," Adelaide suggests on the second night. "We can drizzle flour around your bed and then see how large or small the footprints are."

"Evelyn and Mother are the same size," I argue, "and Mary, too. It would do no good."

The next night, she says, "Perhaps we can string a wire across the floor, just a few inches off the ground. Whoever comes in here is sure to trip and fall, and then we will know who it is."

I consider this for a moment, but then decide against it. "Mary might fall if she comes in to light the fire before we are up, or *we* might forget and trip ourselves."

"What then?" Adelaide asks, but I cannot give her an answer. "Don't you want this to end?" She looks at me in the darkness, and *of course* I do—but I do not know how.

And the needles keep appearing.

What makes it all so much worse is that the noises, too, still arrive—every single night. I wake up just as frozen as the first time, next to my sleeping sister, and can do nothing but lie there and listen as the *something* is dragged across the floor above me, and something else—maybe—is moving inside the walls, knocking and scratching. It sounds as though long fingernails are clawing at the wood, or that there are needles carving grooves inside the boards.

The dark hours have become a nightmare in the truest sense, and whatever *it* is will not give me peace.

When I finally do manage to fall back asleep—I never quite know how that happens—I dream about the shed. It is the very same dream that I have had ever since I was a child: I am locked up in the dark, and I cannot get out. This time, though, the dream is slightly different, because—though the feeling is the same as when I am locked up in the shed—I start questioning if this place I go to in my dreams truly *is* the shed, or if it is somewhere else, just as cramped and unpleasant. When I reach out a hand to touch the walls, it is not the rough wood of the shed I feel, but stone—and that ring is always on my damaged finger: large, cruel, and studded with seeds.

Sometimes as I lie there, terrified and unable to move, I wonder if it is my longing for Jasper Hill that has set all this in motion—if it is a punishment, or a warning, from forces unknown. Perhaps it truly *is* a great sin to covet a married man. And perhaps it *is* the devil who has sent his demons to harass me. Or maybe Jasper, being a reverend, is surrounded by angels or some other good beings, set there to defend him against lustful creatures like me.

Sometimes I imagine Mother on the attic floor, pushing a trunk around, or sitting up on the roof with a poker, knocking it against the outside of the wall. I know such thoughts are silly, and almost certainly not true, but I cannot help but wonder as I lie there, silently shouting to myself to *Get up!* And facing, once again, the horrible reality that my body has lost its ability to follow even simple instructions.

As I lie there, I even consider that I might be dreaming—that it is a simple night terror, like the one about the shed, that holds me captive on the sheets. I even try to force my mind to go elsewhere, to leave the horrid dream behind. Perhaps I can dream about flying, or swimming in the sea. I even try to dream about Jasper Hill, conjuring memories from before, like when I used to sit next to him in front of the piano after the children's choir had left, and he played popular songs from the mainland for me. I remember watching his long, clever fingers, and how we laughed as he taught me the lyrics. The heat of him through our layers of clothes. The way his smile touched my heart.

These attempts at escape never work, however, and I remain held down, by forces unknown, upon the pillow next to Adelaide, whose half of the room never sees one single needle. The nightmare does not end until it suddenly does, and the room is flooded with morning light, the seagulls soaring above the rooftop, greeting the day with their angry cawing. And Adelaide wakes up, rested and refreshed, while I lie there feeling exhausted and wretched.

Every morning before we go downstairs, I take care to disturb my own bed, flinging the covers aside and creasing the pillow, so Mary will think I have slept there. My days are mostly spent pretending to read on the front room sofa, but in reality, I am dozing. I also quite often take long walks along the beach, merely to escape the house. The issue with the latter is that Evelyn wants to accompany me. Though she will never admit to it, the boredom of our house is grating on her now after having led such a lively life on the mainland. I do not want to walk with Evelyn, though, since she always takes the opportunity to berate me—to tell me how ungrateful I am, and how life would be so much easier for me if only I would let Aunt Anne find me a husband. She says I am a fool to let my arguments with Mother influence my choices.

"Spite is a terrible reason to do *anything,*" she lectures as we wander across the smooth rocks, polished and shaped over centuries. She keeps one hand on her head to make sure that the straw hat does not fly away. The waves out at sea dance wildly, licking in the air. "I know how distasteful it is to you to do *anything* Mother would approve of, but perhaps you should consider it, if only just this time? I think you would like your life more if you had your own home, and someone to share it with, too. You are *withering* out here, entertaining wild notions, and, yes, making a *spectacle* of yourself."

My gaze scans the rocky ground, looking for pieces of driftwood among the washed-up seaweed. I am looking for the smaller ones—smooth and hard—while I think of Jasper Hill.

"It isn't *natural* for a young woman to not want anything for herself . . . And why on earth do you wish to stay in the same house as a woman you despise?" Evelyn's words reach me, even if I try not to listen. "She is *damaged,* you know that," she continues, seemingly not discouraged by my lack of response. "Mother doesn't *want* to be cruel, but she is . . . twisted by her own upbringing. She will not get any better, Charlotte. Things will *never* get any easier for you here, so why do you want to stay?"

Because the other option is worse, I want to say. *Because I fear that the moment I go to Aunt Anne's, the choice will be taken out of my hands, and I will never know what could have happened between Jasper Hill and me.*

I recall the last time I was on the mainland, and my aunt had insisted on one of her dinners. We had been sixteen at the table, including my aunt and uncle. Some of the guests were their age but most aligned with me. We were there for my benefit, after all. The candelabras were studded with tall, burning candles, the chilled soup was so cold that it barely had any flavor, and a crystal bowl brimmed with ruby-red punch. The table was laid with silver and china, intricately folded napkins, and an array of tall glasses. The flowers were white: roses and freesias. I was seated between my future brother-in-law, James, and his cousin, Harold, whom I suspected was there to sweep me off my feet.

I looked at the other young women present: there were four of them at the table, two of them married and the other two engaged. I figured the sole purpose for them being at the dinner was to convince me of the happiness found in an appropriate marriage. They wore the same style of dress as I did: made of satin, with square necklines, and crowded with gleaming details. They looked like Greek goddesses escaped from a painting, but the pearls around their necks looked like shackles to me. The jewels on their fingers were glittering locks.

Who might those women be if they ever had a choice?

But I cannot share any of this with Evelyn, because she would not understand. And back at the house, there is a needle waiting in the dregs at the bottom of my teacup.

The secrecy comes to an abrupt halt at breakfast Saturday morning. I am feeling the worst I have all week: my eyes are gritty and my mouth tastes of salt. I try to rinse it out with sweet jam and hot tea, but it does not help. Not even sucking on a lemon wedge can entirely chase the salty tang, which reminds me of soft, cooked meat. We break our fast with Mother and Father on Saturdays, which certainly does not help my mood. Whenever I am reaching for something to eat, Mother wrinkles up her nose and makes her opinion known.

"Not too many sweet berries, Charlotte. You know how easily plump girls like you balloon . . ."

And: "I do believe you have eaten enough butter."

And: "Stop pulling faces like a child."

I do my best to ignore her, although I find it particularly hard today. Father is reading yesterday's newspapers, shipped to him from the mainland, while absentmindedly chewing his toast, so he is of no help. Across from me, Adelaide sits bleary-eyed and pale. Although she seems to sleep soundly enough, the mystery of the needles haunts her and she keeps eyeing our whole family with suspicion. Evelyn has started on the wedding invitations, and even now her gaze is distant as she mentally adds and crosses names off the list, the bread in her hand quite forgotten. Only Sophie is her usual self and chews her food happily, with not a care in the world.

Mary comes inside to leave a bowl of hard-boiled eggs on the table. Both Adelaide and I reach for one, and then, of course, Sophie does, too.

I crack the eggshell by rolling it across my napkin, then carefully peel it with my undamaged fingers. Sophie copies everything, which I find endearing.

I bite into the egg—then cry out.

The pain is so sharp and unexpected that I cannot conceal it. I spit egg and blood down on the napkin, and drop the hard-boiled culprit on the thick tablecloth.

"What is it?" cries Sophie.

"What happened?" gasps Evelyn.

Adelaide starts to cry. "Oh no, not again."

"Did you chew a piece of shell?" Mother asks.

Father folds down his newspaper to see if the situation requires his attention. When he sees the blood on the napkin pressed to my tongue, his eyebrows rise.

With tears in my eyes, I inspect the egg gaping toward me with the yolk on display. I am not surprised to see what I do, but the sight makes me sick nevertheless. Embedded within the egg's yellow core is a needle, with the sharp end pointing to me.

"Is that a sewing needle?" Sophie squeaks.

"Not again, Charlotte," Evelyn chides.

"What is this nonsense?" Mother wants to know.

"*Inside* the egg?" Adelaide looks at me with horror. "How did it get *inside* the egg?"

"Maybe I got one, too." Sophie uses her butter knife to cut her egg in half on the plate. No glinting needle appears.

"Of course you didn't," Mother tells her. "Charlotte put it in there herself."

"She did *not*!" Adelaide bravely defends me, which is a good thing, since I am still bleeding and cannot speak. "*How* would she get the needle in there?"

Evelyn intervenes. "I have seen magicians on the mainland perform astonishing acts . . ."

"She did *not* do it herself." Adelaide sounds exasperated and pulls wildly on her braid. "Why would she hurt herself like that? Tell them, Charlotte!"

I do try, but it is hard. "I . . . did not," I mumble, while drying a dribble of blood off my chin. My tongue is quickly swelling up.

"How would she even know what egg to pick?" Adelaide continues. "*I* could have taken it, or Sophie, but only Charlotte got a needle in hers—"

"Because she *placed* it there herself, using a sleight of hand." Mother sounds slightly annoyed. She wipes her hands with her napkin, over and over again.

"That was a foolish and dangerous trick." Father nods in my direction, decidedly not amused. "What if you had choked on the thing?"

"It would have served her right, I reckon." Mother's eyes are like chips of ice.

"She spends too much time in the house," Father says. "Young women are bound to develop a touch of hysteria if isolated for too long."

I wipe more blood with the napkin, unable to say anything to correct his skewed view.

"I once heard of a girl who cut her own arms and legs with her father's straight razor," Evelyn says in support of Father's assessment. "And our cousin swallowed her hairpins once."

"It's *not* Charlotte!" Adelaide shouts, but no one listens.

I am thinking of Mother again, but I cannot figure out how she could have done it. There were six eggs in the bowl, and I could have picked any one of them—and she had not left the table even once since we all sat down. Mary, then, perhaps? She was the one who had served the eggs. Could she have done something to make sure that I chose the right one? In my chest, my heart is racing wildly. Someone wants to do me harm.

"Mary," I force out between bloodstained lips. The bleeding has lessened, but the swelling has not. My tongue feels like a stranger in my mouth, as large and unwieldy as a whale in a cove.

"Oh, don't you blame *her,*" Mother snaps, throwing her napkin down on the table. Crimson roses have appeared on her cheeks.

"That is utterly unfair, Charlotte," Evelyn chimes in.

"How could *she* have gotten the needle in there?" Adelaide asks, quite wisely.

"Sleight of hand?" Sophie suggests.

Just then, a distinct, clinking noise has us all turning our gazes to the sugar bowl. Sophie, wide-eyed, reaches her fingers inside to retrieve another needle. She holds it up in the air while looking between us all, begging with her eyes for an explanation.

"Where did *that* come from?" Adelaide is off her chair and looks around her with wild eyes. Her hand clutches the braid as she blinks away another bout of tears.

"What trickery are you up to?" Mother shouts at me, just as another plink on the table makes us look to the blackberry jam. Then they follow in quick succession: one needle lands in the butter, another on Father's plate. A third one lodges in Evelyn's toast. Mother cries and joins Adelaide on the floor, pulling Sophie with her. The three of them huddle near the door, seeking shelter in each other's embrace. I want to leave, too, but before I have had the chance, the needles suddenly rain down in a deluge. They rush down from the ceiling, although there is no hole. Some of them hit the chandelier on their descent; others do not stop before they land on the tablecloth, happily bouncing before they lie still. All the food is ruined, studded with sharp needles, and even Father rises from his chair and lifts the newspaper up over his head to shield himself from the onslaught.

Then suddenly, it is silent. Evelyn and I, the last two still seated, look at each other across the table. Both us have needles in our laps.

Then my cup explodes, showering the table in sharp china and oolong tea. One piece hits my hand and draws blood. Another shard cuts Evelyn's chin.

"What on earth?" Mother is livid. She uses her hands to chase Sophie and Adelaide out of the room, pushing their backs out the door. Then she comes at me, arms raised, and would have hit me for sure if Father had not been there to constrain her.

"It cannot be the girl, Hester," he says in a firm voice. But Mother is quite beyond reason. She screeches like a banshee and writhes in his grasp.

"What did you *do*?" she screams at me. "What did you do, you *crow* of a girl! Why did you *do* this to us?"

I quickly rise and back away, needles and china drizzling off my skirt. I spot Mary from the corner of my eye, standing pale and astonished in the doorway.

"Get a grip of yourself, woman," Father barks at Mother.

"We have all had a shock." Evelyn tries to calm us all down, though she is pale, too. Her hand shivers when she grabs a napkin off the table and presses it to her chin, having shaken it free of debris. "What happened here? Where did the needles come from?"

"From *her*." Mother lunges at me again, but Father keeps her in check.

"Get out of here, both of you," he commands, and Evelyn and I readily comply.

Out in the yard, the air is cool, and a strong wind blows from the northeast. The orange barn cat saunters lazily across the yard, sensing nothing amiss.

Sophie and Adelaide sit on the stairs, and both of them are still crying. Evelyn stands in the middle of the yard, brushing her blue skirt vigorously, although I do not think there are more needles. The cut on her chin has ceased bleeding.

"Was it you?" she asks with angry eyes as I stand there by my weeping sisters, waiting for my mind to make sense of what just happened. My breathing is ragged, and it feels as though a sharp, hard claw has curled around my heart, digging into it relentlessly.

I cannot answer with my swollen tongue, but I shake my head in reply.

"She's been finding needles all week," Adelaide says. The secrecy I swore her to is clearly all forgotten. "They have been in her clothes, her shoes, in her bed . . ."

"But where do they come from?" Evelyn sounds amazed. "*How* did they pass through the ceiling?"

None of us know—we *cannot* know—and so she is left without an answer.

We spend the rest of the day together, all of us feeling safer with our sisters within sight. We walk on the beach, and then we knit outside, despite the wind and the cold, perched in chairs on top of the stairs. Mother has taken to her bed, claiming a headache, as she always does when her rage has passed, leaving her feeling weak and regretful. Father comes outside to tell us that we better eat in the kitchen today, seeing as how the dining room might suffer from a flaw. As if it was the wood itself that had opened up and spat the needles onto the table.

Mary and Mrs. Norris look at us with fearful eyes as we dip our spoons into the onion soup and watch the bread dissolve. My belly is a painful knot and I can barely eat at all, and whatever I *do* eat stings, due to the wound on my tongue. We all glance nervously up at the ceiling between each spoonful of soup, at the copper pots and pans, and the rough-hewn ceiling beams. We fear another shower of needles, but it does not come. We inspect every drop of soup and twist our spoons in the murky smudge at the bottom of our bowls, to make sure that nothing is hidden in there.

When the meal is over, we all let out a breath of relief.

"We counted about three hundred needles," Mrs. Norris says somberly. "How the one got in your egg, I cannot say." She looks utterly devastated, seeing as how this is the second time—that she knows of—that a needle has been found in her food. I do not tell her that needles have appeared on my plate all week. I could not even if I wanted to, with my damaged tongue.

The day feels long and grueling, and by the time it finally ends we are all exhausted from walking on eggshells, fearing another assault. Evelyn worries that her cut will leave a scar. Adelaide has been crying on and off all day. Sophie clings to Evelyn's hand and will not let her go.

When Adelaide and I climb into her bed, I fall asleep at once—but then, of course, I wake. I lie there, just as frozen as before, when the noises start up in the attic; and I lie there, just as prostrate, when the knocking in the walls begins. Only my hammering heart and my eyes seem to be able to move.

I have had it with this *thing*. I have had enough! I cannot lie here, night after night, and let myself be tormented so! I cannot use my mouth to speak—I am doubly mute—so I do the one thing I can think of.

Come in then, I say quietly, in my mind. *Come in then, and be done with it!*

The noise abruptly stops.

·13·

jasper

Antonia is better by Saturday. She is up from the bed and dressed before breakfast. Her dress is one of her favorites from before: striped in soft gray and sky blue. She has piled her hair on top of her head to hide its brittle, neglected state, and pearls adorn her ears. There is even a faint blush in her cheeks, but that might be painted on.

She would often use rouge while she was pregnant, to hide how miserable she was. She had so dearly wanted to be one of those flourishing young mothers, brimming with good health and hope for the future. But instead, her body disagreed strongly with the pregnancy. Though she was not always sick in the beginning, food had become distasteful to her, and she was tired all the time, wanting nothing more than to lie in bed. Then came the cramps and the stomachaches, the swelling of her limbs and the odd aversion to light. And then, when it all ended as it did, she promptly blamed herself, although I could not—and still cannot—see how she could have done anything differently. Though I am required by my collar to say that the outcome of a pregnancy is a part of God's plan, I always felt it was a roll of the dice, and no matter how one opts to look at it, Antonia was certainly not to blame.

As happy as I am to see her downstairs and in an excellent mood, I cannot help but worry, though. It is as if I no longer trust this happy and content version of my wife. I fear she is hiding her true feelings, and that they will be revealed at any moment. Then she will be crying again, or scolding me, or withdrawing to her room or inside herself. I fear it must be a lonely place, filled with bitterness and harmful memories, but I do not know how to save her from it. Instead, I offer her toast with honey and milky tea, and kiss her cheek when offered.

"I am thinking I might start a ladies' group," she tells me, "where the women of the congregation can come together and discuss God's word. I could serve tea and invite them to bring along their knitting, and maybe the youngest children, too." She barely even chokes when she mentions the little ones. "I think it would be a good thing for the women to gather from time to time, to care for their souls in the same way that they care for everyone else." She beams at me then sips her tea. "What do you think, Jasper?"

"I think it is a wonderful idea," I say, though I fear that the enthusiasm will be lost when her melancholy returns. I really do wish I could feel more at ease, that I could enjoy this moment more. It is rare now to see her so eager, and I feel as though I should celebrate it, rather than falling into this sulky mood.

"I already talked to Noreen about it, and she said she could make the fruitcake they all like for the first meeting. She also agreed to help spread the word." Her eyes blink rapidly.

Inwardly I groan, but I hope Noreen knows her mistress well enough by now to not go spreading the word just yet. It might lead to disappointment.

"Well, *can* you, Jasper?" Antonia prompts me, and I realize I have missed something, lost in my own ceaseless worry.

"I am sorry, my darling, could you repeat it?" I dearly wish for strong coffee, but all we have been served is the same old tea, which does nothing to invigorate a man.

Antonia sighs. "Could you mention it in church tomorrow?" She speaks with a hint of impatience. "It would be a wonderful way to introduce the group to the community, and it will make it easier for the women to come if their husbands know that the group is approved by you." She blinks again, then again.

"I . . ." I do not know what to say. Of course I want to help my wife—and had she been of sound mind, I would have liked nothing more than to showcase her new and wonderful initiative, which could, as she says, be a valuable service to the women of Margaret's Keep, but I just cannot bring myself to trust her. "Why don't we give it a week?" I suggest at last. "It will give you ample time to plan and make sure this is something you want—"

"Don't you think I know my own mind, Jasper?" She rolls her eyes, as if I am the silliest man in the world. "*Of course* it's what I want. I just told you so."

"Still, good ideas need time to blossom. It might be wise of you to have a plan for the first meeting—what topics you are to discuss—before I make an announcement." Inside, I feel torn. Do I truly want to deny my aid in something that sparks such joy in her? Yet, the fear that it will all fall apart persists. I have seen her like this many times before, and in the early days after the birth I would consider it a blessing—a sign that she was on the mend and about to regain strength and clarity. Time has taught me better, though, and having had to cancel several invitations, and even a few trips abroad, I am reluctant to share in her optimism, and fearful of disappointing my congregation.

She frowns. "I already decided on the topic." The healthy flush in her cheeks suddenly looks out of place—way too red and vivid. "Why won't you help me, Jasper?"

I sidestep the question. "What topic did you decide on?"

"The tenth commandment," she says, dipping a corner of her

toast in the tea. "I can tell that the youth of this island might need a reminder when it comes to coveting that which is not theirs—and who is better to teach them that than their mothers?" She speaks in a light, breezy voice, though the frown remains.

I sigh as my heart plummets to the floor. "Mrs. North would never come to your gathering anyway," I say. "And she doesn't strike me as the type of woman to take advice when it comes to the rearing of her daughters."

Antonia's face falls, but she feigns surprise. "Mrs. North? What does *she* have to do with it?"

"Who else would this be aimed at? Are there many wanton youths on Margaret's Keep?" I cannot help it if a little annoyance seeps into my voice. All of this hope and doubt, and in the end, it was all about Antonia's jealousy.

"There might be." Her voice is suddenly far more subdued. "If one young person does something out of the ordinary, chances are that more will follow. Who knows, maybe in a year, it will be *en vogue* to covet the reverend."

"Nonsense," I say, unable to meet her eyes. "And what about the meeting following the first, Antonia? Do you have a plan for that?" Perhaps she will turn to the seventh commandment, and start raving about adultery, even if there has been none. Just the thought of it makes me shudder.

My wife shrugs. "An idea will arrive, I'm sure. The Bible has many pages."

"There is no need to punish the girl," I snap. "Charlotte has done nothing wrong. She has flirted with me, that is true, but many women do. Had she declared her love in letters or even to my face, your feelings would have been understandable, but Charlotte has done nothing of the sort. She only stares at me from the pew, and gave me some caramels once. Lovestruck women never bothered you before," I remind her, wanting her to see reason. "You even used to laugh at them—or feel pity. Why is it so different this time?"

Antonia straightens in the chair, her face closed and guarded again. Nothing of her earlier enthusiasm remains. "The difference is, Jasper, that this time, you looked back."

• • •

Antonia stays in her room for hours after our spat. I work on my sermon and try not to think of her absence and its cause. It is all so foolish! I have never given my wife cause to doubt my fidelity. In fact, I have made sure to do very little to hurt her feelings. I cannot help if my gaze grazes Charlotte North in church. She sits there right before me in the family pew, and is a part of my flock, too, so I am bound to care for her. I will not ignore the young woman—who clearly needs attention—just because my wife is jealous.

I still feel both guilty and foolish for giving in to Antonia's irrational demands and asking Charlotte to leave the children's choir. She had done a wonderful job, and Monday evenings had been the best part of my week. I will not think of the longing she inspired; the scent of her milky skin, or how I would seek it out, inhaling it deeply whenever I could. Neither will I think of touching her: the smooth warmth of her hand in mine. I will not think of the bodily torment that hounded me back then—which hounds me still on Sunday evenings, after I have gazed upon her heart-shaped face in church.

I go into the kitchen to ask Noreen for coffee, and to tell her to wait with the fruitcake, seeing as how it might not be needed. She nods her head sagely at the message, then informs me that Mrs. Hill will take her lunch up in her room, alone.

I expect to dine alone as well, but to my surprise, Antonia emerges. She is, however, dreadfully quiet, and I instantly feel horrid for having squashed her enthusiasm—even though it would likely not have led to anything good.

She finally opens her mouth to ask, while spearing a potato with her fork, "How come you will help Miss Russel but not me?"

"What do you mean?"

"You mentioned it yourself, how you were going to help her by telling the islanders that the tower was not a 'wicked place.' It is kind of you to help her, but why won't you help *me*? I am, after all, the one who is forced to watch you every Sunday, ogling that girl as if she was a—"

"Stop it, Antonia," I warn her.

"And the worst part is that I'm not the only one who sees it! The whole island does, Jasper. They are all right there in the pews, watching my husband make a fool out of me—"

"Antonia—"

"And a fool out of himself, too. Never mind the girl; she is probably rich enough that reputation doesn't matter. But *you* must watch your steps. Who would want to employ a reverend with a stain on his collar?"

"Your father did well enough for himself," I remark, although I know it is a low blow.

Only the flaring of her nostrils betrays the hurt she is feeling. "Father was a gambler. Gambling is not half as salacious as lust, Jasper. People can *pity* a man under *its* sway."

"But those notions of yours are just *fantasies,*" I blurt out, although I know it is futile. I have said it many times before, but Antonia just keeps hammering on. "She is simply a young woman in my flock. *Nothing* unseemly has happened—"

"*Yet,*" she replies.

I look down at my plate. The mutton chops are distasteful to me now. "Do you want to leave?" I ask her. "Do you want to move back to the mainland? Clearly, the sea air has not had the desired effect upon you—"

"Maybe," she admits as her shoulders sag. Something soft crosses her features, like the gentle wing of a dove.

"Then I'll make some inquiries," I promise, then rise and leave the room, craving said sea air above all else.

I pause outside in the garden—or in the pitiful excuse for one that surrounds the clergy house. Nothing tall can grow in this environment. What the wind does not take, the salt will erode, poisoning the very earth. Is it any wonder my marriage has fared the same? How is a place this desolate, this remote, supposed to bring healing?

There is a stone bench where I often sit to watch the sun set over the sea, bleeding rich gold onto the waves. A few straggling seagulls still soar up there, having missed their curfew, but the sky will soon be blessedly calm, and, hopefully, so will my heart.

What does it say about me, that I revel in this wild roughness that is killing my wife?

How did it ever come to this? How did the happy, spirited woman that I knew before turn into this *irrational* thing?

I know the loss of our son was hard on her—and made even harder by the fact that another child was never to come. The recovery had been long and painful, and she was terribly weak for months. Perhaps it was that time, spent mostly alone in her room, with ample hours to reflect on the things that had gone wrong, which had damaged her so utterly. She had not even had the opportunity to attend her own son's funeral, but lay in her bed—bleeding, alone, grieving.

Yet I had believed that there was reason for hope. The world had many orphans, after all, in need of a loving home. We could fill the whole house with children if we liked. Antonia would not hear of it, though. For her, it had to be her own or none at all, which I had found to be a shame. It was then that I for the first time found myself reflecting on how unfair it was for well-bred women to be brought up to accomplish just this one thing in life: bringing children into the world, becoming mothers. It left so very little room for redemption if one failed.

Since that time, I have thought about this often. So often, in fact, that my pity for my wife has all but obliterated my own desire to become a father and feel a small hand curling around my own.

But I do feel it tonight—in every fiber and every bone.

As a young man reaching adulthood, it had been my biggest wish to raise a child and watch it grow—to teach it and guide it. I could not think of a greater blessing. Yet, when our son died, I locked that desire away, swearing never to touch it again, as it would only bring me pain. Besides, Antonia had needed me so much in the first years after it happened; she had almost been like a child herself. Tonight the old longing is there, and I keep seeing the small, blue face of my son in the tiny, black casket.

The father in me is grieving for the children he never had.

So absorbed am I by my thoughts, that I do not notice at first the white-clad creature standing by the edge of the garden, where the grass-covered dirt meets the salt-licked rocks of the beach. I rise up, startled, and stare as the person comes into focus: curly, dark hair and a heart-shaped face, dressed in what appears to be a nightgown, frilled at the neck and wrists.

Behind her in the dusky night, the waves move restlessly.

"Charlotte?" I say, half in question. Then, I say it louder, "Charlotte!"

She does not respond but just stands there by the sea, looking back at me. She does not even smile or lift her hand in greeting. Could it be that she is sleepwalking?

I start across the lawn and call for her again. I am worried now, my heart is racing.

Then, just as I pass the halfway mark and am close enough to make out the texture of her hair—she is gone.

Inexplicably—*impossibly*—gone.

·14·

ruth

I dread the day as soon as I get up and shuffle through my humble rooms at the back of the schoolhouse. My stomach ties in a knot when I start boiling water for tea on the woodstove and find a hunk of bread in the cupboard. I try to think of an excuse to stay at home, but it is Sunday and church, so I cannot. I will have to go there and weather the storm.

They are not bad, my rooms, only small. Built as an afterthought—or so it seems to me. I have done my best to liven them up: trailed garlands of colorful crepe paper along the rafters, and covered the floors in rag rugs. In summer, I try to brighten the rooms with a smattering of flowers, but nothing can quite erase the flaking yellow paint on the walls or the worn, scuffed floorboards under my feet. In the winter, it is horribly drafty, and with only the one woodstove on an island void of trees, I spend the rest of the year gathering driftwood to get through the January storms alive.

It is my choice, though—not only to come here and work in a place so remote, but to stay in these simple quarters. When I first arrived, the islanders promptly offered me shelter. The last teacher had moved around from farm to farm and enjoyed warm beds and excellent care. He had been a bachelor, of course, and—seeing as how he was a man—unused to fending for himself. He was also not hired for the entirety of the year, like me, but served several different islands, splitting his time between them. I suppose I have the presence of Adelaide and Sophie in my schoolroom to thank for Mr. North wanting a better—more continuous—education for the island children, hence his generous offer to me. And, since I knew I would be on Margaret's Keep year-round, and could not think of anything worse than staying in strangers' homes, with their various odors and customs to keep, being forced to always be polite, I decided I would rather stay here on my own, despite the issue with the stove.

As I open my umbrella and walk briskly from the schoolhouse, I try to steel myself against the day. To make my feelings small and protected deep inside, curled up under an umbrella of their own. There are not many seagulls today, due to the heavy rain, but I meet quite a few sheep, amply protected by their thick coats, clustering together between the stone cottages and barns that make up most of the buildings on the island. I wish I had dressed better, since the damp and the perpetual wind are quickly making their way to my skin. Yet nothing can happen to me today that is bad enough to distract me from the trial I fear awaits me.

Margaret's Keep is my refuge—the rock I cling to. My peace.

I simply cannot lose it.

The congregation mill around the church, waiting for the clock to strike, much like my students do in the mornings. I can spot the islanders a mile off: black silhouettes clustering together like the sheep, or moving around on the emerald grass, as stark against the whitewashed walls as crisp paper cutouts—though sadly they are not. They are people of flesh and blood—the latter possibly whipped to a frenzy by my one careless act. My stomach lurches, but I plaster on a smile as I continue down the road, headed for the church, just like on any other Sunday.

I pass by the few horses tied up outside the gates, next to the Norths' expensive closed carriage, and enter the lush church lawn. No one greets me, or even smiles. I am disappointed to note that even my own students cast their eyes down, with one notable exception. Sophie North, who is standing next to her parents by the entrance, gives me a tiny smile. She even lifts her hand to wave. It warms my heart to see it. Adelaide, on the other hand, standing with her friends Annabeth Ferryman; Norma Fisher; and the latter's sister, Lillian, only shoots me a downcast glance. She looks terrible, truth be told. The girl is pale and has crossed her arms over her black-clad chest, holding herself tightly. If her braids had not been pinned to her scalp, one of them would likely have been lodged in her mouth, just as when we do geography tests.

I am still pondering how best to approach the islanders and their very cold shoulders when the fearsome Mrs. North leaves her husband's broad side to come and greet me. She is wearing a black cape edged with fur, and I can spot pearls dangling from her earlobes. Her curly hair is neatly pinned up under a massive, plumed hat. Her stiff skirts rustle when she comes toward me.

"Miss Russel," she says, grasping my hand in a surprising display of familiarity. Her fingers are covered in gloves, but I can feel their heat through the leather. "You had better sit with us today." She gives me a pointed look.

I let out a deeply held breath as hot and comforting relief rushes through my body. The Norths are on my side in this; it will not be my downfall.

"Thank you," I croak. "It's certainly appreciated."

As we cross the lawn, and people move aside in deference to Mrs. North, she speaks to me in a very quiet voice, "We heard of what happened, and though I myself abhor the tower, I can see why you would not. It must all seem so baffling to you, coming from the mainland. It's an easy mistake to make."

I nod, unable to form the proper words of gratitude, though they are certainly there, stuck in my throat. She guides me to the rest of her family, waiting by the church door. Mr. North offers me a polite greeting, tipping his hat, though it looks as though he has not slept for days. There are dark circles under his eyes, and his face looks very concerned. The whole family looks worse for wear, truth be told. Evelyn, the oldest, hides a yawn behind her gloved hand. She, too, sports purple shadows around her eyes, and Charlotte looks as pale as a freshly bleached sheet. Now that I look for it, I can tell that even Mrs. North carries signs of fatigue on her face, her pallor holding hints of gray. Perhaps there has been a family dispute? I have more than enough to worry about today, though, and chide myself for even wondering about it. I am utterly thrilled that the Norths have deemed me worthy of being taken in under their wing. I simply could not ask for a better shelter.

When the church bells ring and we all file inside, it feels utterly strange to me to take those extra steps and be shown into the Norths' family pew. The seats are no less hard there, but the value of the act is immeasurable. The islanders will notice and take it into account before launching another attack, as none of them wants to be on the wrong side of this family. I doubt the act is enough to entirely quell the gossip, but it will surely make it harder for them to tell it to my face.

It renders the threat of a dismissal null and void.

The church is small, like everything on Margaret's Keep. The white walls are bare save for the polished wooden cross hanging above the altar. Above us, the arched ceiling is adorned with plaster shaped like waves, and the air smells of hot wax and salt. Mrs. Hill—that poor woman—plays the piano, and then Reverend Hill arrives, robed and ready to begin the service. When he opens his mouth to speak, my heart hammers with anticipation, wondering if—and how—he will address my predicament. Mrs. Hill turns around on the stool to watch her husband preach. I have not seen her since the debacle last Sunday, and after the excursion to the tower and its aftermath, I had somewhat forgotten about her disturbing fury. I remember it now, though, when seeing her face. But even as her gaze glides over the congregation, she does not pause on me for a second. Rather her eyes keep moving, and my stomach lurches when I realize that they fasten on Charlotte, who sits just next to me.

Clearly, the girl is still at the forefront of her mind.

To my great delight, I realize that the sermon today is entirely devoted to the topic of seeing demons where there are none. The reverend is quite passionate in his plea for his flock to always consider reason first and fear second when it comes to things that cannot be seen nor touched. The reverend has his own good reasons for choosing this theme, I know, but that does not mean it cannot benefit me as well.

"The imagination is powerful," he says. "That is why God gave it to us, so we can prosper and invent, but sometimes it can deceive us and show us things that are damaging. We must always consider reason then, and strive to keep our mirages in check."

All the while he is talking, his gaze seems to seek out the pew where I sit. At first, I think he wants me to know that I am on his mind while he lightly scolds his flock, but then I realize I am not the one he is looking at. He, too, is looking at Charlotte—and quite pointedly. I cannot understand it. Is this not just the type of behavior that will inflame Mrs. Hill's delusions? Why would he taunt her so?

I dare a look in Mrs. Hill's direction and can tell that she is—quite predictably—moved by it. Her face is pale and as stiff as a mask. The whole affair makes me deeply uncomfortable. I vividly remember the reverend's fierce dismissal of his wife's worries, but now I suddenly realize that the picture might have more shades to it. Perhaps Mrs. Hill has *reason* for concern, even if her words last Sunday were harsh and her demeanor quite unhinged.

I dare a glance at Charlotte. She seems enraptured by the sermon. Gone is the paleness from before, the tired, haunted eyes. She is a blushing flower now, red lipped and pink cheeked, her eyes are dark and shiny. The dramatic curves under her dress are certainly those of a woman, and I wonder if she is aware yet what effect she has on men.

Poor Antonia Hill looks like a dry twig in comparison.

I am not the only one that has noticed. A rustling of fabrics makes me turn my head one fraction, just in time to see Mrs. North, on Charlotte's other side, quickly and precisely pinch her daughter's waist. Charlotte jolts beside me, but then she smiles, wide and dazzling. Before us, Reverend Hill seems to have broken out in perspiration. His forehead appears slick in the light from the flickering candles. His gaze drifts to Charlotte again. He cannot seem to help himself. Antonia Hill looks dead upon the stool—a dead and sad little crow. My heart suddenly aches for her.

So preoccupied am I by this quiet exchange that I nearly miss it when the reverend addresses my situation directly.

"Perhaps it is a thing to celebrate rather than rage against, when a person arrives in our midst to show us that what we feared was nothing but such a mirage. Our brave schoolteacher, Miss Russel"—he extends his hand in my direction—"brought the children to Margaret's Tower in the name of truth and science, and they all returned home unscathed—so perhaps the witch there was nothing but whispers and dust all along?" I can hear a hush behind me as whispers break the silence of the church room. Clearly the islanders do not readily agree. No one dares interrupt the sermon, though, for which I am deeply grateful.

We sing after that, and then are free to go. The reverend and Mrs. Hill stand by the door, shaking our hands as we leave.

"Thank you," I whisper to Reverend Hill when it is my turn.

"I hope it helped," he replies, adding one of his warm smiles.

Antonia Hill, next to him, barely looks at me, so either she has not kept up with the gossip, or it simply is of little concern to her. Perhaps the memory of last Sunday is haunting her, but I do not think so. I notice how Charlotte does not offer Mrs. Hill her hand, and how the latter turns her head when the girl passes her.

Clearly, things have been festering for quite some time.

·15·

charlotte

On Sunday after church, I stand in my bedroom and speak into the air. I have been planning to do this all day, ever since we had breakfast in the kitchen. I even thought about the knocker in the wall during Jasper Hill's sermon, which says something about the importance of the matter. It had been such a wonderful sermon, too, with the reverend's gaze upon me almost the entire time, touching me with fire.

Though I do wish it had been his hands exploring me, and not just his eyes.

My sisters think I am up here to change my dress, but that is not what I have in mind. I believe the knocker is the one dropping needles everywhere, because who—or what—else could it be? And if I could make the noises and the frozen state go away by addressing the thing directly, perhaps it might also take other requests and I can get my bed back, needleless.

That is my hope, anyway.

"Dear knocker," I say with a racing heart, speaking almost coherently again now after the violent pricking of my tongue. "Could you please stop hiding needles in my bed? I would very much like to sleep there, and could you also not put needles in my food—or in anyone's food? It would be best, I think, if you also didn't rain needles down on the table, since it upsets my father." Which is certainly true. He has made poor Mr. Norris check and triple-check the ceiling in the dining room and dismantle the crystal chandelier. Not surprisingly, they did not find anything to explain the torrent of tiny projectiles.

Mother still blames me. She told me on the way to church that she did not know *how* I had done it, but that she was sure it was one of my "juvenile games," like looking at Jasper Hill in church. She also told me that she saw no other reason for me doing these things but to make *her* life a misery. According to my mother, tormenting her is my sole purpose in life, which is nothing but her flattering herself.

The others, though, do believe me when I say I do not know what it is—and that the needles scare me, too, and that something awful is happening to us. Even Father believes me, if only because the physics do not add up.

"Perhaps you can bring me something else," I tell the knocker. "A flower, maybe—or something else that won't hurt me . . ." I hold up my bandaged finger. Under the gauze, the wound is weeping again. "I know I did *that* to myself, but it doesn't mean that *your* needles won't do equal damage—but perhaps that is what you want? Why else would you put them in my bed?" I let out a shivering breath and sit down on said bed, feeling around for needles first. I am still dressed for church, all in black, and the stiff skirt falls in folds around my legs. Outside the window, the seagulls are squabbling, happy now that the rain has ceased. I feel terribly anxious, and am not at all certain if speaking to the knocker is a wise thing to do—but neither can I live in this constant fear of being stabbed.

A loud, single knock sounds above the headboard.

My heart leaps in my chest, and I am as quiet as a mouse while my ears strain, listening intently for more sounds.

When I can hear nothing else, besides the usual noises from the kitchen and the droning of the sea, I ask, "Was that you? Did you knock?"

A second passes, and then it happens again: one loud, single knock above the headboard. Even if I expected it, I startle on the bed and even bite my still-sore tongue. I instantly wince from the pain, and then I feel dizzy. It is astonishing what is happening. I am not sleeping this time, and neither have I lost the ability to move. I am as awake as I can be, and *the knocker is speaking to me.*

Everything suddenly feels eerie, as if the bedroom around me that I know so well has become something strange and uncertain. As if the familiar sight of daylight flooding in between the white lace curtains, and Adelaide's made-up bed by the opposite wall, can no longer be trusted, but might as well belong in a dream.

I scramble for things to ask to keep the conversation going, though I cannot decide if I want it to or not. The thing in the wall is not natural and has proved that it can do harm. Yet, *not* speaking to it seems dangerous, too, like letting a wild thing loose without a leash. It *did* stop last night when I spoke to it in my mind, so maybe this is the way to keep it reined?

"Did you put the needles in the bed?" I ask. "One rap for 'yes,' two for 'no.'" I cannot say if the knocker is a dead person or not, but I have read about séances in magazines and know this is how mediums address the dead. Surely it might work here as well?

Almost immediately, there is a knock in the wall.

I want to ask it why, but the question might be too complicated. "Will you stop putting needles in my bed?" I ask instead.

There is a pause, and then it answers with two knocks in rapid succession, then there is a brief pause again before one single knock lands inside the wooden boards.

"What does that mean?" I ask. "Yes or no—or maybe?"

One knock.

"You will *maybe* stop hiding needles in my bed?"

One knock.

"I suppose that is better than nothing." I ponder for a moment before asking the next question. "Did you create the ruckus up in the attic? The noises?"

One knock.

Again, I cannot ask why, but I try to come up with questions that might bring me a little closer to an explanation.

"Did you want to frighten me?"

Two knocks.

"Did you want me to wake up?"

Two knocks.

"Did you make it so I couldn't move?"

Nothing.

I wait for as long as I dare, fearing that it might disappear at any second, and then I realize that the knocker might not know. "Did you just want me to notice you?"

One knock.

I let out a shuddering breath.

"You could have done that without the needles, though," I cannot help but chide it.

The knocker replies with one knock.

"If I keep talking to you, will you stop with the needles, then?" I ask, suddenly inspired. Perhaps an exchange can be made. I am a tradesman's daughter, after all, and bargains are in my blood.

There is another pause, and then one single knock.

I think we might have struck an agreement. "Good," I say, letting out my breath. "I promise to keep talking to you, then."

A needle falls from the ceiling, and lands in front of my toes with a plink.

I pick it up and pinch it between two fingers. "I thought you were going to stop," I say, too surprised to be mad or even frightened.

One knock sounds inside the wall.

"Was this the last one?" I ask.

A pause, then a knock.

"Good," I say, "or else I might not speak to you again." Although clearly the knocker has its ways to make me, so the threat is somewhat moot. What if the next thing is worse than needles?

"Will you leave me alone at night while I sleep?"

The knocker does not answer.

When I have been sitting in silence for a minute or so, my nerves finally get the better of me, and I flee my bed so fast that it might as well be covered in ants. I run down the stairs, and do not pause or even breathe before I am in the front room, where all my sisters are gathered. They look at me with astonishment as I slump down in my usual chair. Even Adelaide turns her back on the easel to gawk.

"What did you do?" Evelyn asks me, always assuming I have been up to something—although, in this case, I have.

"Did you find more needles?" Adelaide asks, brimming with worry. She has a smear of blue paint on her cheek.

"Why are you still wearing church clothes?" Sophie asks. "I thought you were changing." She is tasked with embroidering flowers again, and the sulkiness comes off her like a stench.

The scene in the room looks so perfectly normal—and so utterly different from how I feel inside. Here there is warmth and companionship, teacups on the table and cookies on a tray. I feel as though I have been dipped into ice-cold water, and then placed before a fire to thaw.

"I . . . talked to it." I force the words out. "The knocker—the *thing* in the walls." I hope that by sharing, it might all feel a little less frightening, a little less unnatural. I tell them what I said, how I made it answer—that it promised no more needles if only I spoke to it more.

"But *why*, Charlotte?" Evelyn groans when I am done. "Wouldn't it be better to ignore it?"

"I don't want more needles in my bed," I say, and realize that I never told them how my nightmares had continued beyond that first day. "I don't want *any* of us to find needles in our beds."

"I'm sure it would just have gone away," Evelyn mutters. A fresh pillowcase rests in her lap, still not adorned by a single stitch. "Now that you have given it the attention it craves, it's sure to linger."

"You cannot know that," I say.

"But what *is* it?" Adelaide has gravitated toward the rest of us. She still clutches a paintbrush in her hand. "Is it a ghost? Or a devil?" Her eyes look large and scared.

"I'm saying my prayers every night," Sophie says. "You don't think it will come for *me,* do you, Charlotte?"

I shrug, as that is all I can do. I have no answers for them.

"I feel safer now, anyway," I tell them at last. "It *is* better to be able to talk to the thing than to have no power at all."

"But what *is* it?" Adelaide insists. "I would rather not have a dead person living in our walls—"

"We could ask it," I say. "If *I* can talk to the knocker, you surely can as well."

Adelaide turns pale. "I'm not sure if—"

"Let's *all* go and talk to it," I insist. "I'm sure you will all feel better if you can speak to it." It had proven true for me, anyway.

Evelyn shakes her head. "I don't know, Charlotte. It just seems sneaky to me. First it says it won't drop another needle, and then one lands right in front of your toes. It doesn't seem like a safe guest to entertain—"

"But it can answer your questions better than I can," and it would feel less lonely, too, if my sisters were a part of the conversation.

Adelaide speaks in a very small voice. "I *would* like to know what it is."

"Not Sophie, though," Evelyn decides. "She is too young."

"I am not," Sophie replies, although I suspect it is mostly for show. I do not think she truly wants to speak to the knocker.

"I will leave if it plays tricks," Evelyn warns.

"It cannot be more dangerous than holding a séance," Adelaide says to reassure herself, "and I have read about plenty of those."

"We should probably be down here praying, rather than indulging that *thing,*" Evelyn huffs, but she, too, follows suit when Adelaide and I move toward the door. I notice how she brings with her the sharp, silver embroidery scissors. I suppose a weapon makes her feel safe.

Sophie is left behind on the sofa, looking quite forlorn.

Back in the bedroom, with my sisters crowding behind me on the floor, I suddenly feel insecure. I look at the blue walls, at the embroidered Bible verses and flowers, at the space around me, flooded with daylight, and it suddenly feels impossible to me that a creature of some kind is hiding in our walls—*even* if I just spoke to it, and even despite the needles.

What if it will not speak when I am not alone, or what if they cannot hear the knocks? Adelaide never woke up before, even if the noises in the room were loud, but perhaps it had been different then, when I was frozen on the bed.

"What do we do now?" Evelyn's impatient voice puts an end to my fretting. "How do we call it?" She sounds angry, but is just tense, I think.

"Before, I just started talking," I say, and do just that. "Are you still there?" I ask the walls. "Can you still hear me?"

It takes a while—my heart is in my throat—but then, finally, one single, distinctive rap sounds in the wall. Not above my bed this time, but right below the window. Adelaide yelps and Evelyn gasps.

"Good." I let out my breath. "These are my sisters." I introduce them to the knocker. "Do you mind if they ask you some questions, too?"

There is another knock, though it sounds more subdued, as if the knocker has doubts.

I turn and look at Adelaide and Evelyn; the former is chewing the tip of her braid. "Do it," I urge them. "Ask." As before, I feel as though time is of the essence, as if the knocker will grow bored and leave unless we keep it entertained. "Only 'yes' and 'no' questions," I remind them. "One knock for 'yes,' two for 'no.'"

"Are you really there?" Evelyn asks, which I think is a pointless question, and tell her so with my eyes. She glares back at me and shrugs.

A loud knock comes from below the window.

We all shudder. It was a very strong answer.

"Can you prove it by moving around?" Evelyn speaks again. "Can you knock from somewhere else?" Perhaps she wonders if there is something outside that is causing the sounds, even if Mr. Norris has checked the walls. Perhaps she still suspects a rat.

Another knock, just as loud, sounds from the ceiling above our heads.

We all look up at once.

"Thank you," Evelyn says. Her knuckles have gone white around the scissors.

"Are you a ghost?" Adelaide asks, still holding her wet braid in her hand.

Two loud knocks sound from under the window. We look at each other, surprised. I suppose we had all been expecting a "yes."

"Maybe it lies—" Evelyn starts, but is interrupted by two more knocks. Clearly, it does not want to be known as a ghost.

"A devil, then?" Adelaide's voice shivers.

Another pair of knocks sound.

"Are you an animal?" I ask. Perhaps there are invisible, clever ones that scientists do not know of.

There is a pause, but then it raps "no."

"Are you just visiting here for a time?" Evelyn is eager to get rid of it.

It says "no" again, and we exchange worried glances.

"Do you plan on staying on here with us?" I ask.

One single knock is my answer.

"It might lie," Evelyn says again, and this time, she is not contradicted.

"Do you want to be our friend?" Adelaide asks, her voice brimming with hope. Now that she knows it is not a ghost, she dearly wants it to be friendly.

She is rewarded with one loud knock.

Evelyn takes a deep breath. "We will be your friends," she says, "as long as there are no more needles or other harmful shenanigans."

It is not a question, exactly, but she still receives a knock in reply. I choose to believe that it is a confirmation that there will indeed be fewer shenanigans.

"I wish we could ask it why it is here," Adelaide whispers.

"Me, too," I whisper back.

Evelyn has regained some of her usual calm. "It only arrived after the earthquake, so perhaps that has something to with it. Did you come from Margaret's Tower?" she asks the knocker.

But the walls seem to have grown silent, and we cannot get another reply, no matter what we ask.

The knocker has gone back into hiding.

When we go to bed that night, both Adelaide and I are wary of our bedroom. The air is warm and stale, as if there had been a dozen people slumbering in there, even if it was aired before bedtime. The room also feels strangely empty; like a ballroom after the guests have departed, leaving behind only traces of scent and the memory of chatter.

In my bed, on my pillow—right at the center—lies a flower, a violet, all dewy and fresh.

·16·

charlotte

"Will I get married on the mainland?" Adelaide asks the knocker. She sits on her bed in a pale pink day dress, twirling her braid in her hand.

"You cannot ask it things like that," Evelyn, next to her, scolds. "It's not a fortune teller, Adelaide." Her own dress is bright blue, matching the glittering stone in the necklace she just received from James.

"You cannot know that," Adelaide protests. "If it doesn't have a shape, it might well be able to look into the future."

Their bickering makes them both miss the single rap in the wall.

We have been doing this for three days now, meeting up as soon as Adelaide and Sophie are back from school, while Mother is busy painting. We slip up the stairs as quickly and quietly as we can, gathering in mine and Adelaide's bedroom to speak to the knocker.

No matter how many times we do it, it always comes as a shock when it replies.

At first, we had meant to leave Sophie out of it, on account of her being just eight, but then she cried and threatened to tell Mother what we did—and seeing as how there had been no more needles since that first conversation, Evelyn decided it was probably safe. She refuses to let Sophie ask questions of her own, though; she is only allowed to watch and listen. Though she so strongly wanted to join us before, she seemed wary when the rapping first sounded in the wall. She pressed herself close to Evelyn and snuck her hand in hers. Today she is even more glued to Evelyn than usual, afraid of losing hold of her even for a second. I wonder if the sessions are harming her in some way, or if she has been having nightmares.

It is Evelyn's turn to ask the knocker, and she clears her voice before speaking, "Were you ever a person?" Evelyn always asks questions like that, curious to know what the knocker really is, while Adelaide seems more concerned with tidbits from the future. Not only for her own benefit either, but for everyone she knows on the island.

The knocker answers Evelyn with two sharp raps. It has never been a person.

I can tell from Evelyn's face that she wants to ask more, but it is my turn now, so she will have to wait. Sophie presses her face against Evelyn's shoulder, too terrified, it seems, to even look at the room she knows so well and where nothing appears out of the ordinary.

"Were you here, inside the house, before I first heard you?" I ask the knocker from my bed. Though it has been days since I last found a needle in it, my sisters are still wary of it, and leave me to sit on the crocheted bedspread all alone.

The knocker gives us two raps again, so clearly it was not here before.

I, too, have more questions on my tongue, but rules are rules, and now it is Adelaide's turn again.

"Will Annabeth and I always be friends?" she asks, and Evelyn groans beside her.

The knocker raps "no" again, eliciting a whining sound from Adelaide.

"Don't ask if you don't want the answer," I say.

"It might be lying," Evelyn reminds our sister, but she nevertheless asks her own next question without any hesitation: "Do you come from this island?"

There is a pause, then a knock comes from behind the blue-painted boards.

"It could be lying about that as well." I give Evelyn a wry smile. "Are you a liar?" I ask the knocker, who either did not hear me or decides not to reply.

"My turn," Adelaide has swallowed her disappointment. "Will my husband have blond hair?"

Evelyn rolls her eyes.

The knocker answers "no."

"Oh, good." Adelaide sounds relieved. She always liked dark hair better, probably because it is different from her own.

"Do you have a shape . . . a body of your own?" Evelyn asks.

The knocker replies "yes."

We all look at each other, surprised and bewildered—except for Sophie, who still hides her face against Evelyn's shoulder.

"Maybe you should leave, Sophie," I say. "Perhaps it is too frightening after all."

She shakes her head with vigor but does not turn her head, just grinds her nose into the blue of Evelyn's dress.

The seagulls cry outside the window. It is the first sunny day in a long while, and normally we would be walking along the beach, or bringing books with us out in the garden to let the sun lick our winter-pale faces. Not today, though. No, today we sit inside and speak to something that should not be—something we do not know what it is. If I pause to dwell on the impossibility of it, my head starts spinning and I feel a little sick.

"Is there a reason why you chose this house?" I ask the knocker.

A pause, then one rap. There is.

"Will Sophie tell Mother about us speaking to you?" Adelaide asks with a sly smile. Evelyn swats her shoulder.

The knocker raps twice and Adelaide giggles. "She would *not* like this." "She" refers to Mother.

"Why?" Evelyn asks, with a look of feigned innocence. "We are just speaking to the air, are we not? There is, after all, no one here—"

She is interrupted by a sharp rap in the ceiling. Our new, invisible friend does not like to be referred to as nonexistent. Whenever Evelyn says something along these lines, it acts aggrieved, and I wish she would let it be.

"Never mind Evelyn," I say to the knocker. "She means nothing by it." I shoot her a dark look across the room, and she stares right back and shrugs.

"I only meant that there's nothing for Mother to see," she defends herself. "I didn't mean that the knocker isn't actually here."

"Did you give me all those needles because of my finger?" I ask, seeing as how it is my turn.

The knocker does not answer. I still have not found out if silence means that it *has* no answer, or if it simply refuses to give it. The rules my sisters and I came up with say that a non-answer is still an answer, however, and so it is Adelaide's turn again.

"Will Charlotte ever kiss Reverend Hill?" she asks, and I grab my pillow to throw it at her. Sadly, I miss by quite a few inches, and it lies there on the floor between us, starched white and lonely.

Adelaide giggles. The knocker knocks, once.

My heart soars. Adelaide gets the pillow off the floor and throws it back at me. Her aim is better than mine and it hits me in the face, making me laugh.

Evelyn rolls her eyes. "Li-ar," she singsongs, and I know she means the knocker. I do not care what she thinks, though. I would rather have hope than nothing at all.

"What can you *do*?" Evelyn asks it. "Can you do more than just throw some needles around?" I cannot fathom why she is doing this: always baiting it, testing it.

The answer is prompt: one knock.

I am curious, too, although probably not for the same reasons as Evelyn. "Can you show us?" I ask. "Can you make something happen in this room now?"

"Oh, Charlotte," Evelyn says with despair. "What if it brings out the needles again?"

"It said it wouldn't," I reply, all the while scanning my surroundings, waiting for something to happen: for a picture to fall off the wall, perhaps, or a drawer to rattle in the dresser. I can tell that Evelyn and Adelaide do the same, their eyes are moving everywhere—but nothing happens.

"Well, that was a promise not kept," Adelaide says with a sigh. "It's my turn now." She straightens up as if she's about to give an answer in Miss Russel's schoolroom. "Will I have more than two children?"

Just then, something *does* happen. I barely notice it at first when my bed starts moving—but it does move! The mattress shakes, subtly at first, then more forcefully, and soon the whole bed frame is shaking, its stubby legs clattering loudly against the floor.

"Charlotte!" Evelyn cries, and rises so abruptly that Sophie loses her grip.

I cannot help but laugh as my bed rattles beneath me; its springs and joints groaning. I even let go of the lip I have been clinging to, so as to experience this marvel fully. It reminds me of being on a boat in bad weather. Evelyn shouts my name again and starts across the floor. Adelaide and Sophie huddle together, both of them crying, while I am still laughing. If the bed shakes any harder than this, it might just fall apart—or both me and the bed will lift off the floor, and—

The door flies open and crashes into the wall. For a split second, I think it is the knocker who does it, but then, just as the bed stops with a bang, I can tell it is Mother.

She stands in the doorway with her pinned hair askew, staring at us with bloodshot eyes. Her mouth hangs open in astonishment, but only for a moment.

"Charlotte!" she cries and barges inside. "Get out of there!" She swats at me, ushering me off the bed. My legs shiver and feel soft when I stand up. Evelyn is next to me with a panicked expression on her face, and a hand pressed to her mouth. Her free hand grabs hold of my sleeve, as if tethering me to her side.

"What is going on in here?" Mother cries.

Evelyn just shakes her head. I am lost for words.

"It was the knocker!" Adelaide shouts from her bed, holding the still-crying Sophie. "It was the knocker who did it!"

"The *knocker*?" Mother looks between Evelyn and me with confusion—and anger, too. There is always anger.

"The knocker did the needle-tricks, too," Adelaide cries. "It dropped all those needles on us!"

"Knocker." Mother mouths the word, then her gaze swivels on me. "What did you *do*?" she demands, jabbing a finger into my chest. "What did you do?"

"Nothing!" I say, but I know there is no use.

Mother has made her decision.

• • •

I am sent to the shed, as I knew I would be, ever since Mother slammed the door open. I really should have known that she would hear the rattling of the bed and come running. Mary, too, had been halfway up the stairs when we left, me held tightly in Mother's iron grip.

"No dinner for Charlotte today," she said as we passed Mary by. "She can dine on dust in the shed."

And so, I am here again, behind these familiar walls, where the scent of dirt and salt is strong, and the light spills in between the boards. I sit down on the stool and let out my breath, wondering how long it will be this time. Mr. Norris has repaired the wall since the earthquake, so escape is no longer an option.

All I can do is wait.

When my limbs go stiff, and unwanted thoughts about the unfairness of it all begin to invade my mind, I get back up on my feet and start pacing, as always.

One, two, three, four, five, six, seven . . . knock, knock, knock.

One, two, three, four, five, six, seven . . . knock, knock, knock.

One, two, three, four, five, six, seven . . . knock, knock, knock.

One, two, three, four, five, six, seven . . . On my fourth foray across the length of the floor, just as I lift my hand to knock, someone does it for me.

Three loud raps sound in the wall.

I immediately press my face to the boards to look outside, thinking it might be Adelaide, but I cannot see anyone. I angle my head this way and that, but there is nothing to see but three circling seagulls.

"Is that you?" I whisper to the wood. "Is it the knocker?"

My heart leaps in my chest when one single rap answers.

"Did you follow me out here?" I ask, even if the answer is apparent, and it *does* feel gratifying when the knocker raps "yes." I am not alone after all.

I sink down on the stool again, resting my back against the wall. "Will you stay until I'm let out?" I ask it.

Again, the knocker says "yes," and I smile in the semi-darkness.

"Thank you," I whisper. "It can be hard being out here, all alone. It's good to have a friend—you *are* my friend, aren't you?"

The knocker confirms it and I smile.

"Since you are so good at fetching needles, how about an apple from the pantry?" I ask. "I'm starving, and Mother has denied me food." It is only fair, after all, seeing as how the knocker was the one who got me in trouble. I am also curious to see what it can do. The needles must have come from *somewhere*.

Almost instantly, objects rain down on me, so hard and fast that I give a sharp yell and guard my head with my hands. There are apples, yes, but also whole onions, a box of sardines, a hunk of ham, a pound of sugar still in the bag, and—inexplicably—a whole fruitcake studded with nuts that I do not think comes from our kitchen.

I cannot help but laugh. This is delightful! I know Evelyn would urge caution and remind me of how we know nothing of the knocker, but this is simply too good. I touch the cake, which has landed in my lap, and can feel how it is still warm.

"Delicious," I say. "This is wonderful, my friend! Thank you!" I break off a piece of cake and smell butter and cinnamon, cardamom and cloves, sweet apples and fat raisins. It tastes just as good as it smells, and I wonder what poor farmwife has lost her treat today. Hopefully, she will blame the seagulls.

I eat cake until I am full, and then I find an empty seed sack on a shelf and stuff the rest of the food down in it. It simply will not do if Mother finds it and thinks me a thief as well. She will never believe that I only asked the knocker for an apple; she does not even believe that the knocker is *real*. Doubtlessly she is already mulling, figuring out ways to lay the blame for the bed at my feet.

As if *I* can make the bed shake—or the walls speak.

"Can you read letters?" I ask, suddenly inspired.

The knocker raps once.

"Good." I am still brushing crumbs off my skirt. "Let us play a game," I say, and cross the tiny floor once more to fetch a bucket of tar and a thick-bristled brush. I clear the wall in front of me, remove the stained work clothes from their hooks, and then—where the faint outlines of my childhood drawings can still be seen—I start painting with the fragrant tar, drawing the alphabet in sloppy strokes, inspired by an article about the spiritualists' talking boards. By the time I am done, my hurt finger pounds, and the whole wall is covered in letters.

"You can spell out your answers for me," I tell the knocker. "This way, we can get better acquainted." I feel wonderful in this moment; joyous and carefree—as if no matter what Mother does to me, I can still outwit her.

Me and my new friend, together.

"Let's start simple," I say, looking at the wall. "Do you have a name?"

"No," it raps from the wall.

"You have to spell it out, see?" I motion to the alphabet. "Knock on the letters, just once."

I startle and take a step back from the wall when something moves to my right. At first, I think it is a trapped moth or a bird, but it is another paintbrush, this one slim and slender. It is lifting off one of the wall-mounted shelves, seemingly all on its own. I know it is not so, though. I know it is held by an unseen hand. The sight sets my heart racing. The paintbrush hovers for a moment, just an inch or two off the shelf, then it moves to the wall in front of me, hangs in the air for a second, then spins around until the bristles face me. Then it knocks the tip of the handle against the wall, first on the *N*, then it glides to the *O*.

"Wonderful!" I am so excited that I clap my hands. This is thrilling beyond measure—now I can get some proper answers. I try to focus, to remember all the questions Evelyn and I asked before that a "yes" or "no" could not satisfy.

"Who are you?" I ask.

Y-O-U, it replies. The brush moves fast, rushing between the letters.

"Yes, but who are *you*?" I try again, but the knocker does not answer, just hovers in the air. "Oh well, never mind that." I feel almost feverish with excitement, and again I have this sense that I must ask now, before the moment is gone—as if the knocker will disappear at any moment and I will never know what I want to know. "Why did you come to our house?" I ask.

Y-O-U, the knocker answers again, and I cannot tell if it is just an echo from before, or if it truly is *me* it means. Perhaps spelling is harder for it than I had hoped.

"That is flattering." I smile. "Can you spell out my name?"

C-H-A-R-L-O-T-T-E, it knocks without hesitation, flying between the letters.

I laugh out loud. "You really *do* know! Where did the cake come from?" I ask next.

C-L-E-R-G-Y.

"The clergy house? Oh, that's an excellent choice. Mrs. Hill must hate missing out on her treat . . . What about the sardines?"

P-A-N-T-R-Y.

"Just where I told you to go." I truly am impressed, but I cannot waste more time on trivialities. "What do you want?" I ask, as that is what we have worked the hardest to try and figure out, besides the question of who—or what—the knocker is.

W-H-A-T-D-O-Y-O-U-W-A-N-T, it spells.

"No, what do *you* want?" I clarify.

W-H-A-T-D-O-Y-O-U-W-A-N-T, it replies once again.

"Are you asking?" I am both flattered and confused. "I want . . . love and riches and everything good," I say. "I wish to live my life just as I see fit . . . and to be with Jasper Hill," I add. "Now it is your turn . . . What do *you* want?"

W-H-A-T-Y-O-U-W-A-N-T, it replies.

·17·

ruth

Adelaide North fell asleep in class today, and Sophie looks bleary-eyed and pale. They have been like this all week: distracted, unfocused, unable to keep up. I have asked Adelaide to take her braid out of her mouth at least ten times. Sophie is barely eating her lunch, but just stares at the winter-wrinkled apple in the tin box as if it is an alien thing that she does not know what to do with.

By the time Friday arrives, I am terribly concerned for them both.

Normally, they are bright students, even if Adelaide is easily distracted by her friends, and Annabeth Ferryman in particular. That is just their age, though. They are all silly headed at thirteen. Sophie is a studious and clever young girl, a little more withdrawn than her sister, but usually happy and content. Their behavior this week is highly out of character, and my impression from last Sunday—that there might be a conflict in the family—has been strengthened. Normally, I do not meddle in family affairs, but the girls' misery is so poignant that I feel I have no other choice but to visit the Norths, and perhaps—delicately—speak to their mother. Even if there is turbulence at home, I am sure that measures can be taken to shield the younger girls, who do need their rest and peace of mind.

I think long and hard on how to best execute my mission. I certainly do not wish to offend the Norths. I am heavily dependent on their good graces and also in their debt. Eventually, I decide to use the kindness they showed me in church as an excuse. Surely, it will only be polite of me to go there to thank them in person, and perhaps even bring a small gift—though what does one give to people such as them?

After a new round of considerations, I dig out an unopened bottle of plum liquor from the bottom of my closet. It has been there for ages, gathering dust. It had been a gift from my colleagues on the mainland when I left, and I have never been able to bring myself to drink it, because it has felt as if doing so would make the severance from my former life complete.

Now I am going to give it to the Norths.

I put on my best skirt of brown tweed and a shirtwaist with ruffles at the neck, and even trade my sturdy outdoor boots for a slightly more elegant pair. My hat and coat are the only ones I have, so there is nothing to do about those, but hopefully I can leave them behind in the hall. I grab my umbrella from the stand and leave the schoolhouse—door unlocked, as is customary on Margaret's Keep.

The weather is warmer, though the sky is hidden behind a carpet of clouds, as thick and opaque as whipped cream. Seagulls circle above my head, belching out hoarse warnings—or so it sounds to me. I start walking, heart in throat, into the sound of the sea washing up against the beach. I clutch the plum liquor in my hand, wrapped in a piece of brown paper.

The shortest way from the schoolhouse to the North residence, lest I brave the fields, is to follow the path to the tower, and then walk along the beach until I reach the harbor, but I do not want to go to Margaret's Tower. It feels as if revisiting the scene of a crime. I cannot afford the wagging tongues that are sure to follow if I am seen there again. Before you know it, Mrs. Fisher and Mrs. Newell will be at my door with torches in their hands, crying about witches and other such nonsense, and so I choose the other way around instead. The walk will be considerably longer, but with my fragile reputation at stake, I suppose it is a small price to pay.

I catch myself slowing my steps as I near the North house. I am worried about overstepping my boundaries and making my existence on this island more difficult. But I am merely visiting, I tell myself, with a bottle of liquor to show my appreciation. If nothing seems amiss in the household—if all I see are happy children—I may choose to say nothing at all. A ragged sheep bleats its agreement as I pass it by.

I approach the house from the driveway that cuts through the grassy fields, and am close enough to see the window curtains when the first projectile hits me from the right, knocking the hat off my head. I yelp with surprise and spin around, but there is nothing to see but the greening grass, the sea and the horizon, and one of the Norths' cows grazing by the barn. *A bird then,* I think as I pick up my hat and dust it off before placing it back on my head.

Then another projectile comes from my left, hitting my cheek with an explosion of pain. I cry out and swivel my head again, but there is nothing on that side either, except sheep and grass and empty land. I look down on the ground, at what hit me, and see it is a jagged piece of rock, stained with lichen. Mica glimmers darkly on the uneven surface.

Then another rock arrives, and another. They come from both sides now, and I hunch down and start running toward the house, all the while screaming for help like a banshee. The rocks come hard and fast—a torrent all of a sudden. My hat is gone again, and the bottle crashes down on the ground, filling the air with sweet fumes. Even my trusty umbrella must go as I sprint toward the North house. I feel as though I am on fire. Every part of me aches—and every time a rock hits, my body winces from the impact. I nearly buckle to the ground when a sizable rock hits my left knee, setting off an explosion of pain.

"Miss Russel!" Someone is before me on the road and comes running toward me with a blanket flapping in his hands. I barely register that it is the Norths' barn master, Norris. When we meet, he throws the blanket over me. It smells of horse and is rough enough to scratch. I think I am still screaming when he grabs a hold of my body to shield me under his arms, but I cannot say for sure. Around our feet, I hear the sharp thuds as rocks land on the road.

Mr. Norris starts running while shielding me. A rock hits my back, and Mr. Norris groans, so he must be hit by one as well. I do my best to keep up the pace under the blanket as we fight our way up the road. Mr. Norris curses plenty, and I cannot say that I blame him. My whole body is pummeled; it burns.

Then—suddenly—it is quiet.

Mr. Norris stops for a moment, and I can feel it when he lets out his breath. He does not free me from the blanket, though, but just keeps ushering me up the road and across the yard, where I can hear women calling.

"Bring her inside!" one shouts.

"Quick!" demands another.

I am not freed from the horse blanket before I am through the front door. I cannot even think of how I must look, all disheveled and beaten. Three women stand in front of us: Mrs. Norris, Miss Boden, and Evelyn North. They all look at me with such concern that I burst into tears.

"Oh hush." Miss Boden embraces me and presses me to her narrow chest. "You have had a shock, Miss Russel. Your tears are perfectly understandable." The housekeeper looks at me with kind eyes.

"Come into the kitchen, Miss Russel," Mrs. Norris says. "We must examine the damage and find you something hot to drink . . . Tea with a little something, I think."

"I will fetch Mother," says Evelyn, and spins on her heel, headed for the stairs. Through my teary haze I see that Adelaide is there, too, dawdling on the steps and looking down at me with horror. And there is Sophie, just behind her, pale faced and serious.

"Go to your rooms," Evelyn commands as she passes them by, her blue skirt lifted high to accommodate the speed.

I am guided into the warm kitchen and placed on a chair by a large, scarred kitchen table. Above me, several pots and pans adorn the ceiling. Mr. Norris has followed us inside as well, and stands by the open door to the hall with his hat in his hands, looking at me with a wrinkle of worry between his eyes.

Miss Boden has handed me a handkerchief, and Mrs. Norris pours tea from a copper kettle. She rummages in the pantry and retrieves a bottle of brown liquor to add to the brew. It makes me think of my own bottle—utterly in shards on the road—and then I start bawling again, unable to stop the tears.

"It's because I went to the tower, isn't it?" I force out the words. "The whole island hates me now—"

"No, no," Miss Boden says gently, brushing my cheek with her rough thumb. "It's nothing you did, Miss Russel."

"But they threw *rocks* at me!" I whine.

Miss Boden gently takes hold of my chin and tilts my head so I look into her eyes. "Who did?" she asks me in a quiet voice.

"I . . . I . . . The islanders," I blurt out. "It must have been them—who else could it be?" Certainly not the seagulls—or the sheep!

"There were no one on the road," Mr. Norris says from his place by the door.

"But there *must* have been. We were *both* attacked, Mr. Norris."

"I'm not saying we weren't," says he, and then his gaze slips away from me.

"But then what happened?" I look between the three, begging for an explanation. The servants just look at one another, though, and Mrs. Norris shakes her head.

"Drink your tea, Miss Russel," says Miss Boden. "We'll find some raw meat to help with the swelling, but it doesn't seem as though any of the rocks drew blood, thank God."

"Small comfort," Mrs. Norris mutters and retreats to the pantry again.

"It doesn't like visitors," a clear voice declaims. Adelaide has come up behind Mr. Norris and peeks around his large bulk.

"*Who* doesn't like visitors?" I ask, feeling chilled to the bone. There is something about the way she said it, and the stark fear on her features. She is wearing a white shirt and a dark blue skirt; her hair is gathered in one single braid. It is the same attire she wore to school today, and the sight of something familiar almost has me weeping again.

"The knocker." The girl whispers the word with fright in her eyes. "Charlotte says so."

"Who is 'the knocker'?" I feel utterly bewildered. None of the servants reply, or even meet my gaze. Mrs. Norris lands a gold-rimmed plate with a slab of beef on the table.

"Does it hurt terribly?" Adelaide's expression turns to one of compassion.

"Quite a bit, yes," I say. "Especially in my knee."

"The tea will help," Miss Boden offers, pushing the cup a little closer to me.

"It shouldn't have done that." Adelaide seems to be battling tears. Mrs. Norris briefly clutches the cross that hangs around her neck.

"Has . . . *it* done that before?" I feel dizzy with pain and bewilderment.

Again, they exchange glances but do not reply.

Something drops from the ceiling and into my tea, hitting the china with a tinkling sound. The servants all draw sharp breaths and Miss Boden whisks the teacup away and empties it in the slop bucket.

"You better ask Mrs. North," Mrs. Norris whispers to me and touches her cross again.

"She will see you now." Evelyn has arrived and stands beside Adelaide. Her face looks just as drawn and exhausted as her sisters'. No one in this house seems to sleep much, and I am starting to get an inkling of why.

I get to my feet—I ache all over—and limp after Evelyn as she guides me across the hall and into a delicately furnished front room. It faces the yard, and I cannot help but glance out the window to inspect the road. My hat lies there—and my umbrella. The brown paper that held the plum liquor flaps in the wind like a wing.

Mrs. North stands by the sofa, tall and straight. Her dress is burgundy and drapes around her neck. The pearl earrings dance when she moves to take my hand, and she gives off a faint whiff of port.

"Miss Russel, I am so terribly sorry." She motions me into a soft, upholstered chair. "I don't even know what to say." She sinks down on the sofa. Her nostrils flare and she wets her lips. "This is certainly not how we usually receive guests."

"I . . . I just came to thank you," I say. "For what you did for me, in church." It feels long ago and far away; everything does right now. It is as if ten years passed me by while I was battling the rocks.

"And a fine repayment we have given you," Mrs. North replies. "I just hope that . . . Perhaps it might be wise not to mention it to anyone—"

"Mention what?" Now it is I who gives an unsound laughter. "I did not see a thing!"

"Just that." She gives a wry smile.

"No . . . I mean, I do not know what happened," I clarify. "Rocks came from everywhere, but I couldn't see anyone in the fields!" Even just saying it out loud makes my heart race again.

"I know." She nods, looking very serious. "She is very cunning."

"Who?" I ask, perplexed. Could this be the "it" that Adelaide spoke of?

"Charlotte." Mrs. North's steely gaze does not leave mine.

"Are you saying that *your daughter* is behind this?" Even on a day full of shocks, the accusation still rattles me. "Surely, one girl cannot—"

"Oh, she can," Mrs. North interrupts me. "She will have her way, no matter the cost—"

"But *how*?" I rub my sore arms. "It's impossible!"

"Is it, Miss Russel?" She arches an eyebrow. "What else would you prefer to blame? Witches? Ghosts? *Surely*—"

"Of course not," I snap, not much caring about Mrs. North's good graces anymore. "Perhaps some sort of weather phenomenon," I suggest. "Perhaps there are gasses in the ground, pushing the rocks up from the soil."

"I hope so." She looks at me coolly. "My husband has sent for a geologist to examine the ground after the earthquake. Perhaps he can find an answer." This, at least, sounds more reasonable than blaming Charlotte.

"I look forward to his results," I say curtly.

"So do I." She gives just a hint of a smile before her face grows dark again. "Charlotte has her sisters whipped into a frenzy." She speaks with some contempt. "She blames this . . . 'knocker' for everything." Her long fingers start kneading her forehead. She, too, is tired, it seems. "I truly wish it is as you say, Miss Russel, and there's a perfectly natural explanation, but I fear it is my daughter." She sighs. "She has always been quite a handful." The unbidden confession makes me squirm in my seat. I had never imagined seeing the mighty Mrs. North so weak.

"I take it you have had a hard time lately," I dare. "Adelaide and Sophie have seemed tired—"

"Yes," she interrupts me. "Charlotte's shenanigans keep them up every night. They cannot sleep for fear of hearing knocking in the walls." She laughs again—a bitter, hopeless sound.

"Do you want me to talk to her?" I offer. Even if I do not believe for one second that Charlotte North was out in the fields pelting me with rocks, it might give me an opportunity to learn a little more of what is going on—and maybe help two of my students.

"What I *want,* Miss Russel, is for you to go home and rest." Her smile is all teeth now. "You must be terribly sore, poor thing." She rises from the sofa and extends a hand to help me to my feet. "I shall have Norris take you in the—*closed*—carriage." Her eyebrow rises again. "And we appreciate your discretion," she adds. "It will only cause a ruckus if this becomes known. You know better than anyone how words spread and twist in such a small place."

There is nothing for me to do but to nod in agreement and gratefully accept the carriage ride home.

And so, thoroughly dismissed—and far more bewildered than when I arrived—I let myself be placed upon the plush seat in the carriage and prepare for the bumpy drive home. My fresh bruises and aches torment me even before the vehicle is set in motion.

Just as the carriage leaves the yard, I catch sight of something from the corner of my eye, and turn my head to look. It is Charlotte, standing in front of a ramshackle shed. She follows the carriage with dark eyes before slipping inside and closing the door.

Some other day, I might be curious to know what she is doing in there, but just today, I simply cannot bring myself to care.

·18·

charlotte

Adelaide and Sophie will not let up about Miss Russel. They keep asking me over and over again why the knocker was so cruel to her, and lament the pummeling she got.

"She was *limping* when she left the kitchen," Adelaide says when the ruckus has died down a bit and we have finally gone to bed. "Poor Miss Russel didn't even *do* anything. She just wanted to come visiting."

"I don't think the knocker cares *why* people come," I tell her, thinking of Father's foreman who had also tried to approach the house and received much the same treatment. "Perhaps it acts like a watchdog, and will come running whenever our border is breached."

"But why?" Adelaide cries in the darkness.

"I—I don't know, Adelaide." Though I asked it many times, the knocker refused to answer.

"We cannot not have visitors, Charlotte. You *have* to tell it."

"Why *me*?" I ask. "You can tell it yourself." Why was it suddenly up to me alone to communicate with it? We had all done it before. I do feel a little guilty when I think of the alphabet wall in the shed, which I have not shared with anyone yet, but find a sweet satisfaction in keeping to myself. It was *my* discovery after all.

"It clearly likes you best," Adelaide mutters in the other bed. "It came to you first and talked to you first, and it only gave needles to you in the beginning." *And a flower,* I think but do not say. I never told anyone about the violet on my pillow either, but promptly put it in my Bible to dry.

"I didn't much appreciate the needles," I remind Adelaide. "If that was an attempt at friendship, the knocker certainly failed."

"Still, I think it will listen to you, if anyone. It *did* stop with the needles when you asked it to."

"Only because I promised to talk to it—"

"Then *do*! Tell it to leave Miss Russel—and *all* our guests—alone," she instructs me.

I sigh and twist in my bed. "We don't have that many guests." I certainly do not feel in a position to make *demands* of the knocker. Besides, it brought me cake.

Adelaide starts another cycle of lament. "Poor Miss Russel. She must be horribly bruised."

I try to comfort her. "There was no blood, though. She won't need any stiches, and will heal up in no time, I'm sure."

"Tell the knocker it made a mistake."

"I don't think it will listen to reason."

"Why do you say that?"

It is just something about the way it is, giving poor answers or no answers at all. "I cannot say if it has compassion."

"What if it turns on us next?" Adelaide asks in a quivering voice. "What if it throws rocks at Sophie and me when we go to school?"

"Have Norris take you in the carriage," I reply. "Then you won't have to fret about it." Though I suspect that the harsh welcome Miss Russel received is reserved for strangers only. Mr. Norris is outside all the time, but before Miss Russel, he had never been attacked with rocks.

"Do you think the knocker is Margaret?" Adelaide asks. "Do you think she broke free like they say?"

"Maybe," I mumble, but I do not truly believe it. Margaret had been a grown woman when she was exiled to the island, and her husband had been rich, so she had been used to being served. She just does not seem like the type of person who would throw rocks or steal a cake.

But maybe death has changed her?

• • •

Mother refuses to let me go to church, though she does not tell me until after I have donned my black dress and come down to breakfast. This is the worst kind of punishment for me, and she knows it, but she would rather that I turn into an ungodly creature than let me sit in front of Jasper Hill for one hour. It is not just my feelings for the reverend that she wants to battle, though. No, this time, I am to be punished for Miss Russel, even if I had nothing to do with it.

"It wasn't Charlotte; it was the knocker!" Adelaide is furious on my behalf. "Charlotte's aim isn't even that good." I suppose she has a point.

Mother and I, standing on the floor, measure each other with our eyes. Her lip is lifted in a sneer, while I battle the fury that rolls in me, since I know that my mother cannot be reasoned with and that any display of anger will be futile.

"There is no 'knocker,' Adelaide." Mother does not turn her head, but keeps her gaze trained on me, as if I am a slippery fish that will escape if not closely guarded. "It's just *Charlotte* who has gotten into your head, and you should know better than to let it happen—"

"Charlotte couldn't have done it all," Adelaide continues. "How, for instance, did she make it rain needles?"

Mother does not deign to answer. She simply does not care. I suppose it is much more comfortable for her to just place the blame with me and be done with it. That way she will not have to consider that we have an unnatural creature dwelling in our walls.

"It's true, Mother," Evelyn says, surprising me. "Charlotte cannot be responsible for much of it—and why would she harm Miss Russel?" After Mother had caught us when my bed rocked, Evelyn had been sickeningly apologetic, following Mother around like a dog and insisting on how she had thought it was harmless. The secrecy had given her away, though. She would not have kept mum about the game if she had not realized what we did was unlikely to be approved of. The tone between the two has been strained ever since.

"Charlotte is capable of a lot more than you think," Mother snaps. "Just look at what a disaster she has been for our relationship with the Hills—"

"That's different." Evelyn can serve a pointed look as well, and sends one in Mother's direction. "It doesn't require magic tricks or invisibility, or—"

"I didn't do it," I cut in. "*Why* would I do something so childish?" Pelting rocks was something young boys did, not a woman of nearly eighteen.

"You always crave attention." Mother uses her favorite barb.

"I would not sleep in a bed full of needles to achieve it."

"It's the knocker," Adelaide insists.

"What is it *now*?" Father booms from the doorway. "What glorious nonsense have we cooked up now to make this Sunday, too, a living nightmare?" He frowns as he looks between Mother and me.

"Charlotte will not be joining us in church," Mother says in a clipped voice.

"Oh, thank goodness." Father lets out his breath. "I suppose she doesn't agree?" His question is for Mother, even if I am standing right there.

"Hardly." Mother snorts.

Finally, he looks at me. "It might be for the best, Charlotte."

"Oh, *that's* not why," Evelyn informs him, referring to my love for Reverend Hill. "Mother thinks Charlotte is responsible for Miss Russel."

"Well, that is highly unlikely." Father sends Mother a questioning look. "How could Charlotte have accomplished something so . . . dramatic? No, I say we wait to hear what the geologist has to offer by way of an explanation, as Miss Russel herself so wisely suggested." He gives Mother a curt nod.

Mother stands her ground. "Charlotte is still not coming to church."

"As I said, it might be for the best." Father shrugs, then finally looks at me. "When you were a child, I had to manhandle you into the carriage to *make* you go to church. You refused it with all your might. I must say, things have changed." A tiny smile plays under his mustache.

"Fine." I let out my breath. "I won't go to church—but I had nothing to do with Miss Russel."

Had this been any other Sunday, I would have felt crushed by this blow, but since the knocker arrived, things have changed. Before, Sunday sermons were the only thing I had to look forward to, and my time spent in church felt sacred to me, but—though I still love Jasper Hill—I have other things now that also feel important, and my family's absence will give me plenty of time alone in the shed. To my surprise, I find that I cannot entirely mourn the lost opportunity to gaze upon the reverend's handsome face.

I have things to discuss with my new friend.

As soon as the carriage has left the driveway, I slip out of the front door and rush across the yard, still wearing my Sunday black. I step inside the shed and close the door behind me. The strong scent of tar envelops me at once, and I can feel that the knocker is waiting.

I sink down on the dusty floor and rest my back against the wall, then let out a breath of relief. For a moment, I just sit there and listen to the sea, then I open my mouth and ask, "Knocker, are you there?"

A single rap in the wall replies, and the faint scent of cooked meat comes seeping in.

"Good," I say. "Mother is blaming *me* for the rocks that hit Miss Russel now. She thinks that I'm responsible." I keep my attention on the wall of letters, in case it wants to reply there, but nothing happens.

"*Why* did you do it?" I ask, though I have already asked it many times before, and never received a good answer. This time is no different. The knocker remains silent.

"Will you keep pelting our visitors with rocks?" I ask.

Two knocks, then a pause, then one single knock. It is undecided.

"It's highly inconvenient," I tell it. "Is there a way to make you stop?"

No answer.

"Can I trade you to stop with the rocks, like I did with the needles?"

Finally, the paintbrush lifts from the shelf, and it knocks on the letters: *N-O-F-R-I-E-N-D*.

"What do you mean?" I ask, puzzled. "Are *you* not a friend, or are *they* not a friend?"

N-O-F-R-I-E-N-D.

"Only because you don't know them, it doesn't mean they can't be your friends," I say, and then think of how highly unlikely it is that Miss Russel should ever befriend something like the knocker. "Perhaps you can make yourself scarce when we have guests?" I suggest.

Two knocks sound in the wall.

"Are you Margaret?" I ask next, thinking of what Adelaide had said the night before.

Two more knocks—and forceful ones.

"Did you *know* Margaret?" I try. My bandaged finger aches.

One single knock sounds.

"Did you like her?"

Another knock in the wall. The paintbrush still hovers in the air.

"Did you help her, too, and bring her things?"

The knocker replies "yes" again, and I get an exhilarated feeling, as if I am a bloodhound on a trail.

"Was Margaret your friend?" I ask, but the knocker is done with talking about Margaret, and refuses to reply. It does that sometimes, goes quiet to change the subject.

"Can you bring me something from the church?" I ask. "Something Jasper Hill has touched?" That way, I can at least feel close to him, even if I am not there.

Immediately, a leather bound book of psalms lands in my lap. When I open it, I am thrilled to see tiny annotations scrawled in the margins. They remind me of his sheets of music, the way he would write little notes to himself. This has to be Jasper Hill's personal book, and I open it to the first page to make sure. As suspected, his name is written in a neat hand on top of the page.

"What a wonderful gift! Thank you, dear knocker. I shall treasure this immensely." I press the book to my chest. "Can you also do something nice for Adelaide, so she won't be so wary of you? And something to make Mother regret blaming me for Miss Russel—though not something dangerous," I rush to add. "Just something to sour her day."

The knocker raps once.

"Thank you," I whisper, and then I ask on a whim, "Is it true that you like me the best?"

Another knock sounds in the wall.

• • •

When my family returns, I am thrilled to see the knocker deliver on its promise.

First there is Adelaide, who finds a mother-of-pearl pendant shaped like a heart on her bed. She grabs it and rushes to find me at once as I sit examining Jasper Hill's psalm book in the front room. I think the pages even smell a little of him: a faint scent of rosemary.

"Did you get this for me?" She holds out the necklace; it dangles from her fingers on a delicate silver chain.

"No." I give her a knowing smile. "I suppose it's the knocker," I say. "It felt sorry for you being so upset about Miss Russel."

"Really?" Her eyes go wide, but then a shadow falls over her. "She looked horrible in church," she says. "Annabeth said she had fallen off a chair, so I suppose that is what she's been telling people."

"Poor Miss Russel," I say, though I feel slightly annoyed that the knocker's gift is so easily forgotten.

"Annabeth said that her mother had said that Miss Russel deserved it, for taking us to the tower."

"What nonsense," I reply.

"Isn't it just . . . and since *we* know what really happened, those rumors feel doubly unfair." Adelaide's eyes fill up with indignation.

"The knocker *is* sorry, though," I remind her, looking at the pendant.

"For scaring *me,*" she replies, "but what about Miss Russel?"

I shrug. "Perhaps it has a gift for her as well? I don't think it wanted to hurt her, Adelaide. I just think it's very protective and doesn't know friend from foe. I have explained it to the knocker now."

That mellows her a little. "It *is* new here," she agrees. "It probably doesn't know any better."

"Exactly," I say, and feel just a tiny bit guilty for deceiving her. I tell myself it is for her own good—to make her sleep better at night. "Do you like it?" I say, looking at the pendant again.

"Oh, I do," she says with a smile, and so I am satisfied.

Mother's "gift" is even better. It happens while we are all seated around the table, enjoying the Sunday roast. I am eating mostly meat again. My newfound appreciation for it has not gone away, and I prefer it above all else—even cake.

Mother eats as normal, but then, when she takes a sip of her glass, her face suddenly turns bright red, and she abruptly spits the wine out, showering both her plate and herself in liquid.

"It's *vinegar*!" she exclaims, wiping her face with the napkin. "Did *you* do this?" Her eyes are like burning dark lanterns when she looks at me.

I shake my head, but inwardly I smile.

Father sniffs his own glass and lifts it to his lips. "Mine is perfectly fine," he says with a touch of wonder. "I thought it came from the same bottle."

"Clearly *not.*" Mother is furious. "*She* has been practicing her sleight of hand again."

"I cannot see how." Father sounds bewildered.

"It was the knocker," Adelaide says, sporting her new pendant.

"It was *Charlotte,*" Mother insists, and goes to change her dress.

·19·

charlotte

The geologist, Mr. West, arrives on one of the fishing vessels on Monday afternoon. Mr. Norris picks him up in the closed carriage, even if it is only a few minutes' walk.

Father will not chance more rocks.

My sisters and I are lined up in the hall: Evelyn first, since she is the oldest, then me, then Adelaide, and lastly Sophie. We are all wearing white today. Mother is, too, as she is the one who decided. Evelyn, who is engaged, has the freedom to choose for herself, but she, too, wears a light, white dress, in solidarity with the rest of us. Father, however, has not felt inclined to don snowy white, but wears his usual gray suit instead. I wonder, if my brother George had lived, would he have been allowed to wear gray as well?

My sisters and I leave our positions to crowd by the window and watch the driveway when the carriage comes within sight. We scan the fields and even the sky, in case a rock should come flying, but the carriage arrives at our door quite safely.

I am secretly disappointed, since I find such visits tedious. It is not due to the guests themselves, but the performance, the display we are made to be a part of. *I* do not care how we appear to people I do not even know. And I find, as I stand there gazing at the road, that I would not much mind a stone-throwing watchdog in instances such as this.

Mr. Norris climbs down from his seat and starts unloading the geologist's luggage. I can see a couple of wooden tripods, a battered leather suitcase, and a sizable trunk. We all hold our breaths when the carriage door opens from the inside to reveal the man himself, wondering if the onslaught of rocks will happen as he crosses the short distance to the stairs—but Mr. West makes it to the door unscathed.

Even Mother lets out her breath before swinging the door open before him, plastering on her best smile. I, on the other hand, sigh from disappointment. I would very much have liked to see a flying rock or two. By the time Mr. West enters the hall, we are all back in line, with white fabric dancing around our ankles.

Mr. West is a blond man in his thirties, with kind eyes and wispy whiskers. He wears a pair of wire-framed spectacles, and a checked flat cap that he promptly scoops off upon entering. His tweed jacket is mustard colored, and his pants are chocolate brown. He greets us all in turn, and thanks Mother profusely for the hospitality, as if she houses him out of the goodness of her heart.

Mr. Norris comes inside with pieces of luggage, and then Mary appears to show Mr. West upstairs. Norris lumbers after them, carrying a heavy load. Once Mr. West is out of earshot, my sisters and I are abuzz, sharing our opinions.

"He seems like a modern man," Evelyn declares. "Just look at the way he dresses."

"He is just dressed for the outdoors," I remark. "That is where he works—"

"His name is 'West,'" Sophie notes with satisfaction. "We are 'north' and he is 'west.'"

"I do hope he won't get any *trouble,*" Adelaide frets.

Mother gives me a warning look. "He won't unless your sister wants it otherwise."

I cannot help but feel it is a challenge. If only she knew how misguided it is.

Mr. West does not come down again for a while. I suppose he needs to rest. Not everyone from the mainland handles the trip well. Our road of salt can be rocky, and bring even grown men to their knees. The island itself can be a challenge, too. When Aunt Anne is here, she often complains that the wind gives her headaches, and that the seagull cries "drill into her brain."

While we wait for dinner to be ready, I leave my sisters in the front room, claiming I have a headache of my own, though instead of going upstairs, I take the route through the kitchen and out the back door, then I slip behind the barn and emerge by the shed. No one notices my stealthy escape but a pair of brown chickens pecking in the dust.

When I am safely inside, I speak quickly to the knocker.

"Why did you bother Miss Russel and not Mr. West?"

The knocker does not reply.

"I know I was mad at you for pummeling Miss Russel, but that is because she is no bother," I explain. "Mother and Father's houseguests *are* bothersome, though, and I would rather they didn't come here. It's tiring to be forced to make polite conversation, and Mother watches me all the time . . . When one of Father's acquaintances was here once, Mother went into a rage because I hadn't eaten the plums for dessert—even if they were sour. If you are going to chase *anyone,* it ought to be visitors like Mr. West."

The knocker still does not reply, and, after having waited for some time, I leave, feeling thoroughly discouraged. I had hoped to at least receive a response, but I realize I know nothing about the knocker. Perhaps it does not like it when I try to decide what it should do. It might not even be here all the time—or perhaps it has left now, for good.

As for Mr. West, I suppose there is nothing else to do but to suffer through.

Mary has made crab soup as a starter and cod for the main course, drenched in butter and drizzled with chopped eggs. I would rather have had meat. For dessert, she has prepared a fruit compote, which Sophie and Adelaide have looked forward to all day. We are all seated around the table in our white dresses. The afternoon sun floods inside through the lace-curtained windows, brightening the room with flecks of gold. Mr. West sits between Father and Evelyn; he is wearing a feisty knitted vest in orange, green, and ocher. The wine flows freely in our glasses, though only Evelyn can take hers without water and Sophie only pretends to drink hers.

"What *is* curious is that there were no aftershocks," Mr. West says to Father. "Although there might have been—only so faint that you didn't notice."

Inwardly, I am already yawning.

"I worry about damage to the cliffs," Father tells him. "It won't do if one of my trawlers goes under them and is hit by falling rocks."

"Speaking of rocks," Mother starts, but then goes mum when Father sends her a look of warning before turning to Mr. West again.

"How will you conduct the examination?" he asks.

"I will traverse the island by foot and keep my eyes on the ground." Fine wrinkles appear around Mr. West's eyes when he smiles. "But if I could borrow a horse for my equipment, it would be a great help."

"Absolutely," Father says, but looks pained. "Or I could have Norris take you in the carriage . . . Wouldn't that be better?"

"It is a generous offer, but it would be hard to see much from within it."

"I'm sure it will be fine." Mother's words are slightly slurred. I do not think the wine in her glass is the first she has had today. "He arrived here in one piece, after all." She does not seem to notice the puzzled look from Mr. West nor the furious one from Father.

Evelyn attempts to save the situation. "We have had peculiar weather. Awful hail."

Adelaide tries to help her, but probably only succeeds in mystifying the matter. "It comes just out of nowhere."

"I wish I were an expert on hail then, too, and not only dirt and rocks," Mr. West says good-naturedly.

"Oh, perhaps it won't happen again." Mother is looking at me.

"It's hard to tell," I say. The smell of fish and butter makes me queasy. I do wish Mother had settled on beef.

"What happened to your finger?" Mr. West nods to my bandage.

"She pricked herself with a needle," Sophie replies in my stead.

Father's eyebrow arches. "It's still the same wound? That was almost two weeks ago, Charlotte."

"It festered," Evelyn says, and drinks a little more of her wine.

"You should have it looked at." Father's brow knits up with concern.

"I do have some medical training. I can look at it if you want," Mr. West offers, and I find I resent the kindness, although I cannot say why.

"That would be of great help," says Father.

Mr. West cuts into a juicy piece of cod. "Tell me more about the island."

"There is not much to tell," says Mother.

"What about the old tower that fell? It must have a fascinating history." The geologist keeps prying. It annoys me for some reason. The tower is none of his concern.

"All I know is that there was not much here when I arrived save for sheep farms and a few fishing vessels," Father replies, and I struggle not to roll my eyes, since I know what is sure to follow. "I invested in steam trawlers, and built the harbor with my family's money. Then I built this house."

"And a magnificent house it is," Mr. West says. Inwardly, I groan.

Mother picks at her fish. "Margaret's Keep used to have a poor reputation."

"But it's flourishing now," Father adds quickly. "The population increase has been significant, too. Instead of moving away to find opportunity, the young ones stay on now . . . If you offer people a way to multiply what little they have, they will take it." He sounds very pleased with himself.

"What made you settle on *this* island?" Mr. West seems genuinely curious, which surprises me. Usually, guests only ask to be polite.

"My grandmother came from Margaret's Keep," Father admits. "She always spoke so highly of it . . . Her father was the reverend here—although back then, there were so few people on the islands that he served quite a few. She used to tell me of how the beach below the church was crowded with rowing boats on Sundays." His face softens as he shares the fond memory. "I always wanted to come here, and when I finally did, I saw the potential." He cuts another piece of cod.

"What about the tower?" Mr. West asks him. "Did she ever mention it?"

"Oh, yes." Father laughs. "But my wife will never forgive me if I tell such stories at the table."

Mr. West is amused. "Is that so?"

"Later, over a port perhaps." Father tries to dismiss the topic.

"A woman named Margaret lived there," I say. "The tower was named after her. She was imprisoned for being a witch—or perhaps an adulteress. No one else lived out here then, so she couldn't do anyone harm. I suppose it was an excellent prison."

"Oh." Mr. West's eyes widen. "That is quite the story—and it explains the name of the island."

"It's just a story," Father says, slightly annoyed. He waves his wineglass in the air. "We don't know how much of it is true."

"The islanders were terrified of the tower," I continue, with the sole aim of embarrassing my parents. "They said that Margaret was buried below it, and that her spirit still lingers there. Many people claim to have seen a ghostly light flicker in the tower's only window.

That was how she signaled to boats if she needed supplies. They said it was a cursed and unhappy place, and that if you stayed there too long, Margaret would come and get you," I finish with a smile.

"Nonsense," Father states.

"It had a certain *gloom,*" says Mother.

"What happened?" Mr. West asks. "If Margaret 'got' you?"

"You were cursed, I suppose." I shrug.

"They say it could drive you mad." Adelaide looks very pale, and her voice is quiet and fearful. "If she got to you, you would be forever drawn to the tower—you could not sleep for thinking of it. My friend Annabeth says that, before, some women threw themselves off the cliff just to make it stop."

"Annabeth Ferryman has a very lively imagination," Mother remarks with a smirk, although I know that she did not like the tower either.

Mr. West looks slightly confused. "But why were they drawn to the tower?"

"Because something there—Margaret, I suppose—wanted to be released from her prison," I reply, and Mother gives me another dark look.

"So her imprisonment never ended?" Mr. West keeps eating his fish, looking amused rather than frightened, which had not been my intention.

"Not according to the islanders," I say.

"They say that she is free now because the tower fell," Adelaide adds, and I cannot help but think of the knocker.

"Girls, please." Mother rolls her eyes.

"Mr. West is *interested,* Mother. It's just a conversation," Evelyn gently reminds her.

"But so *grim*." Mother huffs and drinks more wine.

"Did your grandmother share this story with you?" Mr. West asks Father, just as Mary ferries in the fruit compotes.

Father nods, ruddy cheeked from wine and embarrassment. "She said the islanders would throw pebbles from the beach into the open doorway whenever they passed by the tower, to weigh down the dead and make sure she didn't follow them home." He uses a napkin to wipe his mustache. "There is no evidence that Margaret was buried there, of course."

Mr. West is all smiles. "I have always found such stories fascinating. I find it particularly interesting how natural phenomena—such as earthquakes—might become a part of the lore."

Just then, a loud thump sounds against the wall, behind Father's back.

All of us but Mr. West tense up.

Another sharp rap sounds by the rafters, and Sophie scans the room with frightened eyes. Her much-coveted compote sits forgotten on the table.

Three loud thumps in quick succession sound right behind my back, and then the splintering of glass as a sizable rock comes hurtling through the window to land in a silver dish on the table, sending lemon wedges flying through the air.

My sisters all rise in a flurry of white and start for the door, screaming. Mother, Father, and Mr. West are on their feet, too—and eventually me, although I do not fear the rocks. Who will the knocker talk to if it gives me a concussion? Another rock comes crashing through a window and lands where Father just sat.

"Get out!" Father shouts. "Get out of here at once!" As soon as the words are out, another heavy rock comes flying in through the broken window; and as soon as it lands on the floor, we all rush for the door, accompanied by the sounds of more rocks hitting the walls.

"Oh goodness me!" Mother cries as we rush into the hall, where my sisters, Mary, and Mrs. Norris stand huddled together while listening to the noise. Mary has draped her arms around Sophie and presses the girl to her body, while Evelyn and Adelaide hold hands. I take my place next to them and repress the smile that threatens to burst free.

It seems like the knocker listened after all.

A rock in the dining room bounces off the floor and comes to a halt inside the threshold to the hall. Mr. West quickly retrieves it and holds it up to his eye.

"It is hot," he marvels, staring at the lump. The rest of us look at the open doorway, listening intently as cutlery and china clatter and explode when hit by the rocks.

Then, it is silent.

Mr. West turns to look at Evelyn, hefting the rock in his hand. "*Hailstorm,* was it?" He sounds thoroughly shaken.

"Or something like it," she replies with an apologetic smile.

"Do you know who's behind it?" Mr. West is pale under the whiskers.

"Yes," says Mother.

"No," says Father.

"We cannot *see* anyone," says Mrs. Norris.

"The knocker is angry today." Adelaide twirls her braid between her fingers. The other hand is at her throat, tugging at the heart-shaped pendant. Inwardly, I sigh. I had quite forgotten about Adelaide's fear when I made my request in the shed.

"Certainly, they must be caught." Mr. West's own fear quickly turns to indignation. "They must be made to *answer* for their crime."

"Certainly." Father nods his agreement.

"Do you have any suspects?" Mr. West asks.

"Yes," says Mother.

"No," says Father. "I cannot think of anyone who would do such a thing. Most of our neighbors rely on me for resources and work."

"Oh, my beautiful china!" Mother has dared cross the floor to peek inside the dining room. "We must have the windows boarded up until they can be replaced."

"Perhaps you should hire a watchman," West suggests.

"It has occurred to me," Father replies, sounding unconvinced.

"For now, let's retire to my study, shall we? We can take our port in there."

"After *this*?" Mr. West sounds shocked.

"Certainly." Father forces a smile. "We will catch the culprit in time. Where, after all, are they to hide on an island?"

"I must say, I admire your calm—"

"We have had quite a few 'storms' of late," Evelyn explains.

"Are the police involved?" Mr. West sounds bewildered; his hand still clutches the rock.

"No," Mother says, "but perhaps they *should* be."

"It wouldn't help," I tell her, but she has already turned her back.

Inwardly I am thrilled. The knocker *does* seem to listen to me, even if it does not reply.

• • •

I, for one, sleep well that night; lost in a deep and dreamless slumber—that is until a bloodcurdling scream rips me out of my blissful state and has me on my feet.

Adelaide and I find each other in the dark and grab each other's hands. For a second or two, we just stand there, listening. There are no more screams, but we both startle when a door flies open in the hallway outside, hitting the wall with a crash. Next, we hear rapid footsteps that pass by our door, and then a terrible racket as someone tumbles down the stairs. More doors open, and Adelaide and I move, too.

Out in the hallway, we meet Evelyn, holding a candle high. Sophie is already plastered to her side. Mother and Father come up behind them, bleary-eyed and pale. I can see Father's lips move as he silently counts his daughters: *one, two, three, four . . .*

"What on earth is going on here?" Mother hisses.

Down below, we hear a moaning, as if someone is hurt.

"Mr. West," Evelyn gasps, and that sets us all in motion. We rush for the stairs and Evelyn gets there first. We all file in behind her as she travels down the steps with her shivering candle.

At the bottom of the stairs, we find Mr. West in his pajamas, lying in a heap on the floor. He might be hurt, but he is surely alive, because he makes a series of whimpering noises. The door to the kitchen opens, and there is Mary in her nightgown, carrying another candle.

"Is Mr. West hurt?" she asks, wide-eyed.

"He took a tumble down the stairs," Father announces, then bends down to address the man. "Are you all right, Mr. West?"

"Clearly, he is *not,*" Mother huffs. "Help him up for goodness' sake."

Father supports Mr. West as he rises to his feet, and holds him by the arm even after he has found his footing, as if worried that our houseguest would fall down again. Mr. West looks dazed, and his gaze is unfocused. The spectacles sit askew on his nose.

"What *happened,* Mr. West?" Mother sounds stricken. "Bring him into the front room," she orders Father, then rushes hurriedly in that direction. My sisters and I follow as well, huddled around Evelyn with the candle. My heart beats fast with the excitement of it all.

Just as they are about to cross the threshold to the front room, Mr. West suddenly regains the full use of his limbs and thrashes in Father's arms.

"No! No!" he shouts. "I cannot stay here! I have to get out!"

"It is the middle of the night, Mr. West?" Mother is shocked. "Where would you go?"

"Pull yourself together, man." Father grunts while fighting to regain control of Mr. West's limbs.

"You don't understand," cries Mr. West as Father battles him into the room and down in a chair. "The thing I *saw* . . ." His spectacles reflect the light from the candles Mother has lit, and make his eyes look as if they are burning.

Sophie whimpers next to me, and I place a hand on her head.

"It's not natural," Mr. West whispers. "I cannot stay in this house for another minute—" He is halfway up from the chair again before Father is able to force him back down.

"It's not safe outside either." He looks Mr. West in the eyes while speaking. "People have been pummeled with rocks in our driveway, too." He keeps his gaze fixed on our houseguest for a moment to make sure that his words have sunk in.

"But that . . . *thing,*" Mr. West whimpers.

Mother tries to soothe him. "Just a nightmare, I'm sure." She looks relieved when Mary appears with a tray filled with hot tea, cups, and liquor. Mother serves herself first, then pours for Mr. West. We are not offered any. "I keep some laudanum upstairs," she tells Mary. "Perhaps a few drops would be in order?"

"It was *not* a *nightmare.*" Mr. West clutches his cup. "I cannot—*will not*—stay!"

"You might see it differently in the morning . . ."

"I *know* what I saw!" he bellows.

"He *could* go to the reverend," Mary suggests. "Norris could take him in the carriage."

Mr. West looks hopeful, but Father looks doubtful.

"The thing is, Mr. West"—he speaks in a quiet voice—"we would rather if our fellow islanders did not know about our *hailstorms* . . ."

"Perhaps Mr. and Mrs. Norris can shelter him until morning?" Mary suggests next, but Mother shakes her head.

"Mrs. Norris would get upset, and then we would never hear the end of it."

"There's always Miss Russel," Evelyn says, and Mother looks up, surprised, seemingly having forgotten we were there, clustered by the door. "She already knows what is happening here, and she has kept quiet so far."

Mother nods and drinks deeply from her cup. "That might not be the worst of ideas . . . You girls should go into the kitchen," she continues. "Evelyn will make you some warm milk to calm you down. There is no need for you to stay here."

"Do as your mother says," Father agrees. "You should not be seeing this." They both suddenly seem to have come to their senses, and realized that a grown man falling apart is not a suitable sight for their daughters.

"But what did Mr. West *see?*" Adelaide whispers.

"Nothing," Mother snaps. "He merely had a nightmare." She implores Mr. West with her eyes.

Mr. West, who also seems to have regained an ounce of his faculties, nods. "It must have been." He forces a smile that is clearly only for our benefit.

My sisters and I shuffle back into the dark hall, and Evelyn lights our way to the kitchen.

"What a disaster," she mutters.

"That poor man," Adelaide sighs.

"He looked very sick," Sophie says.

"He looked *scared,*" I reply with some delight, all the while wondering what our houseguest saw.

And if it was I who caused it.

·20·

ruth

The stranger sits at my table, eating my eggs and sipping my tea. He looks too big for the cramped space of my kitchen. Everything in here suddenly looks smaller: the table, the chair, and the cup itself—although I do not think he is all that imposing outside these walls.

I do not like the presence of a man in my home; it makes me wary and uncomfortable, stilted and strangely quiet. It does not much matter if he is nothing but grateful, and if letting him in was the only Christian thing to do when he was dumped on my doorstep in the night.

At first, I had thought there was a fire somewhere when I was woken up by the insistent knocking. And then, when I found Mr. Norris and the Norths' carriage on the other side of the door . . . To say I was surprised would be an understatement.

"There has been an incident up at the house," Norris had told me. "A guest—Mr. West—tumbled down the stairs—"

"Oh my," I exclaimed. "Is he terribly hurt?"

Norris shook his head. "Not that I can tell, but he's mighty spooked and won't stay for another minute."

"Is that so?" I craned my neck, trying to get a glimpse inside the carriage window, but the night was far too dark. "Is he in there?" I asked in a hushed voice.

Mr. Norris nodded. "Mrs. North wonders if you could take him—just for the night."

"Me? Why?" It seemed an odd request. "I am a single woman, Mr. Norris, it is hardly seemly—"

"Well, it's due to your trouble the other day . . ." The old man did not meet my gaze. The wind whipped the hair that peeked out from his blue, knitted cap. "They hope you can be discreet," he said.

So that explained it. "Of course they do. Was the guest pelted with rocks as well?"

Norris shook his head. "Earlier in the evening, yes, but that wasn't what made him leave."

"Then what did?"

"No one knows. Mr. and Mrs. North couldn't make him say."

That sounded both dramatic and discouraging. I was still limping and bruised from my own visit to the North house, and frankly did not want to have anything more to do with the place—but perhaps just because my own "incident" had rattled me so, I could not help but feel for Mr. West. If he was only half as frightened as I had been, he would be in a bad place indeed, and I *was* in a position to offer him a haven, even if it might come with expense to my reputation. And the request came from the Norths, to whom I owed this bed and board. Surely, they would protect me again if the islanders went to war?

"It would hardly be seemly," I said again, in a last, half-hearted effort to wriggle away.

"It would only be for one night," said Norris, "and the circumstances are dire. He could leave in the morning with no one the wiser."

I nodded, as I could not think of more objections, and Norris went to the carriage to fetch Mr. West, who looked terribly shaken as he shuffled inside, still wearing his pajamas under a mustard-colored jacket. Norris followed in tow with a battered, brown suitcase.

Both men thanked me profusely, but I barely heard them. Already, Mr. West looked too big—and severely out of place. Still, I sat him down and made him tea, which he barely touched. Neither did he speak much, just gazed out the window at the dark night that surrounded us.

"Apologies, Miss Russel," he had said at last. "Mrs. North gave me laudanum drops, and it seems they have made me drowsy."

"No wonder," I said, still standing by the stove, unable to make myself sit down yet. "It's the middle of the night, Mr. West. We should both have been asleep hours ago."

"Of course," he replied, seeming to momentarily have forgotten that it was three in the morning.

"I'll make up a cot for you," I said, as it was the best I could do. I do not have a front room, only a small living space that connects the kitchen to my bedroom. I keep a writing desk and a reading chair in there, and now I pushed the desk aside to pile all my excess pillows and blankets on the floor. It seemed a pitiful excuse for a bed, but it had to do.

"Good night, Mr. West," I said, and left him with the burning candle.

When I got up again a few hours later, I had not had much sleep, but neither, it seemed, had Mr. West, seeing as how the pile of blankets had not been disturbed. He still sat by the kitchen table, where he has been ever since.

I must admit, I am pleased to see him eat, and feel relieved when he looks up at me and smiles. It is a brave smile, though, tinged with fear and plastered onto a haggard face. I know that look better than I wish to. I have seen it every day in the mirror ever since I was attacked. It is the aftermath of a shock so violent that it entirely evades comprehension.

I muster some courage and sit down before him. This is *my* home after all, and I should act like it. "I don't know what you went through at the North house, Mr. West, but I think you should know I was attacked there as well, by assailants I could not see . . ." I pause to let him speak if he wants to, but the man remains quiet. I pull up the sleeve of my brown shirtwaist to show him my bruises. "It was quite brutal," I say, "and I cannot for the life of me figure out how it happened."

He inspects the bruising with some interest, though his spectacles are filthy. "Did rocks do that to you?" he asks.

I nod and pull the sleeve back down again. "My whole body is battered," I say, "and I did nothing more than to walk up their driveway."

"For me, the rocks came in through the windows yesterday." He speaks calmly, as if recounting an everyday occurrence. "They landed on the dining table, sending the china flying. Yet the Norths acted most strangely, as if it was nothing at all."

"And you could not tell who did it?" I ask for confirmation's sake.

He shakes his head. "I thought Mr. North would go outside to look, or that the girls would run upstairs to surveil the garden from the windows, but they *didn't*. It was as if they could not care less who was doing it." He sounds utterly astonished.

"Were all the girls at the table when it happened?" I ask, thinking of Mrs. North's absurd allegations. "Was Charlotte with you when the rocks came flying?"

"Yes." He looks surprised. "All their daughters were there."

I sigh and lean back in the chair. I always knew that Mrs. North's explanation did not make sense, but this confirms it.

"Yet you didn't leave then?" I prompt the man. I do not wish to cause him discomfort, but I do have a feeling that he *should* talk, since horrible happenings have a tendency to fester if buried in the mind, then later make themselves known in unexpected—and unwanted—ways.

"No." Mr. West shakes his head again. "I drank port with Mr.

North," he says, then gives a short laugh, unsound and brittle. "Forgive me, Miss Russel, but it seems so absurd now, that we went to drink and chatter away as if nothing was amiss, when the dining room had just been smashed to pieces."

"They didn't hit you, the rocks?" I pour myself more tea. I dearly need the warmth and the sugar.

"No." He sounds surprised. "They didn't hit me."

"That is a blessing at least," I say.

"Oh, but I have plenty of bruises of my own." He gives me a pointed look. "I *did* take a tumble down the stairs."

"Of course," I say, ashamed to have forgotten, if only momentarily. "How is your head? Does it ache?" I have had a few students with concussions in my day.

"Not terribly so," he replies. "My shoulder, hip, and knee got the worst of it."

"I suppose we will both be limping, then."

"All the way to the boat," he agrees, as something dark crosses his features.

"You won't be staying?" I am jealous that he can just leave—I have been thinking of little else since the pummeling. So far, I have been able to convince myself to stay by focusing on my duty to my students and how much this island means to me—how it has been my rock. Sometimes, though, and usually at night, I am itching to pack up my belongings, board the *Seagull,* and put as much distance between me and the North house as possible. Surely there are other positions? Perhaps not ones as lucrative, but worthy endeavors nevertheless.

"How can I?" Mr. West looks at me with stark terror in his eyes, then he seems to get ahold of himself. "I admit it's not convenient. I came here to work and am not ashamed to tell you that I need the money. Mr. North was very generous in his offer to me—though I suppose it was hard to find someone with my credentials to come out here on such short notice."

"What were you going to do for him?" I ask, although I have already figured out that Mr. West must be the geologist.

"I was going to examine the ground after the earthquake, make sure that the cliffs are sound—but I cannot possibly stay with the Norths now."

"Was it truly so awful?" I prod gently. "Cannot some fresh air and sunshine change your mind?" I feel like a hypocrite, but my loyalty is first and foremost to the Norths—or at least it is for the time being. Outside the window, the seagulls have begun their day, circling the sky and looking for breakfast.

"It was terrible! At first, I thought I was dreaming, Miss Russel—that I had a nightmare, and then, when I realized I was not, it was . . ." He trails off as his eyes grow distant.

"What did you see, Mr. West?" I ask gently. "It would help me, too, to know."

He snaps back to the moment. "Oh, I don't think so, Miss Russel. No one would benefit from that."

"I will believe you," I assure him. "No matter what it was."

"No, you will not." His lips twitch, and he uses the tip of his fingers to smooth down his whiskers. "It was a *demon*, Miss Russel—an ugly black thing. It hung upside down in the corner of my room, staring at me with red, glowing eyes."

I all but spit out my tea. "A *demon*?"

"See?" Mr. West arches an eyebrow. "I told you it was hard to believe."

"Are you sure you weren't dreaming?" It seems the most logical explanation. "The imagination can be *very* vivid," I remind him, "and it *had* been a stressful day."

"Oh, I'm sure. I lay there for quite some time waiting for it to disperse. I even got my spectacles from the nightstand, thinking my poor eyesight might be to blame. Instead of vanishing, however, the thing stretched out its very long limbs and started crawling toward me on the ceiling. I did not wait for it to arrive." He looks terribly unhappy as he picks up his spoon and starts stirring in his tea.

"How big was it?" I ask. "Could it have been a cat?"

"Upside down on the ceiling?" His lips quiver as if he is about to smile. "I assume you teach biology and simple physics, Miss Russel. You know that isn't possible. Besides, it was as big as a man—if slight."

I do not know what to say, so I keep quiet. Mr. West fidgets on the seat before me. After a moment of silence, he speaks again.

"Believe me, Miss Russel, I know how it sounds, and I wouldn't have believed me either." His cheeks have grown a little red. "I wouldn't have told you at all if you hadn't had your own unpleasant encounter."

"But a *demon,*" I splutter.

"Well, I cannot say for sure if that is what it was, seeing as how such creatures are not known to science, but I cannot think of a better name for it either. It was *not* human—that much is certain."

I sit quiet for a very long time, my mind churning with a thousand questions. "Well, *something* peculiar is happening at the North house," I concede at last. "Something violent. The North girls call it 'the knocker.' Because it knocks, I assume."

"Whatever it is, it isn't natural," says Mr. West. "Or at least not *yet known* to be a part of the natural world."

The dryness of his delivery puts me a little at ease. It makes me trust that he is not a madman. And I do appreciate his scientific approach; it makes it all seem a bit more digestible—and a bit less frightening.

"I thought it might be gasses in the earth or some such that threw the rocks up at me," I say.

"That should be considered," he agrees, "though I have never heard of such a phenomenon before."

I do refrain from noting that a *demon* seems just as unlikely.

"Perhaps you could stay with the reverend?" I suggest. "Reverend Hill is a kind man, and a . . . a demon would probably not bother you in the clergy house. That way, you could still do your work and receive payment from Mr. North."

"Maybe," he replies, but sounds doubtful. "Although Mrs. North seemed most adamant that no one on the island should learn of their troubles."

"Silly, if you ask me," I huff. "The reverend ought to know more than anyone. He could actually be of help or comfort. Or you could stay here," I surprise myself by saying, and want to take the words back at once. They should never have slipped out. Perhaps it is the sleepless nights that have me craving company to such a degree that I am willing to risk what little is left of my reputation.

"Miss Russel?" He looks at me with astonishment.

"Yes, I know." I feel flustered and can feel my cheeks reddening. "I should not have asked. It was a foolish suggestion—but I am old for a woman and my bedroom door locks. It would be quite safe for both of us." I blush. "I suppose it's just a relief to have someone to talk to about these things . . . They seem more frightening to me now than any blow to my reputation." I hate to sound so weak, but it is nothing but the truth, and something about Mr. West puts me at ease, despite the horrific circumstances. Perhaps it is the warmth he emits—the compassion I see in his eyes.

"I would never do anything to endanger your reputation, Miss Russel." He speaks very calmly. "I, too, must admit that you are to me a godsend: an educated, intelligent human being appearing as by miracle on the darkest night of my life. Together, we might even be equipped to make sense of what we witnessed—or did *not* witness, as in your case."

"I have thought about leaving as well," I admit. "To pack up my things and seek work elsewhere, but, like you, I would rather stay here and do my work. *I* need Mr. North's money, too."

"Perhaps I *should* stay." There is compassion in his eyes again. They are utterly void of pity or disdain. "*If* you think it's seemly."

"Well, it's not," I reply. "But we have both been through some extraordinary ordeals, and, truth be told, it has been hard for me not to be able to speak of it. I would feel safer with someone else here."

He gives another broken laugh. "I didn't manage to do much to save myself."

"Well, you *did* get out of there," I remind him. "I'd say that was a feat."

"And I will *never* set foot in there again," he swears. "Something is terribly wrong in that house."

I cannot argue with that.

·21·

jasper

I am working in my study, preparing a sermon, when I am surprised by visitors. This is not uncommon; it is a part of my daily life to welcome parishioners and offer guidance in both spiritual and practical matters. Truth be told, it is one of my favorite things to do, and I consider it a privilege to be of assistance. It provides a much-needed respite on long workdays that are usually spent alone. I suppose my sociable nature is not entirely suited for my line of work, but then I chose it to be of service and not to please myself.

I hear my visitors before they arrive—some bustling in the hall. Then comes Noreen's familiar knock on the door before she opens it to let the guests inside.

I must admit that I am surprised to see Mrs. North cross the threshold, closely followed by her housekeeper, Miss Boden. Both women have left their coats and hats in the hall. Mrs. North wears a purple dress with an elegant diamond brooch, while Miss Boden's dress is a simple beige that seems to be of good quality. I rise to greet them, and then busy myself with clearing my desk and finding more pillows for their chairs while we wait for Noreen to bring tea.

I notice that both women look tired, and that Mrs. North barely offered a smile when she clasped my hand. Whatever they have come to discuss, it must be of a grave nature—especially given how rarely the Norths pass through my doors.

Could it be about Charlotte?

Her absence from church has worried me, and I have been haunted by her appearance in the garden—and sudden vanishing after. Perhaps it is the sleepwalking her mother is here to speak to me about, although, if so, it seems strange that Charlotte herself is not present.

When we are finally all seated, and cups of tea steam before us on the hastily cleared desk, I place my folded hands on the polished wood and lift my gaze to Mrs. North.

"What can I do for you today?" I ask, assuming she is the one who needs guidance.

Mrs. North, unusually quiet, looks to her housekeeper and wets her lips. Her eyes, when she looks back at me, are frightened. I give her some time, since I sense that she struggles to find the words. Miss Boden loses her patience before I do.

"There's something terrible happening at the house," the woman blurts out, eyes wide. "It has been happening for some time now—all *sorts* of terrible things—"

"*Mary,*" Mrs. North snaps. "You have to excuse her," she says to me. "This whole . . . *ordeal* has her quite upset."

"I can tell." I give them both a puzzled look. "What exactly is it that's happening at the house?"

Again, I wait for Mrs. North to reply, but again, she seems to have lost her tongue, and Miss Boden speaks in her stead. "There are rocks flying through the windows, and people are being attacked on the road. They arrive at the house beaten and terrified!"

This is indeed astonishing—and not at all what I expected. Who on this island would ever attack the Norths? I look to Mrs. North for confirmation, and she nods her head so slightly it can barely be detected. Her lips are tightly pressed together and her nostrils flare just a bit. The pearls dangling from her earlobes shiver but do not swing.

"Do you have any idea who is doing it?" Perhaps this is a case of someone being out of their minds—not cruel but sick—and that is why the Norths have come to me instead of calling in the police on the mainland.

Mrs. North nods her head, but Mary says, "No. That's just the thing, Reverend, we cannot *see* the culprit. It's as if they are invisible! There is no one in the fields around the road, and no one outside the house, but the rocks still fly. And then there were the needles." She pauses, and Mrs. North snorts. Her gaze is glued to the window behind me, to the restless sea outside.

"The needles?" I ask, while thinking that this must surely be some elaborate, misguided boys' prank.

"They rained down from the *ceiling,* Reverend, hundreds of them! And not only that, but they turned up in the food as well, at the bottom of cups and even inside an egg!" Mary's bottom lip shivers. I can sense from across the desk how relieved she is to speak of it. She can barely contain her words. Her mistress, on the other hand, seems to have left us. Her gaze is staring at the horizon, and she does not react at all.

I, however, do—and, despite my profession, my first instinct is a strong and powerful disbelief. "Are you sure you are not mistaken?" I ask the housekeeper. "Or that it isn't someone doing it out of spite—or even a poor sense of humor?"

Mrs. North snorts once more. Her hand dips into her purse to retrieve a delicate white handkerchief, which she twists between her fingers.

"It cannot *be* done, Reverend." Miss Boden looks at me as though I am less than bright. "How can *anyone* make it rain needles from the ceiling? There were no holes up there."

Mrs. North, next to her, blinks several times, as if just waking up.

"There has been some theft in the kitchen," she says. "Sieves and ladles have gone missing—and a cheese."

"Oh, but that is *nothing* compared to—" Miss Boden abruptly stops speaking, likely realizing it is her employer she is arguing against. "Yes," she says quickly. "Things have gone missing, and we cannot see how, as Mrs. Norris keeps it orderly in there. And we can all swear that we saw the ladle where it's supposed to be—and then, all of a sudden, it was gone."

"And you never saw it again?" I ask, struggling to keep up with the sudden shifts in the conversation. I recall the recent theft from my own kitchen, where a fruitcake apparently upped and went away. Antonia and Noreen had both been quite upset.

"Well, sometimes," Miss Boden says, sounding lost. "Sometimes the thing comes back again, often where we left it, but other times not. I found a carrot under my pillow once, and a rolling pin in Mr. North's closet. Mrs. Norris even discovered a hunk of ham in her husband's shoe one morning, and he *swears* he never put it there. Why would he even do something so foolish?"

This certainly sounds like a prank. "Could it be the youngest girl?" I ask. "Sophie?"

Both Mrs. North and Miss Boden shake their heads.

"How could an eight-year-old girl pelt Miss Russel with rocks on the road and not be detected?" Miss Boden counters. "The landscape is quite flat, and the rocks had both speed and aim. Besides, the girl was in the house at the time."

"Miss Russel, you say? She has gained some enemies here since venturing with the children to the tower—"

"Well, that has nothing to do with it," Miss Boden interrupts me, which is quite uncharacteristic of her. "Mr. North's foreman was pelted, too, and the geologist ran off to the schoolhouse in the middle of the night, seeking shelter with Miss Russel. None of us know what happened to him."

This story certainly has its twists and turns. "Has he left the island?" I ask, thinking I might speak to him. Perhaps a man of science can make more sense of it.

"He is still with Miss Russel," Mrs. North offers. "Norris was there today with a bed. He refuses our hospitality, for reasons unknown." Although the expression on her face suggests that she *does* know why it has come to this. "Look, Reverend," she says, and some of the usual steel is back in her voice. "I'm only here because Mary threatened to leave if I didn't come to see you. She and the other staff blame witches and ghosts and whatnot. I, on the other hand, am convinced that the culprit is *very* much of flesh and blood—someone intent on making my life miserable. I suppose I don't have to tell *you* who that is." She gives me a sharp look.

"*Charlotte?*" I am astonished. "I cannot see her display such vehemence," I say. "And why would she attack poor Miss Russel?"

"You don't see her as she is," Mrs. North informs me. "My daughter is crafty—and too bright for her own good. I can always *feel* it when she is up to something . . . A mother *knows,* Reverend." She nods sagely and takes a deep breath.

"Sorry, Mrs. North, but *how?*" The housekeeper sounds exasperated. "Even if Charlotte was a prankster as a child, she's a grown woman now, and I cannot see how she could have done *any* of this."

"She does it to punish me." Mrs. North's gaze is back on the window, her lips pursed. Her fingers tug at the handkerchief. "She will not go to the mainland and let my sister introduce her to potential suitors, though that is absolutely what needs to happen. Clearly, staying at home with her family rots the girl's mind."

Again, I remember Charlotte in the garden. "Perhaps you should wait," I tell Mrs. North. "There could be other reasons for Charlotte's strange behavior. I did not want to tell you this, but I saw her outside one night, on the beach in her nightgown. Have you considered that she might be sleepwalking?"

Miss Boden looks at me with disappointment on her face. "Even if she did, how would that explain—"

"She is not sleepwalking." Mrs. North snorts. "She is *very* cunning, Reverend. I am surprised that you of all people cannot see that. If you saw Charlotte on the beach, it was because she *wanted* you to see her there."

"Oh, I cannot believe that," I say.

"Not even after what she put your wife through?" Mrs. North's sharp gaze fixes on me.

"If you think that Charlotte is . . . disturbed," I say, "there might be help for that. Please forgive me if I overstep, but could a psychiatrist be something to consider?" Antonia saw one after our son died, and, though I cannot say for sure if he helped her or not, it is still worth a try—then as now.

"She is *difficult,* Reverend, not mad," Mrs. North replies coolly. "As soon as she is married, I am sure she'll be just fine." I feel a quick jab in my heart at her words and instantly loathe myself. I have no right to feel possessive of Charlotte; *of course* she will marry in time. Yet the heart is a fickle thing that does not always listen to reason.

Miss Boden shifts in her seat. "But how could she possibly—" She stops herself. Thinking there is no use, perhaps. I, too, find it hard to believe that Charlotte should go to such lengths just to punish her mother, but Mrs. North seems quite decided.

"Sometimes fear can make us susceptible to all sorts of mirages," I tell Miss Boden. I may not be able to give her answers, but at least I can try for some comfort. "It might not be as mysterious as it looks. Perhaps there's a good explanation for it all."

"The girls call it 'the knocker.'" Miss Boden looks at me with fearful eyes.

"*It?*" I cannot help but shiver. It is not so much the name but the way she said it: full of dread.

"The thing doing it," Miss Boden clarifies.

"Nonsense," Mrs. North cuts in. "It's just something Charlotte has told them."

"Does it knock?" I ask.

"Sometimes." Miss Boden drops her gaze. "At night."

"It's just Charlotte," says Mrs. North.

"What would you have me do?" I ask, realizing how the conversation is unlikely to reach a conclusion, with my guests being so at odds. "Do you want me to speak to Charlotte?" I ask Mrs. North.

"*You?* Goodness, no!" she exclaims. "*You* should stay away from her. It's bad enough that she sees you in church."

My cheeks instantly redden with shame, although I know I have done nothing wrong. "What, then?" I ask, a little sharper.

"Perhaps you could pray for us," says Miss Boden, "or even bless the house?"

I look to Mrs. North, who sighs and shakes her head. "There is no need for such theatrics, Mary. Everything will be back to normal when Charlotte goes to the mainland. You'll see."

"Still"—Miss Boden's voice has dropped—"I would feel better—we *all* would."

"I can certainly visit," I offer, thinking that some prayer never hurt anyone.

"Not while Charlotte is at home," says Mrs. North. "Wait until she has left for my sister's."

I would never say so, but I certainly think it is peculiar that she is more afraid of inflaming her daughter's misguided passion than providing her household with much-needed comfort.

"And you must come by closed carriage," says Miss Boden, "lest you be attacked on the road."

"Of course," I say, mostly for her benefit. I still find it hard to believe that the Norths' driveway is in any way dangerous. "Just send word—and please encourage Charlotte to come back to church. If she is as disturbed as you say, this is no time to stay away." Now it is I who give Mrs. North a stern look.

"I will tell her." Mrs. North smiles stiffly, then rises to leave. "And we appreciate your discretion in this, Reverend," she adds. "We don't want the wagging tongues of Margaret's Keep to get hold of this story."

"Of course," I say again, only slightly offended. "Not a word will escape these walls."

"Especially not to Miss Russel." She narrows her eyes. "She has suffered more than enough already. I should think she just wants to forget it all."

"But the geologist stays at the schoolhouse with her?" That is certainly an unusual arrangement—and luscious fodder for those wagging tongues.

"Oh." Mrs. North notices my puzzlement and waves it away. "Miss Russel is well above thirty, and a lifelong spinster for sure. If you ask me, she will only appreciate the help Mr. West can provide."

"She is still limping," Miss Boden supplies. "After the attack."

I am taken aback by that. I had not realized it was so serious—and had clearly not been paying attention in church. Perhaps because all I had thought about was how Charlotte was not there.

Again, I experience a wash of shame.

"It is good of him to stay with her, then," I say, thinking again that it is strange. Miss Russel has always struck me as such a solitary woman. "Should he change his mind, he is always welcome here."

"And with us." Mrs. North arches an eyebrow. "But he seems to prefer the schoolhouse."

"Probably because they both encountered it," Miss Boden suggests in a voice full of doom, just as I show them to the door. "They have both met the knocker, and have bruises to prove it." Mrs. North only huffs in response. "You will pray for us, though, won't you?" Miss Boden pleads again before leaving. She looks only slightly relieved when I assure her that I will.

When I have closed the door behind them, I am left with a foul taste in my mouth. Not only due to the terrible story about torrents of needles and invisible assailants but also the callousness of Mrs.

North, which I find repulsive. How can a mother not love her child better? How can she not aim to protect her? I like to think that, had my son lived, he would never have received such coldness from me. I am deeply puzzled that Mrs. North has decided to lay the blame so squarely at her daughter's feet. Certainly, Charlotte would never have attacked another human being—or chased the geologist from their house in the night.

According to Miss Boden, she *could not* have.

I am already regretting the vow of silence; it is highly inconvenient. Miss Russel, if anyone, might be able to shed a light on this murky affair.

But I swore not to speak of it, and so I will not.

·22·

charlotte

"You can ask it whatever you want," I say, as I shepherd the girls into the shed. It is a Monday and they have just finished school. Adelaide is there, of course, along with her friends Annabeth Ferryman; Norma Fisher; and the latter's younger sister, Lillian.

Adelaide leads the way, seeing as how she has already been in the shed and seen the alphabet wall. It was the knocker who told me to bring her when I complained of how tiresome it was that she feared it so. I was happy for the suggestion, as it has been trying to share a room with someone who always questions and cowers in fear, when the knocker is such a wonderful discovery. True, it was terrible with Mr. West, who fled the house, but that was entirely my fault; and the knocker would have left him alone if I had not made that wish in the shed. I just have to be more specific in the future—tell it not to go overboard. A scare is fine, but nothing so severe that it leaves a mark on the body or frightens someone out of their mind.

The knocker seems to me a blank canvas. Like a child, perhaps, or a puppy. It does not understand how to behave, so I figure it is my job to teach it. Seeing as how it does not wish to leave, *someone* has to guide it, and when it is not misbehaving, the knocker is a wonderful friend. It brings me all sorts of gifts, and makes sure that I never get lonely. Sometimes I wonder what it wants in return, but I have still not been able to get a good answer. It puzzles me, as in the stories there is always a price—something to be worked out in a bargain—but the knocker does not seem to *want* anything, besides my attention, perhaps.

I do believe it when it says it loves me, and has *chosen* me to be its friend. And it is cunning, too, when it needs to be, like when suggesting that I bring Adelaide to the shed so she could speak to it herself. Not surprisingly, she had changed her tune by the time she stepped back out again. The knocker had been on its best behavior, promising her suitors and a future rife with happiness. It had also spelled out, by knocking with the brush, that it would never hurt Miss Russel again—although for reasons I cannot explain, that did not feel sincere to me.

But Adelaide *loves* the knocker now, so I suppose the lie served its purpose.

"It smells bad in here," Norma Fisher complains as she enters the shed. Her knitted jacket hangs off one shoulder, and her mousy hair has worked itself loose from the braid. Her freckled nose twists up with disgust.

"It's just the tar," Adelaide says with some impatience. "You will get used to it in no time."

"I *swear,* Adelaide," Annabeth says in her booming voice, "if you are lying about this, I will *never* forgive you."

"I'm *not.*" Adelaide sounds slightly offended. "Why would I make up something so strange? If I am to lie about anything, it will be something that people would believe."

"Oh, Mother would not like us coming here," Lillian huffs as she slips inside and comes to stand next to her sister, facing the alphabet wall. She has the same unremarkable features as Norma, and wears the same ill-fitting knitwear as well.

"Mother is afraid of *everything*." Norma shrugs. "I thought she would *kill* Miss Russel after she brought us to the tower."

"Poor Miss Russel." Annabeth sighs. "She's had a hard time going *anywhere* after she fell off that chair." Adelaide and I exchange a brief look. It certainly is a good thing that few people know what really happened to Miss Russel. *No one* would come here if they knew the truth. I never worried about the girls coming up the driveway, though. They are the knocker's own guests, after all.

"So what do we do now?" Lillian asks. She looks at the wall with puzzlement.

"We ask about things and it answers," Adelaide replies with a touch of pride. She is tremendously excited to share this gift with her friends. It had taken some convincing to make her swear not to tell Evelyn about the shed, but now she seems fine with the secret. She, too, knows that our older sister would not like what Adelaide uses the knocker for.

"We just ask it outright?" Annabeth asks.

"Yes"—Adelaide nods—"when Charlotte has spoken to it first."

Three pairs of eyes land on me, displaying both excitement and doubt. I certainly cannot blame them—I would be hesitant to believe in it, too. I give them a reassuring smile.

"It isn't dangerous," I say. "It's no different than when Reverend Hill speaks to God—only it isn't God, and it answers right away." Next, I step up in front of the girls and speak to the alphabet wall.

"Knocker, are you there?" I know that it is—it always is—but sometimes it takes a while to answer. This time, however, it does not dawdle at all, and a single rap sounds from within the wall.

"Someone is knocking from outside," Annabeth cries, unable to believe anything else.

"*No,*" Adelaide hisses. "There is no one there."

I can hear the girls shuffle and shift on the floor behind me.

"Prove to them that you are not 'someone standing outside,'" I say with a sigh. When you know something is real, it is very tiresome when someone else questions it.

The knocker dutifully does as I say and lifts the paintbrush off the shelf. It flies quickly up in the air and knocks twice in the slanted ceiling, then it lands on another shelf inside the shed, toppling over a can of old paint. The girls all shriek, and Lillian starts for the door. Norma catches her, though, before she can flee, and holds her in a tight grip.

"Don't be a *child,* Lillian," she wheezes into her younger sister's ear. "Adelaide *said* this could happen." Lillian sobs but goes limp in Norma's arms. Adelaide rolls her eyes at Annabeth, as if to say that Lillian is *indeed* a child.

When they are all back in line, we begin in earnest.

"Knocker," I say, "could you be so kind as to answer some questions from Adelaide and her friends?"

A single rap sounds from the ceiling, and I hear Norma whisper, "One knock means 'yes.'"

"Good," I say to the knocker. "Then we can take turns . . . You can start, Adelaide," I decide, since the whole reason why I agreed to this was to make my sister feel special. *I* would rather not spend my afternoon with Adelaide's friends, but it means a great deal to her, and anything that makes her fonder of the knocker is worth it. Adelaide has sworn them all to secrecy, but personally, I do not much mind if the knocker enters the island gossip. Nothing would displease Mother more, and now that she is determined to send me to Aunt Anne again, nothing would please *me* more than seeing her embarrassed.

Adelaide clears her throat and her voice sounds more serious than it has ever been before when speaking to the knocker. She must feel the weight of her friends' presence.

"Knocker," she opens, "can you tell me where I left my comb this morning?" This is a trick question. She hid it herself before going out, and has doubtlessly already informed the other girls of its whereabouts. She aims to prove how the knocker knows things it should not. The paintbrush immediately rises in the air, and glides through the air to the wall.

U-M-B-R-E-L-L-A, the knocker knocks. I say it out loud as well, in case the girls find it hard to follow. It does move very fast.

"Yes, that's right! The umbrella stand!" My sister is utterly thrilled.

"Annabeth," I say, "you are next."

"Um . . ." The girl seems to have lost her tongue, and stares at the hovering paintbrush as if petrified.

"Come on," Adelaide urges her.

"Um . . . Where is my brother John now?"

B-O-A-T, the knocker replies, and I repeat.

"That's right." Annabeth grins. "He went to the mainland this morning and is expected back tonight." In all fairness, Annabeth's brother is a fisherman by trade, and spends *most* of his time on boats, but I do not point that out.

"Can you ask it about things that happened before?" Norma wants to know.

"Of course," I say. "Ask it anything you like."

"About the future, too," Adelaide adds.

"What happened to my gray kitten last fall?" Norma's voice quivers.

W-E-L-L, says the knocker.

"Did it fall in?" Norma sounds aghast, and seems to have forgotten the one question rule.

The knocker raps once, from the ceiling this time, and not with the paintbrush.

"Oh," exclaims Norma.

"Lillian?" I move the game on.

"What will we have for dinner today?" the girl asks in a thin voice, and the others groan, deeming it a boring question for a spirit.

C-O-D, sounds the answer, which is also no surprise.

"Again?" Norma sighs. The knocker raps in the ceiling once, although it was not a real question.

Inwardly, I chuckle.

It does not take long before the girls ask the questions they *really* need answering.

"How many years until I get married?" Adelaide asks.

S-I-X, replies the knocker.

"Will I ever live anywhere but on Margaret's Keep?" Annabeth asks.

The knocker raps twice in reply, and they all embrace Annabeth, making compassionate noises.

"Which one of us will get married first?" Norma asks.

A-N-N-A-B, the paintbrush spells, and now all the girls squeal and pat Annabeth's back.

"Will Miss Russel ever walk properly again?" Lillian asks, and my heart speeds up its pace. It just will not do if they start asking too many questions about Miss Russel.

The knocker replies with one knock on a shelf, and I let out my breath.

"Is Mr. West her *special* friend?" Adelaide asks, cleverly moving the conversation away from the teacher's damage.

The knocker does not reply.

"It doesn't know," I say. "Or it doesn't understand what you mean by that."

"Do Miss Russel and Mr. West sleep in the same bed?" Annabeth asks with a giggle.

The knocker raps twice, leaving them all disappointed.

"Will I have a daughter or a son first?" Norma asks.

T-W-I-N-S, the knocker spells, and the girls are squealing again.

"Will my grandmother recover from her pneumonia?" Lillian asks.

The knocker raps twice.

"I figured as much," Lillian remarks with a sad expression.

"Is Richard Newell in love with me?" Adelaide asks.

The knocker raps twice and all their faces fall again.

"Why are you here in this shed?" Annabeth asks.

C-H-A-R-L, says the knocker, to my great satisfaction.

"Do you like Charlotte very much?" Norma asks.

The knocker raps in the ceiling once, and I smile.

"Is she your sweetheart?" Annabeth asks, ignoring that it is Lillian's turn.

I hold my breath until the knocker raps twice, then I let it out.

"Why Charlotte?" Adelaide asks.

The knocker does not reply.

• • •

When the girls have run out of questions, we go into the fields by Margaret's Tower. None of them is allowed to go there, of course, but they feel daring today. We chase away the sheep that have gathered by the ruin and sit down in the grass. The animals never went there before the tower fell, and seem to enjoy exploring their new territory. The flowers arrive late on Margaret's Keep, but there are a few bluebells hiding in the growth. The afternoon sun is glorious, warm and bright, and even the wind is barely a hush. The sea looks like a glittering carpet: deep blue and restless as it laps against the cliffs. We all smell of tar and dust. Adelaide's pink dress has flecks of grime on it.

"How lucky you are, Charlotte, to have a friend like that." Annabeth sighs. Her red hair gleams copper in the sunlight. She has gathered straws and bluebells in her lap and is busy with her fingers, twisting and braiding.

"Is it true that it brings you gifts?" Norma asks.

"It does," I say. "Anything I ask for." The young girls promptly gasp.

"Could it bring you breakfast from Paris?" Norma asks. Her mouth hangs open and her eyes are wide.

"Maybe, but probably not. I don't think it can fetch things from afar. I tried to have it bring me my aunt's locket from the mainland once, but it didn't work." Or perhaps it simply does not want to leave my side.

"What *does* it bring you?" Annabeth asks.

"Trinkets, sweets, and books," I say. "Flowers and seashells from the beach."

"It must really love you," says Norma. "I wish someone brought *me* gifts."

"Why *you,* though?" Adelaide repeats the question from the shed with just a smidge of jealousy.

"Luck, I suppose." I shrug.

"Maybe it is because you aren't afraid of it," Lillian suggests.

"I was at first," I admit. "But then I realized it was nothing to be afraid of."

"Do you think it watches over you when you sleep?" Annabeth's fingers are still busy, working down in her lap.

"I should think so." It is always around.

"I think it came from there." Adelaide looks at the ruin. "You were the first one to come here after the earthquake, Charlotte. Maybe it got loose then, and followed you back home like a duckling."

"Maybe." I shrug. I have long since stopped wondering where the knocker came from. Perhaps one day it will tell me.

"Do you think it is Margaret?" Lillian looks pale.

"It says it's not," Adelaide replies. "And it says that it isn't a ghost."

"Perhaps it's a fairy." Norma gasps.

"Aren't they just ghosts?" Annabeth asks.

"Not always." Norma shrugs.

Annabeth has made a wreath of grass, straw, and bluebells. Now she rises to her knees, and places it on my brow. All the girls look at me and smile.

I am not looking at them, though. I am looking at the thing sitting in the grass between us and the tower: spindly and long, its skin charcoal gray. Its outline is stark against the blue sky above. It looks to be neither a man nor a woman. It has no hair, and its skin looks uneven, as if it is burned. Its eyes are red, and glowing. I know I should fear it, but I do not. As strange as it looks, there is something familiar about it, too, as if I have always known, deep inside, that this is what the knocker looks like. A sense of dreaming comes over me as I sit there, staring, with the crown upon my head—as if none of this is truly happening, although I know it is. The girls around me laugh and smile, so I know they do not see it. This display is just for me, because it trusts me now.

When I lift my arm, it lifts its own.

When I turn my head, it does, too.

When I adjust the wreath of flowers and straw, its spindly fingers follow suit, grasping at the air.

It is a perfect mirror image of me.

·23·

ruth

After nearly a week of shared accommodations, Mr. West convinces me to bring him to the tower. I cannot say exactly how he did it; I have shunned the place like the plague ever since the ill-fated excursion, and have been determined not to give the islanders another reason to question my conduct. But, then, Mr. West's presence in my home has probably already blown what was left of my reputation to smithereens, so perhaps I feel I have nothing to lose.

Or perhaps he just has a way of convincing me.

I cannot deny that Mr. West has been a great comfort to me. I feel better—more *balanced*—since he arrived. It was not until I had a companion with whom to discuss the happenings at the North house that I realized how pushing the fear and questions away had only made the damage worse. The more I had tried not to think of it, the worse the anxiety had grown—and with my foolish promise not to speak of the attack always present in my mind, I had been both fearful and muzzled.

Mr. West, being a victim himself, did not fall under the vow of silence; and once the floodgates were open, it was hard to stop talking. I learned early on that Mr. West felt the same way as me: terrified and baffled in equal measure. In fact, he kept thanking me for being so willing to listen to him while he theorized and wondered—trying, like me, to make sense of the senseless, to transform the terror into something small and easily digestible. Something we could ascribe to—*believe* in—like the laws of physics, all while we waited for our bruises to heal and the aches to disperse, leaning on each other as we hobbled between the kitchen table and the cooking stove. We even took turns to inspect the other's injuries—though his were far fresher than my own.

With him, the horror that had befallen me became a mystery—an equation to be solved, something we could pick apart and hopefully get an answer. Every night after school, Mr. West and I sat by the candlelit kitchen table and discussed what this *thing* could possibly be, all while downing cups of hot tea and munching pieces of crumbling fruitcake. We brought up old myths and legends about household spirits and trickster fairies, ghosts we had heard of in our youth—usually tame specters who did little more than to drift through a room. We also spoke of the spiritualists' claims to call back the dead and of demons from the Bible. The problem, though, was that neither Mr. West nor I was an expert in the field. Between us, we covered geology, botany, biology, history, and literature, but neither of us was well-versed in folklore or religion. And since we could not talk of it to others—and the island has no library—our efforts sadly came up short. Yet we simply could not stop prying and pondering—both of us still reeling, I think, from the way our worlds had been utterly shaken by something we could not grasp.

I did feel better, though, from talking it through with another resourceful human being. And in the end, I found that that fact mattered far more to me than what the people on Margaret's Keep might have to say about my having a male houseguest. It even mattered more to me than my own hard-won privacy. Being pelted with rocks by an invisible assailant can, as it turns out, make you change your mind about a number of things.

In the first couple of days after Mr. West's arrival, a trip to the store had taken us all morning, with all our various aches, but now that his body is healing, he has started on what he came here for: assessing the island and looking for fissures. So far, he has found none, and he does not think Margaret's Keep is particularly prone to earthquakes. What happened seems to have been an anomaly. His work is not why he wants to go to the tower, though. It has entirely to do with our own investigation. Though I am certainly wary of the place—not the least because of its proximity to the North house—it does feel safer when I am not alone, and curiosity is strong in me, too, now, ignited by Mr. West's hunger for knowledge.

As we cross the field and walk toward the tower, slowly and with me still leaning on a sturdy stick, I notice how Mr. West, too, keeps glancing toward the North abode. We are both treating the immaculate building as if it were a wild animal—one we are uncertain to trust. The house looks calm enough, though: flanked by barn and stable, and proudly rising toward the overcast sky. A seagull perches on the house's roof, and a lace curtain has drifted out of an open upstairs window, rising and falling with the wind. Below the house, in the harbor, a fishing vessel drifts slowly to shore between the steep cliffs, aiming for the red building where the fish is taken in.

"I wonder how they are doing in there," Mr. West says in a quiet voice, mirroring my thoughts exactly.

"I worry for Mrs. North," I say. "Her . . . grasp of the situation isn't sound."

"Blaming her daughter, you mean?"

"Just that." I look up at Mr. West and meet his kind eyes. He looks quite the peacock in these sparse surroundings, with his colorful attire of mustard yellow and forest green. The flat, checkered cap on his head makes his wispy blond hair stay in place. I cannot help that my eyes sometimes linger on him in an admiring way, and I chide myself for it after, silently in my head. I decided a long time ago that such things are not for me.

"I wonder why she insists that her daughter is the cause when it is so apparent that she simply couldn't have done it." Mr. West gently kicks a small rock. It dances for a second before coming to halt against the grass.

"Perhaps it is her way of protecting herself," I suggest. "Perhaps it is better to name a known foe than accept the unknown. Or there are other, deeper issues that we know nothing of," I add, somewhat nervous to speak of it here, where something might be listening. Something we cannot see. I tell myself it is a foolish notion—but then, I know it is not. All the muscles in my body are tense, fearing another onslaught of rocks.

Mr. West must be sensing my trepidation, because he gives me a reassuring smile before offering me his arm. "I am immensely grateful to you, Miss Russel, for joining me," he says. "I must admit that I am nervous as well, although I know it's not very manly of me."

"Oh, pish," I say. "You wouldn't be human if you weren't nervous. In fact, I would have called you a fool if you were not."

"I know how the tower got you into trouble before—"

"It's *nothing* compared to the trouble that followed—"

"I just very much want to see it for myself—and preferably not alone. With all the stories about this place, we should at least consider that the—the *creature* came from here. That the earthquake somehow let it loose."

"It is what my students say, that the witch is up from her grave," I add ruefully.

"The thing I saw was not a woman," he notes.

"Or not a woman *anymore,*" I say with a shudder.

"Perhaps she had devils at her beck and call?" He gives me a playful smile, but it does not reach his eyes.

"I rather believed the other story," I say. "That she was an unfaithful wife. Rich men do things like it all the time: find ways to sideline and restrain their willful women."

"Perhaps she found something out here." His eyes light up. "Perhaps she was merely an unhappy wife when she arrived, but then found something out here to keep her company." The words make me shudder again.

"It must have been awfully boring for the demon, though," I note in an effort to lighten the mood. "Being out here all alone just waiting for someone to turn up."

"Perhaps it came in from the sea," he says just as we reach the ruin, and I find myself, once again, surrounded by the rubble that used to be Margaret's Tower. "It did perhaps have an aquatic quality to it," Mr. West muses, as we step into the naked square between the fallen walls.

I am exhausted from the walk—my knee has pained me a great deal since the attack—and, though I do not want to, I have no choice but to slump down on the jagged edge of the ruin. On my way there, I gingerly sidestep the pile of pebbles that I now know to be the remains of a ritual meant to keep the islanders safe from an invisible, tower-dwelling foe. I remain seated while Mr. West has a look around. He scans the ground with his keen eyes, and even walks closer to the cliff's edge to have a look at the foaming sea far below. My heart starts racing in my chest when he—quite without hesitation—drops to the ground and begins edging closer to the abyss.

"Do be careful," I call out.

He turns back with a smile on his face. "I know my field, Miss Russel," he says. "The ground is perfectly safe." I want to say that in this particular environment, nothing is safe, but then I think better of it. One of Mr. West and my joint missions is to make sure that neither of us lives the rest of our lives in fear, and the best way to do that is to go where terror might be lurking and to endure the discomfort of being afraid.

I surely have ample opportunity to practice as I sit there, watching Mr. West slowly crawl toward the drop. What I fear will happen is unclear, and that in itself is worrying. One second, I imagine the black creature crawling up the cliff toward him, ready to pull him over the edge. The next, I imagine a hail of rocks pummeling his prostrate body. I look at the remains of the tower walls instead—finding those shallow grooves again—and wonder at what quirk of nature made them so many moons ago.

When I finally look up to see that Mr. West's head and shoulders are hanging freely in the air, I cannot be quiet any longer. "What exactly is it you're looking for?" I ask.

"Fissures," comes his muffled voice. "A cave, perhaps."

He is looking for the creature's home, I realize, and for a second a cold hand of panic squeezes my heart. "It's not here anymore," I say aloud, more to ease my worry than anything else. "It's moved in with them." I nod toward the North house, though Mr. West is in no position to see it.

"If it even was here to begin with." Mr. West finally pulls back, rises to his feet, and wipes his hands on his thighs. I let out a deep breath of relief. "I couldn't see anything out of the ordinary," he says, as he comes to sit beside me. "Maybe if we could examine the fallen rocks, perhaps that could give us a clue."

"We would need a boat," I say, "but that isn't hard on Margaret's Keep."

"The tide would have to be out," he notes.

"Do you really think Margaret was out here all alone?" I say, scanning the vast sea, the pale horizon, and the whitecaps rushing to shore. It seems so desperately lonely.

"I wish we knew," Mr. West says quietly, having pulled out a handkerchief to wipe his fingers more thoroughly. I worry about the state of his clothes, but then he seems to have an ample store in the luggage Mr. Norris brought with the bed. "The tower was built a long time ago, though, while they still courted other powers than the Lord's.

Even my grandmother often left small offerings outside: milk and honey—bread, sometimes—to appease whatever dwelled nearby."

"Do you think it worked?" I ask.

"I never even considered it. I used not to believe in anything at all." He shrugs. "I certainly didn't believe that there were nonhuman creatures existing around us. Margaret's Keep has changed that."

"Perhaps Margaret made an offering, and it was answered," I say, with another violent shudder.

"Perhaps someone else has made an offering more recently," he replies, not helping my discomfort the slightest.

"Charlotte North?" I ask.

"Or someone else." He shrugs. "But it's just speculation, of course."

"I wish we knew more," I say. Knowing might disperse the spell and make my world feel normal again—or at least, as it was before.

·24·

charlotte

What happened in the shed remains a secret for four days. Then Mrs. Fisher comes to speak to Mother.

I should rejoice in this turn of events. It is what I wanted after all: Mother's embarrassment, her fury and shame. Instead, I feel nothing as I watch from the stairs while Mother and Mrs. Fisher step into the front room. I consider eavesdropping at the door, but I already know what they will say: Mrs. Fisher will be respectful but driven by righteous anger, she will speak of her daughters' innocence and my own corrupting influence. Perhaps she might even mention the devil.

Mother will be shocked and apologetic at first, and then—as Mrs. Fisher continues talking—her pride will get the better of her, and she will become haughty, maybe blame the Fisher girls or sow doubts about their story. Perhaps she will even question Mrs. Fisher's intentions, and imply that she has come here to blackmail us. They will part ways cordially, but also secretly as enemies.

Mrs. Fisher can ill afford it, though. Father owns their trawler.

I go into my room to wait for Mother. I know she will come when her guest has left to confront me with my wrongdoing. Perhaps she will even send me to the shed—though perhaps that punishment is ruined for her now.

I do not have to wait long before I hear Mother on the stairs, her feet working like pistons. She barrels in through the door without knocking, and has my arm in a grip before I have had time to rise. She yanks me up from the bed, her face as hard and unyielding as marble. Her eyes are as cold and harsh as the sea in a winter gale. When she speaks, droplets of spittle rain down on my face.

"How could you?" she rages. "How *could* you?"

I cannot help but laugh—I find her quite ridiculous—which only makes her tighten her grip and even shake me a little.

"Do you mean to ruin me?" she cries. "Is your family of *no* importance?"

"It did no harm," I shout back. "The girls were just amusing themselves!"

"No harm?" Mother's voice rises in pitch. "They think you have *the devil* in the shed! What on earth were you *thinking*?" She shakes me again, and this time it hurts.

"It's harmless," I insist again, although I am not entirely sure. "And it wasn't me who spoke to them. If you are to blame someone, blame it on the knocker."

"The *knocker*." Mother spits the word; the pearls in her earlobes dance a merry jig. "It's bad enough that you're poisoning your sisters and the servants, but now you are luring in the neighbors as well. I *see* you, Charlotte! I know who you are! I carried you and bled for you—do you really think you can hide from me?" Her eyes look quite crazed now. The storm has turned into a hurricane.

"The knocker is real, and you know it! You have *seen* what it can do . . . You saw Miss Russel and Mr. West. You saw the needles rain down from the ceiling—"

"And I *know* it was because of you!" Mother shouts into my ear.

"Adelaide would *never* have gone into the shed alone—would never have brought her friends! Whatever curse has befallen this family, it starts and ends with you!"

"*I* cannot control the knocker—"

"And yet it seems to serve you well!" More spittle leaves her mouth to land on my chin. "You are a *danger,* Charlotte, to yourself and to others. You will go to the mainland, tomorrow. I will take you to Anne myself—"

"But I haven't prepared!" I try to make her see sense, even if I know I cannot.

"I don't care if you travel in your shift. Tomorrow we will both be on the boat."

An icy fury rises in me; it grows from the pit of my stomach and spreads out through my limbs, culminating in a blinding flash of a headache. "Do you think it's wise?" I ask. "Do you think it is wise to *make* me do *anything*?"

"I am not afraid of you."

"The knocker, then? Are you afraid of *it*?"

So fixed am I on Mother's face, that I do not notice Evelyn arriving before she speaks. "What on earth is going on in here?" she asks from the doorway. "Should I get Father?" She looks between us.

"Your Father cannot help Charlotte now." Mother snorts.

"What did you *do*?" Evelyn looks at me. She carries fabric samples in her hands: thick white silk and beige taffeta. She is to choose for her wedding dress today.

"*I* didn't do *anything*. It was the knocker who—"

A terrible crash, followed by another, suddenly interrupts me. We all turn our heads to look in the direction of the noise. It comes from this floor, but farther down the hall. Evelyn is the first to move, then Mother and I, on her heels. We all lift our skirts as we run down the hallway, to where more crashes and bangs can be heard.

It comes from Mother's room, as I somehow know, even before I see the drift of smoke coming out from under the door. By the time Evelyn has her hand on the handle, the hallway has filled with the scent of burning.

Smoke pours out when the door is opened. My heart beats rapidly in my chest, and my entire body shakes when I look inside. Everything is upended in there: Mother's bed stands on its side; the blankets heaped on the floor. Her dresser has flown across the room to crash into the wall. Her vanity is on its face in a pool of glass and perfume. The little stool that goes with it balances rudely upon its fallen friend's back. The floor is a sea of gleaming strands of pearls, glittering rings, brooches, and crushed port bottles.

On an easel stands Mother's newest house, intricately painted and on fire.

·25·

ruth

Mr. West abruptly rises from the ruin, staring in the direction of the North house.

"What is that?" he asks with alarm. "Do you see that, Miss Russel? Is it smoke?"

I jolt up as well and follow his gaze, to see that, yes, there is indeed a ribbon of smoke rising out the open window on the house's upper floor.

"Good Lord," I say, clutching my heart. "Is there a fire?"

No sooner are the words out of my mouth than the lace curtain is eaten by a vicious flame.

Without exchanging another word, we both start racing across the fields as fast as we can. I am still in too much pain to run, but Mr. West is more agile and sprints ahead. Knowing the strength of his fear, I am both amazed and strangely touched to see him rush toward the house. Clearly, his need to assist in a crisis overrides the terror in his heart.

I am even amazed at *myself,* truth be told, though my progress is slower.

The ribbon of smoke is a shroud now, streaming out of the window. As I come closer, I hear voices, too, shrill and loud, then something black and smoking is tossed out the open window. It is large, flat, and rectangular. I think it is—or was—a painting. It falls down on the ground with a thud and lies there on the grass, still smoking.

The other windows upstairs are opened in quick succession, and the acrid scent of smoke in the air is strong. I can see no more flames, so hopefully it did not spread from the curtain.

As I turn the corner from the barn, I see people out in front of the house: Adelaide and Sophie are there, alongside Mrs. Norris and Mr. West. The girls look pale and stunned, and their eyes are glued to the red front door—anxiously waiting for news, I assume.

I go to them at once.

"What happened?" I ask, as I place one hand on each of their shoulders.

"Oh, Miss Russel!" The relief on Sophie's face is unmistakable. "Mother's painting caught on fire!"

"How?" I ask.

"We don't know," Adelaide says. "Mother wasn't even there. She and Charlotte fought in our room."

"Could it have been the turpentine? It ignites so easily."

Adelaide shakes her head. "Mother only paints with watercolors."

"A candle, then—or a cigarette, perhaps?" I suggest, but Adelaide looks doubtful.

"Oh, I do wish they would tell us what is going on!" Mrs. Norris huffs, wringing her hands before her.

"They threw the painting out," I say, "and there would have been more flames and smoke by now if the house itself had caught fire."

"Is Mr. North inside?" Mr. West asks.

"No, only Mr. Norris, Mrs. North, Miss Boden, Evelyn, and Charlotte."

"Has he been told?" I ask, and Mrs. Norris shakes her head.

"I can go," Adelaide says, undoubtedly relieved to escape it all.

"Yes," says Mrs. Norris. "Run down to the harbor and find your father."

Adelaide is gone the same moment, slipping from my grasp like a wriggling fish. Sophie takes my hand in hers and holds it tight. The girl smells of smoke and ashes.

Other islanders have come drifting into the yard. Mrs. Fisher is there with her husband and two of her older boys. Mrs. Newell is thankfully absent, but her husband is there, with three other men. They all eye the North house and sniff the air, waiting, like us, to see how bad it is. Something slams behind me and I startle. When I look, I can see that the door to the ramshackle shed has flown open, subject to the whims of the wind.

"Let's take a look in the garden," Mr. West says to Mr. Newell. "In this windy weather, it will not do if there are smoldering embers on the lawn." More men join them as they go around the corner, headed for the singed painting. Soon I can hear a woman's voice calling out to them from a window. It is Miss Boden, I think, but I cannot hear the words.

"Are you very afraid?" I ask Sophie, giving her hand a squeeze. "It will be all right, I'm sure."

Sophie looks up at me with her big blue eyes. "I think the knocker did it." The girl is clearly uncomfortable; she fidgets and cannot look straight at me. I realize that she, too, must have been told not to speak of it. I squat down before her and place my hands on her shoulders, making her look me in the eyes.

"It's all right, Sophie," I tell her gently. "I already know what is going on, remember?"

Relief breaks through on her face, like the sun's return following rain. "It is what they fought about," she whispers, "before it started to burn. Mrs. Fisher had been at the house before, and Adelaide said it was because Norma and Lillian had met the knocker in the shed, and Mrs. Fisher found out."

"Oh dear." I sigh. "That's not good." As fearsome as Mrs. North is,

Mrs. Fisher is no spring breeze either, and I do not think discretion is her strongest suit. *Not* that I would mind a little gossip in this case. "Are Norma and Lillian all right?"

Sophie nods. "Adelaide said they *liked* the knocker, and she does, too, now. She and I listened in on the argument from the stairs when it started to burn in Mother's room. No one was in there, though, so it *must* have been the knocker." Her gaze shifts away, and my heart gives a painful twinge when I realize that Mr. West and I are not the only ones who are wounded by this place. My young students are aching, too. The door to the shed slams again, and this time it causes a violent shiver through my body. Had not Sophie just said that the girls met the knocker there? Could *it* be in there even now? I refuse to look at the offending building, even if my eyes strain to go there and assess the possible threat.

I embrace Sophie and hold her tight, feel her tense body slowly go limp against mine as her slender arms come to curl around my neck.

"It will be fine, Sophie," I say into her ear. "I'm sure that things will be fine again soon."

I lie, though—because I do not know. And perhaps I should not make such promises, but I sense that the girl needs hope more than terrifying reality.

Mr. West and the other men who went to inspect the garden re-emerge. I can see relief in their faces, which leads me to believe that the danger is contained.

"Mary says that the flames are out," Mr. Fisher declares, and the gathering responds with whoops and even some scattered applause. Mrs. Norris looks faint with relief. "The only thing lost is a painting and some curtains," he adds.

Mr. West comes up behind him, wiping his hands on the handkerchief anew. I wonder if I will have to draw him a bath when we get home. We both could use one, truth be told, to scrub the scent of smoke out of our hair. Thinking of Mr. West in the bath makes me blush.

I give Sophie another squeeze. "See?" I tell her. "It's already over."

Sophie lets go of my neck and nods, but does not look particularly happy. Rather, she looks doubtful, as if she does not trust the peace. It utterly pains me to see it.

Then the red door opens to reveal Evelyn and Miss Boden. As soon as they step out, Sophie leaves my side to run to her older sister. Evelyn North looks tired; she barely even manages to smile and lift her hand to greet the onlookers. Above their heads, the few remaining closed windows on the upper floor pop open, one by one, and I catch a glimpse of Charlotte as she works her way through the house.

"Do you want to leave before Mr. North arrives and puts us all to work?" Mr. West says as he reaches me. Around us, the islanders have relaxed and started speaking to one another, discussing the day's dramatic event. I nod and feel a deep relief when we leave the Norths' yard behind. I will not walk down the driveway, though. I will never go that way again. The memory of the rocks is too vivid in my mind. Instead, we leave the way we came: take the path to the tower and then across the fields.

As we move toward the schoolhouse, both of us dazed from the day's upheaval, I share what Sophie had told me.

"If Mrs. Fisher knows, the whole island will soon. I wonder what the Norths will do then." Secretly, I hope it will dissolve my promise to keep mum.

"It could still be blamed on young girls' imaginations," he says. "And we don't know what happened when they met it—or what 'meeting it' even means. I assume they were not pelted with rocks."

"As far as I know they are both hale. The islanders would rather believe their own stories than listen to reason, though, so the Norths will have a hard time explaining it away if the girls experienced something unnatural."

"Or something not yet known to science," he corrects me with a smile.

"Neither will it ever be if they keep insisting on secrecy." I return his smile with one of exasperation.

"Mrs. Fisher could make that choice for them. Besides, a sudden fire might just be serious enough to make them reconsider."

"Sophie could be wrong, though. It could have been nothing but a cigarette left behind."

"Of course," he says, but his eyes have grown distant. A smear of soot mars his cheek. "Am I a coward for not going inside?" he asks.

"No, of course not. What would you go in there for? Mr. Norris and Miss Boden had it all in hand."

"But I didn't know that at first," he protests.

"And so it was wise to wait until you knew." I do understand why it bothers him, though. He does not want to be a slave to his fears, does not want the *creature* to affect him. "Mr. West—" I begin, but he cuts me off.

"Benjamin," he says with a quick smile. "I think that sharing a house—and a mystery—it is time that you call me Benjamin."

"Benjamin," I agree, and find myself smiling.

·26·

charlotte

Despite what Mrs. Fisher told her, Mother sends me to the shed again. I suppose she had no other option. I do not for one second believe it will be the end of my sentence, though. No, she will find a different—better—way to punish me, and my heart races when I think of what might come. The few slaps she gave me when the fire was out were just a taste of what awaited.

What makes it even worse is that not even my sisters seem to entirely believe that I had nothing to do with the fire. I suppose it is because Mother and I were arguing when it happened. I count my blessings, though, and I am happy that Mother no longer thinks that I have secretly become a gifted stage magician. There is no more talk of sleight of hand, for which I am grateful. She believes in the knocker now—but she still thinks that everything it does is orchestrated by me, which is not entirely true. I never know *how* the knocker chooses to respond to my pleas, and certainly never asked for the fire.

All I do is wish.

It *is* sweet, though, to finally have something—or someone—to use against her. Even the shed has been transformed and taken from her grasp. This place is no longer a punishment. It feels safe to me now, with its familiar scent of tar and salt. The droning of the sea is nothing but a comfort. Even my nightmares have ceased.

The shed is no longer Mother's cage; I have made it my refuge.

"Knocker, are you there?" I ask, and sigh with relief when it raps in reply. "You made quite a ruckus," I say. "They are all mad at me now."

This is especially true of Evelyn. "I swear to you, Charlotte, if the knocker ruins my wedding, I cannot answer for what I will do to you," she said to me as soon as the fire was out. James is soon to arrive here, and she is increasingly worried that the knocker will chase him away, just like it did Mr. West. As if I would do *anything* to jeopardize Evelyn's wedding. Adelaide, too, was quite distraught, and I do not think she likes the knocker anymore. So much for winning her over by entertaining her friends.

A dozen wrapped caramels from the grocery store come raining down from the ceiling to land in front of my feet, making me feel better at once.

"Thank you," I say, and start picking them up. "You, at least, know how to lift my spirits." The caramels are hot to the touch and they melt on my tongue, sticky and buttery. I will never stop talking to the knocker. Sometimes I feel it is the only one who stands by me—the only one who appreciates me and never berates me for being who I am. I do my very best to return the gesture, and whenever it does something outrageous, like the fire, I remind myself that it does not know our rules.

It is nothing like us at all.

This is why I do not blame it for what happened today; I just do not think it would be very useful. "How is Jasper Hill?" I ask it instead, since the reverend is always my best cure for gloominess. The paintbrush lifts from the shelf and flies to the wall.

D-R-E-A-D-F-U-L, the knocker spells out.

"What do you mean? Does he *feel* dreadful?"

One rap in the wall—"yes."

"Why is he feeling dreadful?" I sink down to the floor with my caramels and rest my back against the wall.

W-I-F-E, says the knocker.

"Is she cruel to him?" I ask, not without glee.

S-I-C-K, the knocker spells out.

"Yes, she is that. Can you tell what is wrong with her?" It has always been such a mystery.

The knocker hovers for a moment, then it replies, *C-H-I-L-D.*

"She doesn't have a child," I remind it.

D-E-A-D, says the knocker.

"Oh, the dead child," I realize. "Yes, I have heard about that. Is she barren now?" I ask, as that would explain why they never had another.

I am answered by a rap in the ceiling.

This is certainly useful information. "Does *he* know that she cannot have another?" I ask next, since the knocker sometimes knows more than the persons themselves.

Yet another rap sounds.

"Does he still think about me?" I am done with discussing Mrs. Hill.

Another single knock, and my heart swells in my chest—but then, not even the thought of Jasper Hill can entirely keep the unpleasantness of my situation at bay.

"Mother wants to punish me severely, doesn't she?"

Once again, the knocker says "yes."

"Will it be bad?" I ask, somehow hoping it will say "no," even if I know better.

The knocker does not reply at all. The paintbrush just hangs there in the air.

"Will my sisters forgive me?" I ask next.

The knocker does not reply to this either.

"No one *died,*" I complain. "One would think they had *some* sense."

I eat another caramel. "Will you protect me from Mother?" I ask. "Without fire," I quickly add. "She hit me today. It was painful." It still aches when I touch my cheek.

The knocker hesitates, but then it says "yes." I think it really likes fire.

"You can find another way to do it, I'm sure—but don't hurt her too badly," I add with sudden fear. "I won't have her *death* on my conscience." I give a nervous laugh. The knocker would not go as far as to *kill* her . . . would it? "*How* will she punish me?" My thoughts keep returning to the question, much like a tongue prodding a loose tooth.

H-E-L-P, it replies. The paintbrush rushes between the letters.

"She will help?" I laugh again, just as nervous as before. "How?" I just cannot see it.

J-A-S-P-E-R-H-I-L-L, it replies.

·27·

ruth

The fire at the North house is on everyone's lips the following day. Even if it was just a small fire and quickly put out, such an event is still dramatic and frightening to young minds. Adelaide and Sophie are quickly surrounded when they arrive, as their peers want to know everything there is to know about the incident.

Mr. West—Benjamin—is not in the schoolroom this morning, although he often is. He has proven to be quite an asset when it comes to the children, able to teach them a little beyond the curriculum. He has taught them plenty about the island, for one, and the dirt we all walk on. He has even brought the children outside to demonstrate a compass and collect mineral samples from the cliffs, far, far away from Margaret's Tower. I think it is important that he is out in the open where everyone can see him—that we do not make a secret of our unusual arrangement. Whatever the islanders might think, it is harder to make accusations when no one appears to be hiding something. My injury buys us goodwill, too. I am clearly infirm and need help.

"Did the whole painting burn up?" Annabeth Ferryman now leans on Adelaide's desk. Her eyes are as round as marbles while she prods her friend for information.

"Most of it," Adelaide replies. "There was a lot of smoke for just one painting."

"Did someone light it on fire on purpose?" Alfred Anderson asks.

"I don't think so." Adelaide squirms. "Father thinks it might have to do with the paint—that it caught fire in the sunlight, even if it's just watercolors."

"That is some dangerous paint." Norma Fisher gasps.

"It never caught fire before," Sophie says from the adjacent desk. "Mother has made many paintings and they never caught fire before." The girl briefly shifts her gaze to me, then drops it to her desk. It must be terrible, I think, to be so young and burdened with such a dark secret as the knocker. My gaze seeks out the Fisher girls, both of them hovering around Adelaide. None of them seems harmed—or even spooked. If they did indeed meet the knocker, none of them seems to think it had anything to do with the fire, because they appear just as delightfully curious as the rest.

"Father will send the paint to the mainland to be examined," Adelaide tells her friends.

"It was lucky that Mary knew what to do," Norma says. Apparently, Miss Boden had been the one to throw a blanket over the canvas, preventing a devastating blaze.

"She saved the house," Adelaide agrees.

"I hope your father gives her a raise—or more days off," says Annabeth.

"Mother gave her a brooch," says Sophie. "It's shaped like an elephant and has rubies on it."

"The whole room must be repainted," Adelaide offers. "The walls all have soot on them now, and it smells terrible."

"It must have been a big painting," Alfred says.

"It was," Adelaide confirms. "It was a big canvas, and some of the easel burned as well."

I clap my hands together hard. "How about some algebra?"

• • •

The day is fine—or as fine as it can be in June on Margaret's Keep—so I let the children outside to eat their lunch in the grass while I clean the blackboard and prepare the books we will need for the next lesson.

When I hear a commotion outside the window, my first thought is that the sheep are bothering the children, although the latter usually consider their woolly neighbors entertaining company. It is not before I hear crying that I realize something is amiss, and then Benjamin comes into the schoolroom, having been disturbed by the shouting as well.

"I think there might have been an accident," he says as he enters. "I saw through the window how all the girls are flocked around Adelaide and Annabeth, and the two of them seem horribly upset."

I put down the books in my hands and follow Benjamin outside. It is not only the girls now, but all the children who have gravitated to the wailing pair like iron shavings to a magnet. Annabeth and Adelaide clutch at each other as they cry.

I fight my way through the throng of small bodies until I reach the two in the middle. "What is it?" I ask them. "What is going on?" I have to see their faces, I decide, to properly assess the damage, so I use my hands to separate the girls, who are reluctant to let each other go.

Annabeth and Adelaide are red-faced and teary, but look otherwise unharmed. The first one sobs and the second one sniffles, but neither seems to have as much as a scratch. I catch Benjamin's gaze over the children's heads. He looks quite alarmed, and I suppose I do, too.

"Everyone but Adelaide and Annabeth, follow me," he says, and starts marching back toward the schoolhouse.

"Do as Mr. West says." I use my sternest voice, and after some cajoling, they listen. Normally, this would be a treat for them, as they all adore Benjamin, but I cannot fault them for being curious. Annabeth and Adelaide are certainly in a state, and now it is up to me to find out why. Has something serious happened to them, or are they merely cursed with the cruel fate of being thirteen-year-old girls?

"What happened?" I ask again, gentler this time. I place one hand on each of their shoulders and look them in the eyes. "Why are you so upset?"

Adelaide's braid is in her mouth once again, and I carefully pull it out. She purses her lips and shakes her head, but Annabeth has found her voice.

"We saw Charlotte in the field," she says with a sob.

"All right," I say, patting the girl's shoulder. "What did Charlotte do in the field?"

"She just stood there." Annabeth shudders violently. "She just looked at us, and then she went away."

"All right," I say again. "That doesn't sound so terribly frightening—"

"You don't understand!" Adelaide shakes her head with vigor. "Charlotte *couldn't* be in the field! She *couldn't*!"

"No?" I ask, alarmed by the girl's sudden passion. "Why is that, Adelaide?"

"I think maybe she died," Adelaide whispers, and wipes tears with the back of her hand.

"What?" I blurt out. "Why?"

"Because she just vanished," Annabeth wails. "She stood there in the field and then she was gone!"

"She left?" I cannot make head nor tail of it.

"She *vanished,*" Annabeth repeats. "One moment she was there, and the next she was not—and she isn't even supposed to get out." She looks to her friend for confirmation, but Adelaide just cries.

"Get out?" I look at Adelaide as well. "Get out from where?" I feel very uncomfortable now. Icy needles rush down my spine.

"Our room," Adelaide says in a very thin voice. "Mother locked her inside." The girl will not look at me, but studies the dust on her shoes.

"Since when?" I ask, heart hammering wildly.

"Since last night," Adelaide whispers. "Because of the fire."

Annabeth takes Adelaide's hand in hers. "At first, Mrs. North locked her up in the shed, but then Adelaide reminded her that it was better if she was inside, because she wouldn't set fire to the house if she was locked in it herself." The girl is clearly well-informed.

"It was Evelyn who said that," Adelaide corrects her, wary of taking credit for someone else's quick thinking. "Mother wanted to send Charlotte to Aunt Anne, but she cannot do that now, because what if she sets fire to Aunt Anne's house, too?"

I'm reeling from the onslaught of information, delivered in chopped, rapid sentences. "So Charlotte is now locked in her room?" I ask, to clarify.

"Uh-huh," says Adelaide, "so she cannot be here—"

"But she was—and she *vanished,*" Annabeth says again. "Like a ghost."

"So I think she must have died in there." Adelaide wipes tears again.

"I'm sure Charlotte is fine," I assure them, in lieu of something better to say. I cannot believe that Mrs. North would lock up her daughter—and for something she simply *could not* have done, based on my conversation with Sophie. The fact that Adelaide and Annabeth say they have seen Charlotte in the field is of less concern. The girls are impressionable; they could have made it up. Although I have become reluctant to disbelieve *anything* of late.

"But how can you *know* that Charlotte is fine?" Adelaide pulls me from my jumbled thoughts.

"I cannot," I admit. "But sometimes we see—or experience—things that are not what we think. Perhaps you just *thought* of Charlotte, and then you imagined that you saw her. Maybe you were talking about her?"

They shake their heads in unison.

"We talked about the knocker, though, before," Annabeth admits.

"The knocker . . ." My mouth has turned as dry as parchment. "I think it's best if you don't speak about the knocker," I tell them, as calmly as I can muster. "I think it's best if you pay no attention to it at all."

"But what about Charlotte?" Adelaide's voice is thin and small. "What if she is *dead?*"

"As long as you don't know for sure, you should assume she is not," I say, although an eerie feeling has come over me, too. "Dry your tears and go inside," I tell them. "I will be with you in a minute."

When the girls have vanished from sight, I walk around the corner of the schoolhouse and lean my back against the wall. I just stand there, breathing heavily, until I feel certain that my equilibrium is somewhat restored.

I look around me. At the endless grass fields. The grazing sheep. The one single—stunted—oak.

I do not see Charlotte out there.

• • •

The rest of the school day feels like walking through mud: hard and slow. Though both Adelaide and Annabeth have perked up a little by the end of the last lesson, I myself am exhausted. I feel thoroughly relieved when the schoolroom is empty and I can limp into the kitchen, where Benjamin waits with the soup ready. I never even knew that men *could* cook before I met him.

Over the meal, I fill him in on what the girls told me. I shudder again as I recount the tale. The sheer *unnaturalness* of what is going on still makes my skin crawl.

"Do *you* think the fire could be natural?" I ask him when I am quite done.

"It's hard to say." He dips his spoon in the soup. "It does seem peculiar, with the cause being so vague."

"I have never heard of watercolor paints catching fire before," I say.

"And with so much else going on in that house, I would be surprised if the fire wasn't a part of it." He chooses a piece of bread from a wooden board and starts buttering it. "I'm worried about the girl, though." Benjamin looks as pained as I feel. "Her mother should not be locking her up."

"I couldn't agree more. It's just horrible what Mrs. North is doing to her—it's as if she has lost all reason. If Adelaide and Sophie are anything to go by, the North girls are all feeling the pressure. And to be blamed for it all must be excruciating."

"Do you think Charlotte was in the field today?"

"No. The girls said she *vanished,* so it must have been a story. Perhaps . . . perhaps Adelaide was concerned and made something up to have an excuse to tell me about Charlotte's situation. Maybe she was asking for my help." A dark, helpless feeling descends. What can *I* do against Hester North? "The discretion the Norths so value is unraveling, though. Adelaide has never been one to keep a secret, and she shares *everything* with Annabeth Ferryman. The latter was well-informed about Charlotte's dire circumstances."

Benjamin chuckles softly. "Felled by a thirteen-year-old."

"And their own daughter, at that." We smile at each other over the soup bowls. "Perhaps, if the knocker becomes common knowledge, we could speak to the locals—especially the elder ones—and maybe find out more about the tower." To no longer keep it a secret would certainly be a relief.

"Do you think the stories about the tower are true?" Benjamin asks me, serious again.

"Perhaps." I shrug. "But I don't think it's Margaret, though—the knocker."

"What I saw at the North house was certainly not a woman," he agrees.

"And the stone throwing on the road was most unladylike," I add.

Benjamin adds more pepper to his food. "I do hope Charlotte is all right."

"So do I," I agree, but a bad feeling has taken hold, and simply will not let go.

If Adelaide had been asking for my help, should I not at least try?

·28·

ruth

I make up my mind during the night, while listening to the wind wailing against the schoolhouse walls. It is my duty as a member of the community, I decide as I lie there fretting—knowing very well that the result of this particular meddling might be that I find myself unemployed.

For a long time, this has been my greatest fear. Margaret's Keep has seemed to me the perfect haven: a place that asked very little of me, and where I would be left in peace. No one here knows where I come from, and no one, quite honestly, cares. My family's history is my own business here, and no one will even think of questioning my choices—save when I bring their children to the tower, that is. The island has provided me with freedom from the past, and battling its winds has made me stronger. So I have been very reluctant to jeopardize my existence here, but the knocker has changed all that.

Or perhaps it is Benjamin, with all his talk of not being ruled by one's fears, that has changed my outlook and made me a little bolder—a little less afraid to lose what I have.

In the pit of my belly, I recognize a fire that has been all but extinguished ever since my youth. I had not been afraid to leave things behind back then. I had not been afraid of vulnerability. True, I had also known very little of what hardships a woman alone had to face, or what it truly meant to lack bread and butter—but I prevailed.

Perhaps I should take a lesson from that young, bold woman I had been, rather than regard her as a cautionary tale. I had sacrificed much for my freedom on this island, but what point was there in freedom if one never used it? Again, I find that spark of a younger me deep inside, and recall her pride and her stubbornness—how she had refused to bend her neck. Just an ounce of that power could perhaps be enough to make life a little better for the North girls.

Perhaps I wish that, when I was a child, someone would have done the same for me.

• • •

The next morning, I inform Benjamin of my plans over breakfast.

"It's the only thing I can think of," I say. "He is the only one that holds sway."

"Do you want me to come with you?" he asks, stirring his tea.

"No, I think I should do it alone. He owes me a debt—or he thinks he does, anyway—and I mean to remind him."

"I suppose you are referring to the terrible tea party?" He arches an eyebrow.

"Exactly," I confirm. "It's better if he doesn't know I shared that sorry tale with you."

"For such a small island, there are a lot of secrets," he notes.

"Perhaps it is *because* it is so small that secrets must be kept tight to uphold the status quo," I reply. "It's harder to remain both king and bishop when the number of pawns is small."

"And now you are out for the queen?" he asks, giving me a slight smile.

I groan. "I was always terrible at chess."

"I think you do fine," he says. "Charlotte North will surely thank you."

"*If* I can even do something," I remind him. "*If* I can talk him into it."

"If it's true as you say and he has some sort of sordid history with her—"

"Not sordid. Just . . . questionable."

"Then he might not be that hard to convince."

"No. At least he, too, must realize that locking up a grown girl is utterly reprehensible." Knocker or no knocker.

I leave the students in Benjamin's care and set out directly after breakfast. I worry that, if I wait too long, the fire will go out of me, and my boldness will turn to dread. Had it been any other family, I would not have felt this way, but the Norths are mighty and I am small.

Fortune favors the bold, I remind myself, as I limp down the potholed dirt road, leaning on my walking stick. *Nothing ventured, nothing gained,* I say, as the church comes within sight. *Endure the discomfort of fear,* I tell myself as I walk up to the clergy house and gingerly raise my hand to knock. *The Norths are mighty, but so am I,* I try to convince myself, as my knuckles hit the wood.

I do not truly feel it, though. Not really.

I am surprised when the reverend himself opens the door. A delicate, small cup in his hand emits the scent of strong coffee.

"Miss Russel," he says. "Apologies for the informality. I saw you arriving through the window and thought I might greet you myself to save Noreen the trouble."

"How thoughtful of you," I mutter as I step inside and lean my walking stick against the wall. I sorely miss my sturdy umbrella, which has always been my shield. Now that I am here, the nervousness is so powerful that I can barely speak. "I trust that you are well," I say, "and Mrs. Hill, too."

I say it only to be polite, but he instantly takes on a pained expression. "Yes, yes, we're both well enough," he says, though his face speaks another truth entirely.

Noreen comes rushing to take my coat, and then I am shown into the reverend's office: a small room lined with shelves carrying books and various knickknacks. Most prominently upon a shelf sits a model of the church made entirely of matches. Between the two windows behind the desk hangs a cross made of white seashells and a photograph of the previous reverend and his wife.

I have barely even had time to sit down before Noreen is there again, offering me some of that strong coffee. I do not normally indulge, but figure that, in this case, a taste of something strong and bitter might just be in order. She pours the black liquid into a cup no larger than the bottom half of a chicken egg, and not much thicker either. When the housekeeper has left, the reverend turns his attention to me.

"What can I do for you, Miss Russel?" His brown eyes look very kind—an expression I am sure he has perfected over the years. Behind him, through the window, I see the ruins of the tower.

"Well," I start, searching for my voice. The small cup in my hand is scalding hot. "It's a rather delicate matter, Reverend. Perhaps I shouldn't have come to you, but I don't know where else to turn."

"Is it about your houseguest?" The kind eyes peer at me, brimming with understanding.

"What? No!" I am so surprised that a fiery hot drop of liquid escapes the china to land on my hand. "It has nothing to do with that. You must believe me when I say that Mr. West and I are merely good friends."

"Oh, *I* believe you," he replies, handing me a napkin from the tray, "but others might not be so inclined. Has anyone said anything unkind to you?"

"No. I had assumed they might, but Benjamin—Mr. West—has been such an asset. He has even donated his time to teach the children. It's just that he will not stay with the Norths," I say, trying to edge closer to the matter at hand.

"How *did* he end up with you?" Reverend Hill sounds genuinely curious. "I would think the clergy house a more appropriate destination if he was uncomfortable at the Norths'."

I had not expected being questioned about this either, and it takes a moment to compose myself. "It was because I knew what ailed him," I say quietly, looking down.

"You had been afflicted, too?" His voice is very gentle.

I eye him with sudden interest. "Do you *know*?"

"My lips are sealed," he says good-humoredly. He has picked up a sword-shaped letter opener and is passing it from hand to hand, quite relaxed.

"So are mine," I reply with an exasperated sigh. "I wish now that I never made that promise." Though it *is* good that he knows. It will make this so much easier.

"Is your limp from that . . . affliction?" Reverend Hill asks.

"It is," I confirm. "It is a particularly grave . . . situation the Norths have." I place the coffee on the edge of the desk. Cup and saucer gently rattle. "And that is what I wanted to talk to you about—or at least about something related."

Reverend Hill bends forth in his chair, looking at me with interest. "Please do share," he says. "Hopefully, I can be of assistance."

"It's about Charlotte," I say, and the man instantly tenses up.

"What about her?" he asks in a thick voice.

"I have learned from her sister that Mrs. North has locked her up in her room since the fire. You do know there was a fire?" I look at him.

"I do, yes." His voice is even thicker than before. "No one was hurt, thank God."

"Mrs. North seems to blame Charlotte for the ordeal," I say, "though the youngest girl, Sophie, is adamant that her sister was nowhere near the painting when it started to burn." I lift my gaze to make sure that I still have the reverend's attention—that he understands what I am trying to convey. "It is not natural, Reverend, to lock up a grown girl. Neither is it sound to blame her for something that she clearly had no hand in. Truthfully, Reverend"—I am gathering steam now—"this is not the first time Mrs. North has placed the blame for something *impossible* at her daughter's feet."

Reverend Hill is quiet for a very long time, deeply lost in thought. I am elated that the words are spoken, yet anxious about his verdict.

"What do you want me to do, Ruth?" he asks at last, surprising me by using my given name. His voice is not unkind, though, just curious.

"I want you to find out if Adelaide is telling the truth," I tell him. "And if she is, I want you to speak to the Norths. This is no way to treat a young woman." It is a bold thing to ask of him, but this is a day for boldness.

"I agree," he says, but looks pained again. I assume the reason is that it concerns Charlotte. "I must be careful, though. Tread delicately."

"I worry that the . . . ailment has had an unfortunate effect on Mrs. North's state of mind," I tell him.

"Having had no experience with this *ailment,* it is hard to believe in it," he notes. "But I cannot deny its effects. I will certainly look into it—and in on Charlotte," he adds.

"She must be let out."

"Indeed, she must, if she truly is captive."

"Do not underestimate the cruelty of the wealthy, Reverend." My boldness seems to suddenly have caught a wind and set sail. "Pearls and finery are no guarantees of virtue."

"That is certainly correct." A hint of humor has come into his voice. "Still, we cannot judge before we know for sure."

"Of course," I say. "But you will look into it?"

"That I will," he replies.

·29·

jasper

I cannot say what I expect when I enter the Norths' yard. Nothing, I suppose. I have been looking around for flying rocks ever since the beginning of the driveway, but none have appeared.

I honestly find the whole affair baffling, and have spent most of the morning since Miss Russel left reading up on mass hysteria. I still have quite the library of books on afflictions of the mind, bought during the first few years of Antonia's illness. I do believe that is what has happened here: a seed has taken root and sprouted leaves, insidiously affecting even the balanced and strong of mind, like Miss Russel. Doubtlessly, she was attacked—she even has a limp to prove it—but the reason for the damage, I fear, has become shrouded in superstition and fantasies. This is certainly not Miss Russel's fault. Such ideas will spread like wildfire, and are—indeed—an affliction.

Could it also be what ails Mrs. North?

I do find it hard to believe that they would mistreat their daughter, because Mr. North seems to me the very epitome of reason, and would surely have put his foot down. The family has its share of challenges, of course, undoubtedly made worse by the fact that they are somewhat isolated from the rest of Margaret's Keep and crowded with young girls at that. I suppose conspiracies can easily be hatched in such an environment, and demons be born from juvenile games. I hold on to this sobering thought as I battle the wind to reach the red door, worrying all the while about Charlotte's well-being. Can it truly be that she is in dire straits? Just the thought of it makes me feel nauseous.

Miss Boden looks surprised when she opens the door, but also pleased. She promptly invites me in and takes my hat and coat.

"It's long overdue that you come to see us, Reverend," she says in a quiet voice. "Things aren't getting any better since we saw you. I suppose you heard about the fire?"

I nod. "That must have been very frightening for you."

"I'm only glad I was here," she tells me. "None of *them* could put it out; they simply don't know *how*. If I hadn't been here, the whole place would have burned to the ground."

"It's lucky for the Norths that they have you, then." I smile at her. "God surely did well in placing you here."

A shadow crosses her features. "Perhaps," she mumbles, and I briefly wonder if Miss Boden is not as happy with her lot in life as I had previously assumed. But then, circumstances in the household have changed.

The housekeeper leaves me waiting for her mistress in the hall. It is a fine, large room, but something seems different since the last time I was here. I have not been waiting for long before a feeling of unease comes creeping in. I cannot say exactly what it is that rattles me, but there is a sense of gloom that not even the daylight from the windows can whisk away. The usually pristine home seems to be coated in a sheen of dust, though when I discreetly inspect a flower-carrying side table, I can see only the gleaming surface of polished wood and the immaculate crystal of the vase. I find it all very peculiar, and wonder if it has something to with the fire—soot particles or lingering smoke.

"Reverend." Mrs. North enters the hall with her hands stretched out in greeting. I clasp them both and squeeze them gently. Mrs. North is dressed all in white, and has a blue ribbon tied in a large bow around her neck.

"Mrs. North," I say. "It is good to see you."

"You, too, Reverend. Very good, indeed. I was just thinking of calling on you," she says, eyes uncommonly serious. "I was thinking of accepting your generous offer at last." Her voice has fallen to a hush. A brief flash of fear on her face makes my heart start thumping hard in my chest.

"Offer?" I ask, momentarily confused.

"The house blessing," she says so quietly that it is barely a breath. She will not meet my eyes. Perhaps she feels that merely making the request is shameful? I give her my best reassuring smile—the one I use to put people at ease.

"I take it that your problems have not ceased?" I say, relieved not to have to be the one to bring up the recent unpleasantness.

"Sadly, no." Mrs. North's hands flutter like little birds in the air. "On the contrary, Reverend, they have grown worse. We have *fires* now." She sounds utterly crestfallen. Unlike the last time we spoke, when she and Miss Boden sat in my office, Mrs. North seems to have lost her confidence and assurance. This version of Mrs. North is nervous, uneasy, and somewhat brittle.

Unstable enough to lock up her daughter?

"I heard about the fire," I say. "Such a terrible shame. Thankfully, no one was hurt."

"Only my painting." She gives a thin laugh. "I was very pleased with it, too. But then, she probably knew that."

"Who?" I ask, though I fear I know the answer.

She gives me an overbearing look, as if I were some hopeless toddler. "Charlotte, of course. The scourge of my existence." Mrs. North laughs again, and I catch a faint whiff of port on her breath and belatedly realize that she is drunk. This certainly does not bode well.

I clear my throat and gather my thoughts. "Surely, you are not suggesting that Charlotte set the—"

"No, not directly. It is complicated, you see." She flashes a quick smile. "Charlotte might not even *know* what she is doing."

I give her a puzzled look, but feel some relief as well. At least she does not seem to be so utterly convinced of Charlotte's guilt anymore. Perhaps she can be led to reason.

"Where is Charlotte now?" I ask, hoping for a reassuring answer.

"In her room," says Mrs. North, and my stomach drops. "We keep her locked up in there—for her own safety, as well as ours."

"Locked up, Mrs. North?" I cannot believe it is true. "Surely that cannot be good for her state of mind—"

"I don't care, Reverend." She lifts her chin. "I will do what I must to keep this all contained." Her frightened gaze has turned as sharp and steely as a knife's blade; she will not be challenged in this.

"But there *must* be other ways," I protest. "Have you given a psychiatrist any thought?"

"What do you think that would do to Charlotte's reputation, Reverend? Who will want to marry a madwoman? No, we will wait it out, that is all. Sooner or later, it will pass."

"Afflictions of the mind rarely pass," I say gently. "It might go into hiding, but will not entirely disperse on its own."

"Nevertheless, it *must,* or all my daughters will be damaged goods. And then what will we do?" Some shrillness has come into her voice. Behind her back, I can see Miss Boden slowly shake her head, warning me not to proceed down this path.

I quell my protests—though it is hard—and give Mrs. North a brief smile. "Perhaps a house blessing will be of comfort," I say. "Perhaps it can help you all heal." Perhaps I can calm her enough to let her daughter out of her room.

"At least it cannot hurt," she concedes.

Mr. North joins us in the hall then, which certainly is a surprise, since he seems the kind of man to stay away from domestic issues. He looks drawn behind his mustache, and his eyes are serious as he takes my hand. I cannot help but notice that he reeks of brandy and cigars. Mrs. North is clearly not the only one to have embraced the bottle of late.

"It's a terrible thing to welcome a man of God into my home under such terrible circumstances," he says. "I never before believed in stories about devils roaming wild."

"But now you do?" I ask, taken aback.

"I cannot deny my own eyes," he replies.

"What exactly did you see?" I continue my inquiry, but the man is not inclined to answer. He just pats my back good-naturedly. The reek of brandy is very strong. I never thought I would see the day when a man like him welcomed me in to swipe devils and ghouls from his door, but here we are. A blessing was not what I came for, but it certainly seems to be what they need.

We start the blessing in the front room, where Evelyn sits, stitching monograms onto silk. She is quite alone, so I suppose the younger girls are at school. The young woman looks very serious as she rises from the sofa. I notice how her sky-blue dress has a few spots on the sleeve. She, at least, does not hide the tarnish.

"Have you come to speak sense to my parents, Reverend?" she asks with an ounce of bite. "You must tell them how they simply *cannot* keep their daughter locked up in a room."

"First and foremost, I'm here to bless this home," I say, conscious of the Norths following me. My heartache intensifies when I see the despair on Evelyn's face and realize how worried she must be for her sister. When I feel certain that the Norths cannot see it, I give her a reassuring smile, wanting her to know that I *do* grasp the direness of the situation and *will* do something to rectify it. She might not get my meaning, though.

I make the Norths and Miss Boden join me, and we form a circle. I recite the Lord's Prayer before adding a wish that the house and its inhabitants shall be protected from evil forces, that the walls may withstand any attack. Miss Boden sighs deeply when the prayer has ended.

"It feels better in here already," she remarks.

I am quite pleased with the performance, and we proceed to the dining room and repeat the little ritual in there. I am surprised to see that most of the windows are boarded up, leaving the room dark and gloomy. I wonder if Mr. North's "devils" are to blame.

I am still confident as we step into the kitchen, with its scent of heated copper and boiling meat. Mrs. Norris, the cook, is there, waiting. She rises from her chair and takes a few quick steps toward me when we arrive. The relief is apparent on her features.

"Oh, thank goodness," she declares. "Finally, someone that can help!"

"Calm yourself," Mrs. North mutters. "You have wanted the reverend to come for ages, and now he is here. Hopefully, this will satisfy you."

Mrs. Norris quite rudely ignores her employer. "It has been such a horrible time, Reverend." She wipes away a few tears with her knuckles. "We do what we can, but it's not enough."

"What do you do?" I ask, curious, while taking her free hand in my own.

"Oh, we pray, of course, and light candles—though *that* has become quite a hazard." She gives me a telling look. "And we carry our crosses and bless the food . . . Oh, and in the morning before dawn, I go up to Charlotte with a seashell of seawater, honey, and salt. She drinks it, too, but it doesn't help."

"Why do you do such a thing?" I am utterly mystified.

"It's something my grandmother mentioned. Four things not 'made of man' are supposed to get rid of such afflictions."

"What affliction is that, Mrs. Norris?"

"Oh, devilry and such . . . *Unclean spirits,* like the ones in the Bible." Her eyes still leak tears, and I do not have the heart to set her straight.

It is a quiet sound at first, barely a tinkling—a faint little song of metal that reaches my ears while I listen to Mrs. Norris—and then, without warning, it is a clamor. I quickly spin around to see the copper pots in the ceiling dancing wildly on their hooks. I am barely able to stifle the shout of surprise that threatens to erupt from my throat when the chair Mrs. Norris has just vacated shoots backward across the floor to crash into the wall by the window.

The Norths, Miss Boden, and Mrs. Norris run for the door at once, but I—new to this—do not. I just stand there, dumbfounded, and stare, not even having the good sense to utter the Lord's name. This is surely no "demon of the mind"!

As I stand there, frozen, the strangest thing happens. Just as the clamor of the pots dies down, it starts raining violets from the ceiling. They are tiny things, fresh with dew, though hot to the touch when they brush against my skin. They land on the floor by my feet, the petals looking immensely delicate and soft against the roughness of the wooden boards. There must be two dozen of them in all. I grab one as it floats by and smell a heady scent. I drop it again at once.

"Oh, *look* at that." Mrs. Norris is full of awe. She speaks from the doorway, where all my companions huddle together. "Even the spirit recognizes a man so close to God," she says.

"Flowers? That is new," Mr. North marvels. "It's usually needles that fall from the ceiling."

"It must have a liking for you, Reverend," says Miss Boden.

Mrs. North, though, is not so easily impressed. "*It* might not," she snorts, "but I certainly know who does."

"Surely, you cannot mean—" I start, but then I think better of it. Words fail me, truth be told. I cannot comprehend what I just saw with my own eyes. Though I have chosen a spiritual profession, I have never before been faced with something so arbitrary to logic. I am not frightened—not truly—but I *am* puzzled, and deeply worried.

"Your daughter is not a *witch,* Mrs. North," I manage at last. "Has it ever occurred to you that the . . . *spirit* might *want* you to blame your daughter? Perhaps this is all a ruse, and Charlotte is nothing but a victim." The violets are just *too* poignant, too much on the nose. It is the same type of flower that Charlotte used to leave for me, tied with a neat little bow.

"*I* believe the reverend speaks truth," Mrs. Norris says at once.

"Charlotte says she has no control of it," Miss Boden adds.

"She is in dire need of help—of *care*." I am looking at her father. "Can you imagine how frightened she must be?" Suddenly, I am grateful for Mrs. Norris and her seashell. At least the woman tried to do *something* to ease Charlotte's suffering. "I must see her. How long has she been locked in her room?"

Mr. North sighs deeply. "You better come into my study, Reverend. I think this requires a private conversation."

I could not agree more.

We leave the servants behind in the kitchen, cross the hall, and step into Mr. North's smoke-infused study, where the brandy decanter has been left out on the untidy desk. Mr. North refills his glass, then pours generously for me and Mrs. North as well, picking fresh tumblers off a silver tray. Mrs. North instantly brings the glass to her lips and empties half its contents. The woman's nerves must be overwrought, but I do not blame her anymore.

Mr. North sits down in a broad swivel chair while Mrs. North and I seat ourselves in the two leather chairs positioned across from the desk. I sip the liquor; I sorely need it.

"The reverend is right." Mr. North speaks to his wife. "Charlotte *cannot* stay up in that room. It's inhumane, and she *is* our daughter—and nothing has changed in the house even if we lock the door. The devil is still about—"

"What do you suggest we do, then?" she fires back. "Just let her roam and spread fire in her wake?"

"What about an exorcism?" Mr. North speaks to me now. "Surely, in such dire circumstances, that can be arranged?"

I shudder at the suggestion. "Perhaps our cousins in Rome are so inclined, but it's not—"

"There must be *something* you can do," Mr. North booms, and now I can see the ruthless businessman behind his benevolent exterior. "What is the point of you, Reverend, if you cannot help in matters of the soul?"

"We do not even know what this *is,*" I protest. "It *looks* like a malevolent spirit, but we cannot know for sure—"

"What else could it be?" he asks me. "You yourself just denied that my daughter is a witch—"

"But she is, though, isn't she?" Mrs. North speaks in a harsh voice. "When she was a child, she *saw* things, even before she could walk. Journeys past the graveyard were a nightmare! She would point and laugh at nothing at all, and draw crude pictures of whatever she had seen among the graves—"

"Children have wonderful imaginations," I say.

"But she *knew* things." Mrs. North's voice drops, and is suddenly so soft it is almost a whisper. "She knew what we were giving her for her birthday, or what her sister had dreamt of at night . . . And she was *obsessed* with labyrinths, Reverend, and drew them *everywhere*—built them out of pieces of cardboard and pebbles from the beach . . . She forced Evelyn to read to her about the Minotaur and Ariadne's thread over and over again, wanting to know the trick of how to let the monster *out*." Her words trail off as her gaze turns distant. "She unnerved me as a child—and she still does. I have so longed for her to get married and leave—"

"What did you do, Mrs. North, when Charlotte *saw* things?" Though I use a gentle voice, my insides are seething with fury. *How* can a mother not love her child better?

"Oh, I locked her up in the shed." She straightens up in the chair. Some of the strength has come back in her voice. "I would have locked her in there now as well, had it been safe—"

"But why?" I interrupt, and politeness be damned. "What good does it do to lock your daughter up?" What was the point in having a child only to punish her so severely?

"She had to learn." Mrs. North suddenly sounds haughty. "Just as *I* did. My father never cared for wayward daughters either—and it *did* stop after I put her in there." There is triumph in her voice. "Charlotte stopped seeing those . . . *people* in the graveyard, and she stopped obsessing about *labyrinths*. It's a cure, Reverend, and it will work now as well. A little time to herself, and the wickedness will stop." I think she says it mostly to convince herself.

"What I think Charlotte needs is rest, fresh air, and prayer," I say. "What she *does not* need is to be left on her own in that room. How long has she been there?" I ask Mr. North once again.

"Ever since the fire," he mumbles, looking somewhat ashamed.

"Let her stay with Antonia and me in the clergy house," I suggest. "It will give you all some time to heal and reflect."

Mr. North looks as if he is considering it, but Mrs. North has her verdict ready. "No," she snaps. "You *know* how she feels, Reverend—it would be a *disaster*!"

"I can handle Charlotte," I say. "She and I used to be good friends—"

"But it's *dangerous,* Reverend," Mr. North interrupts. "We almost lost our house to fire, Miss Russel was pummeled with rocks, and the geologist I hired fled the house in the night . . . You have just seen for yourself how mad things can get, and chances are that you'll get the spirit, too—"

"I'm not afraid of it," I say, though I do feel a tightening in my chest.

"Only because you got violets, not needles," Mrs. North remarks curtly.

"I am close to God," I say, feeling only slightly ashamed of making such a bold claim. "If anyone is capable of subduing what has attached itself to Charlotte, it is I." I know this sounds terribly boastful, but it is nothing but the truth. "I can lead her in prayer and help her unburden her soul."

"It will only tempt her to more mischief." Mrs. North fills her tumbler anew, with hands that are shaking badly.

"She *would* be out of that room," says Mr. North. His father's heart is obviously torn.

Mrs. North tries a different approach. "Mrs. Hill would never allow it.

"Antonia is a godly and charitable woman," I say, even though I fear that Mrs. North is right.

"No," Mrs. North says, and the word has an air of finality to it. "I will not allow it. She would see it as a victory! She would think that she had *won*—" A large glass paperweight shaped like a cod flies off the desk and hits her in the head. She topples from the chair and lands on the floor. A large gash on her forehead gushes forth blood.

"My God!" I cry out, feeling as if struck by lightning. My heart races painfully hard in my chest as Mr. North and I rush to kneel down next to her, pressing damp fingers to her neck in search of the throb of life.

Her eyes stare up at the ceiling, quite empty.

·30·

charlotte

Jasper Hill comes to my rescue like a knight from one of Evelyn's books. Though I might have dreamt of something like this happening in the many idle hours I was locked up in my room, I had not thought it would truly happen. But then, following an awful ruckus from downstairs, the key is twisted, the door springs open, and there he is.

My savior.

I have not seen him for so long, and cannot not help it if tears come trickling when I throw my arms around his neck, bury my face against his shoulder, and inhale the scent of him: brine and rosemary. I let him lead me down the stairs and into the closed carriage.

Mother is still unconscious when we leave. While the carriage rattles along, Jasper tells me how he and Father had very carefully moved her to the sofa in the front room before Father left to send for a doctor. Jasper is pale when he tells me what happened; something haunted flickers in his eyes. I suppose it must have been a terrible thing to see the paperweight lift and hit her. He keeps saying she might have a fractured skull.

I place my hand on his and enjoy the warmth of his skin. "Mother will live," I say. "The knocker wouldn't kill her." It had promised me, after all. Because I have not been entirely alone in my bedroom. I have had a friend with me at all times. Perhaps the true knight in this story is the knocker, doing what must be done to free me—not just from the room but from my mother's house and rule. The former could have been easily breached by the knocker unlocking the door, but then where would I go? No, I needed Mother gone—or incapacitated at the very least, to perform a successful escape. I did not *want* to see her hurt, but it was the only way. There is a war between us now, but she is the one who instigated it.

All *I* do is defend myself.

It is already afternoon when we arrive at the clergy house. It is a fine wooden building with roses climbing the white-painted walls—though the flowers on Margaret's Keep never grow large but look like miniature versions of their cousins on the mainland, if they even bloom at all. The double front doors are chocolate brown, and the small pane windows reflect the low sun in flaming hues.

One of the doors opens just as we arrive, and Mrs. Hill steps out to greet the carriage. She is wearing all white and reminds me of a wraith with her skeletal build and light hair. When she sees me emerge, her face twists up and her pale eyes come to life with anger.

"What is the meaning of this?" She looks from me to her husband. The latter has also climbed out of the carriage and stands there in his black attire, looking for a moment like a child caught in mischief. Then he straightens and puffs out his chest.

"We must take care of Charlotte for a while. Mrs. North has been injured—a concussion, if not worse. Charlotte is in need of *care*." He emphasizes the last word just as the carriage rattles away. Mr. Norris is undoubtedly relieved to leave us behind. It is clear that a storm is upon us.

"No," says Mrs. Hill, and now *she* is the one appearing like a child: lost and abandoned in a deep, dark forest.

"Yes," says he, still moving. "This is not a time to be selfish. We must do what we can to help."

Mrs. Hill entirely ignores me. "But none of this makes *sense,* Jasper. If her mother is injured, shouldn't Charlotte be at home to help?" Her gaze finally darts in my direction. "Unless *she* was the one who did it. I've heard plenty of stories of what's been going on at the North house. Noreen is well-informed," she adds, in a voice thick with bile. "Have you brought a *criminal* to our home?"

"Of course not," he scoffs. "I *saw* Mrs. North being injured myself, and Charlotte was locked in her room at the time."

"From what I've heard, that means nothing." Mrs. Hill shoots me a look of pure hatred—but not fear. Her utter dislike of me seems to override any other emotion.

"I will not claim your husband's time, Mrs. Hill." I cannot help it if a tiny smile forms on my lips. "I only seek sanctuary until matters between my mother and me can be resolved."

"Claim his time?" Mrs. Hill sounds baffled. "I'm far more worried about you burning down my house!"

"That would hardly serve my purpose, would it? Where would I go if my sanctuary is burned? There's nowhere else on this island."

"See?" Jasper arches an eyebrow at his wife. "Charlotte will be perfectly safe. She has been through an ordeal and needs peace and calm—and prayer, too. Plenty of that."

"Noreen will quit in protest," Mrs. Hill grumbles.

"And lose a lucrative post? I think not."

Mrs. Hill does not seem to appreciate his flippant tone. Her brow knits up, and her pale hands curl into fists by her sides. "She ought to go to the mainland if there is no place for her on Margaret's Keep."

Jasper's voice turns stern. "Remember our Christian duties."

"This has nothing to do with Christianity!" Mrs. Hill's voice teeters on shrillness. "You *know* that I would gladly have opened our doors to anyone else but *her*!"

"And yet, you will do as I say," he barks, and I have never seen him angry before. Even I take a tiny step back.

Mrs. Hill does not move nor speak for a while. She just stands at the top of the stairs with her fists pressed to her belly, her chest moving fast with her breathing.

"All right," she says at last, in a thick, pained voice. "I'm aware it's my duty to obey, but I will not help and I will not *see* her. She can stay in the attic, out of my way."

"You *will* help," he snaps, "but the attic is acceptable for now. Come along, Charlotte." He forces a smile as he turns to me. "Everything will be fine, you will see."

I know the clergy house well, though I have only been here a couple of times since the Hills moved in. Before that, while the old reverend still lived, we would visit weekly. The house is as it has always been, with the same old scent of brine and smoke, but now a hint of rosemary has mingled with the familiar. I suspect that Jasper keeps sachets with his clothes. There is lavender in the air, too, and I think that scent belongs to *her*. She probably has sachets of her own to keep insects out of her closet. Lavender is a widow's scent for me, reminding me of my grandmother and her heavy, black garb. I am happy that Jasper chose rosemary.

Despite my familiarity with the place, however, I have never seen the attic before; it was always forbidden to us children. A scent of sun-heated wood and dust envelops us as Noreen and I climb the steep stairs from the kitchen with a candle. I am pleasantly surprised to discover that the attic is not the jumble of crates and castoffs that I had imagined, but contains several furnished rooms and has plenty of space below the slanted ceiling. Soon, our feet tread on thick rag rugs, which cover the floor of a narrow hallway. Noreen opens the first door on the left to reveal a simple bedroom with an iron bed and a washstand placed under a circular window. A simple rag rug hides some of the scuffed floorboards, and there is a large, wooden chest for clothes. The walls are painted gray blue, and there is a framed painting of Jesus handing out fish. It is a maid's room for sure, and Noreen confirms it.

"I used to stay up here in the beginning, before I married," the housekeeper says. "It's not much, but it suffices." She eyes me warily while she speaks, as if I am about to burst into flames myself. "You will not have to cross paths with Mrs. Hill very often," she continues. "The stairs to the kitchen are the only ones, and you can take your meals down there. Also, the back door will take you to the garden, which Mrs. Hill never uses. I think it's best if she doesn't have to see you at all," she says bluntly. "And, yes, I question the reverend's wisdom in bringing you here in the first place." She sends me another frightened look, but I am not offended by her frankness. If anything, it makes me like her more.

"I will be as quiet as a mouse," I promise. "Mrs. Hill won't even know I'm here."

"Oh, she'll know," Noreen states, arching an eyebrow. "And, as Mary tells it, not even lock and key can keep your *spook* at bay."

"It isn't *my* spook," I say. "I have nothing to do with it. It might not even know where I went. I could be free of it now." But I do not really think so, because a whiff of cooked meat is teasing my nostrils. "Besides, it never hurt Mary," I add, since it is nothing but the truth.

"If it had, I would have refused to care for you." Noreen's lips tighten. "But my niece speaks well of you, and thinks none of it is your doing. I trust my Mary a great deal, so I will feed you and air your bed—and even pray for you, if you like—but the spook is not why you being here is *wrong,* and I think you know that as well."

"That was a long time ago," I say, assuming she remembers the debacle with the caramels.

"Not that long ago," she replies.

When Noreen has left, I sit down on the hard bed, let out my breath, and listen to the churning of the sea outside and the cries of the seagulls above. In one way, it feels as though I have simply traded one room for another, one furious jailor for more of the same. But I know it does not much matter, because I will always have the upper hand, as long as the knocker is with me.

"Knocker, are you there?" I ask the blue-painted walls.

A hard rap sounds in reply.

"Good." I let out my breath. "Will Mother live?" I ask next, and surprise myself by feeling relieved when the knocker promptly raps "yes."

"I said no more fire, and you found another way," I acknowledge with some pride. "Thank you for listening to me." I shift on the bed and inspect my bandaged finger, which is weeping pus again. "Now, could you bring me some books?" I ask. "I think I will be dreadfully bored, spending my days up here."

Immediately, four books fall from the ceiling to land beside me on the mattress. Two are about church history, one is religious poetry, and the fourth is a romance, like Evelyn's. With three out of four being religious, I think they must come from downstairs.

"Thank you," I murmur into the ether, then lie back and open the romance. I am in Jasper Hill's house now—at the heart of his life.

And the knocker is the one who made it happen.

·31·

jasper

"It's our duty to help," I remind Antonia over dinner. I am still shaken from what happened at the North house. I have a piercing headache and my nerves are frayed. It has been a flurry of activity ever since Norris deposited us in the yard, and my mind has become a windy place, prone to shifts and sudden gusts. And Antonia's jealousy does nothing to settle me. In fact, it only whips the winds to a frenzy. Should she not console me? Help me to make sense of it all?

Can she not tell that I am unnerved?

"A duty we share with every Christian soul on this island," Antonia harps on, while calmly peppering her steak. "Why is it *we* who must open our doors? Is it because the Norths are rich? Won't a humble cottage do?"

"We *do* have more space," I remind her, as calmly as I can muster. "Empty rooms are a luxury we are obliged to share, yes." I refrain from pointing out how a priest can be of help and comfort. Antonia has grown up among clergy, and is fully aware that we are not holy. In fact, the cross and collar I wear does nothing to impress her.

"What about the grocery store?" she asks next, still trying to wriggle out of the commitment. "Don't they have spare rooms there?"

"She needs peace and prayers," I say. "A busy retail environment cannot provide the necessary calm—"

"I still don't see why she had to leave her home," she interrupts. "She is a grown woman, as well you know. She should be with her sisters, caring for their mother."

"Her remaining at the North house would not have contributed to *anyone's* healing." I cut the beef, which tastes of nothing at all.

"Would you have brought her here if it were anyone else? If it was one of her sisters, would you still have taken her here and installed her in the attic?"

"No, because *she* would have been deemed worthy of a guest room," I snap, still sore that Charlotte had been offered only the attic. "She should at least be able to take her meals in here with us."

"Do you really want that, Jasper?" Antonia swirls the wine around in her glass. "I cannot see how that would be pleasant for any of us." She sounds so devastatingly calm. Can she not see how something *horrible* just happened?

"You are not a gracious hostess," I note, but refrain from pushing the matter, far more concerned with other things, like the violent power I encountered at the Norths'. "I will write to Dr. Crown," I say, just as I make up my mind. "I will ask him to come posthaste to examine Charlotte." Dr. William Crown had been the psychiatrist Antonia saw after our son died, and he seems to me a lifeline now—a man of thought and reason.

"Is she insane?" Antonia glances up at the ceiling. "I thought you said she was 'just' haunted."

"Of course she's not *insane,*" I huff. "But the . . . *peculiarities* surrounding her require a keen eye, and Dr. Crown knows much about the human mind, as *you* know better than most." Secretly, I hope it is my *own* mind he will soothe, by offering me an explanation for what I just saw with my own two eyes. I never believed in "the devil's emissaries" before. I never believed in the stories of old. *My* God is one of light and rationality.

"*Peculiarities.*" Antonia laughs. "Like *arson*?" Her gaze meets mine with the warmth of a glacier. "Or *assault*?" She laughs again—a brittle, worrying sound. Suddenly I realize that Antonia, too, is scared; and for the first time since I whisked Charlotte away, I consider the implications if the spirit—devil, *knocker*—has followed her across the island. In my mind's eye, I see the heavy glass paperweight flying through the air once more, and experience a strange sensation, like cold water running down my back. Was I too rash? Too determined to save her? It was all I could think of in the moment, while Mrs. North lay bleeding on the floor, but perhaps it had been poor judgment—a decision made by a shocked and frightened man. Perhaps I did not save *her* as much as I saved the Norths.

Have I put us all in danger by bringing Charlotte here?

"Dr. Crown might not be the answer." Antonia jabs her fork into a piece of meat. "As I recall it, I felt more like a stabbed pig on a butcher's block than a valued patient," she continues. "He kept asking me about the *wound*." She rolls her eyes. "How we had to find 'the place that bled,' as if I didn't know where that was already. I ruined many a good dress after the birth."

"Don't be vulgar, Antonia." I feel both sick and annoyed. I need peace to think, but her voice keeps grating. "He told me of how you deliberately resisted treatment, so any failure is on you and not the doctor." I send her a reproachful look; my head has started pounding like mad. "I am confident that with Dr. Crown's knowledge and my faith at her disposal, Charlotte will have all the help she needs in overcoming this . . . *affliction*. Yes, she is right where she needs to be," I say, feeling quite pleased with my reasoning, even if my heart disagrees by pumping out warnings.

"And her red lips and black hair have nothing to do with it?" A wicked-looking smirk spreads on my wife's thin lips. "The fullness of her bosom and the blush on her cheeks play no part in your decision whatsoever?"

"Antonia!" I gasp, entirely exasperated. "The girl is under some sort of attack—"

"Yes, from a lustful, married man!"

"If you had seen what I saw—"

"I did not, but I *do* know there's nothing *noble* about this pursuit!" She abruptly rises from the chair and throws her napkin down on the table. "Do you think she will love you better if you exorcise her demon?"

"I think it is my duty—"

"Your faith may not be strong enough for that!" Her chest heaves under the froth of white lace, and again it strikes me that Antonia is afraid, but tries to hide it beneath a veneer of outrage. "If you truly mean to take on this task, you better make sure that there is *nothing* standing between you and the Lord. No weakness, Jasper, none—or it might be *you* that is pelted with rocks!"

"I feel quite confident," I say stiffly, ignoring the alarm bells. The headache will not let go, but feels like needles piercing my scalp.

Antonia sends me a scorching look. "You're a fool. You lie to yourself, Jasper, and you will not hear the truth—"

"Enough!" I bellow, and rise as well. "*I* know my heart, wife, better than you ever did."

"We'll see about that," she replies, quite cold.

• • •

When Antonia retires, I remain at the table, drinking wine until the headache subsides to a dull ache. Then I cork the bottle and gather what little is left of my courage before rising to see to our houseguest.

Noreen is still in the kitchen when I pause to fetch a candle for the stairs. At first, she does not speak at all, just stares at me darkly from her place by the table.

"I just want to make sure she's comfortable for the night," I say, then inwardly reproach myself for feeling a need to explain. I am nothing but a gracious host—a caregiver. I do nothing but what my conscience tells me.

"She seems quite snug up there," says Noreen. "I brought her some dinner earlier, and she will have breakfast with me in the morning."

"She might need a bath, too," I say.

"I shall see to it," Noreen replies. "It's a shame, though," she adds, but does not specify what exactly deserves this label.

I ascend the stairs slowly, with a heart that is beating fast in my chest. My palms are sweaty by the time I stand outside the closed door to Noreen's old room where we decided to put her, and lift my hand to knock twice.

"Come in," she calls, and when I do—heart in throat—I find her comfortable upon the bed. She has changed into a nightgown from her suitcase, hastily packed by Evelyn before we left, and there is a candle burning on the nightstand. I see an empty teacup there as well, and a collection of books that Noreen must have brought. I recognize a couple from my study. In her lap rests a rather rowdy romance that I believe belonged to the last reverend's wife. I should not have read it, and yet I had, during the long winter nights while Antonia thought I was working on a sermon. For some reason, seeing it lying there on Charlotte's white-clad thighs makes my throat constrict.

"How are you settling in?" I ask, when I have somewhat regained my bearings.

"Fine, I suppose." A touch of sorrow tinges her voice.

"I'm sorry I cannot accommodate you better," I say, mouth dry. Looking at her sitting there, so serene, the happenings at the North house suddenly seem oddly distant.

As if none of it had happened.

"I will be just fine up here." She smiles up at me. "At least the door isn't locked."

"And it never shall be," I promise.

"I just worry about Mother." She shifts upon the bed, and the lace on her nightgown rustles.

"I will ask after her health in the morning," I say.

"I *am* grateful, Reverend, and I hope you know that. I am grateful to both you and your wife for taking me in. My sisters would have let me out of the room eventually, but Mother would have locked me up again as soon as she was able."

"I fear that is the truth," I admit. "Mrs. North must have succumbed to the strain of all that has happened of late."

"She feels it. We all do." Charlotte looks utterly unhappy. "I'm glad that the knocker didn't attack you, too, Reverend. That would have broken my heart."

"On the contrary," I say, still astonished by the fact. "It brought me flowers . . . violets."

"Oh." Charlotte blushes prettily, remembering, perhaps, the little posies she used to bring me. "It does that sometimes; brings something nice." Her gaze briefly grazes the slim stack of books, which sends a wash of cold down my spine. Did the knocker get them for her?

"Did it follow you here?" The question shoots from my mouth like a bullet—needlessly hostile, perhaps.

Charlotte's gaze shifts. "Knocker, are you there?" she asks, and my heart leaps painfully when a single, assertive knock sounds from the ceiling right above us. "It did." She rests her eyes on me.

Is there a challenge in her gaze?

"But why?" I stare at the spot where the knocking sounded, and see nothing but the slanted, white-painted boards. "Does it truly belong to you?"

"It belongs *with* me." She shrugs. "I cannot tell you why, but it does—or *it* thinks it does, anyway."

"But does it . . . obey you?" I ask, with terror wrenching my gut. The headache is back with its needles and thorns, prodding at my temples.

"No," she says. "It is its own master. You can ask it yourself if you like," she offers. "One rap for 'yes,' two for 'no.' It's quite simple."

"Oh, I better not," I reply, though it is surely tempting. Who would not feel an ounce of curiosity when faced with something so nature defying? "The Bible tells us that such beings are liars," I caution her. "They cannot be trusted to tell the truth." Whatever the thing is, I feel quite certain that the warning applies.

"That's what Evelyn says, too," Charlotte admits, "though in my experience, its answers and predictions make sense."

"That's how lies are best sowed," I tell her. "They hide in truth like weeds in rye. If you trust the liar, it can better deceive you."

"But why would it do that?" She looks up at me with her big eyes. The nightgown makes her look like a child, hiding the fullness of her torso.

"Who knows why such creatures do what they do?" I am terribly aware that said creature is likely listening in, but still feel that the words must be said. "If you asked my father—who was also a reverend—he would say it is here to corrupt and to reap souls for its master, the Devil. *I* say that we don't know that for sure. Science has yet to tell us."

"If it is of the Devil, wouldn't it have had problems entering here?" she asks. "Wouldn't it have welcomed you with daggers, not violets?"

"Oh, but a priest's home is no holier than he is," I say. "Underneath the collar, I am still just a man." I cannot help but feel a burst of shame as I say it, although there is no reason to.

Charlotte smiles. "I know you are, Reverend."

"Will you pray with me, Charlotte?" I ask, turning to the safety of ritual.

"Of course." She does not hesitate, which feels strangely reassuring.

I place my candle next to hers on the nightstand, and Charlotte puts her book away. Then she climbs out of the bed and we both kneel, side by side, our knees on the chilly floor. We place our elbows on the mattress and fold our hands. She does not look like a child anymore, and I try not to notice her breasts, or how her dark lashes fan out when she closes her eyes. A thick tendril of hair brushes my arm, as a scent of perspiration and oolong tea engulfs me. Her radiating heat seems to soak through my clothes and caress my naked skin. I curse the knocker for leaving me so raw, and then I curse the wine for making me susceptible to fancy.

I pray for delivery with a strong and even voice, not letting up before my voice grows hoarse. By the time I am quite done, we are both covered in a sheen of sweat; it glistens on her brow like dew.

"Thank you, Reverend." She smiles shyly. "I do feel much stronger now."

I do not, though. I feel weak—exhausted by fear and tormented by shame.

"Get some sleep, Charlotte," I say, then I rise to fetch my candle. "Our work has just begun," I add. "It will not end before the spirit is gone and bothers you no more."

"I know." She climbs back onto her bed. "I will sleep much better tonight, though, knowing that you are close, protecting me."

"I'm glad to hear that," I say, though my voice is not only hoarse but brittle, and the flame on my candle flickers wildly, due to an unsteady hand.

When I close the door behind me, I let out a breath of relief that has nothing to do with devils.

·32·

charlotte

On the third day since the paperweight flew off the desk, my sisters come to the clergy house to celebrate my birthday. It is a fine day, if windy, and I meet them in the garden, which no one but me ever uses. It is not much of a garden, truth be told. Compared to Aunt Anne's abundant crop of flowers on the mainland, none of the gardens at Margaret's Keep have much to offer. The Hills keep a few flower beds, and the grass is cut; some berry bushes have been planted and somehow survived, though they yield very little fruit. It is mostly the stone furniture—benches and tables scattered in the green—that makes it stand out from the surrounding fields. And where the grass ends, the beach begins: a field of its own, made up of smooth, gray stones.

Beyond that lies the whitecapped sea.

I feel at home in the garden and frequently spend my time there, reading a book or just thinking. It keeps me from crossing paths with Mrs. Hill, and it also keeps me out of the attic room, which, despite being a refuge, is horribly small and cramped. I tell myself that this situation will not last forever, and that the promise of seeing Jasper

Hill every day more than makes up for the discomfort. Yet, I am happy for the garden—for the salty air and open space. And the knocker, too, seems to rejoice in it, and moves through the grass like a snake, leaving ribbons-like tracks in its wake.

I meet my sisters by one of the benches next to a circular stone table, whose concrete base is set with pretty fist-sized rocks from the beach: pink specked with silver, green run through with black. It *is* good to see them and they must feel the same way, because they all embrace me and hold me tight. Adelaide weeps a bit, and even Evelyn seems touched. Sophie clings to my waist like a monkey.

We all sit down and Evelyn brings out gifts from her basket: soft honey cake—my favorite—and bottles of lemonade. Though Noreen is no novice, I have missed Mrs. Norris's cooking and do appreciate the familiar taste of home. Evelyn also has a book on homemaking for me, which I will never read, but know is given from a place of love. Adelaide and Sophie have drawn greeting cards. Adelaide's is excellent, as always. It shows a cat sleeping under a tree, next to an open picnic basket. The basket's contents have all been consumed: fish bones and milk bottles litter the ground, and there is even a tiny mouse skull. *Best Wishes on Your Birthday* is penned underneath the drawing. Sophie has drawn a tree as well: an apple tree heavy with ripe, red fruit. Sophie always draws trees, on account of there being so few on the island. They are exotic to her.

"How is Mother?" I ask, when satisfactorily fortified with honey cake. Jasper has told me she is better, but he has not seen her for himself. I believe she turned him away.

"She is on bed rest," Evelyn answers. She has donned one of her many blue dresses, and wears her dark hair pinned up at the nape of her neck. Her straw hat lies on the ground, held in place by a lemonade bottle. With the sea rising and falling behind her, she looks much like a mermaid, doling out sweets from her bottomless basket.

"She has a *severe* concussion," says Sophie, likely having picked up the words from the doctor. She does not look too troubled by it, but sits ramrod straight on the bench in her green-checked attire, ripping pieces off the sticky cake and popping them into her mouth.

"The doctor thinks she will heal," says Evelyn. "She just needs some time and plenty of rest—and she is not allowed her port, which bothers her a great deal."

"We haven't heard it since you left." Adelaide sounds out of breath.

"No," I say, "because it's with me."

"That's what we figured." Adelaide nods. "The house feels just like it did before. There's nothing peculiar about it. Mrs. Fisher tells everyone that you kept a devil in the shed, though, and the islanders are happy that you live with the reverend now. They think he can defeat it."

"Norma and Lillian shouldn't have told," I say, even if I am secretly pleased.

Evelyn lets out a deep breath. "You are just lucky that Mother is on bed rest, and has not heard the gossip yet. Though I imagine that when she does, the Fishers might lose their boat, unless they agree to take it all back or blame it on their daughters' imaginations."

"Do you really think Father would do that?" Adelaide's mouth hangs open.

"Certainly." Evelyn sounds curt. "What else is all his power for but making us feel safe? He does not want a scandal any more than Mother does."

"Oh, poor Norma," Adelaide laments. "I would not have brought them at all if I had known the knocker was still wicked."

"Not wicked," I say. "Just different from us. It does not have a conscience," I explain.

"Because it is not of God." Evelyn's sharp gaze bores into mine.

"Has it bothered the reverend and Mrs. Hill yet?" Sophie looks up at the clergy house's stern facade.

"Not yet," I reply, though it is not entirely true. "It is mostly up in my room, and seems to have behaved, since Mother."

"But you still talk to it?" Evelyn frowns.

"Yes," I admit reluctantly. "It just seems safer." Somehow I cannot bring myself to tell even my sisters how close I feel to the spirit now, how much I have come to rely on it. "As long as I talk to it, maybe I can temper it somewhat," I continue, in the hope that it might be a satisfactory answer.

"I think that's a foolish notion." Evelyn's frown deepens. "It certainly showed no restraint when it attacked our mother."

That is not true, though. It *had* shown restraint—but I can never let Evelyn know that.

"Do they treat you well here?" Adelaide asks, eager to change the subject.

"Well enough," I admit. "Mrs. Hill hates me, of course, but I rarely see her and the reverend comes to pray with me every night." I can barely contain the blush when I say it, thinking of those moments together in the intimacy of the attic room: the darkening of his eyes when he looks at me, and the light shivering of his hands. "He has written to a doctor to come and see me," I add, to let my sisters know just how committed he is to helping me.

"Why?" Adelaide asks. "You're not sick, are you?"

I shake my head. "Not that I know. Perhaps he just wants to make sure."

"It's good that you are here, though," Evelyn says. "Mother was furious, of course, when she learned that he had 'stolen you away.' Listening to her now, you would think that *the reverend* is the villain, rather than the spirit. She always spoke so highly of him before—blaming the affair with the children's choir on you—but she seems to have had a change of heart. She feels that he took advantage of her illness to abduct you." She rolls her eyes. I cannot help that her words—condemning as they might be—make butterflies form and flutter in my belly. "I don't think you should be in the same house as Mother right now," Evelyn continues. "God only knows what she could come up with. She is not handling any of this particularly well."

"And Father?" I ask.

"Concerned for Mother," Evelyn replies, then suddenly looks bothered. She bites into her lip as a faint color rises in her cheeks. "James is still set to visit," she murmurs, and I know what she is thinking even without asking, and decide not to force her to say the words.

"I suppose you would rather not have me at home while he is there." I try not to let the hurt seep into my voice.

"Perhaps it would be safer—" She shifts on the seat. "Perhaps it would be easier for all of us . . . just until he's gone." Her gaze moves restlessly, looks at everything but me.

"Evelyn, that's *so* unfair!" Adelaide rises from the bench, her brow knitted in anger. "Charlotte *lives* with us, and James does not. It's *her* house, not his!"

"No," I say, grabbing hold of her wrist. "Evelyn is right. I better not be at the house right now, for *many* reasons—"

"But it's not your *fault*!" Adelaide protests. "You didn't want any of this to happen, and now it's ruining your whole life!"

"That's just why I should stay here," I say. "If anyone can help me, it's Reverend Hill. Besides, just because the knocker gives *me* grief, it doesn't mean that you all have to suffer."

Evelyn gives me a grateful look. "Just be careful, Charlotte . . . with the reverend." And again—despite the direness of her voice—I cannot help but feel a thrill pass through my body. She would not have issued the warning if she did not suspect that something *might* happen and that my nighttime fantasies could finally come true.

I, for one, will *not* be careful.

"I still think it is terribly unfair." Adelaide sits back down again, frowning all the while.

"You just don't want to sleep in our room on your own," I tease.

"Well, it's scarier than it used to be," she admits.

Evelyn flashes a quick smile. "Adelaide sleeps in Sophie's room now."

Sophie has long since stopped listening to us; her gaze is glued to the horizon. "The view of the sea is so strange without the tower," she remarks.

"It was old and in poor repair," I say. "Perhaps it wasn't much of a loss."

"Do you think *it* came from there?" Adelaide looks unhappy again.

"I don't know," I reply, since it is the truth, and I have long since stopped wondering about the knocker's origins.

Evelyn seems to agree with me. "It doesn't matter where it came from. The only thing I care about is ridding us of that thing."

"Me, too," says Sophie.

"Me, too," says Adelaide.

I say it, too, even if it is a lie.

·33·

ruth

Six days after the attack on Mrs. North, Evelyn comes to the schoolhouse to speak with me, and I am instantly in turmoil. As I fuss with hot water and cups for tea, my heart hammers wildly in my chest. I think the hour of reckoning has come for sure, and that she is here to berate me for sending Reverend Hill to their door.

It had ended in disaster, it truly had—and I cannot help but feel responsible.

It was Miss Boden who filled me in on what had happened, when Benjamin and I met her on our way to the grocery store, just two days after the incident. I had asked after the girls' health, since both Sophie and Adelaide had been missing from school, and Miss Boden, looking small within the folds of her headscarf and shawl, had taken on a grave expression.

"There's nothing wrong with the girls, Miss Russel, but Mrs. North is gravely injured. I'm sure the girls will be back at their letters as soon as the shock has settled."

"Oh, but Miss Boden, what happened?" I asked, instantly rattled.

My thoughts went to the knocker at once—to rocks and fire and black creatures in the ceiling.

"She was hit." Miss Boden had lowered her voice. "I know she wants me to say that she took a tumble down the stairs—like you did, Mr. West." She looked up at Benjamin. "But we all know it was the glass paperweight in Mr. North's study that hit her. I had to clean the thing myself."

Benjamin and I looked at each other, mirroring each other's horror.

"Did it hit her . . . by itself?" Benjamin asked, looking stricken, and Miss Boden gave a curt nod, looking around her, up and down the dirt road, as if worried that her employer—or even the knocker—should be nearby to hear her tattle.

"What about Charlotte?" I asked, thinking of the girl's plight, locked up in her room.

"Oh, the reverend brought her to the clergy house, and we haven't seen her since—not the . . . *thing* either, truth be told. We cannot *feel* it anymore, either; that sense of someone watching is gone. Mrs. Norris thinks it went with Charlotte."

"So the reverend was there when it happened?" I tried to make sense of the tale.

Miss Boden nodded. "He came to bless the house, as we had asked him to do. It all happened while he was in the room—in the study, that is, discussing Charlotte with the Norths. He was quite angry, you see, that Mrs. North had decided to lock her up."

Benjamin and I exchanged glances again.

"In the ruckus after Mrs. North fell unconscious, the reverend freed Charlotte and brought her to the clergy house," Miss Boden continued with wide eyes. "She has stayed there since. It was a good thing, though, that she left, because Mrs. North wasn't happy when she came to—not that she can do much, in her state." Miss Boden sent another uneasy look up the road, although it was void of traffic. "Mrs. Fisher's girls had been with Charlotte in the shed and spoken to that ungodly creature as well—or at least that's what they say, and Charlotte doesn't deny it." She gave us a pointed look. "That's what set Mrs. North off on the day of the fire. She did her best to swear Mrs. Fisher to secrecy, of course, but there is already talk and none of it good, so yes, it's a good thing that Charlotte isn't home."

"And Mr. North?" Benjamin asked. "I suppose he agreed to Charlotte's leaving?"

"He was relieved, I think, with his wife being injured, that someone else took care of his other problem. Norris drove Charlotte and the reverend to the clergy house in the closed carriage." An expression of insecurity suddenly crossed her features. "Mrs. North seems to think that the reverend took advantage of her injury to spirit the girl away." The words sounded strangely ominous, and caused a cold claw to curl around my heart—even if I was relieved to learn that the reverend had freed Charlotte from captivity, as I had asked. I suppose I just had not imagined that he would bring her home—to Mrs. Hill—who had no love for the girl.

"And you, Miss Boden?" I asked her softly. "What do you make of it all?"

"I think she is better off with the reverend." The housekeeper gave me a tired look. "I think he stands a better chance against the forces of hell than Mrs. North."

And now I cannot think of any other good reason why the oldest North girl should seek me out, besides berating me for my undue meddling. Aside from delivering Benjamin to my doorstep, the grown-up Norths have stayed clear of me ever since the rock incident, and I suppose I cannot blame them. The embarrassment they feel must be immense, and they clearly have enough trouble to handle. In a way, it feels like a relief to finally come face-to-face with one of them. Benjamin and I have spent many hours since our meeting with Miss Boden discussing the implication of the latest turn of events. I had even considered going to the clergy house myself, just to see how things were going, but did not want to appear unduly curious. Besides, the last time I meddled, it ended in concussion and—according to Mrs. North—an abduction, so I figured it was safer to sit on my hands.

Evelyn does not seem angry, though, as she sits by my kitchen table. Rather she appears pensive, and—to my surprise—I notice an extra sparkle in her eyes, and a hint of blush in her cheeks. The reason for this enhancement soon becomes clear.

"My fiancé, James, arrives tomorrow," she tells me, while taking the offered cup of tea. Benjamin has made himself scarce for the occasion, and is outside, chopping slender logs of driftwood into smaller pieces. He says he enjoys the manual labor, the feel of the sun on his skin.

"That must be exciting for you," I reply. "Is it safe, though?" The words slip out of my mouth unbidden, as I envision the poor man pelted with rocks.

"Well, yes . . . It's quite safe *now,* with Charlotte staying at the clergy house. I'm sure you already know she is there?" She fixes me with her gaze until I give a nod. "The timing of his visit is still not ideal," she admits, "with Mother recovering from her . . . *accident,* but we'll make do, and I'm committed to giving him a good impression."

"Charlotte is not coming home, then?" I ask, somewhat surprised, since I cannot imagine Mrs. Hill being too thrilled with the current arrangement. In fact, I am astonished that she agreed to it in the first place.

"Not for the moment, no." Evelyn smiles at my bafflement. "It is peculiar, I know, but it is only for now. We are all very grateful to the Hills for showing my sister such hospitality." I know this cannot be entirely true, but still manage to nod and smile. "Reverend Hill has arranged for a psychiatrist to come," Evelyn continues, and manages to take me aback anew. This is not normally something one shares over tea, and especially not with someone practically a stranger. Evelyn seems not to care about this breach of etiquette, though, but continues unperturbed. "He has asked me to sit in while Charlotte is being examined, seeing as how Mother is indisposed, but I would rather not have this . . . *darkness* pollute James's first visit to the island." Her pretty face turns grim, and she sips the hot tea with a thoughtful expression. "It simply will not do if I have to leave him alone for hours to attend my sister's *psychiatric* examination. I'm sure you understand, Miss Russel." She looks at me with her pretty brown eyes—so very much like Charlotte's.

"I do," I confirm, "but why do you share this with *me*?" I decide on a frank approach, certain there must be something behind it. Evelyn North did not come just to visit.

"Miss Russel, could you go in my stead?" She places her hand on mine on the table, her eyes most imploring. "You already know what is going on, and you know Charlotte, too—"

"Barely!" I protest. "Such examinations are personal. *Intimate*." I gently pull my hand away.

"But you are such a levelheaded woman, Miss Russel. You have such a calm demeanor, and will not lose your head over nothing. Charlotte would feel safe with you, and she *must* have another woman there." She is begging me with her eyes, a tiny sapphire pendant glittering on her clavicle.

"What about Mrs. Hill?" I ask.

"Oh, she won't." Evelyn shifts her gaze away. "You know how she doesn't care for my sister."

"Adelaide, then?" Though even as I form the words, I realize that the girl is far too young, and Evelyn shakes her head.

"There is no one else but you, Miss Russel. The staff is too immersed in their own superstitions, and there are no other appropriate women on the island." She shifts in the chair and finishes her tea. "You must have ample time now as well, since the children have started their summer break." She raises one eyebrow slightly, as if to say that I have no excuse. "We have appreciated your discretion over the last few months," she continues, "and hope to be able to rely on it in the future as well. Father wanted me to mention that you will be duly compensated for your time."

"I don't need money, Miss North," I tell her, forgoing her Christian name. "Most of all, I would like to not get further involved." Discussing the matter is one thing, but I would rather not come face-to-face with the knocker, boldness and courage be damned!

"But you *are* involved," Evelyn reminds me. "Your limp is proof of it—as well as your handsome houseguest." A tiny smile plays on her lips, and her gaze wanders to the wall, where the chopping of wood can be heard from outside.

And so, with a slight feeling of being tricked, I agree to it. I do.

Because Charlotte has nobody else.

• • •

The examination is to be held on the following Friday, and I predictably fret the night before. Had I been alone, I would have been in my bed with a stomachache, cursing the Norths up and down. Thankfully, though, I am not, so instead I find myself by the kitchen table, where Benjamin plies me with tea, rum, and assurances.

"There's no doubt that Charlotte needs you," he says. "She must be under a lot of strain, taken from her home and battling something unknown. She is young, too, barely more than a child."

"I know," I reply unhappily. "I know I must do it, but that doesn't mean that I don't fear the thing that follows her."

"We have spent a lot of time, you and I, wondering about this phenomenon," Benjamin says. "Perhaps this way, we can finally learn more."

"I would rather learn from a distance," I admit, which makes him laugh.

"The reverend must have a reason for bringing in a psychiatrist. Perhaps it will be a fascinating exploration—"

"Well, that is the other thing," I admit. "I cannot *stand* psychiatrists.

In fact, I *abhor* the profession." I speak with such vehemence that the teacup jiggles in my hand and spills a few sweet drops down on the table.

"Oh." Benjamin sounds surprised, unused to seeing me in such temper. "May I ask why?" he says cautiously.

I sigh and put the teacup down. "I don't speak of this—ever—but the circumstances force me this time, and you have become such a wonderful friend." The last word is tinged with sadness. A part of me wishes that I were young and inexperienced—untainted by the cruelty of the world. Perhaps I would have allowed myself some hope then. As it is, however, it is better to let this notion wither on the vine before it can blossom into something dangerous. "It concerns a great injustice." I force the words out between tight lips. "One that quite ruined my childhood."

"Oh, dear Ruth." His hand squeezes mine. "Please, do tell. I'd be honored to listen." His eyes behind the spectacles are nothing but good and kind, and the sight of them almost makes me weep.

"Do you remember how I told you that my father was a successful businessman, and how I grew up in circumstances quite similar to—if not better than—the Norths'?" I wait until he nods his confirmation. "I could see it on your face then—the wonder, the question: How did I end up here, an unmarried schoolteacher on a remote island, if I was born to such wealth? You were too polite to ask me what happened, and, needless to say, the answer is grim." I pause while searching for the courage to continue. "The journey of my . . . decline, started when I was a child, and my mother had an affair." I look up at him briefly, unable to meet his gaze. The words are hard to find, and even harder to express, but I have started down this path of honesty, so now I must follow through.

"It wasn't a great love story." I give a thin laugh. "She was just unhappy and bored, and found some solace with the coachman who used to bring her around. He was young—or younger than she—and handsome, too. I suppose the secrecy was a part of what made it an adventure for them both. It was a dangerous game, though, and my father eventually found out. Perhaps he had been suspicious for a while . . ." I trail off, momentarily lost in the past, seeing it all so vividly again: the large brick house we lived in, the green velvet drapes in all the windows, and the carved wooden furniture in every room. I see my collection of milky-skinned porcelain dolls, the silver cutlery on the crisp white tablecloth, and remember the scent of cigars and misery that always infused our home.

"Many men in my father's position—busy and rich—do not mind if their wives find themselves discreet amusements, but my father was of a different ilk. He was the jealous type, driven by spite both in business and in private, so when Mother's affair became known to him, he decided that she ought to be punished." I take a deep breath before forming the next words. "He used the affair against her, and had her declared insane."

"Could he *do* that? How?" Benjamin sounds surprised, which surprises me in turn.

"*Of course* he could," I tell him. "There was no shortage of doctors willing to support his claim that a woman acting so 'at odds with her nature' could clearly not be sane, and she was certainly not fit to raise a child." My lips twist up in a bitter smile. "My mother spent the rest of her life in an asylum," I continue. "I rarely ever saw her, though we did visit every Christmas. I had no brothers or sisters, so it was a very lonely childhood after she was gone."

"Oh, Ruth," Benjamin says again. "What a terrible story—and what a horrible thing for a child to live through." His hand around mine is warm and firm, anchoring me to the here and now. "No wonder you don't appreciate psychiatrists—or marriage."

"Yes, what happened to Mother certainly gave me ample reason to examine the institution, and find it lacking. I resolved I would never marry. I even gave up my inheritance for it." My bitter smile turns wry. "Father knew of my resolve, and added as a condition in his will that I had to marry by the age of twenty-five, or forfeit his fortune. I, of course, refused to let a dead man decide on my behalf, and became a schoolteacher instead." I give a rueful laugh. "I would not so easily abandon my power."

"And neither should you have to." Benjamin sounds sincere.

"I must admit that I regretted the decision often, when money was scarce and my future uncertain, but I could not go back on it. My cousin inherited the fortune in my stead, so the money is utterly gone."

"I don't blame you for the regret," he says, "but you are nevertheless an enormously brave individual, Ruth, to fight so hard for your principles." The admiration in his voice seems sincere.

"Brave is one thing, foolish another. I did not know what the world was like, Benjamin. I did not know how you had to fight tooth and claw—"

"Yet, if you *had* married, the money would not have been yours—not truly."

"I know. And on good days, I tell myself that is why the decision I made was sound. I could never thrive living under another's thumb. Sharing a roof with my father was a harsh lesson in that regard."

"My mother died so early that I can barely remember her, but I do hope she never felt like that." Benjamin squeezes my hand again.

"I don't think our fathers were much alike," I say.

"Mine was a gentle soul," Benjamin admits. "Kind and enamored with nature."

"Just like his son."

"I can see why you feel a certain responsibility for the North girls, however," he remarks. "I suppose they hold up a mirror."

I nod. "That is why I have to help Charlotte. I have to be there to make sure that she will not be swallowed up and mistreated. She *does* need an advocate—and, under the circumstances, only I can be that for her."

"She is lucky to have you," he says. "You will not let yourself be so easily swayed by the opinions of powerful men."

"No," I say. "But I still fear them—almost as much as I fear the spirit."

"You are a very brave woman, Ruth Russel," Benjamin declares again, although I do not much feel like it.

Mostly I feel lost and scared—like a mouse about to enter a lion's den.

·34·

ruth

We gather in Reverend Hill's office on the ground floor of the clergy house. There is the reverend and myself, Dr. Crown and a *Mr.* Crown, his assistant, who also happens to be his nephew. Mrs. Hill is nowhere to be seen.

Noreen serves coffee in those tiny little cups as we settle in around the reverend's massive oak desk. Dr. Crown turns out not to be as old as I expected, but carries a full head of dark hair, with just a little silver at the temples. He is a tall man with a prominent jaw and green eyes that would be beautiful had they not belonged to a psychiatrist. His nephew, *Mr.* Crown, is a nondescript, light-haired young man of about twenty-five. He has the air of someone believing himself to be the best and brightest in any company. I blame this on his youth, and promptly decide to ignore him.

The reverend looks tired. His pretty face holds an ashen pallor, and I cannot help but notice the liquor on his breath when he greets me. He is also uncommonly jittery, seeming to easily lose his focus, which does not bode well for the day's undertaking. Having Charlotte at the clergy house must be a challenge for him—and not only because of her invisible companion. I remember Benjamin's description of the demon in the ceiling, and a chill passes through me, even if the room—and the coffee—is quite warm.

I dearly hope the creature will not show itself.

"Our first task in this initial examination will be to establish if there are, in fact, phenomena occurring that defy the laws of nature," Dr. Crown declares in a drawling voice. His nephew takes down every word in a notebook, writing at impressive speed. "Reverend Hill, a reputable witness, has made such a claim, and so it must be examined closely. Hoaxes in this field abound, so we must be absolutely certain—"

"What field is that?" I ask, before I have had time to think better of it.

"Psychical research." His green gaze lands on me, and I do not like it.

"I thought we were here to examine Charlotte's mind," I protest, refusing to let the pompous psychiatrist intimidate me. "I thought we were here to *help* her."

"All in good time, Miss Russel," the psychiatrist says with a twinge of impatience. "First, we must establish what exactly we are to examine: a young woman who has her family fooled, or . . . something else." He gives a self-satisfied smile, and I am unsure if I should be relieved that Charlotte is not yet entirely blamed, or if I should be worried that he even considers the possibility of a hoax.

Clearly, he has not yet met the knocker.

"I was pelted with rocks in the Norths' driveway," I say, wanting him to face reality. "There is simply no way Charlotte could have orchestrated the event. She wasn't even there—no one was."

"And now we have *two* reputable witnesses." Dr. Crown sounds giddy, almost gleeful. "A reverend and a schoolteacher," he notes with even more satisfaction. "I know we asked you here for the girl's comfort," he says to me, "but now I think Mr. Crown must take down *your* statement as well. This is indeed a most interesting case . . ." He rises from his chair and starts pacing the small room, seemingly deep in thought.

"But we *are* here to help Charlotte?" I look to Reverend Hill, who sits behind the desk.

"Of course we are, Miss Russel." He gives me a reassuring smile. "Dr. Crown has some interesting theories, though, that I think are worthwhile to examine."

"If you don't mind, Miss Russel"—the doctor spins around until he faces me—"I would rather not share them just yet. I would prefer if we waited until *after* the examination, just to avoid any bias."

I still feel puzzled—and I do not trust him—but feel I have no choice but to nod in agreement. I have not even seen Charlotte yet.

"Good." Dr. Crown pauses by the desk, while the nephew still writes with pomp and fury. "As I said, our first task will be to establish whether there are nature-defying forces at work, and if so, what—exactly—they are."

"Nothing good," I murmur.

"Excellent," says Reverend Hill, listening only to the doctor. He rises from the desk to go and get Charlotte.

I feel tense while we wait; a faint taste of bile fills the cave of my mouth.

I just know they will blame Charlotte if they can.

She looks very small as she enters, but then she was never big of stature. It is only in my mind that she looms large, due to all that has happened. She is wearing a nice yellow dress cut in the latest fashion, and has tied her hair back with a piece of white ribbon, matching the gauze twined around her left ring finger. Her gaze moves restlessly—curiously—between the men, before it comes to rest on me.

"Good morning, Miss Russel," she says, as if she is a student in my schoolroom.

"Good morning, Charlotte." I smile at her. I notice how the reverend takes care not to touch her; how he makes sure to always stay at least two steps away from her, as if he fears her—and maybe he does. But that is not what his eyes are saying, caressing her quite shamelessly. He cannot be aware or he would surely avert his gaze, rather than letting it linger on her mouth. The tense feeling inside me grows stronger and is joined by its steady companion, the stomachache.

I do not like this at all.

Charlotte is placed on one of the straight-backed chairs that litter the room, meant for members of the congregation when they come to seek advice. They are not built for comfort, but rather to make the sinners feel the aching of their flesh. Perhaps they are built to remind us that living is equal to suffering—to make us long even more for the soft clouds of the beyond.

Charlotte does not complain, though, but sits down when told to. She even looks slightly amused as she takes us all in. Mr. Crown and I have turned our chairs around to get a better look at her. He is balancing the notebook on his knee. Even now, when looking at the woman placed so vulnerably in front of him, the young man has an arrogant tilt to his head, the hint of a sneer plastered on his lips. I wonder if anyone but his uncle would have given him a job.

Reverend Hill and Dr. Crown stand before Charlotte. The latter creases his brow with concentration, while the former has something lost about him as he stares at the pretty young woman in the chair. Charlotte herself smiles at them and smooths her skirt with her hands. I regret the coffee, which I now blame for the taste of bile flooding my mouth.

Dr. Crown starts his examination. "Good morning, Charlotte." He is trying for a gentle smile, but it falters. For a moment, I wonder if he, too, is afraid of the spirit, but then I think he has another agenda—an ambition to fulfill—and that is why he is staring at her like a wolf about to devour a sheep.

"Good morning, Dr. Crown," she says quite calmly, and I am suddenly reminded that Charlotte is a North. It will take more than a fancy title to scare her; and for once, I am grateful for the arrogance of the rich.

"Remember, Charlotte, this is nothing to be afraid of," Reverend Hill assures her nevertheless—blind, perhaps, to the young woman's power. "Dr. Crown is here to help, that is all. Together, perhaps we can make sense of the knocker, and put all the unpleasantness to rest." He smiles.

"Of course," she says, utterly unfazed.

"Now, Charlotte." Dr. Crown takes over. "You seem like a bright young woman, so I will not insult you by treating you like a child." He effortlessly throws this barb in the reverend's direction. "We—Mr. Crown and I—are here due to the spectacular claims made by Reverend Hill about you harboring an entity referred to as 'the knocker.' In your estimation, are these claims accurate?" He paces in front of her with his hands laced behind his back, feeling quite the detective, for sure.

"That is accurate, yes."

"And this creature—this 'knocker'—how would you describe him?"

"It's not a man," she says. "I don't believe it has any gender."

This stops the doctor in his tracks. "What makes you say that?"

"Well, it doesn't feel like either," says Charlotte.

"But you have not *seen* it to confirm either way?" Now he is pacing again

"No," she replies as her gaze shifts. "It's just a feeling I have."

"Do you think it is a ghost?" He pauses briefly while waiting for her answer.

"It says it's not," Charlotte replies. "And not a devil either."

"That *is* most curious." Dr. Crown gives a thoughtful nod. "Could it be something new? Something never heard of before?"

"I cannot say," Charlotte admits. "I can only tell you what it tells me."

"And how—exactly—does it communicate with you?" Dr. Crown sounds sarcastic, though I do not believe he intends to be. I suppose it is just in his nature.

"Through knocking, mostly," Charlotte replies. "For a while I had an alphabet painted on a wall, and it would knock on the letters."

Dr. Crown grins. "That must have been exciting for you. Do you enjoy speaking to the knocker?"

"At first I did," she says. "Then, when it became violent, I stopped. Then I started speaking to it again because *not* doing so seemed to make it worse." I find I am leaning forward in my chair. This is all news to me, and despite myself, I am intrigued.

"So it keeps you hostage— Is that correct?" Dr. Crown starts pacing again. His nephew scribbles with vigor.

"In a way, yes." Charlotte drops her gaze to the floor, her voice suddenly sad.

"What are you afraid of? What will happen if you stop?"

"Oh, there are the needles, of course. It hounded me with needles for a while. I found them in my food, in my bed, and even in my shoes. But mostly I worry that it will set another fire or throw stones at someone, like it did to Miss Russel." She briefly lifts her gaze to me.

Dr. Crown stops abruptly and spins to face Charlotte. "Why *you,* though, Charlotte? Why does it so desperately want to communicate with *you*? Why not one of your sisters?"

"I don't know," Charlotte replies, looking very confused. "It says it's because I was the first one to notice it was there."

"And how *did* you first notice—and when?"

"It was just noises at first, from the attic. Then came the knocking in the walls. It started two days after the earthquake." She gives her answer with an air of duty, and reminds me again of a girl in a schoolroom being questioned about her homework.

"So, by your estimation, it could have been any one of you who caught the knocker's attention, but you just drew the unlucky number?"

"I suppose so, yes," she mutters.

"Can you tell me why it is that you came to stay at the clergy house?" Dr. Crown asks her next.

"Of course. My mother had locked me in my room because the knocker had set fire to her painting. While Reverend Hill was at our house, the knocker threw a paperweight at my mother, causing a concussion. Reverend Hill then thought it would be safer for all if I was here." She says it matter-of-factly, as if recounting a day spent wandering on the beach. I find myself baffled, but also impressed.

"That is quite the story, Charlotte." If Dr. Crown shares my feelings, he does not show it. "Why do you think the knocker harmed your mother?"

"I cannot say," she replies. "I do not control the knocker."

"Were you angry at your mother for locking you up?" His green eyes glint in the sunlight flooding in through the windows.

"Of course I was," she replies, "but mostly I was concerned, because I didn't know what the knocker would do next. The fire had frightened me, too." She takes a shuddering breath.

"Quite understandably." Dr. Crown nods. "Did you ever ask the knocker why it threw stones at Miss Russel?"

"It said it didn't like visitors," Charlotte answers, and I shiver in my seat.

"Did you ask it about the fire?"

"No. I had given up by then. I didn't think it would tell me."

"Why?" Dr. Crown measures her with his fox-like gaze.

"It stopped divulging its reasons shortly after Miss Russel." She gives me another brief glance, which seems somewhat apologetic.

"Is the knocker an evil creature?" Dr. Crown starts pacing again.

"Not necessarily," Charlotte replies to my surprise. "It's more like a child. It doesn't know the difference between right and wrong."

"Not even if you tell it?"

"It doesn't listen to me," she says. "The knocker does as it pleases."

"And it has nothing to do with you?" the doctor asks.

"Of course not." Her red lips curl into a tiny smile, as if she finds the question ridiculous. "I don't control the knocker. If anything, it controls *me*. I wouldn't be in trouble at all if it hadn't taken a liking to me."

"You think it likes you, then?"

"It says that it does. It says that it loves me," she adds, and I suddenly feel sick.

"Why do you think it set fire to your mother's painting?" Dr. Crown asks next, changing direction once again. I do wonder where he is headed.

"I cannot say," Charlotte replies.

"If you had to guess?"

"I do not know its mind." She shifts on the chair, looking bored more than anything else. I cannot fault her for growing tired of the relentlessness of his questions. "Perhaps it wanted a spectacle? Perhaps it disagreed with the motif?"

"Where were *you* when your mother's painting caught fire?" Dr. Crown asks.

"In my room, with Mother," she replies at once.

"Were you two arguing?"

"Yes, in fact, we were."

Dr. Crown stops abruptly. "Can we speak to the knocker now, do you think?" He looks back at Charlotte on the chair, and I suddenly find myself highly alert. I do *not* want to make the creature's acquaintance—and yet I remain seated, unable to react. Perhaps it is the shackles of duty that keep me rooted to the rock-hard seat.

Charlotte shrugs on her own terrible chair. "If it wants to," she says.

"Wonderful." Dr. Crown smiles. "So how do we do this? Must we hold hands?"

"No. I'll just make an introduction."

Dr. Crown nods. "Go ahead."

Charlotte takes another deep breath, then speaks loudly. "Knocker, are you there?"

What feels like an eternity follows. None of us move, we just listen intently. I hardly dare to breathe. Then, faintly, from the bookshelf: a knock.

Our heads all swivel in the sound's direction, but I look back at Charlotte just in time to catch her rolling her eyes. She, for one, is not impressed.

"Knocker, are you there?" she asks again, with even more volume.

Now the knock from behind the bookshelf is as sharp and loud as a rap on a drum. Mr. Crown, next to me, blanches and finally stops his eager scribbling.

"Wonderful!" Dr. Crown laughs and claps his hands together. "Well done," he says to Charlotte, who gives him a puzzled look.

"Will you speak to Dr. Crown?" Charlotte asks the unseen entity.

Two raps sound in quick succession. They come from the ceiling this time.

"Two knocks? That means 'no,'" Charlotte tells us. "One knock means 'yes.'"

"Ask it why not," Dr. Crown urges.

"Why will you not speak to the doctor?" Charlotte asks the empty air. "Are you afraid of Dr. Crown?"

Two more knocks sound, this time from the wall by the windows.

"Do you dislike Dr. Crown?" she asks.

One single, hard rap can be heard from the desk. I cannot help but yelp and pull away from the possessed furniture. Reverend Hill looks awestruck as he follows the sounds with his gaze. Dr. Crown, however, seems as giddy as a boy, smiling all the while. He does not seem discouraged at all that the knocker will not speak to him.

"I'm sorry," Charlotte says to Dr. Crown. "It seems it doesn't care for you."

"Oh, no problem at all," the doctor says with a chuckle. "Can you ask it to do something else? Move something, perhaps?"

Charlotte gives him another puzzled look. "Knocker," she says, "can you move something for Dr. Crown?"

Two quick, sharp raps sound from the floor.

"I'm sorry," Charlotte says again, with her eyes on the doctor. "I cannot make it do anything." But this time I do not believe her. There is something about the way she says it, as if suppressing a smile or keeping a secret—the way contempt briefly flashes in her eyes as she looks up at the smug doctor. The sight of it stuns me. It feels as though I've been hit in the chest with something hard and heavy.

"What if we try this?" Dr. Crown says, and before any of us have time to react, he is by Charlotte's side, grabbing her hand and squeezing her bandaged finger.

Charlotte wails like a banshee just as the little china cup I had so daintily placed on the desk suddenly flies off its plate and crashes into the doctor's head. More projectiles follow in quick succession: a book of psalms—also from the desk—and the model of the island church made entirely of matches, which flies from its spot on the bookshelf to firmly hit Dr. Crown's jaw.

Reverend Hill is most distraught. "Stop this at once!" he commands the doctor, then steps forth to pry him off Charlotte's damaged finger. When the doctor finally lets go, I am shocked to hear him laughing. Reverend Hill, by his side, looks utterly stunned and quite furious. I finally remember why I am here, and rush to Charlotte's side. I kneel next to her chair and take the bandaged hand between my own to inspect it for fresh damage.

I look up at her pale, pained face. "Are you all right, Charlotte?"

"I am *now,*" she says, sending the laughing doctor a very dark look.

"Wonderful, Charlotte." The psychiatrist sounds almost deranged. "What a wonderful, stellar performance," he cries, as redness blooms on his forehead.

"Uncle?" Mr. Crown squeaks from his chair, his scribbling forgotten.

"Do you want to leave?" I ask Charlotte. "Go up to your room?"

She nods, looking unhappy. She retracts her wounded hand and cradles it gently in its unharmed twin. Her eyes shoot daggers at the crowing doctor.

"Do you want me to come with you?" I ask.

"No, I can manage. I'd rather be alone."

I do not blame her one bit.

I rise back to my feet. "Charlotte is leaving now," I declare.

Dr. Crown looks at me as if only now noticing my presence. "But we have only just begun."

"Charlotte is leaving now," I repeat in my sternest schoolroom voice. "Shame on you, doctor," I continue, quite unable to contain myself, "treating a young woman in such a way. This is nothing but an *assault*!" I pause to let my words sink in. "Reverend, do you endorse this behavior?"

The reverend shakes his head. "No, of course not! I promised Charlotte she wouldn't be harmed." He sends Dr. Crown a furious look. "You *should* go, Charlotte," he says, and the young woman slips out at once. "You owe her an apology," he says to Dr. Crown, as soon as the door has closed behind her.

The doctor seems to have finally come down to earth. "Oh, I do apologize," he says, but does not sound sorry at all. "It is just that—well, the temptation was too strong to resist. I wanted to prove a point, you see. I had a theory that I wanted to put to the test, and, by God, I think I did!" He chuckles again as the rest of us frown.

Reverend Hill's voice is very quiet, the expression on his face unusually cold. "Explain yourself."

Dr. Crown sinks down in my vacated chair, pulls a handkerchief out of his pocket, and starts mopping his brow. "It is *her,*" he declares in a voice brimming with amazement. "It is *her*—don't you see?"

"See what?" I ask, quite done with this man.

"She is *doing* it," he states with another sharp bark of laughter, before gathering his wits and putting on a more serious expression. "It has been a theory for a while now, among some of my more daring colleagues, that such phenomena are caused by spontaneous telekinesis. That a person—usually a young woman—in rare cases can develop such talents, and this *proves* it, don't you see? It was not some spirit from the beyond knocking on the walls; it was *her*! And when I hurt her, she defended *herself* by throwing objects at me!" He looks between us—waiting, no doubt, for the moment when the reverend and I would grasp the importance of his words.

"Of course it's not Charlotte!" the reverend snaps.

"That is highly unlikely," I agree.

"Charlotte is a tormented girl, distraught." Reverend Hill gestures wildly with his hands.

Dr. Crown chuckles. "But that is the beauty of it. She might not even know that she is doing it; the act can be utterly unconscious. She describes this 'knocker' as a child, yes? A child that loves her very much; a child that will go to battle for her and pull petty pranks, like burning her mother's painting while they quarrel." Dr. Crown is up from the chair again and resumes his restless pacing. "But it is revenge, don't you see? The knocker is Charlotte herself in a childlike state—a phantom of her own making!"

"Nonsense," barks Reverend Hill. "Pure speculation!"

"Why would she pelt me with *rocks*?" I ask.

"Because she *could*!" Dr. Crown beams at me. "Because this monster she has created knows no bounds—"

Reverend Hill cuts him off. "You have lost my trust, Dr. Crown. You have violated my hospitality and my welcome. I didn't invite you here to assault my houseguest, and I must ask you to leave my house at once!"

This seems to cool the doctor down a little—enough to grasp for a reprieve, at least. "Oh, but we have only just begun. This is a *groundbreaking* case, Reverend."

Hill renews his stance. "None of it is Charlotte's fault. She is the victim in this."

"Well, in a sense, yes." The doctor nods several times. "She is a victim of her own splendid *mind*—"

"No," Reverend Hill snaps. "I will *not* have you doing more experiments—"

"But she is a perfect candidate for a study! We could write a book—together, if you like. This could solve a number of the mind's many mysteries—"

"Her father would never allow it," I interject. "He is a rich and powerful man, with no interest in scandal. I'm surprised he even allowed this examination. You must pray, doctor, that Mr. North never learns of what you did and said here today. It might well be the end of your career." After this tirade, I have to sit down to catch my breath, as the whole room seems to be spinning around me.

"Miss Russel is right," the reverend agrees. "Leave now and never speak a word of this. It's the best you can do to save your own reputation."

"But you don't understand," the doctor pleads. "I *can* help her. If only we find the cause for her affliction—the *wound*—we can right what is wrong, and make the symptoms—'the knocker'—disappear."

Although I, for one, think the doctor finally speaks some sense, the reverend will not hear it. "There is nothing wrong with Charlotte," he booms, and strides out of the room.

I suspect that he is headed for the liquor cabinet.

I straighten up and turn to the door, thinking I should leave as well. "You should have kept your ambition better hidden from view," I tell the psychiatrist. "No one likes being taken advantage of."

"But surely you, too—and the reverend—must see the value of such a study . . ."

"Yes, but we do not *know,*" I say. "And as long as we don't know for sure that what you say is true, we cannot let you do it."

I feel as though I've been pelted with rocks again by the time I leave the clergy house. My insides feel like raw wounds, cut open by fear and left bleeding by doubt. Instead of helping, the doctor has made the confusion even worse, and I no longer know what to believe when it comes to Charlotte and her spirit. I want to trust her sincerity, but it is suddenly hard.

My steps are even slower than usual as I make my way home.

• • •

It is as I finally sit at my own kitchen table, enjoying Benjamin's stew of cod and carrots, and slowly relay the day's dramatic events, that I become aware of some unusual traffic on the road by the schoolhouse. First, I see the youngest Newell boy come sprinting past and do not pay it much mind, although the boy is red in the face and runs as if the devil himself was hot on his heels.

Next, Molly Boyden and Simon Fisher come running in the opposite direction, also red in the face and obviously excited. Still, I have no energy to spare, and keep chewing my fish and filling Benjamin in, until he, too, is suddenly distracted by something on the road.

Slightly annoyed, I turn my head to see Norma Fisher and Annabeth Ferryman come charging past, their braids dancing wildly on their backs.

"Oh no." I sigh. "The children are running. That means something terrible has happened." My heart starts racing in my chest, and my taste for fish has suddenly vanished.

Benjamin sounds puzzled. "How can you be so sure?"

"It's how news travels on this island. They send children to spread the word." I sigh again and empty the glass of beer Benjamin had poured for me.

"How can you be certain that it is bad?" he asks, just as John Newell comes running past again, with the shopkeeper's son, Eric Samuelson, in tow.

"When is it not, these days?" I reply, sounding like an island grandmother all of a sudden. "We better go see what it is."

We have not stood on the schoolhouse steps for long before Herbert Newell, John's older brother, comes rushing by, and I call out his name to make him stop. When he does, he is so exhausted that he has to pause on the road to catch his breath before coming toward us with his cap in his hands.

"What is happening, Herbert? Why are all the children running?" I ask when he is close enough that I can see the shine of sweat on his brow.

"There has . . . been an . . . accident on the road," the boy manages to utter with some difficulty. His eyes are wide and shiny with excitement.

"What kind of accident?" I ask, while my stomach starts hurting again.

Herbert has regained some of his composure, and speaks more coherently. "That doctor from the mainland, Miss Russel . . . The carriage he rented from the store toppled over on the way to the harbor."

"Oh no," I say, and grab hold of the doorframe as I sway. Benjamin's hand comes to steady me, pressing gently against my back.

"What happened?" he asks the boy, who shakes his head with vigor.

"No one knows, Mr. West. It just capsized on the road. The horses must've gotten spooked or something."

"Are people hurt?" I croak.

The boy nods, looking solemn. "But alive, though," he quickly adds. "The reverend and some other men are with them now." He fidgets on the spot, clearly eager to be on his way and not miss any of the excitement.

"Thank you for telling us," Benjamin says to the boy, who takes this as his cue to charge off.

As we step back into the schoolhouse, I cannot help but see her before my inner eyes: Charlotte North in the clergy house office, and the lightning-quick flicker of contempt on her face when she looked at the doctor's turned back.

·35·

charlotte

Jasper sits in the leather-upholstered chair that he has added to the attic room, looking at me. I am on my bed, dressed only in my nightgown. It is dark outside the window, but a candle flickers on the nightstand, washing the small room in gold. I note that the reverend looks tired; dark shadows fan out under his eyes. His scent of rosemary and salt is mingled with that of brown liquor.

I hate to see him tormented, but I know it cannot be helped. *A little pain will only make the sugar taste better,* Mary used to say, before pulling our loose baby teeth and then rewarding us with cookies.

"Did you question it about the carriage?" Jasper asks, as he has done for the past three nights, ever since Dr. Crown and his nephew had that accident on their way back to the harbor. The good reverend is terrified that the wreck happened because of the knocker.

"It won't answer," I say, and it is the truth. My friend has remained stubbornly mum on the topic. "Any number of things could have happened to their carriage," I say, just as I do every night. "Maybe they were just unlucky."

"The driver says that the horses were spooked," he recounts, not for the first time. I, for one, wish we would speak of something else. Neither the doctor nor his assistant *died,* and both reached the mainland in one piece, if not entirely unscathed.

"The driver *would* say that, if his recklessness caused the accident," I tell Jasper.

"But it *could* have been the knocker."

He will not let it go. Perhaps it is due to him being called to the scene after the wreck to help organize a boat for the wounded. Seeing the damage up close must have been jarring. Both Dr. and Mr. Crown had been carried on board the trawler on stretchers, but they had both been conscious at the time, so the damage could not have been too severe. Listening to Jasper, though, one would think they had both died a gruesome death. I suppose he feels guilty, because of the knocker.

"*If* it was the knocker," I say, "it must have changed. The knocker enjoys a spectacle. It throws stones and causes fires, but there were no stones thrown at the carriage. Maybe it was the seagulls that spooked the horses."

"The horses were born here, so the seagulls wouldn't have spooked them," he argues, swaying a little on the chair. "It's just that the knocker was so terribly angry at Dr. Crown. It seems peculiar to me that an accident should happen right after the knocker attacked him in my office—"

"Even if it *was* the knocker, there's nothing we can do," I remind him. "That is the cause of all my troubles: I *cannot* make it disappear."

"I know," he says, and his expression turns soft. "I suppose I just want an accurate measure of it—want to know what it's capable of. If it *was* the knocker, it's more covert now, as you say, and that means it is learning stealth—which, in turn, makes it far more dangerous."

I cannot disagree with that, but I am rejoicing, too. This proves that I have been right all along: the knocker *can* evolve. It means that I can teach it, and guide it. "I know it has a mind and a will of its own, and despite what Dr. Crown theorized, they don't always align with mine." I still become furious when I think of the doctor, and what Jasper had told me of his "theory." I never asked the knocker to punish him, but that does not mean I do not feel that the punishment was just.

"But does it have a *purpose*?" Jasper muses. "Does it have a singular goal?"

"I don't know," I admit, just as my eyes snag on a tall shape standing behind the reverend, just by the circular window. The candlelight only reaches so far, but it is bright enough that I can make it out: a young woman just my size, wearing a nightgown just like mine. Her dark hair falls in curls around her face—just like mine does.

"There are rites," Jasper says, "used by the church in the past. I didn't want to go there, but perhaps we must."

"Will they work?" I ask, with a slight twinge of worry.

"We shouldn't leave any stone unturned." Jasper shrugs. "As long as we don't know exactly what will work, we should use all the weapons at our disposal."

"Then I'm lucky to have a priest by my side," I say, though my mind is elsewhere. Behind Jasper, the girl by the window has come closer. She is almost by his shoulder now. She smiles, and I see that it is *my* smile curling her lips—*my* smile in *my* face, like a mirror image. It is eerie and unsettling, but not as frightening as it should have been, because I know who it is that is coming toward me. A scent of freshly cooked meat teases my nostrils, and I suppress an impulse to greet it.

"Antonia speaks of 'spiritual leeches.'" Jasper's voice reaches me, but I am no longer listening. I am far too preoccupied with looking at my twin—the darkness of her eyes and the paleness of her skin. "She worries that the knocker might feed off us—and off you. But you don't feel *drained,* do you, Charlotte?"

Reluctantly, I shift my gaze away from the figure, "No, not at all," I say. I could add that the reverend himself looks worse for wear, but I know there are good reasons for that. "I am strong and healthy," I say. "Noreen feeds me well."

"And your wound?" He looks at my bandaged finger. He has been overly concerned with it ever since Dr. Crown assaulted me.

"It's better now," I assure him. "Noreen has washed it and added a poultice."

"I cannot *believe* that he did that to you."

"Perhaps dealing in madness has had a poor effect on his mind," I suggest. My twin has not moved again, but still stands next to Jasper. Her hand hovers just inches from his shoulder, as if she might touch him at any time. I check her other hand, and note that she, too, has a bandage there, twined about her ring finger. It reminds me of a dream I had the other night. It was about the crude silver ring. The dark seeds set in it had opened up, sprouting glossy red leaves.

I wonder that Jasper does not see her, but it seems he does not.

"I think we're *all* going slightly mad." He gives me a gentle smile. "The strain is taxing, to say the least."

"I'm sorry," I whisper, averting my gaze.

"Oh, it's not your fault, Charlotte," he assures me at once, just as I had hoped he would. He abandons the chair to come and sit on the edge of the bed, extending a hand to brush his fingers through my hair. I lean into the touch like a hungry kitten. "You mustn't blame yourself for this. We are battling forces far outside your control."

"Yet perhaps if I hadn't spoken to it—encouraged it—none of this would have happened," I complain, all while watching from the corner of my eye as the twin comes gliding closer, until it stands next to Jasper by the bed.

"How were you to know?" He soothes me, still with his fingers buried deep in my hair. I can see his chest rise and fall, faster now than the moment before. "No one can fault you for wanting to end an onslaught of needles in your bed." His voice falters on the last word. "It's an entanglement, that is all, and we will untangle it, together."

The scent of liquor on his breath is very strong up close, but I do not mind it. If anything, the brandy makes him less wary of me, less inhibited by my presence. I purr on the inside when he pulls me close; rejoice in the sensation when his arms wind around me, and I savor the scent as well as the warmth when his cheek meets mine, raspy and firm. A lock of his brown hair tickles my nose. Suddenly, I am terribly conscious of wearing nothing but my nightgown. No lacings or hooks hide me away, just this one layer of fabric trimmed with Irish lace. The embrace lasts much longer than it should. When we finally do part, his face is red.

The twin still stands there, watching, smiling.

"I find flowers on my pillow every night now," he whispers hoarsely. "Always violets. Antonia says she find needles in her bed. It makes her quite upset, as you can imagine. Do you think it is the knocker's way of initiating communication, as it did with you?"

"Maybe," I reply, but I know it is not so. The violets and the needles are just gifts—tokens. I take some pride in the fact that the knocker now seems to have learned the difference between good and bad. Needles are for those we do not like, while violets are for those we cherish.

I taught it that difference.

"Should we pray for our delivery?" he asks me in a husky voice.

I nod and kneel before the bed at his side. The warmth of him and his rosemary scent still lingers on my skin. I cannot help but smile as the chill of the floorboards soaks through the nightgown to cool my shins. It is uncomfortable, kneeling like this, but I do not care. All that matters is the man beside me.

As we fold our hands and place them on the bed, I notice the third of our party again. The twin kneels, too, right next to me, and has her hands folded just like mine. When I bend my head, it does, too. When I whisper the prayer in time with Jasper's voice, the twin mouths the words as well. Only in its eyes can I see a difference: mirth. But perhaps that, too, is a mirror.

Jasper prays with vigor and passion tonight, and so it goes on for a while. I suppose he has demons to exorcise—flesh to discipline, a heart to punish for its sins. I inch a little closer on the floor to feel the heat radiating through his black attire, and watch the muscles flex in his jaw as he speaks. The twin follows suit, moving when I do. It feels much like having a fully fleshed shadow.

"Is the knocker here?" Jasper asks after the last amen.

"Always," I say, glancing at the twin, who glances back at me. I wonder if it is Dr. Crown's wild "theory" that has inspired it to take on my likeness.

"The prayer does not keep it away?" Jasper asks without much hope.

"No," I reply. "It remains."

Jasper sighs and places a hand on my back—to comfort me, perhaps, but it does not feel that way. His thumb makes circles on the fabric of the nightgown. Then a sharp inhale sounds beside me, and he abruptly retracts the offending hand, as if I am made of burning coal.

"We must be careful," he says in a rough voice.

I know he is no longer speaking of the knocker.

·36·

ruth

"The worst thing is that we will never know," I say to Benjamin. The two of us sit on the rocks, looking out over the sea. We have crossed the island today and are as far as we can be from the tower ruin, the Norths, and the clergy house. We walked until the sea stopped us, barring further progress with its vast expanse of frothing blue. Only the seagulls can breach that border, and gleefully do so, too, soaring beneath the blue-gray sky. A couple of fishing vessels drift toward the horizon.

I am talking about the accident, of course. Dr. and Mr. Crown. Both of them unpleasant men, but that does not mean they deserved to get hurt. What truly bothers me, though, is that we do not know if the knocker was behind the wreck.

"I cannot help but think of what he said at the end," I tell my companion, who looks very fancy today, wearing his mustard-colored jacket. "At first, the idea that Charlotte is somehow responsible for the knocker seemed outlandish, but then—when he mentioned a root cause—it suddenly made more sense."

"From a psychological perspective, yes, but why did the spirit appear at the same time as the earthquake?" Benjamin's dark eyes are lost in thought. He has found himself a slender stick and is prodding pebbles and empty crab shells half-buried in the sand between the rocks.

"Perhaps there is some 'unconscious' reason for that as well," I speculate, placing a hand on my head to prevent the wind from snagging my hat. "But there is no proof that the human mind is even capable of moving things at will, and even if Charlotte *does* have that ability, I don't think she is aware in the slightest."

"You don't trust her, though." It is not a question. Benjamin and I have discussed the matter relentlessly since I came home from the examination four days ago, so exhausted and bedraggled that I could barely stand on my feet.

"I don't trust that there is no allegiance," I say. "I don't trust that she has no control over it. It was the way she looked at the men . . . the way she rolled her eyes."

"The way it seems to pave the way for her," he notes.

"Do you think she *wanted* to go to the clergy house?" I ask, then check myself. "Right; of course she did." According to the Hills themselves, she has been pining for the reverend for months. "If she *does* control it—or if it *is* her—then Charlotte is a dangerous person," I note, with a fresh stab of fear in my gut. "I cannot *believe* that Mrs. North was right."

"We don't know that for sure, Ruth," Benjamin says lightly. "It could still be a demon—a ghost—a spirit. Something that came from Margaret's Tower. Maybe it achieved some sort of power over her."

"We know too little." I sigh—and not for the first time. "I truly wish I had paid more attention to the islanders' superstitions and not just outright dismissed them."

"Me, too." He laughs. "I never thought science would fail me like this, and I had to look to old wives' tales for answers."

"I wish we could speak to the locals, but—"

"The precarious situation we are in, I know." He gives me a reassuring smile.

The only good thing to have come out of the accident and all the trouble with the Norths was that no one on the island has had time to build any outrage against Benjamin and me. I knew it was just a matter of time, though, before Mrs. Newell and Mrs. Fisher stood at my door again, demanding that I redeem my sinful ways. Never mind that the most sinful thing Benjamin and I did was buttering each other's toast and stirring the other's tea. People will be people, and always imagine the worst. Reason and truth have nothing to do with it.

"I should have left Margaret's Keep a week ago." Benjamin's gaze follows the sea again, travels on the waves that hit the shore. "My work here is long since completed," he adds, and then falls silent.

I instantly feel a twinge in my heart. "I would miss you," I say, barely breathing.

"You would also not get into trouble on my account," he says. I want to say that it does not matter and who cares what the islanders say, but my position is at stake, and there is no point in pretending otherwise. My desire to flee the island is still there, but quieter now, like a murmur. Being with Benjamin has been a balm for my soul, calming the raging waves of my fear. What used to boil so hot has turned into a simmer: still hot enough to scald, but not enough to send me running.

"We should have told them that you were my brother," I say, trying to make light of the situation. To my relief, Benjamin laughs—although the laughter is tinged with sadness, which only makes my own heart feel even heavier. My feelings toward him are not at all fraternal, no matter how much I try to convince myself. It is his kindness that does me in. He is so different from other men I have known. I do not think he would ever hurt me—but then again, those are dangerous thoughts, and I have long since decided that the wisest course of action is to solely rely on myself.

It will pass, I tell myself. Whatever feelings bloom in my heart, they will pass, and then I will have peace again. "What will I do without you?" I ask nevertheless. "The knocker—Charlotte—will still be here."

He gives me a teasing look. "I am clearly no match for the knocker."

"No, but it helps to have someone to discuss it with. I might have given in to my fear and left Margaret's Keep myself had you not arrived that night."

"Our discussion will not have to end when I leave," he says. "In fact, I dearly hope it will not. On the mainland, they have what we are sorely lacking: books and annals, records and resources. I mean to keep looking into it, Ruth. I mean to keep prodding until something gives." I note how his jaw clenches.

"You mean to exorcise the demon," I say quietly, and do not refer to the knocker, but the one that lives on in Benjamin's mind.

"I do," he says with conviction. "I will not go to my grave not knowing what it was that spooked me so badly. And honestly, Ruth, I just cannot see how Charlotte's subconscious mind would be able to conjure the creature I saw."

"No," I admit. "It does seem unlikely." But then, what do I know of the uncharted quirks of the psyche? "If you *do* go, you must write to me often, fill me in on what you discover." My voice has grown thick, and I feel as if I am about to cry.

"Of course." He gives me a smile. "I will let you know every detail—and hopefully something useful will come of it, too."

Before me lies a loneliness as vast and deep as the sea.

Benjamin must have sensed my melancholy, because he suddenly takes my hand and squeezes it. "Take heart, Ruth. Sooner or later, an answer will appear." He does not yet understand that my gloominess has nothing to do with the knocker. "And if you ever come to the mainland," he continues, "you must let me know. We can go for tea or a walk in the park." His eyes do not match his tone; they are about as sad as I feel. He must realize, too, because suddenly the smile is gone. "Why do you live out here, Ruth? Why is it so important to you? If you lived on the mainland, we could meet all the time."

I want to answer, but my throat constricts, and I fear I cannot utter as much as a word without unleashing a torrent of tears. I do want to, though—want to explain how this island is my rock, a place where I could drift ashore and find an ounce of peace again. It had not been easy to give it all up: the fortune and the life I was used to. There had been so many nights filled with doubt and regret when I came to realize how all I knew—even my relatives—shunned me, and pushed me out in the cold, because I was no longer one of them.

The poverty, too, had been a shock. I had used what little I had inherited from my mother to put myself through school, living in poor quarters and with very little food. Seeing fine houses, carriages, and motorcars put me in a foul mood, reminding me of what I had given up in my wild and stubborn quest to follow my own heart. Seeing people that I had known before could leave me reeling for days. It had seemed childish at times, what I had done, like the tantrum of a spoiled girl who did not know what was best for her—just as Father had said. Being on the mainland, I could not escape who I had been before. My former life, my fateful choice, glimmered on every street corner.

On Margaret's Keep, though—this blessed rock—I could simply be Miss Russel through and through. No one would roll their eyes at me for being an utter fool. The only chink in my armor had been the North girls: rich and unhappy, stunted in their development, and unable to stray from the beaten path.

My mirrors, as Benjamin had put it.

"You have been a perfect friend to me, Benjamin," I say at last. "I will never forget how you made this all bearable." My heart beats painfully with regret as I speak, but I am not Charlotte North, untried and easily swallowed up by infatuation. I am a woman grown, and this affliction, too, shall pass.

"Likewise, Ruth. I will never forget you," he replies, which only makes the grief so much worse.

·37·

jasper

"How long do you mean for this to go on?" Antonia stands in the doorway to my office, wearing a red-striped shirtwaist and a long blue skirt. She does not look well, but whatever discomfort she might be feeling, it does nothing to suppress her temper. "Two weeks now, Jasper! Two weeks!" She slaps her palm against the white-painted doorframe. "Two weeks with that devil's *whore* living up in the attic, and what do you have to show for it but needles in my bed and an injured doctor? Whatever it is you do up there at night, it *clearly* does nothing to purge the demon!"

I refrain from pointing out that putting Charlotte up in the attic had been Antonia's choice—one that had undoubtedly been a mistake. She is hidden from Antonia's sight, true, but that is not necessarily a good thing. At least it is not for me.

"I never said this would be easy—or fast," I reply from my place by the desk, and notice how my voice is not as steady as it should be. I know this is due to the liquor, but I am in need of it. The pressure of it all—Charlotte, Antonia, the knocker—is simply more than a man can bear. I had honestly believed myself to be stronger, and am ashamed at how fast I crumble. I do not understand the knocker at all, but then I do not understand *myself*. I feel tawdry every time I enter the attic to gaze at the young woman on the bed, and yet I cannot help myself. She is there, after all, all alone, and hidden away from my wife's eagle eyes. Through her jealousy and distrust, Antonia has created a situation that is far more precarious than it needed to be.

But I cannot blame her. This is all on me.

"*You* allowed that devil into our home," Antonia keeps pestering me. "Noreen combs my bed for needles every night, and yet I find them there in the morning, quite often lodged in my skin—and to make matters worse, the bed *shook* all night; tossing me around like a pebble in a tin can!" She looks at me as if expecting an apology.

"I do not control the knocker," I say, unconsciously repeating Charlotte's words. "And neither does the poor young woman in our care," I add for good measure. "It is our duty to help her." I have grown tired of this as well: the constant repetitions. I pick up my silver letter opener, shaped like a crusader's sword, and clutch it in my hand for comfort.

"Her mother seems to think differently." Antonia's narrow face twists up with disgust. "According to Noreen, she speaks as though you have *kidnapped* the girl, against Mrs. North's wishes."

"Her father was in agreement, and that is all that matters." Though I cannot deny a slight twinge of discomfort when I recall how distressed Mr. North had been at the time, with his wife lying unconscious and bleeding on the sofa.

"Mrs. Fisher says—"

"That is just a story, Antonia—twisted and corrupted by the minds of young girls and a fisherman's wife. A grain of truth that has become something else. Charlotte would never expose young minds to something wicked. She helped me run the *children's choir* for heaven's sake." I find my handkerchief in a pocket and mop perspiration from my brow.

"According to Noreen—"

"Well, Noreen is wrong," I snap.

Antonia falls quiet for a moment, and I dare hope the storm has passed. Then she finds her voice again, "It is only because of Evelyn's fiancé that they have not fetched her back already. I cannot wait for the young man to leave." My wife looks sick. A frown is plastered on her face, and her eyes appear dull. "What will you do, Jasper, when they take your plaything away?"

"This is beneath you," I declare. "Who else would the Norths turn to but their priest at a time of crisis? I offer nothing but solace to Charlotte, and my only aim is to help her get rid of the spirit—"

"Well, you fail spectacularly," Antonia declares from the doorway. "Not only did Dr. Crown end up in a hospital—"

"That had nothing to do with us—or *it*."

"But you make a laughingstock of yourself, keeping the girl up there like a *concubine*—"

"That was *your* choice!" This time I cannot help but say it. "I wanted her to stay in one of the guest rooms."

She laughs and it is an ugly sound. "I didn't want her here *at all*. The mere suggestion was an insult! And now look what has happened: our house is haunted and we are falling apart! Can you not *see* the devil, Jasper, even as he is staring you in the eyes?" Her own eyes are pleading with me, and her pitifulness cuts far deeper than her anger ever could.

"I see him, and I challenge him," I reply, mustering what dignity I have left. "That is my duty as a reverend. What chances does a young woman stand, alone and faced with evil? She *needs* my help, and I will give it to her."

"Oh, I think you give her more than that." Antonia lifts her chin. "Anything she wants, I reckon."

Her vulgarity makes me cringe. "Nothing unseemly has happened—"

"Yet. But you cannot convince me that your feelings are *pure*. I have seen you besotted before, remember? Once, it was *I* who had you pining—"

"But you are still my wife," I interrupt, vexed by an argument that only ever goes in circles. Even the letter opener seems to taunt me with the inscription running down its slender blade: *The Lord is my shepherd,* it says, but in truth, I feel quite lost.

"You don't deny it, then." Antonia looks victorious. "You don't deny that your thoughts stray—"

"You put words into my mouth," I protest, though the guilt writhes like a snake in my belly. Outside the windows, the seagulls cry. "Perhaps you ought to go somewhere to rest for a while. To your sister's, perhaps—or somewhere else on the mainland."

She laughs again, mocking and loud. "What, so that you and your mistress can have the house to yourselves? No, Jasper, *I* still have some dignity left."

"If you could only overcome your jealousy and find some compassion—"

"Oh, Jasper. You *cannot* be this naive—or perhaps you are merely lying to yourself, which seems the likelier option."

"Charlotte is not the enemy," I implore. "The knocker is."

The spirit promptly replies to the statement by toppling a stack of books off my desk. In the next second, a portrait of the former reverend is pushed so it hangs askew on the wall.

Antonia's fingers flutter nervously before her, before coming to rest on a button on her shirtwaist. "This cannot go on, Jasper." Her voice is suddenly calm, which somehow unnerves me more than her shouting. "You only believe what you want to believe. You will lie to yourself if need be to protect the man you *think* you are, but in truth, you are no match for this. I know you better than you know yourself—"

"You do not know me at all!" I shout.

"You are a man in love with your lies. You dare not even *touch* the person living underneath all your layers of Scripture and polish, for fear he will not be to your liking—"

"Enough!" I slap my hand against the desk, battling a surge of fury. "How dare you speak to your husband in this way?"

"All men are worms," she says, "writhing in the dirt. You are no different, Jasper Hill." With that profound insight, she finally leaves the doorway, and I let out a shivering breath when I hear her footsteps on the stairs.

In the sudden quiet, I fill my glass from the bottle I keep in my desk, then lean back in the chair and try to dispel the lingering discomfort from the argument. I remind myself, again, that Charlotte is not the agent of disruption—the knocker is—but it is still her face I see whenever I close my eyes.

I know I should not be in her room at night, when the house is empty save for Antonia, and no one can overhear us. I certainly should not be there when she is dressed in nothing but her nightgown, modest though it might be. I should not embrace her, or caress her hair. Should not touch her just to feel her warmth—and yet I know I will do it again tonight.

Though my steps on the attic stairs might hesitate, and the hand I lift to knock will shiver, I will be there, like clockwork—drawn by desire. I will loathe myself and hate myself, and yet I will go.

Antonia is entirely right—and that makes me loathe her, too.

The knocker is the issue, I remind myself again. There is no doubt that Dr. Crown's visit stirred it from a more docile state and set it loose in the building. Books move, teacups clatter, and then there are the flowers and needles that show up in our beds.

Noreen is terrified because things disappear from the kitchen, and she says she can hear it knocking, too, moving around inside the walls. We keep buckets of sand in every room, knowing how it might cause fires; and the sheep that have been such a menace, grazing around the house, are now gone. They will no longer come near the building. I never once thought I would miss the brash and burly things. The seagulls remain, though, ever circling and crying.

They do not seem to mind the spirit at all.

But of all the tricks the knocker has played on me so far, the crying infant is doubtlessly the worst. I hear it every night as I make my way down from the attic, but so faint that it might just as well be the wind. It makes me long and yearn again. Makes me see his little blue face, makes me feel the weight of his body nestled in my arms . . .

My thoughts once again stray to Charlotte—as they so often do. I remember what she told me when I asked her about the future, what she saw for herself once the knocker was gone. *Love and riches and everything good,* she had said and laughed. *And I want to have children, at least three or four.* I see it now, whenever I look upon her: how the roundness of her body would blossom with a child; how her breasts would swell with milk. She would surely be able to have a whole clutch of strong and ruddy-cheeked offspring—as many as she likes, without being torn asunder. They will have her dark curls and button nose; the boys will be wild things, running about; the girls will be clever but sweet. I long to feel their little hands in mine, to lift them onto my knee and read them stories from leather bound books, to kiss them good night and greet them in the morning. But it will not be me who does any of those things.

Though my restraint is wearing thin.

Antonia's wedding portrait on my desk is mocking me. A spiderweb of cracks runs through the glass after the knocker threw the brass frame against the wall. Antonia is happy in it: bright-eyed and hopeful. I had loved her then and I love her now—though more as a concerned sibling than a husband. I want her to do well—I want her to *thrive*—but the dreams we made when we were younger we both know now will never come to pass.

It bothers me, the crying infant. It tickles those dead hopes and dreams back to life, and nothing that is dead should rise again, except on judgment day.

The knocker is the issue, but I do not fear the knocker.

I *do* fear Charlotte, and the promise in her eyes.

·38·

charlotte

I speak to the knocker while waiting for Jasper to come and pray with me. I have washed and changed into my nightgown, and sit on the bed, looking out in the room. The knocker is not visible tonight, but it quite often visits in my guise now. Last night, it settled down next to me in bed, mimicking all my movements. We lay there like sisters, side by side, sharing the same blanket. Though when I reached out to touch my own face on the pillow, the knocker was suddenly gone. This new thing is both unsettling and captivating, but I do feel even less alone when I have a twin there with me, so maybe that is just why it is doing it.

Or maybe it is not.

"Did they quarrel about me?" I ask the knocker. I had heard a terrible row from downstairs, and though I could not make out the words, I knew it had been passionate.

The knocker replies with one rap in the wall.

"Does she hate me very much?" I ask.

Again, the knocker raps once, and I smile.

"Does she want to throw me out?"

The knocker confirms with a tap in the ceiling.

"Will she succeed?" I ask, holding my breath.

The knocker does not reply, which is not the answer I was hoping for.

"Can I prevent her from throwing me out?" I ask instead.

The knocker raps once—yes.

"Will you help me?" I ask, and am rewarded with another sharp yes.

"No fire, no stones," I remind it, as I have done every day since I came here. "Just little things, like needles."

The knocker confirms with one extra knock.

I smile again as I lie back on the bed, staring up at the ceiling. "Does he think about kissing me?" It is gratifying, if not unexpected, when the knocker tells me that yes, he does.

"Does he think about me right now?" I ask, though it feels a little wrong to use a power such as the knocker to answer something so mundane.

The knocker nevertheless confirms.

"Do you enjoy looking like me?" I ask it next.

A knock sounds in the wall above the window.

"You are very good at it, too," I say. "I cannot see any flaw."

The knocker does not respond to that. It is hard responding to a compliment when all you can say is "yes" or "no."

"Thank you for being my friend," I whisper hurriedly when I hear Jasper's footfalls on the stairs. The knocker, ever perceptive, replies with a quiet tap by the headboard—one that only I can hear.

Then another knocking sounds, this time on the door.

"Come in," I say, still lying down. The intimacy of the attic room is such that decorum has no place. We are naked in here, even if clothed. We are alone within the soft glow of the candle, where nothing can be heard but our voices, the wind, and the waves. It is hot tonight, though—quite stifling—even if the room has been aired. Or perhaps it is just myself I feel: the burning of my need for him.

Jasper looks worse for wear as he enters. Perhaps the argument with his wife has worn him out, or perhaps the liquor is taking its toll. He barely even smiles at me before thumping down in the leather chair, staring at me with haunted eyes.

"Charlotte," he says, sounding awfully tired.

A pang of worry goes off in my chest. Will he send me back home?

"Are you quite well?" I ask Jasper as I sit up on the bed. "You look tired," I add with concern. He really does look disheveled tonight; his shoulder-length hair is mussed, and his face has not seen a razor for days. He does not seem drunk as much as defeated; his shoulders are slumped and he slouches in the chair, yet there is an expression of grim determination on his face that I cannot tell is a good thing or not. He is about to either throw me out or devour me whole; I simply cannot say.

His eyes have narrowed to glittering slits as he watches me in the dark.

"Charlotte," he says again, adding a sad smile.

I am beginning to feel concerned and place my feet on the floor. "Is something wrong?" I ask. "Did the knocker do something?" I try to catch his gaze, but it is hard. He is not very sober.

"No." Jasper shakes his head; locks of dark hair tumble down on his brow. "Nothing more than usual."

"Is it Mrs. Hill?" I ask. "Does she want me to leave?"

"Antonia always wants you to leave." He gives me another sad smile.

"Then what is it?" I ask, more puzzled by the second.

He takes a moment before replying. "I cannot . . . lie," he says at last. "Not anymore. Not to you, and not to myself."

Another pang goes off inside me, but this one has tendrils of fire. "What do you mean?" I whisper.

Instead of answering, he rises from the chair and crosses the short distance to the bed, then kneels down before me on the floor and bends his head.

"Do you want to pray?" I ask, uncertain. It is a strange thing to see a man so subdued, if that is what he is.

I startle when I feel his hands grab hold of my naked feet. He keeps them there for a moment and I savor the feeling, expecting him to release me at any moment. He does not. Instead, he slides his hands upward, dips them under the hem of my nightgown, and caresses my calves. The excitement makes my breath hitch in my throat.

Next, he moves his head to rest it in my lap, and I feel his hot breath against my thigh through the cotton. I feel a sudden, unexpected urge to weep when my fingers lace in his hair, before sliding down to his face, tracing the angles and lines that have previously been forbidden to me. He moans when I touch his lips.

"Charlotte," he whispers, and turns his head to bury his face in my lap. The warmth of his breath is almost unbearable. Under the nightgown, his hands climb higher. I braid my fingers in his hair again to nudge his head upward. When I can see his face again, I bend down and kiss his lips.

They are softer than I thought they would be, and dry. I wind my arms around him to pull him closer, and then I kiss him again. He groans when he gives in to it, kissing me back with passion. His hands leave my legs to hold me instead, and he pushes me back on the bed before climbing onto it himself, straddling my body and kissing me all the while.

These are not the kisses of fairy tales, but those of Evelyn's novels. His lips and tongue are everywhere as he kisses a trail from my mouth to my neck and back. It is wetter—messier—than I had imagined, but not in an unpleasant way. It is different, though—*he* is different. No longer imprisoned by the white collar, he is like a stranger to me—a wild thing let off its leash.

His fingers touch my breast through the cotton, and I turn into a wild thing myself, straining against his hand. He pulls at the ribbons at my neckline, but I swat his hands away and push his weight off me, so that I can sit up and pull the nightgown off.

I figure we are way past modesty at this point.

It feels even better when he touches my breast without the bothersome cotton, and with his lips on mine, the sweetness becomes an aching itch. Between the kisses, I chuckle with excitement. It is finally dawning on me what is about to happen: the *impossible* thing that was simply not to be, and a strong sense of triumph mingles with the desire, as I impatiently tug at Jasper's shirt and do not relent before it is gone.

I grasp for him; he grasps for me; hair mussed and mouth slack. We roll around on the narrow bed, rubbing, touching, and moaning. When I first hold him in my hand, it seems to me a newborn thing: smooth and straining, weeping in my hand.

"I can stop," he whispers with burning eyes. His face is slick with perspiration and traces of moisture from our kisses. I only shake my head in reply, then smile when he rolls on top of me and parts my legs with his.

It takes some time for him to enter me fully but I can be patient when it counts, and when he succeeds, the sense of triumph is there again, bursting forth like foaming sea waves.

"Are you in pain?" he whispers. "Does it hurt?"

I shake my head, even if it does sting. What little pain I feel does not compare to the joy, though, and so I ignore it and twine my legs with his, savoring the sweetness of the moment.

As Jasper starts moving inside me, rocking his hips back and forth, I catch sight of the knocker, standing by the bed. It is wearing my guise and its face matches mine—every twinge of pain and every breath of pleasure. I smile at it over Jasper's shoulder, and the knocker smiles back: a perfect mirror.

The rocking has become more intense as Jasper's pleasure mounts. He grunts and he groans and clutches at me as he pounds into my body. It does not last very long, and he whimpers as he finishes. The candle on the nightstand goes out with a puff, leaving an acrid smell in the room.

Jasper lies perfectly still for a moment, breathing into my ear, then he gently rolls off my body to lie next to me, leaving behind a coating of sweat and a spot of sticky residue between my legs. He takes my hand and holds it, but his face is turned against the wall. I cannot say for sure, but I think perhaps he is weeping.

In the blue darkness, the knocker and I lock eyes and smile.

·39·

ruth

"He is turning people away." Noreen's voice is quiet. She sits at the kitchen table at the clergy house, with a large, steaming mug of tea in her hand. "Reverend Hill has never done that before. He has always made time for his flock." The old woman's face is drawn with concern. "And *her*." Her gaze shifts to the ceiling above us. "I can barely get her to eat. Meat and cake, that is all she will have. I cannot recall the last time she consumed a cabbage leaf or a piece of apple. I wonder how she's still standing with so poor a diet."

"It takes a toll, I'm sure, living with something so . . . unusual." I am still wearing my coat and hat; the umbrella rests on the table. I have stopped to pick up Charlotte and escort her to church at the reverend's behest, but I arrived early and she is tardy in coming down, so now I have tea with Noreen.

The housekeeper looks worse for wear. Her eyes are sunken and her hands shake when she pours the fragrant beverage. I am surprised by Noreen's candidness, but the poor woman clearly needs to unburden herself, and seeing as how I am already involved, it is better that she talks to me than some less understanding neighbor.

Ever since Dr. Crown's catastrophic examination, I have been concerned for all who dwell within these walls, so when Reverend Hill sent a note asking me to help once again, I was happy for the opportunity to check on them—even if just crossing the clergy house threshold has become an act of boldness. I also need the distraction. The days have been long since Benjamin left, and it has not yet been a week. I imagine him being proud of me now, for entering the lion's den once more, and not succumbing to my fear.

"I would've left if it wasn't for Mrs. Hill," Noreen says next. "I have enough saved that I could retire, but she's fragile, and having spent so much time with her—just the two of us rattling around in this house—I feel as though I cannot leave her." She sips her tea with a thoughtful expression. Her hair is pinned at the nape of her neck, and the white collar of her black dress is neatly starched and pressed.

"She is grateful for it, I'm sure," I say. "Poor Mrs. Hill didn't ask for any of this. I'm surprised that *she* hasn't left. I know she has family on the mainland."

"Oh, I think she worries that there'll be talk." Noreen glances up at the ceiling again. The day outside is bright and plenty of light floods in through the windows, yet the spacious kitchen around us appears both gloomy and dark. Not even the scent of baking bread seeping from the stove can quite lighten the mood. "I don't know what exactly the reverend *does* up there, but it usually happens after I have left at night. I can only tell because he leaves his candle on the counter, and I can see how much it has burned."

"They are probably just praying," I say, and feel my cheeks redden. Who am I to question the morals of a man and a woman spending time alone together? Benjamin stayed with me for three whole weeks before he left.

"If they do pray, it doesn't seem to do any good. The spirit grows bolder by the day. Yesterday, it was in the laundry basket when I hung the wash to dry, throwing garments around. Only *hers,* though—only

Mrs. Hill's. I had to pick her skirts out of the bushes." She shakes her head. "Rodents I can handle, and flies and fleas, too, but this infestation is something different, and seeing what happened to Dr. Crown . . ." Her voice trails off and her eyes grow distant.

"The wreck could have been an accident," I remind her, daring some of the tea.

"Mr. Newell is a good driver, and he's sure something he couldn't see spooked the horses," Noreen argues. The carriage had belonged to the grocery store and could be hired with a driver by visitors to Margaret's Keep. That day, poor Mr. Newell had been hired on by sheer unluck, since Mr. Samuelson was busy with the store. He had fared better than his passengers, though, and only sustained small injuries. They say the carriage was in good repair, but clearly it was not if spooked horses could make it topple over.

"The important thing is that Dr. Crown and his nephew will be all right," I say. "The recovery will take time, but at least none of them was hit in the head, like poor Mrs. North." That was the wrong example to give, though, as Noreen visibly blanches, and I wish I had picked a better one that had nothing to do with the knocker.

"It is a hellish thing, this spirit." Noreen lowers her voice. "It's like a cancer in the home, Miss Russel. The reverend is not himself, and he drinks—more than is good."

I have noticed this myself, so I can only nod in agreement. "He may turn around when the spirit—and the guest—are gone," I say.

"According to Mary, Mrs. North didn't want her daughter to come here." Noreen lowers her voice, as if sharing a secret. "She was strongly set against it before she was injured. She doesn't trust the reverend with her daughter—or perhaps it's the other way around." She smirks. "Mrs. Hill worries, too. They have terrible rows, and it's not all about the knocker." The housekeeper gives me a telling look while sipping more tea.

"It's easy to think the worst when a beautiful young woman is involved," I say, though I am very aware of the tension between them.

"For what it is worth, I for one believe that the reverend's intention is to vanquish the spirit. Why else would he invite Dr. Crown?"

Noreen's forehead creases. "There is something that's not right, though, and Mrs. Hill knows it. She has a terrible time with it all. The spirit bothers *her* more than anyone else, drizzling needles in her bed and setting her bathwater to boil. It wants her gone, and I cannot help but wonder why."

I get a sinking feeling in my gut when I realize what she is implying. "Charlotte does not control the knocker." I repeat the well-worn phrase, ignoring Dr. Crown's theory. "But my previous lodger, Mr. West, is on the mainland now, looking for answers. Perhaps he will find something useful."

"Hopefully something that is a little more effective than the reverend's *praying,*" Noreen huffs. "There's another thing, too, that I think is strange. I keep finding seashells and flowers on the back stairs. At first, I thought it was Charlotte who had gathered them, left them, and forgotten about it, but the other day, I saw the Fisher girls and Annabeth Ferryman sprint away from the house. When I went outside, I found flowers and *bones,* Miss Russel, laid out on the stairs. Bird bones. Likely from seagulls. Not that those are hard to come by around here."

A sense of deep discomfort comes over me. "What are you saying, Noreen?"

"Oh, I don't know—but I suppose you have heard the story? The devil in the shed?"

"I have," I confirm. "We don't know if it is true, though, or what exactly happened. They are young girls and impressionable. Perhaps they just want to comfort Charlotte." She is after all sick in a way, even if her affliction is unusual.

"By bringing her *bones?*" The housekeeper gives me an incredulous look.

"Perhaps they thought them pretty," I say, even if it is a weak explanation.

Noreen shakes her head and tuts, which leaves me with a sinking feeling, as if I have disappointed her—but what else could I have said? I do not know why the girls left those things on the stairs.

Thankfully, she moves on. "I do agree that Mrs. Hill should leave here, for the sake of her own sanity. I have told her, in gentle words, that nothing is more important than her own well-being, but I think she worries what will happen if she's gone." I take it from her expression that it is Charlotte and not the knocker that is the bigger issue in this instance.

"Charlotte *will* go home, though," I remind her, "when Evelyn's fiancé has left."

"Oh yes, and we're all waiting for that day with bated breath," Noreen replies, and I assume she is speaking of herself and Mrs. Hill. "I even asked Mary to plead with Mr. North to bring Charlotte home sooner, but Mr. Eckhardt's visit is important to Miss North, so they won't do a thing as long as the reverend is willing to house her."

"They appreciate the calm, I'm sure." I smile to soften the sarcasm. "For a reverend, this must be a most singular challenge. Sending her back with the spirit still intact must seem like a defeat."

"Sending her back with his wife still intact should be of bigger concern," she replies. "Mrs. Hill is not *well,* Miss Russel. You saw it yourself when you came here for tea. We both know why they never invited you again."

Noreen rises from her chair to get the bread out of the oven. Unlike most people on the island, Noreen rarely has a Sunday off, being tied to the reverend's schedule. She still goes to church, though, and will accompany us there. The reverend and his wife are already in place, readying the church for the service.

Noreen goes to fetch her coat and hat, leaving me alone by the table. I listen for sounds from upstairs when a movement outside the window suddenly grabs my attention. It happens very fast—just a glimpse of a person passing through the yard—but I am sure it is Charlotte I see, wearing her Sunday black. I rise from my chair to get a better look, wondering what she is doing—why she is outside—but then there is Charlotte behind me, coming down the attic stairs. I hear her before I see her: her high-heeled shoes on the steps, so she could not have come from anywhere else.

I check the window again and see that the yard is utterly deserted.

Once again, I feel as though the world has shifted, unsettling me in ways I had previously thought impossible. I remember Adelaide and Annabeth's claim that they had seen Charlotte in the field, and experience a feeling of shivering weakness that spreads all through my limbs. I do not let Charlotte see it, though, but plaster on a pleasant mask and hide my trembling hands in my sleeves before I turn to greet her.

"Charlotte," I say, grinning like a fool. I feel a sudden, strong need to sit down, and retreat to the safety of the kitchen table, where I can better conceal my flustered state.

"Good morning, Miss Russel," she chirps in reply. "It's a glorious day, isn't it?" She flutters to my vacated spot by the window, her black-clad, dark-haired silhouette stark against the blue and cloudless sky outside. From what Noreen had told me, I had expected her to look emaciated or timid—even sick—but that is certainly not the case. The young woman is *radiant*. Her skin looks clear and healthy, her hair is lustrous, and her eyes sparkle with life, so even if her diet is poor, it does not seem to disagree with her. She is also in an immensely joyful mood—which is a sharp contrast to the last time I saw her with Dr. Crown.

She wears her hair up in a fancy knot; there is no childish ribbon to be seen in it today. The little cross around her neck glints golden when she spins around. "Are we ready to leave?" she asks, and then, without waiting for an answer, "I haven't been to church in quite some time, but Jas—Reverend Hill thinks it's time. It's better to show myself, he says, than to just let the gossip flow. I don't think my soul has suffered, though, with Reverend Hill praying with me every night. In fact, I think I'm closer to God now than I ever was before. I was never very good at my prayers, you see; I always just daydreamed when folding my hands. But with the reverend I have put my heart and mind into it, so I don't think the absence from church has hurt me in any way."

"That sounds good, Charlotte." I give a faint smile, and refrain from pointing out how their shared prayer has done nothing to discourage the foe they seek to exorcise. It *is* good to see her so happy. I had not been expecting it.

"I wonder where the sheep are at," she continues. "They were such a menace when I first got here, but now they have disappeared entirely. Perhaps they found greener pastures elsewhere. I hope July will be as warm as June has been, even the wind has let up—"

She abruptly stops talking when Noreen reenters the room, wearing a thick black coat that must be way too warm for the weather. Charlotte, though, forgoes a coat altogether, and settles for a fringed, black shawl draped over her shoulders.

"It's such a very short walk," she says, catching my puzzled expression. She looks better suited for a night at the opera than church, truth be told. "Mary brought some clothes by, and it *would* be a shame not to use them . . . I cannot wait to see my sisters," she continues, as she slips out the back door. "I haven't seen them for weeks, and we are usually together all the time." Noreen and I exchange worried looks. This does *not* seem like a haunted woman; tormented and plagued by a wicked spirit. And her good mood continues, too, all the way to the church, where black-clad islanders and an assortment of seagulls—big and small—are waiting by the door.

The Norths are already there. Mr. North stands closest to the entrance, seeing as how he always is the first one to enter. He is accompanied by three of his black-clad daughters and a strapping young man with blond hair. I assume this is James Eckhardt, and when Evelyn loops her arm in his, I know that I am right. The eldest North girl wears a fancy hat with bows and feathers that must be the latest fashion. I expect she wants to impress her more worldly fiancé. Mrs. North has not been seen since her "accident," and is likely still recovering.

Charlotte strides over to her sisters at once, ignoring the cautious looks of the islanders. The Norths have certainly failed to quell Mrs. Fisher's tongue. I suppose that means I am free to speak as well, but now that I finally can, I realize the desire to do so has died. What would my story be now, other than fodder for the island gossip—bound to be twisted out of shape. No, I will rather discuss it with someone like Benjamin, who will carefully examine the evidence rather than rush to blame the devil.

Charlotte's reunion with her sisters is heartwarming, though. Both Adelaide and Sophie embrace her, and even Evelyn lets go of her lovely man to clasp her sister's hands. The oldest North girl moves on to me next, showering me in praise for caring for her sister, and even introduces me to her fiancé. Charlotte's smile is so bright that it could light up the sky, and not even her father can help but smile back. When the church door opens and we are ready to enter, I see him gently place a hand on Charlotte's shoulder and squeeze. He must be pleased to see her so happy and healthy.

"How is your mother?" I ask Adelaide as the two of us slip inside.

"Better now." Adelaide beams. "She sits up more often and paints a little, but she still has to be careful. The doctor says that her neck took some damage as well."

"Does she miss your sister?"

Adelaide shrugs as we move up the aisle. "It is better this way," she says cryptically. "James will be leaving again soon." I smile and nod, but inwardly I sigh. I do not think Noreen and Mrs. Hill should live with the knocker for even one more day. They are unravelling quickly.

"Perhaps she could come home anyway," I say, though I know perfectly well how little say in the matter Adelaide has. I am merely voicing an idle wish.

"It's better for *Charlotte* to stay away," Adelaide clarifies, in a voice that leaves me cold. "*I* miss her, though," she adds softly. "Mother doesn't want us to go to the clergy house anymore. She says that Charlotte doesn't deserve the pleasure of our company. I write her letters, but don't know if she gets them." The girl looks desperately unhappy, and for once I am at a loss for words.

I am about to slide into my usual pew, a couple of rows down from the front, but Adelaide will not have it.

"Sit with us," she says. "We have plenty of room, and you escorted Charlotte."

It feels a little precarious to accept the invitation of a thirteen-year-old girl, whom I know has not conferred with her elders, but the throng is such by then that I quickly relent and follow Adelaide. Thankfully, no one seems to think this strange, and Charlotte even waits for me so that we can sit together, close to the aisle. Adelaide, seated on her other side, promptly takes Charlotte's hand in hers, and does not let it go before it is time to pray.

The service, at least, is reassuring in its normalcy. Mrs. Hill plays wonderfully, and a few sunbeams find their way inside to shoot shafts of light through the room. The scent of warm wax from the many candles is like a comforting blanket, and the knocker seems awfully far away. I think about Benjamin again, and miss him keenly. Sundays with him had been for exploration, and we had spent many hours together on the beach after church looking for fossils and other peculiarities. Now all that awaits me at the schoolhouse is empty rooms and quiet hours. I do not even have my work to focus on, with the children running free through the fields all summer.

I am so focused on my own longing that it takes me a while to notice that Reverend Hill's eyes have fastened on Charlotte again, just as they did the last time I sat here. I can hardly turn my head to check if she is looking at him as well, but I figure that she must be, since he *is* the focus of attention in here. Mrs. Hill frowns on her broad stool and I am puzzled. One would think that the reverend should have his fill of Charlotte now that she lives under his roof, but apparently not.

If anything, the gawking seems to have grown worse, and a pained expression of shame—which I know only too well—flashes on his features whenever his gaze lingers on her.

And yet, despite the shame, his eyes sparkle, too—just like hers do.

A cold fist forms in my chest and stays there like a lump of ice. When the reverend's voice falters for moment, the ice expands and makes it hard to breathe.

I look at Mrs. Hill, who is looking at her husband. Her face is a rigid mask, every line etched with a sharp blade. When she turns her gaze on Charlotte, the mask cracks for a brief moment, and the rage I see beneath it makes me gasp.

·40·

charlotte

The heady sense of triumph has me walking on clouds for almost a week after Jasper first climbed into my bed. He has climbed into it again every night since, forfeiting prayer for desire. In the wee hours he leaves me exhausted and wet on the sheets, if not entirely satisfied. Sometimes he cries, but I do not mind.

I figure it will pass in time.

I suppose my satisfaction, too, is something that will come in time. As for now, the victory itself keeps me happy and content. They said that I could not—but I *did*, and every night when he comes to me, it is another laurel leaf for my crown.

My days are spent waiting for night, building up a hunger—which is why, I suppose, I often find myself in the clergy house pantry, scavenging for meat scraps and pieces of rock sugar. Sometimes, while I wait for him, I undress on the bed and use my hands to mimic his caresses from the night before. The knocker is often with me then, touching its own mirror body. It is not hard to find satisfaction when I am on my own, and when the touches bring me to ecstasy, the knocker burns, too, beside me. We turn our heads to each other on the pillow and kiss. It feels like nothing but air, but smells of cooked meat. Its eyes sometimes, briefly, turn red.

When Jasper is with me, the knocker is drawn like a dog to the scent of our coupling. It watches with glee as we wrestle on the sheets, and seems to take as much delight in the victory as I do. When I walk in the sunlit garden, I sometimes see it dancing, spinning, and leaping down on the beach, wearing my naked body. I rejoice in its joy, and it rejoices in me.

We are much the same now, the knocker and I, thriving in our unholy covenant.

It is on the sixth day it happens. I have just been in the pantry for some ham, and am making my way upstairs with the laden plate. It has been a quiet day, with Jasper gone to visit a dying man on the other side of the island and Noreen busy with laundry. I have spent all morning outside, sitting in the grass and dreaming of the future, letting the sun lick my face. I am sluggish and warm as I walk upstairs, but not so much so that I fail to notice how the door to the attic room is cracked open. This is highly unusual, as I tend to take care to close it, having seen a mouse on the stairs one day. The knocker might have left it ajar, though—it does not mind the mice—and so I am not overly cautious as I enter the attic and push the door fully open.

My heart stops in my chest when I see Mrs. Hill in my room.

This has never happened before—the woman avoids me like the plague—and yet there she is, wearing one of her frilly white dresses and standing just in front of the bed, which was tidy when I left it, but is not anymore. The sheets and the pillows are a jumbled pile on the middle of the mattress, and the face Mrs. Hill turns to me is red and wet with anger and tears.

I stop right inside the door. I dare not move a muscle.

"What is this?" she rages. Her hand has snagged the edge of a sheet and holds it up in the air. "What is this mess?" She pulls the sheets with her as she crosses the floor, and holds it up for me to see. The pristine cotton is marred with stains from our lovemaking, and a little bit of blood, too, frozen in reddish-brown smears. "Tell me it's not my *husband* who's soiling your sheets!" More angry tears come pooling from her eyes.

"Mrs. Hill," I say, both shocked and amused—though I am not ashamed. She does not own him if he comes to me, no matter what her wedding ring says. "You shouldn't be up here. It will only hurt you."

She laughs at that—a cackling sound. "Are you *mad*? This is *my* home—*my* house! I go where I like!" She drops the sheet to the floor as if it is on fire, then rips the plate of ham right out of my hands and throws it against the wall. Shards of china and slices of pink meat join the sheet on the rag rug. I barely flinch, though, being used to Mother.

"Cocky little harlot," Mrs. Hills exclaims, "serving yourself from *my* stores. Who do you think you are?" Her eyes meet mine, burning wild. "What have you been promising him? Children? Solace? Escape? I knew you were up to something, ever since the first time I saw you ogling him in church, but I *never* thought you were shameless enough to do it *here,* under my roof! Have you no respect?"

"Perhaps he is in love with me," I say. "Perhaps there is no other reason—"

"*Love?*" Her eyes go wide, and she spits out the word as if it is the most ridiculous thing in the world. "My God, Charlotte, are you truly that naive? It's not *love* that makes a man find comfort in the arms of a younger—and simpler—woman. It speaks of a lacking in *him,* don't you see? A failure, an insecurity—"

"Unless it's *you* that's lacking," I say, admittedly not as calm anymore. I do not like what she is telling me, and I do not like *how* she says it—speaking to me as if I were a child.

"Charlotte." Her voice is brimming with exasperation. "Day after day, night after night, he has denied his attraction to you when I asked him. He has *lied* and refused to admit that this is even happening. Is that *love* to you? Is that worth throwing your life away for? He is a *man of God,* Charlotte; he will *never* divorce me. Even if you give him children, he can *never* claim them." Her burning gaze is firmly glued to mine; her shallow breathing comes rapidly. The words make me feel as though I am being slapped or submerged in ice-cold water.

"You are young," she says more calmly. "I was, too, not long ago, and I remember how powerful emotions can be when you lack the experience to temper them. I don't blame you—not deep down—but neither do I blame myself. It is *Jasper* that is to blame for this. He should have been able to resist temptation, especially with a *devil* on the loose!"

"You cannot say for sure that it isn't love." I know that I sound like a sullen child, but I cannot stop the words from coming. "But even if it's not, it's of no concern. Does *my* desire count for nothing?"

This makes her flinch. "You are young and beautiful. You can have *anyone*. Why would you choose a married *priest*?"

"To see if I could?" I suggest.

"Are you truly that cold?" She shakes her head. "Would you willingly cause all this pain just for your own gratification? No, Charlotte, I don't believe you are that selfish. I think you are a foolish girl, led astray and grappling to keep your dignity. But if there is one thing I have learned, and gladly will pass on, it's that the most important lesson in life is to let go of things you *cannot have*. Clinging to them will only cause you pain—"

I cut her off. "*I* am not pitiful. *You* are!" Seeing as how miserable she is all the time, she is hardly the right person to give advice.

"Tell me that again," she bites out, "when you are disowned by your father and abandoned by your lover, and sit there alone with children that you cannot feed—"

"You are forgetting one thing," I say.

"I am?" Her eyebrows rise. "What is that, Charlotte? That he *loves* you?" She says it mockingly, rolling her eyes.

"No. That I am *not alone.*"

The knocker comes then, like a wind. It lifts the soiled sheet and makes it dance in the air. The shards of china littering the floor fly up and are thrown at Mrs. Hill's face. She cries out and lifts her arms to protect herself, but she is barely more than skin and bones, so it does very little in the end. She cries out again when a shard cuts her cheek, and another one lodges in her thumb. The sight of blood calms me down. It feels utterly—entirely—just.

I step aside when she runs for the door, followed by more jagged shards and even a slice of ham, dusty from the floor. When the door slams shut behind her, the pieces clatter to the floor, quite useless.

"That was immensely foolish of her," I huff as I slump down on the stripped bed. "She should know better by now than to test me." The knocker agrees with a firm rap in the floor.

Her words do bother me, though. They are like buzzing bees in my head even as I try to swat them away and tell myself that she is merely a desperate woman, clinging to what little she has. The picture she drew of my future was grim, and certainly not one I want. I do have the knocker, that is true, but what if it one day decides to leave? Who will feed me then, if I have no spirit to fetch cake for me?

"You wouldn't do that, would you? You wouldn't leave me all alone?"

The knocker raps twice—no.

I let out my breath in one long exhale.

"She will throw me out for sure now," I complain. "She will go to Father—or Evelyn—to make sure that I leave this house."

The knocker confirms with a rap in the ceiling.

"She must clean her wounds first, though. Treating me as a silly girl," I mutter. "Treating me as if I'm nothing at all . . ." The anger is seething, writhing in my belly. "*She* must go," I say. "Today." She is known to be ill, so perhaps to an asylum. "Frighten her," I say. "Make her lose her mind. Do what you like, but just get her out of my way—although no fire and no stones," I remind my friend. "Be stealthy, like I know you can be." I think of Dr. Crown's accident.

There is another reason, too, that this must happen. Mrs. Hill knows my secret now. She knows that I am friendlier with the knocker than I have let on and that it does, to some degree, do my bidding. The thought of anyone else finding out makes my stomach tie up in a knot. "Make sure she tells no one what happened up here," I whisper to the air, and give a relieved sigh when the knocker replies with a rap.

It will save me, again.

When I have calmed down enough to put the bed back in order, I swipe up the china shards with one of the psalm books and carry them downstairs to the kitchen in my skirt. I want the room to look as it always does when Jasper comes to me tonight—*if* he comes. Mrs. Hill may be speaking to him this very moment, telling him of how she found traces of us on the sheets, and how the knocker attacked her when I wanted it to. Or she could be crossing the island, headed for my father's house. Adelaide will be frightened for sure if she learns how close I have become to the knocker. Perhaps I will lose *all* of my sisters if they find out how things are with the spirit and me—and that I let Jasper Hill come into my bed, night after night after night.

I feel sick when I think about it. Sick and dizzy.

That is why I am relieved to see Mrs. Hill outside the kitchen window, crossing the yard in the afternoon sun. Jasper seems not to be home yet, and that certainly adds to the sense of relief. She may not have spoken to anyone yet, and there is still a little time to stop her. I go to the window and watch as she paces back and forth, seemingly looking for someone—probably Noreen. Her face under the elaborate hairdo is a stiff mask of despair.

The cut on her cheek glistens red.

Then, suddenly, halfway across the yard, she abruptly lifts up in the air—at least three feet off the ground. Her body flips horizontally and her limbs begin to flail. Her mouth opens, trying to scream, but she never emits a sound—at least not one that I can hear. She just hangs there suspended for a second or two, then her body convulses violently, before falling back down on the ground, heavy and hard like a sack of potatoes.

Even before I run outside, I know that she is dead.

·41·

ruth

Noreen sends the youngest Newell boy to alert me. He must have run all the way as fast as he could, because his face is red and his breathing labored when I open the door, already anxious from the ferocity of his knocking.

The terror in his eyes does nothing to put me at ease.

"You must come at once!" the little boy cries. He is so flustered that he forgets to take off his cap, and his hands are everywhere, flying through the air, unable to settle for even one second.

"What is it?" I say, already grappling for my coat on the hook by the door. "What has happened?" I fetch my hat and umbrella as well before stepping outside where the boy is waiting, jumping from foot to foot. I imagine his pregnant sister bleeding—or his old grandfather outside the barn with a broken foot. The strongest image of all, though, is one of the clergy house set ablaze—and after the horizon yields no smoke, of some poor creature crushed beneath a pile of flying rocks.

"It's Mrs. Hill," the boy says breathlessly. "She is dead—or at least they think so. She keeled over in the yard," he informs me. "Aunt Noreen said you must come at once."

My heart is already racing in my chest, and my breathing comes quick and shallow. I waste no more time interrogating the boy, but follow as fast as I can in his track when he sets off again, taking the shortcut across the fields.

I can feel it long before we arrive. There is a darkness in the air, thick enough to cut, even if I cannot see it—as if the place is polluted, laboring under a cloud of toxic smoke. Or perhaps it is just that news of the death already has me in despair.

There is no one out in the clergy house yard. It is utterly deserted but for one lone seagull, ogling us with vicious eyes. When we near the entrance, it takes flight with a cry. Noreen opens one of the double doors before we have had time to knock. The housekeeper looks pale and her eyes burn black, wide with shock.

"Oh, Miss Russel." Her voice is thick with grief, and she comes out on the stairs to embrace me. "Oh, what a tragedy," she wails. "What horrible, horrible wickedness!"

"What happened?" I ask against her shoulder, noting how shrill my voice sounds.

"She just fell over," the Newell boy answers from behind me.

"Is that true?" I ask Noreen, who nods against my shoulder, still holding me tight. I have a feeling of being a raft for the poor woman—a crutch she uses to keep herself upright.

"You must help us," she says, sobbing. "I feel so useless, and I couldn't think of anyone else."

"Of course," I say. "Of course." I gently push her away from me so that I can see her face. "Where is the reverend? Where is Charlotte?"

"Inside." She nods to the open door and the looming darkness.

"Let's go inside, then." It takes all my courage to say those words, and I do not *want* to go inside—but if not me, then who? Noreen is right; there is only me.

The housekeeper shows me into the day room, where Mrs. Hill lies on the plum-colored sofa. I barely notice that the reverend is there, too, sitting in a chair with his face hidden in his hands, and Charlotte is behind him, wearing a yellow dress. But they are of no importance to me. The only one I see—that I cannot force my gaze away from—is Mrs. Hill herself, dressed all in white, which matches her pallor. Her eyes are still open, looking up at the ceiling, but they are as vacant and dead as pebbles on the beach. For the first time, I notice their pretty color: pale blue, like the sky or the sea in cloudy weather. Her blond hair is still pinned up, but holds pieces of debris: grass and dirt. She should have looked peaceful—calm in death—with all her muscles slack and all wrinkles gone, but she does not. A glistening gash mars her pale cheek. Her lips are parted to show her teeth in sort of a snarl, and her hands on her chest are tightly curled up, like talons.

She looks like a madwoman, ready to strike.

"She just . . . fell over." Charlotte sounds astonished. "I saw it from the kitchen window."

"Had she ever done this before?" I let out a shivering breath. "Fallen over, I mean? Or did she complain about pain?" I *need* to find a cause for this. I *need* to be able to explain what has happened, so that my dark suspicions will not take hold and grow.

"She took headache powders every day." Reverend Hill's head rises from the cup of his hands, his gaze dazed and unfocused. A half-empty tumbler of liquor stands before him on the polished table. "She also served herself generously from the laudanum bottle."

"It looks as though she has had a seizure," I note. "Did you see anything like that, Charlotte?"

"She twitched, once," the girl responds.

"What is that?" I point to the wound on her cheek, and notice several smaller cuts besides, littering the canvas of her face. Her long-fingered hands, too, have tiny wounds, as if she has been bitten by something small and angry.

Noreen shakes her head—she does not know, and Charlotte mirrors her movement.

"It could have happened in the fall, perhaps," the reverend suggests.

"Might have been her heart that did her in," Noreen says. "It was quite broken."

"That is not how the body works," the reverend notes. He reaches out a hand for his glass, but his movements are sluggish and slow. "She never complained of chest pains," he informs me.

"Perhaps she served herself *too* generously from the laudanum bottle," Charlotte suggests. "They do say that excess use can take a toll on the body." I do not like her calm. She should be distraught—shaken and tearful. Even if she and Mrs. Hill had not gotten along, the latter's death should warrant something more than the slight disdain I see in Charlotte's eyes.

"Perhaps it was that *devil*." Noreen's sharp voice cracks through the air. "Perhaps it was done with taunting her with needles and decided to kill her instead!"

"We don't know that," says the reverend.

"It has never killed before," says Charlotte.

"Mrs. Hill never asked for any of it." Noreen sobs, pressing a handkerchief to her eyes. "What fool lets a devil in through his doors?" She looks at the reverend, quite unashamed, and a part of me is proud of her for speaking so candidly—and for voicing my own thoughts so perfectly.

"If nothing else, it couldn't have been good for her nerves," I agree. The laudanum was news to me, though not a surprise. And letting a troublesome spirit into the home of a sickly woman had, indeed, been foolish.

"I only meant to conquer it," the reverend mutters. "It was my Christian duty—"

Noreen interrupts him. "She *begged* you not to. She *begged* you not to take her in!" The look she sends Charlotte is anything but friendly.

"That's quite enough, Noreen." Reverend Hill slams his empty glass back on the table. "And Charlotte had nothing to with it," he adds before rising from his seat to start pacing the floor. "Antonia had some affliction—she *must* have had." He steers his steps toward the door, and Noreen and I part to let him out. We all remain quiet as he crosses the hall, and slams the front door behind him with such force that the walls reverberate. Shortly after, we can see his retreating back through the window as he makes his way through the garden, toward the sea below.

"We should clean her up," I say, when the silence has stretched for long enough. "She should wear something else—something black—and perhaps we can find a cross to place around her neck?"

"I'll find something," Charlotte offers at once, seemingly happy to escape the room and the presence of the corpse. I would have figured Noreen was better suited to choose attire for Mrs. Hill, but the housekeeper does not protest, and so I do not either. Perhaps Noreen would rather that Charlotte left, too. Perhaps she does not want her to touch the body.

Whatever the reason, it is Noreen and I who carry Mrs. Hill from the sofa to the cleared dining room table. Though she was lithe in life, she is heavy in death, and we struggle to make it a dignified transition, huffing and puffing all the way. I do my best not to look at the face—at the frozen, ugly grimace—as we lay her upon the gleaming oak and light all the candles in the room.

Next, we close the curtains and stop all the clocks in the house, before heating water in the kitchen. We fetch scissors from Mrs. Hill's own sewing set and begin to cut the body loose from the long, white dress. Noreen has brought a bottle of brandy from the reverend's store, along with two sizable glasses for us. I do see the wisdom in the act. We certainly need all the fortification we can get to make it through the long hours ahead.

Noreen sniffles softly as we wash the skin and comb the hair. I cannot help but notice the red stretch marks running down Mrs.

Hill's abdomen. We are quick to uncurl the talon-like hands and close the staring eyes—erase the ugly grimace as best we can—before rigor mortis sets in, yet it is hard to make her look completely at peace, especially with the blue tint that has come bleeding into the white of her skin. Though there is some warmth in her yet, she will soon be utterly cold. We can do nothing about the wounds, though.

"At least *she* will have to go now," Noreen says grimly while moving the damp cloth across the pale skin. "He *cannot* allow her to stay with only him in the house. *No one* would think it seemly, even if he is a reverend."

I nod. "Her father will never agree to it."

"And certainly not *Mrs.* North." Noreen gives me a dark look. "I used to feel sorry for their daughters, living under her thumb, but I've come to see the wisdom in keeping them on tight leashes—"

"No," I interrupt. "*You* cannot blame Charlotte for this." Those are serious allegations that should not be made without ample proof.

"Mrs. Hill knew, though." The housekeeper seems not to heed my advice. "She *knew* there was something wrong from the start. She could *feel* the rot from the beginning—"

"It was never a secret that Charlotte had a stowaway."

"Oh, that *thing*." Noreen spits out the word. She is teary again, sniffling incessantly. "It drives me *mad* not to know where it is or what it'll do next. Even now my skin crawls just from thinking about it. It could be in here with us this very moment! It could do to us what it did to Mrs. Hill!" Her eyes are wide with fear when she looks at me, and suddenly I feel it, too: the uncertainty and the terror. My heart works fast in my chest.

"She might have taken too much laudanum," I mutter.

"Laudanum makes you sleep," says Noreen. "Mrs. Hill was walking around."

"A damage then, from overuse." I will not—*cannot*—let myself believe that the knocker has such power.

"Don't be naive, Miss Russel." Noreen's voice is as harsh as I deserve. "Just because you don't want to believe it doesn't make it any less true."

I nod once and hold out my glass, needing more brandy to soften the sting.

We finish our unpleasant task in silence, and when Charlotte arrives with her hands full of black fabric, Noreen excuses herself and goes outside with the washbasin, leaving me alone with her. Though I have never been afraid of Charlotte before, I find her presence today unnerves me, and I wet my lips nervously as we set about looking through the dresses she has chosen. I am grateful for the brandy now. It nests like an amber-colored egg in my belly, radiating strength and heat.

As we hold up the garments to inspect them, I notice how Charlotte often looks back at the table, at the prostrate corpse at the center.

"This must be very hard for you, Charlotte," I say gently. "Mrs. Hill was so generous to you, letting you into her home."

Her gaze snaps to me, quick as a viper, blazing with suspicion, if only for a second. "Yes," she says in a sweet voice. "Mrs. Hill was very kind."

"It's hard when someone dies unexpectedly," I say, folding up a skirt. "It's easier when it follows a sickness, or if the deceased is old."

Her eyes are full of wonder. "She just walked out in the yard, then—suddenly—she was gone."

"Noreen thinks the knocker had something to with it," I say carefully. Even if I am emboldened by the brandy, I still know to watch my step. "Do you think that could be true?"

Charlotte shrugs. "I don't control the knocker, but I cannot see why it would suddenly kill someone when it never did before. Rather, it might have been a broken heart." She gives a thin smile. "As Noreen said."

"Why would Mrs. Hill have a broken heart?" I ask, with my own heart in my throat, thinking of the precarious relationship between Charlotte and Reverend Hill.

"The child, of course." Charlotte motions to the corpse with her hand. "It died before they came here."

"Oh," I say, almost disappointed by the simple explanation. "But you cannot say for sure that it *wasn't* the knocker. Did it have anything against Mrs. Hill?" Again, I can hardly breathe. The idea is just too tremendous—too overwhelming to comprehend—even if it once pelted me with rocks.

"It didn't like her," Charlotte admits. "But, then, it doesn't like many people."

"Why is that?"

"I cannot say, but I don't think it killed Mrs. Hill."

When the body is dressed in somber black, and we have clasped a cross around her neck, I leave Noreen to tend to the candles and step outside in the darkening night. My feet are heavy as I cross the garden and approach the still figure perched upon a rock on the beach. The reverend does not react when I arrive, though he must have heard my steps. His gaze is glued to the cold, lapping water, to the dark waves rolling rhythmically to shore.

I sit down next to him on the large stone slab and place my hand on his on the rough surface. His skin is very cold—almost as cold as his wife's.

"A dead whale washed up here once," I tell him. "I brought the students here to see it."

"I remember," he says in a rough voice. I am happy to notice that he does not appear to have brought a bottle with him.

"The islanders will come soon to verify the news," I say. "Young Newell and his friends must have spread it far and wide by now. You should be there to give them answers."

He nods slowly but does not reply.

I take a deep breath before my next question. "Noreen thinks that the knocker—"

"Charlotte had nothing to do with it," he interrupts me.

"I spoke of the knocker, not Charlotte."

"Well, it's hers, is it not?"

"Charlotte does not control the knocker." I repeat the words that I have heard too many times to count. "Unless you think Dr. Crown was right after all?"

"Of course not," he scoffs. "But I will have Antonia sent to the mainland for an autopsy. That should bring Noreen some peace."

"And you, too, I reckon," I say. "You must be wondering, too." He would be a fool not to. "Did the knocker have a reason to dislike your wife?"

"This is beneath you, Miss Russel." The reverend's voice is as cold as ice. "I know what you are insinuating, and it's *not* appropriate with my wife lying dead."

"I'm not insinuating anything," I counter, although I certainly was. "It's no secret that Charlotte has a fondness for you. She has been besotted for a while . . ."

"That is all in the past," he declares. "Her childish longings have *nothing* to do with our relationship now." Somehow, I do not like the sound of that one bit.

"But if it *was* the knocker—"

"What of it, Miss Russel?"

"Might it not be worth it to consider if Charlotte—quite unconsciously—gave it an incentive?" The brandy has made me bolder than is good for me.

"Dr. Crown was mistaken," the reverend says, his gaze still on the waves. "Charlotte is a victim, not a foe."

"But if it killed your *wife,* Reverend. Isn't it worth it to—"

"No!" He is up from the rock in one fluid movement. "I thank you for your help today, Miss Russel, but you must refrain from making *dangerous* accusations. It will only come back to haunt you when it is proven that Antonia died of natural causes."

"But what if it was *just* the knocker," I venture, "without Charlotte having anything to do with it? Doesn't it make this a *very* dangerous being? Something you cannot fight all on your own?" After all,

Noreen complained that the praying alone did not work. "A spirit that strong might require more than *one* priest—"

"I will consider it," he says, in a voice that tells me he probably will not. "We don't know *what* happened to Antonia."

"That is true," I admit. "But whenever there's been unexplained occurrences on this island recently—like the attacks on me and Mr. West—it has always come back to the knocker."

"And yet, we cannot *assume*—"

"Of course not, but we must *think* it."

"Must we?" His breathing comes hard. When he speaks again, after a good long while, his voice is calm, but forcibly so. "I thank you again for your assistance, Miss Russel, but I would like to grieve my wife in peace now."

"Of course," I say, rising from the rock. "Be kind to Noreen. She has had a difficult day."

"I will," he promises, but does not come to take my hand as he usually does when parting. "Good night, Miss Russel. I will repay your kindness some other time."

"Good night, Reverend," I reply. "And God rest Antonia's soul."

When I arrive home that night, I am broken. The walk has mellowed the buzz of the brandy, and the loss of it makes me feel naked and cold. I sit down by the kitchen table to weep, then I make tea that goes cold before I taste it. It all feels so awful—the possibilities so frightening—that I fear I will not sleep. I rub my hands against my face in an effort to expel the images crowding in my mind: Antonia's ugly smile, her hands curled like talons; Charlotte at the window, quite calm.

The dark silhouette of the reverend on the beach, as lost a man as I ever saw.

I find a piece of paper and start penning a letter to Benjamin. My hands shake while I write, but hopefully he will understand the scrawls. *Come back to Margaret's Keep,* I write. *I cannot do this without you.*

·42·

jasper

On the second day after Antonia's passing, I have her crated with ice to go to the mainland. I stay away from the dining room while the men I hired nail down the lid and carry the sorry casket outside. The crate and the ice come from the harbor, and the former carries George North's name on the side.

Antonia would have hated that fact.

None of the men looks me in the eyes as they pass me in the hall. This is not how things are done on the island. The deceased is supposed to lie on display while friends and neighbors come to say their goodbyes. Corpses are to be temples for the living before they are lowered in the ground. They are not meant to be shipped off like barrels of fish, or cut into with sharp knives—and yet, it is the only reasonable thing to do.

None of us will know peace until we know what killed her.

I beg for a faulty heart or an enlarged liver. I beg for an aneurism or epilepsy. I want it to be anything but what Noreen is thinking and Miss Russel fears—and what I fear, too, in my darkest hours, nursing the bottle alone in my office. But how does one prove interference from a spirit? Will there be markings inside the body? Some anomaly that does not make sense? I dream of an answer that leaves no doubt, but know from experience how hard it can be to obtain such a thing from the knocker. Perhaps it is simply in the spirit's nature to be always elusive and vague.

The worst of it all is that I miss my wife. Despite all our quarrels—and how our marriage had derailed—I miss her presence in the house. I know how it is common after a death that the rooms seem suddenly vast and empty without the noises and smells that accompany a person. How the air itself seems to shift. It is more than that, though. I miss who we used to be, when we were both young and life was easy—who we still *could* have been, if said life had not dealt us a terrible blow.

I remember how Antonia used to laugh, when I first met her in her father's parlor. It had been such a thrilling sound, reminding me of sunshine and butterflies. She had been such a perfect match, too: the daughter of a reverend, so she knew what to expect. And I, just starting out in my career—still so eager to make a difference, so hungry for a purpose. I remember how I thought that she was perfect: a blond angel on my arm. I remember how my chest swelled with pride on our wedding day when I could finally declare that, yes, she was mine. I had loved her dearly then, and she had loved me, too. I remember how we said that we were lucky—that a well-suited match like ours rarely came with the gift of true love.

We could not wait for our life to begin, and now hers has ended in tragedy.

The knocker responds to her death with a flurry of activity. It is giddy, I think, unable to hold still. Perhaps it is rejoicing in its victory—though I try not to let my mind go down that dark, winding path. It opens drawers and rummages through the contents, moves my pens, and topples candles. It will not leave Antonia's belongings alone, but throws her dresses on the floor and litters the garden with her fine satin shoes. Yesterday, we found her pearls and brooches in the soup Noreen was making. Charlotte could not help but laugh, which made me gasp like some pious elderly lady.

I know it is just the shock of it all that makes her behave inappropriately. Charlotte has been through so much already, and this sudden death—which she witnessed—must weigh on her immensely. We have been eating together in the kitchen now, like peasants, while Antonia's corpse has claimed the dining room table. There is a rustic charm to it that I might have appreciated if everything else had not been so terrible. I have offered Charlotte one of the guest rooms instead of her attic chamber, but she has so far declined. She has stayed for so long in the attic, she says, that it feels like home now. She prefers it there, she claims, even if the sun heats the roof tiles and makes it almost unbearably hot.

I still go up there at night. I cannot seem to stop myself. I truly should be able to—especially with Antonia lying dead in the dining room—but my godless desire seems to know no bounds. So to Charlotte I go—not to pray, but to rut, driven as much by shame as by lust. It is as though my own depravity is beckoning me as I make my way up the attic stairs, as if I long for the self-loathing that follows in the debauchery's wake. As if the sin is somehow delicious to me, and I rejoice in my own fall from grace. Perhaps I deserve no better. Perhaps I am finally embracing the ugliness within. Antonia had certainly seen it clearly, pointing out my failings daily. I feel silly now for having so vehemently defended myself. My wife *had* known me better than I know myself.

Or perhaps it is all due to this simple truth: if you are told enough times that you are rotten, what used to be a spot can grow like mold on bread, until everything you are is rot.

When our battle on the sheets has come to an end, and I leave the young woman—whom I have sullied and defiled, despite my solemn promise to protect her—I make my way down the stairs, accompanied by the sound of the crying child. It is a different sound now, though, more *hopeful* than before. Especially in the days since I became a widower, its siren call has taken on a more joyful timbre. In my more charitable moments, I think it might be what is pulling me back to the attic room and Charlotte: the dream of a child, another little boy, but then I know I am only fooling myself. I go there because I am so warmly received, and because the pleasure is like a potent drug that I cannot—*will* not—be free of.

Charlotte makes it easy to sin, though the guilt is riding me as soon as I have left the warmth of her sheets. Her father entrusted her to my care. I was supposed to banish her wicked spirit, not ruin her heavenly soul—and yet, I still go, every night, to add more fuel to the flames of hell. Perhaps Antonia's death was a punishment—or a warning—but, even if so, I know it will not help. I will still go—to rut, then cry, soaking her pillow with the salt of my shame.

"You are a widower now," she says, trying to soothe me. "The sin cannot be as grave when you are no longer married."

But she does not understand, and she has no care for *herself*. Perhaps the hold of the spirit grows stronger now that she sins with me? I am, after all, still a priest.

"Think of what might change for the better, now that Antonia is gone," she whispers.

"You deserve a stronger man than me," I reply. "You deserve someone unsullied."

"I would rather have you. God forgive me, but I would rather have you."

She might not see the extent of the rot. Might not see what it truly means that the knocker is still here, wreaking havoc and pulling pranks. Might not see it for what it is: my utter, devastating failure.

Instead of helping her, as I should, I keep serving myself greedily, like a pagan king at a feast.

·43·

ruth

I miss the children and the chatter of the schoolroom. I miss Benjamin, too—desperately. Every morning I go to the grocery store to check if a reply to my letter has arrived, but so far, it has not. I wonder if my words were too much—too unhinged. If he would rather not think of the horrors that dwell on Margaret's Keep now that he is back on the mainland. Perhaps he has decided to leave it all behind him. I would not blame him if he did. Self-preservation is a worthy endeavor—but I miss him. I do. Every hour of every day.

Mrs. Hill's passing has left me in agony. Though I fight it with all my might, it has been hard to escape the fear and keep the dark speculations at bay. I worry for everyone—myself included. Worry for our sanity more than anything. It rattles you, being faced with a danger that cannot be seen or predicted. Though my leg is much better, the wound on my soul still festers, and I have trouble sleeping and concentrating. It is hard not to let my thoughts stray to the clergy house and Mrs. Hill's death. I worry about Charlotte, too, wondering if she is victim or foe—and, if the latter, what that means. Yet I do not go to see them or seek out any news. I stay here at the schoolhouse, stewing in my misery. It is not good and it is not healthy, but it seems to be all I can manage.

I long for fall and normalcy, but fear that nothing will ever be normal again, because *I* have changed through all of this. My sense of security will be forever rattled. This is nothing like losing a fortune or a gaggle of friends. It is losing your trust in the physical world: the very ground you tread on and the air that you breathe.

What other hidden threats might nature conceal?

When a knocking on the door disturbs me, shortly after I have consumed the bread and soup that seems to be the only sustenance I can stomach these days, I am instantly alert. My heart starts racing in my chest, and it feels as though I am suffocating. I instantly recall eight days ago, when the boy came to my door to tell me of Mrs. Hill's passing, and cannot help but imagine fresh tragedies. Has something happened to the reverend or to Mrs. North? Is there a fire or a new death? To my credit, I do not hesitate but go to the door at once, and do not even pause to calm myself before flinging it open.

The daylight outside is blinding, flooding my poor eyes, but not so much so that I do not recognize the man standing right outside the door: his mustard-colored jacket and unruly whiskers. The glint of metal in his spectacles.

"Benjamin." I breathe his name, then I throw myself at him, quite unashamed. I wind my arms around him and press my cheek to his left side, then his right side—and then, to my great surprise, I press my lips to his.

"Oh, Ruth," he breathes, when the kiss has ended. There is surprise in his voice, but he seems pleased, too, and is smiling when he carries his suitcase inside. I, however, am both flustered and mortified. I cannot believe what just happened, what I did.

"I'm sorry," I mutter, as I lead the way into the kitchen. "I don't know what came over me. I have been so alone since you left, and . . . I missed you." My hair has come quite undone, and I push stray tendrils back behind my ears.

"Oh, Ruth," he says again, and places a hand on my shoulder, stopping me in my tracks. He spins me around on the scuffed kitchen floor, and kisses me again—more thoroughly this time. "I have missed you, too," he says, holding me close, gently pressing my head to his chest. Holding me as if I am precious.

We stand like that for a while, enjoying the other's presence. When we let go of each other, we do so only reluctantly. All the fear and worry in me has momentarily fled. It feels as though I have rid myself of a heavy burden.

"Tea?" I ask, adding a tiny smile. It feels strange now to go through our usual rituals. Everything has changed.

"Of course." He smiles, and I think he can feel it, too, how the new intimacy has charged the air and instantly transformed our little world. My hands are shaking when I open the cupboard and find his cup.

"I didn't bother with replying to your letter," he says from behind me. "The message seemed so dire that I figured it was better if I just came."

"I am immensely glad that you did," I say, unable to contain the joy. I even find myself smiling as I measure out the tea.

"I can tell," he says good-naturedly from his usual place by the table. "I shouldn't have left in the first place. I can see that now. It wasn't fair to leave you alone with it all."

"No one had died yet when you left," I remind him. "And it isn't your responsibility to take on the burdens of Margaret's Keep."

"Neither is it yours," he tells me gently. "I suppose, most of all, I came back to beg you to leave with me. Going back to the mainland did wonders for my sanity. It quite restored my equilibrium, and I think it could do the same for you. Now that I am here, though . . ." He takes a deep breath.

"Now that you are here?" I prod when he remains silent.

"I suppose it has a certain pull, this . . . spirit. And that it isn't in your nature to just leave when you might be needed."

"It's still tempting, though," I say, and place the empty cup before him. "The mystery has turned deadly, and I'm hardly equipped to handle something of such magnitude. The problem is that neither are *they,* and I worry they will drown in the knocker's wake: the reverend, Noreen, the Norths, and even Charlotte. Me being here might not prevent that from happening, but perhaps I can do *something* to steer us all clear of a complete disaster." I feel emboldened now that he is with me—strong again, because I am not alone. I loathe myself slightly for feeling this way, and yet it is the truth, warts and all. Perhaps we all have a limit for what we can shoulder by ourselves. Perhaps it is easier to face your fears if you are not doing it all alone.

"You are quite certain, then, that the knocker is behind Mrs. Hill's demise?"

"Well, it's impossible to know," I admit, "but even if the autopsy should say it was her heart, for instance, how do we know that the *cause* of the heart failure wasn't the knocker? It is Charlotte more than anything; the girl seemed so utterly cold after the fact, and the animosity between them was no secret." My hand moves nervously on the tabletop while I speak, until Benjamin catches it in his.

"I did as I said I would and looked into it," he declares. "I didn't get as far as I would have liked, but I spoke to some acquaintances and did some reading. As you know, I am quite the man of leisure now, being between assignments."

"And what did you find out?" My heart is racing again. I want to know and do *not* want to know, all at the same time.

"Well, Dr. Crown was right in that there are other cases like Charlotte's—spirits attaching themselves to young women—and young men, too, at times. He also told the truth when he said that psychiatrists and other scientists are doing research, working under the assumption that the subjects of the hauntings are in fact creating the phenomena. There is even a name for the type of spirit that is able to physically move things. From what I could glean, there have been stories about such 'knocking spirits'—or poltergeists—for as long as there have been people, from all over the world."

I am paying attention now, eagerly sucking up his words. "That is a good thing," I exclaim. "It means there must be a cure—or at least that others have fought them before."

"They have, yes. The 'cure' has changed over the years, of course. Back in the olden days, the pranks were attributed to household spirits and the afflicted tried to appease them. Then, when Christianity arrived, the pranks were blamed on demons or ghosts, but prayer does not seem to work very well against them."

"A month at the clergy house with nightly prayers has certainly done nothing for Charlotte." I laugh, then lift my gaze to his. "What *does* work? Did someone ever succeed?"

Benjamin shrugs. "Usually, they disappear on their own. Perhaps they—whatever they are—grow bored, or if scientists like Dr. Crown are to be believed, the youth at the center of the haunting grows out of it. None of the knocking spirits I read about had *killed* anyone, though. But I did read about stone throwing and things falling from the ceiling, so I do believe it is the right creature—or phenomenon, depending on your stance."

This is both encouraging and discouraging. "What about the demon?" I ask. "Did it say anything about the black demon?"

"Alas, that was all very vague." I can tell from the expression on his face that just thinking about the creature in the ceiling makes him feel uncomfortable.

"At least we know we are not alone," I say, though it feels like cold comfort. It is useful to know there are others, but it does not solve the problems at hand. "Maybe it is sated now that Mrs. Hill is gone?"

"I suppose that depends on Charlotte. None of the cases I read about at the university library ever mentioned what would happen if the people at the center of the haunting *befriended* the spirit. Rather, they seemed tormented by its presence, or they simply grew used to it. I read about other things, though." His eyes grow distant. "Witches' 'familiars,' otherworldly spirits in a witch's service—"

"Surely you don't suggest that Charlotte is a *witch*?"

"No." He gives me a quick flash of a smile. "Not as such, but I wonder if the knocker—in its lack of wisdom—perhaps believes that it is so."

"That Charlotte is a witch?" I lift the teacup to my lips, and barely even notice that the brew is scalding hot.

Benjamin nods. "If it came from the tower . . ."

"Margaret," I say, feeling cold.

"I looked into her as well," he admits, "and I found something that might be helpful, if disturbing."

"*All* of this is disturbing," I remind him in a carefree voice, but when he clears his throat and begins to talk, I steel my heart and guard my soul.

"When I first started the search, I was hoping to find something helpful that the islanders were not aware of. Margaret must have come from *somewhere,* after all; and though sources from her time are scarce, the legend is so dramatic that I figured there had to be *some* trace."

"And did you find anything?" I prompt when he falls silent.

Benjamin blinks as if waking up from a vivid daydream. "I *did* find Margaret—or at least I believe I did. A connection of mine at the university's history department let me access the old archives, and I found something astonishing in the correspondence between the abbess of a local convent and a bishop. Or rather, my colleague, who knows the archives well, found the letters. All *I* did was make sense of them." He smiles sheepishly.

"And?" I find that I *am* hungry for this knowledge. As terrible as the knocker is, it has not yet quelled all of my curiosity. Besides, I have always believed facts to be formidable weapons.

"Well." He clears his throat again. "Apparently, Margaret—who was indeed married to a very rich man—was sent to a convent in an effort to vanquish an 'evil' that was said to be following her around. But it did not work out. The nuns were plagued by knocking in the night, and things started to go missing. The abbess also mentioned 'the spirit' throwing milk pails and attacking one of the novices at prayer. That did not ruffle the abbess's feathers, however. It seems she expected no less from the devil, but she couldn't abide how the thing seemed to cater to Margaret's every whim and brought her precious gifts and rich food in the night—things that had no place in a convent. The abbess said that Margaret used the spirit to her own selfish ends, and that all who dared speak against her met with terrible misfortune. She does not say exactly what that misfortune was, but I imagine they were accidents."

"A fair assumption," I note, thinking of Mrs. North.

"The abbess, feeling the weight of responsibility, decided that Margaret posed a threat to her charges—and especially, she wrote, to the young ones, who seemed to be mesmerized by Margaret and her specter. The priest must have warned her in a previous letter that an accusation of witchcraft was out of the question, due to her husband's donations to the church, because the abbess suggested that they build a 'holding' far from other people, where Margaret could live out her days."

"The tower." I feel cold again.

"It seems likely." He takes off his spectacles and wipes them with a piece of cloth. "I cannot say for certain that *this* Margaret is *our* Margaret, but the odds are in our favor. The events took place before the church was reformed, so a little earlier than expected, but everything else fits."

"Yes, it does seem unlikely that there should be two Margarets around that time who had to be exiled," I manage at last. My mind is in turmoil, buzzing with new information. I think about the nuns—then I think about my young students meeting "the devil in the shed," and placing flowers and bones on the clergy house stairs. Might the abbess have witnessed something similar? "So what now?" I ask Benjamin.

He shrugs. "We still don't have a cure, but at least some answers."

"To think that the islanders were right all along!"

"Yes, it's devastating, isn't it?" His lips turn up at the edges. "*If* it is the same Margaret, and the knocker *did* come from the tower. We still don't know for sure," he reminds me.

"No, of course not," I agree, "but for the first time since I was hit by the rocks, it feels as though some of this makes sense. Instead of only fragments, there is now the outline of a picture."

"Which, I agree, is satisfying." He smiles at me across the table, then he reaches out a hand and captures mine. "Ruth," he says, suddenly serious. His kind blue eyes meet mine and set my heart fluttering. "What happened between us before. The kiss," he starts, and the flutter turns into a painful thumping of my heart. Is this the moment when he tells me that it cannot be? That he thinks of me only as a friend? That an old spinster like me should be beyond such longings? I take a deep breath. Whatever comes next, I trust him to deliver it with his usual kindness. "I never dared presume," he says. "Not that I didn't think of it, but you were so adamant—I wanted to respect your wishes."

"And I am grateful." I am flooded with feelings of relief and tenderness. "Not everyone would have been so kind—although, I will not—do not expect . . . You should not just to be kind. I am no youngster," I blabber. "You should not just to spare my feelings—"

"Should not what, Ruth?" He gently interrupts me, and I feel my cheeks burning.

"Should not . . . should not—" Suddenly words evade me.

"Should not love you, Ruth?" His lips curl into a soft smile. "I'm afraid it is far too late for that. I don't know if it is your courage or the magnificent umbrella, but I think I was yours from the first time I set foot in this house."

"Really?" I say, utterly surprised. I look for mockery on his face, but of course there is none. "So the islanders were right about this, too?" I cannot believe it!

Benjamin chuckles. "It seems so. Though I *do* know your stance on marriage"—he turns serious again—"just know that I will never ask that sacrifice of you, even if I might wish for it to happen."

"Then what *do* you want?" I examine his face. Who *is* this most unusual man that fate has delivered on my doorstep?

"I just want to be with you." He shrugs and looks a little abashed all of a sudden. "Perhaps there needn't be any plans beyond what we will eat for breakfast tomorrow."

"Those are the words of a scoundrel," I say, arching an eyebrow playfully. When he becomes flustered, I laugh. "Breakfast tomorrow is as far as *anyone* should plan," I say. "As recent events have shown, you never know what foe might be lurking behind the next corner. I find this ordeal has given me a whole new appreciation for the present moment."

"Yes, hasn't it just?" He speaks softly. His thumb makes circles on my wrist, causing all kinds of pleasurable sensations.

"How is your bed from the North house?" I ask. "I suspect the mattress is better than mine."

"Quite soft," he replies with a twinkle in his eye. "I am sure you will find it to your liking."

·44·

ruth

The next morning, I wake up in Benjamin's arms in the bed on loan from the Norths. It takes up most of the space in my small sitting room, but has proven to be far more comfortable than the lumpy one I keep in my bedroom. It had been such a natural thing to do the night before: curl up next to him and let our shared warmth keep the demons at bay. It had felt equally natural to shed our clothes and let our bodies give in to nature. Though I had made mistakes in the past—as a young and vulnerable student who could easily be taken advantage of—I had never been with someone like Benjamin before. First of all, it had been no mistake, and with him already so firmly rooted in my heart, it had felt like such a small leap to let him into my body as well. There had been lust, yes, but also comfort and a desire to make the other happy. In our blissful nest of blankets and pillows, there had been no place for dread.

When I first opened my eyes, my face had been nuzzled against the nape of his neck, and our limbs had been tangled together. Now we have untangled, and Benjamin has padded to the kitchen to make tea while I still linger in bed, unwilling to let harsh reality catch up with me just yet.

"They are bound to talk, now that I am back," Benjamin says from the doorway to the kitchen. He is, of course, referring to the islanders.

"Doubtlessly." I chuckle. I do not feel any guilt, though. Neither of us believes in sin—or at least not in the biblical way, and I find I would rather sin against God than sin against myself. If that makes me a heretic, so be it.

Benjamin smiles at me from across the room. The new thing between us hovers like something shimmering and invisible that is nevertheless very real—like the knocker. "Mrs. Hill's death will probably keep their attention for a while."

"They are angry about the autopsy," I say. "The islanders are very respectful of their dead."

"I admit I am curious to know what it might reveal."

"As are we all." I finally sit up, leaving the bliss and the warmth behind. "I wonder what you and I would talk about if the knocker upped and left," I say.

"Oh, I'm sure we would find something else to occupy our minds," he replies with a smile. "Hopefully something a little less disturbing."

"Perhaps we should open our own detective agency," I joke.

"We would be excellent detectives," he says with a chuckle, and I join in.

It does not take long, though, before my thoughts drift back to the trouble at hand—to what Benjamin had told me about Margaret. "We ought to go and see her," I say.

"Charlotte?" He is fussing by the stove now.

"Yes, Charlotte," I confirm. "We should meet her, assess her. Perhaps we are painting the portrait of a monster while in reality there is just a sad young woman in despair. I could be entirely wrong, you know. I might have thought I saw callousness in her that simply wasn't there."

He appears in the doorway again. His shirt is half-buttoned and he is holding a piece of toast. "You are right that we should be cautious," he admits. "Our forefathers cried 'witch' too many times, for no good reason, and with terrible results. We must be absolutely sure before even *suggesting* that she cannot be trusted."

"Yes," I decide as I slip out of bed and let my toes meet the floorboards. "We must definitely go and see Charlotte."

"We might offer her our assistance," he says. "Or at least share what we know. She, more than anyone, could use the information."

"And if she doesn't want our help?"

"Then at least we will know where she stands."

I nod as I shuffle toward him. "If she truly wants to be rid of the thing, she will be grateful for the help."

• • •

After breakfast, we go straight to the North house. It feels different now, to walk together, even if we have crossed the island side by side many times before. It is as if I am more aware of my companion. When our hands brush against each other, or when we walk in step, the whole world seems brighter, infused with a new, heady clarity.

I barely even mind walking up the driveway, though I take Benjamin's arm when offered, and we both walk uneasily—and fast. Any unexpected sound would have made me turn back and leave at once, but there is nothing but the seagulls, the waves, and the bleating of sheep.

So I face my fears and march on.

We are surprised to find the North house deserted, and our knocking goes unanswered. When we walk around to the back, however, rapping on the kitchen door yields a better result, and Miss Boden peeks her head out.

"They have all gone to the mainland," she says. "Mrs. North is to see a doctor, and the girls will do some shopping for the wedding. I think there will be tea with Mr. Eckhardt as well."

"Charlotte, too?" I ask.

"Oh, no." She shakes her head. "Charlotte is still at the clergy house."

"Is that so?" I can barely contain my astonishment. "I was so sure she would be back home by now." There is no good reason why not, with Evelyn's fiancé gone and all the praying proving futile.

"Yes, you would think so, wouldn't you?" Miss Boden swings the door fully open and leans against the doorframe. "It's none of my concern, of course, but now that Mrs. Hill is no longer with us, it doesn't seem appropriate, does it? I haven't resented the decision before, on account of Evelyn wanting the devil gone from the house while Mr. Eckhardt was here, but a young woman alone with a widower is not something I can condone." A tightening of her lips underlines the word. I think of the night Benjamin and I just shared and blush.

"Then why do Mr. and Mrs. North allow it?" I quickly ask, to cover up my embarrassment.

"Well, Mr. North and Evelyn went there to pay their respects the day after the death, and they spoke to Charlotte then, and apparently she said she *would* come home. But so far, we haven't seen her."

"But Mr. North could just go and get her," Benjamin remarks, looking unusually chic today in a double-breasted red jacket and brown pants. Under his arm sits a leather bound journal that contains his notes about Margaret.

"He *did* go there again, the day before yesterday, but I cannot tell you what happened then since he didn't tell me. The only thing I know is that Charlotte wasn't with him on his return—*and* he was in a foul mood." Miss Boden's eyes narrow and her voice drops.

"It could be that they allow it from pity," Benjamin muses. "With the reverend being so recently bereft, perhaps he finds comfort in Charlotte's company."

Miss Boden snorts and arches an eyebrow. "All the more reason to bring her home."

We certainly agree on that.

We say our goodbyes and continue our journey, following the path to the church, but taking a detour across the fields to avoid Margaret's Tower. I just cannot stomach the jagged ruins today.

The clouds gather as we approach the clergy house, obscuring the sun. They are dark and threaten with rain, and I wonder if there is a thunderstorm coming. The gloom has certainly not lessened around the place since Mrs. Hill's death, and I can feel it even by the church, surrounding me like an invisible fog.

"Something is very wrong here." I long to take Benjamin's hand in mine, but settle for his arm, seeing as how we are in public.

"It's just the sudden darkness from the clouds," he replies, trying to soothe me, but it is impossible that he does not feel it, too.

I dread what we will find when we knock on the front door, and am relieved when it is Noreen who answers. I am not prepared to speak to the reverend today, since the two of us have not exchanged a single word since our awkward encounter on the beach.

Noreen informs us in a tired voice that Charlotte is out in the garden. The woman is pale and carries dark shadows under her eyes, so is clearly still smarting from the loss of her mistress. I promise her that I will come for tea at the earliest convenience, and I mean it, too. I feel terrible for the faithful housekeeper, who has found herself caught up in such a nightmare.

We find Charlotte sitting on a stone bench behind the house, reading a book, unbothered, it seems, by the sudden clouds. She looks surprisingly radiant: her cheeks glow rosy red, and her lustrous dark hair is pinned up in her new style. She is wearing a simple black dress, but a colorful shawl in shades of blue is draped across her shoulders. I think it used to belong to Mrs. Hill.

"Miss Russel." She beams at me as we approach on the gravel path. "And Mr. West." She rises from the bench, leaving her book behind on the stone. "What brings you here? Did Noreen offer you tea?"

I cannot help but notice how quickly she has taken on the role of hostess, and it makes my skin crawl.

"No need for that." I plaster on a smile. "Where is the reverend today?"

"Oh, inside somewhere. It is hard for him, you know . . . with his wife."

"Of course," Benjamin and I both mutter, bending our heads slightly in respect.

"There's no news from the autopsy yet?" I ask.

"No. Jas—Reverend Hill says it might take a while. Do you want me to go and get him?" Her gaze flickers to the house behind us.

"Oh, no. Leave him in peace. We came here to talk to you," I say.

"Really?" Her eyes widen with surprise. "Now I am *intrigued,*" she replies, though she honestly looks more worried. "What can I do for you?" She sinks back down on the bench, and I sit beside her. Benjamin remains standing in front of us both.

"We wanted to tell you about the tower," I say, forgoing more pleasantries. Although we are there to assess her, it is equally crucial to let her know what Benjamin has found.

"The tower?" She looks at us with an expression somewhere between curiosity and annoyance. "What about it?"

Benjamin suddenly seems nervous; he fidgets on the spot and his skin looks damp. Perhaps it is Charlotte's presence he finds unnerving, or he worries that she will dismiss the information without proper thought. "I found something," he says, and opens the journal, holds it out in front of him like a Bible.

"There is new information," I clarify. "Perhaps it can be of use."

"Please." Charlotte looks at Benjamin with expectation. A small smile plays on her lips. Clearly, she is not yet convinced that our offering will be of assistance.

Benjamin clears his throat, and then he begins. He tells her about the Margaret he found in the archive, and her unfortunate stay at the convent. About the holding that was built for her to live out her days in. When he has reached the end of his notes, he finally looks up, considering his mission complete. He has found the facts and given them to Charlotte; now all we have to do is watch and learn.

At first, though, she just seems confused. "I see how you think this story is similar to what has happened to me, but how does it help?"

Benjamin and I exchange looks.

"Mr. West thinks it might be the same creature," I attempt to clarify, in case it makes any difference. "He thinks Margaret's unruly spirit *is* the knocker, and that it has been trapped in the tower. When the earthquake happened, it got loose."

"I can see that." She sounds impatient. An angry little wrinkle has appeared on her forehead. "It doesn't change anything, though, to have it down in writing. We always figured that it might have come from the tower . . . Or do you suggest that I lock myself away, too? That I build myself a tower far from people?"

"No." I quell an urge to laugh. "Absolutely not!"

"We just thought you might want to know," Benjamin explains. "We figured it might be useful to you."

"How?" she demands, looking at us. "It's just another story of misery—"

"Well, haven't you been wondering—?" My voice falters, faced with her anger.

"Margaret never escaped, did she? If the legend is true, she *died* there." Charlotte rises from the bench again, and this time she brings her book with her. "How is that going to help *me*? The knocker wasn't even the true villain of that piece," she declares, then turns her back and marches along the gravel path, away from us.

"Not the villain?" Benjamin mutters, then he repeats it louder, aimed at her retreating back. "How is the knocker *not* the villain? It caused misery among the nuns, and it was the *reason* behind Margaret's cruel fate."

Charlotte spins around on the gravel; her face is a mask of anger. "Her *husband* was the reason behind Margaret's 'cruel fate.' The abbess, too, and the bishop. Perhaps they should have *helped* her instead of locking her up."

"Of course," I say. "That is exactly the point! We must find a way to—"

"The reverend is helping me," she interrupts. "We will get rid of it together."

"But, Charlotte, prayer will not help," I say. "Margaret lived in a *convent*."

"Perhaps Margaret's devil *isn't* my knocker." She lifts her chin in a defiant stance. "Perhaps Margaret's priests weren't as *powerful* as Reverend Hill is."

I shake my head, momentarily speechless. "You cannot truly believe that," I manage at last.

"What business is it of yours anyway, Miss Russel? Do you want compensation for the damage to your leg?" Something utterly wicked has come into her expression.

"Of course not!"

"When people get hurt, it is *everyone's* business," Benjamin adds in a stern voice. "The spirit is not just your problem, Charlotte. The spirit is *everyone's* problem now."

"But mostly mine, though. I don't see you or Miss Russel suffering through its knocking night after night "

"If it truly bothers you so, why will you not even consider our help?" I say it as a test, to provoke a reaction.

"The reverend is helping me," she replies.

"The reverend needs help himself." I am serious now, meaning every word. "The death of Mrs. Hill—"

"Had nothing to do with me." But she says it a tad too quickly, a little too rehearsed.

"Do you *truly* want to get rid of it?" Benjamin launches an even stronger challenge. "Or does it have you entirely under its sway?"

"*Of course* I want to get rid of it," she huffs. "That is why I am here, sweltering up in the clergy house attic—"

"Then please *listen,*" I plead. "Listen and grow wiser. We know things that might help—not only about Margaret, but *all* such spirits."

"I don't need your help," she declares, in a voice so hateful that I reel from it. She turns her back to us again and hastily makes her way down the path.

"Did you ever see it?" Benjamin calls after her back. "Did it ever show you its true face? Because *I* did see it, Charlotte, and nothing good can ever come from such a creature!"

She does not stop, though, and she does not turn back. She just keeps walking, back ramrod straight, until she reaches the kitchen entrance to the house and is gone.

"Well," Benjamin says, "that did not go as we had hoped."

"You think she is utterly lost to it?"

"I do now, yes." He takes my hand and squeezes it. The journal is back under his arm. "What now?" he asks. "Where do we go from here?"

"Now, we go home," I say and start walking down the garden path, keeping his hand in mine. "We can heat the soup, butter some bread, and drink a little bit of wine. Then you can tell me silly stories from your childhood, and we can listen to the thunder, quite content."

For a few blissful hours—just a moment in time—I would like for us both to be rid of the knocker.

·45·

charlotte

Father's closed carriage comes up the road again. It passes by the church as the knocker and I watch from the clergy house stairs. This is his third attempt. It has only been a day since the last time he came to bring me home, and I had been hoping he had learned his lesson.

Clearly, he has not.

The wheels move faster as the carriage veers like a scuttering beetle between the bright green fields, its coat of black varnish gleaming in the blazing sun. The rain that had lasted all weekend is gone, and summer has found Margaret's Keep once again.

Above our heads, the seagulls are circling.

The knocker and I look at each other and our identical eyes lock. Father has no business here, and we mean to let him know. I have never openly opposed my father—only Mother—and I suppose it ought to make me feel an ounce of guilt to refuse his request, but I cannot see any other way. I am too close now to having my own way, to grasping and holding the freedom I have been yearning for all my life.

I will not let anything derail me.

The knocker's gaze slips away as the carriage embarks on the last leg of the journey, which will bring it all the way into the yard. The wheels spin even faster now; Norris, at the reins, snaps the whip. They are trying to outrun what they know is coming, futile as it is.

It will not end any differently than the last two times.

When the knocker leaves my side, the grass in the fields bends under its wind; dust and debris, tufts of greenery and clumps of soil hurtle through the air to hit the carriage walls. Then come the rocks, dozens of them—though none of them big enough to cause serious harm.

I hear Norris cry out and he lifts his hands to shield his face. The carriage veers on the road as the horses get spooked, for even more rocks are raining down on the carriage from above. Norris cries out again as the hat is knocked off his head and falls to the dusty ground. He is clasping his hands on top of his head now, trying to protect his balding scalp. Father's voice sounds from within the carriage, barking out orders, but it is far too late. The horses have already left the road, headed for the field, pulling the carriage across the uneven ground.

I imagine it cannot be pleasant in there, despite the plush, upholstered seats.

Just as the carriage makes a sharp turn, headed for a flock of sheep who abruptly stop their grazing to scatter, I catch a flash of blue through the carriage window. Evelyn is in there, too—undoubtedly brought along to talk sense into me, or tug at my heartstrings and remind me of my duties. It does not matter. Evelyn cannot sway me, and she will be safe enough inside the carriage.

The knocker chases the carriage halfway across the field, then the wind suddenly stops blowing and the rocks fall powerless to the ground. Slowly, the vehicle comes to a halt as the horses sense that the danger has passed. The beasts stand lathered and shivering before the vehicle, wondering, perhaps, what just happened. I think Norris is bleeding, using the sleeve of his shirt to wipe his cheeks and forehead.

I feel sorry for him, I do, but it just cannot be helped.

When the carriage starts moving again, it sets a slow and rickety course back toward the road and away from me, passing the church anew.

This attempt, too, has failed.

My sense of satisfaction lasts only as long as it takes for me to step back inside, where Noreen is waiting in the hall. She sends me a dark look, full of contempt, but says nothing before returning to the kitchen. She is frightened of me now, and has been so ever since Mrs. Hill died. It is unfortunate the old housekeeper is so important to us or I might have convinced Jasper to let her go. Sadly, my cooking skills are meager, though, and so Noreen must stay. I do fear that she will tell the other islanders what she has seen here of late and whip their fear into a frenzy, but then she might have already. No secret is safe on Margaret's Keep.

I am about to follow Noreen and ask her for some tea when Jasper enters the hall from his office. He looks worn and pained as usual, and the reek of brandy wafting off him now obliterates the fragrant scent of rosemary. He gazes at me with bleary eyes and leans against the wall.

"What's the ruckus?" he asks in a slightly slurred voice. "Did someone come into the yard?"

"No. All is well, Jasper."

"I thought I heard something, like thunder." He is doubtlessly referring to the rain of stones on the carriage.

"It's such a difficult time you're going through," I say. "Your mind must be playing tricks on you." I pull Mrs. Hill's shawl off my shoulders and hang it next to his coat on the wall.

"Did Noreen bring back any letters from the store?" he asks, thankfully letting the matter go.

I nod. "They are on the table in the front room as usual," besides the note from Father, which I have kept for myself. I have quite a few of them now, hidden away in the chest in my room. They all say the same thing: *Charlotte must come home*. There are letters from Dr. Crown there as well, begging for Jasper to facilitate another examination.

One of these days, I will burn them all.

When Jasper disappears into the front room, I let out a breath of relief. Despite my calm when it happened, the knocker's attack has left me feeling slightly ragged. I am tired all the time now, from both keeping up the charade and protecting myself. I know this situation cannot last forever. Sooner or later, the gossip will reach a pinnacle and people will seek action. They fear powerful women on this island—and fear witches most of all—and I have the power of a witch now. Miss Russel and Mr. West are already on the hunt, wanting to take my friend away from me. The knocker belongs to me now, no matter where it was before, and I will never go back to being just Charlotte, a foolish girl with no power at all.

Miss Russel and her companion could cause me problems, though, like telling Jasper what they know, and he—weak as he is—might even listen. They can speak to Father, or even the church. They can go to the newspapers on the mainland. Their meddling is no good at all, and ought to be stopped. The knocker has known all along that Miss Russel is not a friend.

It told me so plainly, back in the shed.

It has left the schoolteacher alone ever since the rock incident—because I disapproved, I suppose. But now I am starting to believe that perhaps it was a mistake to discourage it so, and that Miss Russel *should* be chased.

She and the geologist both.

My family is of more immediate concern, though. On the two church days that have passed since Mrs. Hill's demise, the islanders have contented themselves with lighting candles and singing hymns, but they will not be deprived of their Sunday sermon forever—and who will be there in the front row but the Norths? Father will speak to Jasper for sure, will tell him of how he has tried to reach me and how it is imperative that I return home. Jasper will undoubtedly be shocked to learn of this and eager to satisfy Father's demands. The worst thing that can happen is if he starts asking himself why the knocker is attacking my family now, or what might have swayed it to do so.

Not even Mrs. Hill's death was enough to make me safe, it seems.

The knocker is already in my room, waiting by the round window. It is wearing the same black dress as me, and when I unpin my hair and slump down on the bed, it does so, too. We lie side by side—twins in black—with our dark curls pooling on the crisp, white pillows. The sheets smell of rosemary and sweat. I think of Mrs. Hill's words to me, of how my future may be grim indeed. The chances have lessened with her out of the way, but Jasper is not stable. He has not talked of the future, and he has not declared his love for me. He is only concerned with how he has failed me. It is quite tiresome, truth be told—and it makes the knocker more important than ever. Though I like having Jasper, because he is my victory, he is not the exciting company that I had imagined before. I swore back then that I would save him, though, and leave the island by his side—and so I will, though the foe I seem to be battling now is the man himself in place of his wife. Only the knocker remains consistent.

Will you stay with me forever? I ask it in my mind.

The knocker replies with one rap against the windowpane.

"Do you promise?" I ask.

Again, it replies with one knock.

"I would *die* if you left me." Suddenly, I am sobbing, and the twin by my side does, too, soundlessly and without tears. "What would I be without you?" I ask. "Someone for the world to chew and spit out." If knowledge of my long stay with the reverend should ever reach the mainland, I might not even be able to find myself a husband there. I might already be pregnant. I dare not ask the knocker if I am.

What will I do if Jasper deserts me, and the knocker disappears?

"How can I make him stay with me?" I ask the knocker, and it replies by showing me a picture of myself and Jasper in church, standing before a different priest.

"Marriage? Yes, I suppose that makes sense." At least I will not starve then, if the knocker leaves me. I cannot help but think of Mother, though, of Aunt Anne, and even Antonia. Marriage had not made any of them happy, but then perhaps it will be different if *I* have the upper hand. Being a priest's wife is surely better than being none at all?

"How can I hold you to your word? How can I make sure that *you* stay with me?" Of the two of them, the knocker is by far the more important. My friend is what will make the rest of it bearable. It *is* my upper hand.

The knocker replies by slipping the knowledge into my mind again. Suddenly it is there: the answer to my plight.

Would it be forever? I ask it in my mind.

The knocker raps once on the window.

"And you wouldn't diminish, but stay the same?"

Again, it raps once: yes.

"Show me your face again first," I whisper, thinking of the thing I saw in the field. I need to see it again to remember it clearly. "If I allow you to do this, the least you can do is reveal yourself to me one last time." If we are to make a bargain, at least there should be honesty between us, and no more masks to hide the truth. I look at my twin—at her oval face just an inch from mine; at the dark brown of her eyes. I watch them as they bleed to red, and then watch the face as it turns rough and black, with a texture reminiscent of charred wood. Then it is over, and it is me again—my own familiar face staring back at me.

"You *always* wanted to be me, didn't you?"

The knocker replies with one single rap.

My heart beats rapidly, but I am not afraid. We both want each other, and that is the truth of it. It wants my flesh and I need its power. We can both satisfy each other.

"Come then," I whisper into the brightly lit room. My eyes are on the slanted roof, not on Charlotte by my side. "Come," I say—and it does.

It appears like a thick mist, reeking of cooked meat and brine. It kisses my mouth before it slips between my lips and slithers down my throat, leaving behind it a taste of burning and something else, like iron. I keep seeing leaves for my inner eyes—glossy and red, growing on vines—and for a second I am convinced that it is *them* I feel moving through my body, that the slick, slender vines twine with my bones, put down roots in my flesh, and drink from my blood. The leaves are shaped like spears: very sharp.

The mist is so thick that it almost chokes me, but then, just when I think I cannot stand it any longer, it stops as abruptly as it began and I am left wheezing and gasping for air, with debris like ashes littering the bed.

Alone.

·46·

jasper

"We must leave the island," Charlotte says. She has come into the office at dusk and stands with her back to me, staring out at the darkening garden and the rolling waves beyond.

"I thought you didn't like the mainland," I say, swirling the contents of my glass around and around. Before me on the desk lies the unfinished sermon that I am meant to give this Sunday, but what little I have managed to get on the page seems nothing but gibberish. I struggle to gather my thoughts and follow my own reasoning to coherent conclusions.

I blame my confusion on the liquor. I blame it on Charlotte. I blame it on the death of my wife. I blame it on the knocker, too, though it has—strangely—become a problem of lesser concern. I am not blind, though, to the possibility that the knocker is the soil from which all my other problems grow. The seed of the rot. The adversary.

I pray for strength and comfort, but guilt stifles my words, just as it stills my pen.

I am a sorry creature of late.

Charlotte is not sorry, though. Charlotte is a picture of health and beauty tonight, with her long, lustrous hair tumbling down over her shoulders to blend with the thick, black silk of her mourning dress. When she turns to look at me, I see the roses in her cheeks and the glistening red of her lips. Her skin is clear and without a blemish; her eyes are bright and gleaming like jewels. I can see the roundness of her bosom rise and fall as she breathes, and even now—in my sorry state—it stirs the hunger in me. I want nothing more than to tear off the silk and have her right there, on the desk.

Sometimes I feel she is quite the disease.

"I didn't like the mainland before," she answers, "but that was when going there meant grueling hours spent at dinner parties while my aunt did her best to marry me off. I always knew that my fate waited here, on Margaret's Keep." Her smile is as sweet as a piece of chocolate, and she looks at me adoringly.

"What would we do on the mainland?" I lean back in the chair and look at her. She truly is unusually vibrant tonight, and I am reminded of how women often look in the middle of their pregnancies: the epitome of health and more beautiful than ever. It feels as though a painfully sweet dart pierces my heart when I allow myself to form the thought that maybe—just maybe—Charlotte finds herself in such a condition. Maybe the crying infant I have heard is a harbinger of good, rather than a spirit's cruel trick.

"We should get married," she replies unashamedly. "We should get married as soon as possible, just in case." Her hand flutters across her belly—might it be that she is reading my mind? Then I notice how her ring finger is free of the gauze that has marred it for so long. She follows my gaze and gives a small smile.

"It finally dried up," she says. "There is barely even any scarring." She holds up her finger for me to inspect. The skin is, indeed, surprisingly smooth. "It must be Noreen's poultice."

"I cannot just leave," I say, tearing my gaze from her finger. "I have my post here, and the flock—"

"The church cannot fault you for wanting to leave the place that claimed your wife. Surely, they will find another reverend for Margaret's Keep." She sounds very certain, and for a moment she reminds me of the formidable Mrs. North. "Yes, we should leave, as soon as possible."

"But your father—"

"Cannot say a thing once we are wed."

"I cannot condone such dishonesty, Charlotte. I cannot willingly deceive an honest man—"

Her eyes flash with anger. "You seemed quite content to deceive your wife, and was she not an honest woman?"

Shame washes over me, thick and ugly. "Of course, but—"

"You keep saying how you have wronged me, that what we do is sinful and damaging. Well, here is your chance to set it right, Jasper. Take me away from the island and give me your name. You know it is the only honorable thing to do."

Her words hit me like daggers. I do not feel like an honorable man anymore. I do not believe I deserve redemption, but that is what she is offering, is it not? A chance to put things right—with God, at least, and Charlotte, if not with Mr. North.

And if there is a child . . .

My protest is weak. "Antonia just died. Would it be seemly, so fast?"

"No one would have to know on the mainland. We could settle somewhere far from here—in a city, perhaps, where it is easy to hide."

"And . . . the knocker?" I look up at her. She looms so large in my vision: an angel of honey and shadows, painted by the flickering light of the candle.

Her red lips split in a smile. "I don't think the knocker will bother us on the mainland."

"How can you know?" I ask, perplexed.

She shrugs. "It's just a feeling I have." She crosses the short distance between us and leans down to kiss my stubbled cheek. "It will be *good,* just you see . . . a new start for both of us. A new life." When she retreats, a faint whiff of cooked meat—like a roast—follows in her wake. I grab her arm and pull her close to me again, seeking out her mouth with my own, while burying my free hand in her mass of curly hair. The kiss is long and hungry, and I whimper when we part.

"You must give me some time," I whisper hoarsely. "Just a couple of weeks to settle my affairs. Give me *that* at least."

"What affairs are there to settle?" she asks.

"*Antonia's* affairs. Finances. I should at least *notify* the church . . ."

She seems to think it over. "Ten days," she agrees, "and only if you give no more sermons."

"Why?" I honestly should; I owe it to my flock.

"You are not a liar," she says, though we both know that is not true. I am a great deceiver—and especially of myself. Charlotte's finger traces my face, and a gentle smile has appeared on her lips. "Can you truly stand before them all and not feel a need to tell them you are leaving? Can you look my father in the eyes and not admit that you are taking me away?"

"No." I shake my head with shame and fumble for the tumbler on the desk.

"We should not speak to my family at all," she decides. "It will be better this way."

"Yes," I whisper, hoping with all my might that it is true. And yet, when Charlotte leaves me to go upstairs, I cannot help but feeling duped.

Duped, and utterly lost.

·47·

ruth

Evelyn North is in my kitchen again. The young woman looks composed but slightly the worse for wear. The hand that lifts the chipped teacup shivers. There was a time when I would have been ashamed to offer the oldest North girl poor china, but those days are long past, and Evelyn does not seem to care. There is something in her eyes that I do not like. They seem crushed, somehow, like spiderwebbed glass. The healthy glow I had seen on her cheeks in church has been wiped from her skin.

It is just the two of us, per Evelyn's request. It is a *private* errand, she said. Both Benjamin and I know what that means. She is clearly here to talk about Charlotte—to ask another favor perhaps—though after the scene in the clergy house garden, I strongly doubt if she will accept my help with anything. And, to be honest, I am not sure if I will be offering Charlotte my help again. At least, not in any way she likes.

Evelyn gets her privacy, though. Benjamin goes for a walk, down to the harbor and the grocery store, to check for letters and buy a few commodities, leaving me alone with the broken-looking young woman and whatever fresh horrors this day has in store.

"What can I help you with, Miss North?"

"Oh, Miss Russel." She sounds unhappy. "I am *so* sorry to be bothering you again, but I simply do not know where else to turn." A faint smile twitches my lips when I hear the familiar words. Who would have thought that the Norths would become so dependent on the poor spinster in the schoolhouse?

"I assume it is about Charlotte," I say. "And, if so, I must inform you that I don't believe I find myself in her good graces anymore."

"None of us are," she says. "Her devil will not even let us into the yard, but blows the carriage off the road. Father is immensely distraught. We all are."

"I *have* wondered why Charlotte isn't back at home," I admit.

"It's certainly not for lack of trying. We have tried to go there several times—our last attempt was yesterday—and Father has written letters to the reverend, but nothing happens. The knocker can be quite fearsome in its fury, and Norris refuses to drive to the clergy house again. We have even considered the police." She sends me a telling gaze. The fear of scandal usually makes law enforcement a last resort for the wealthy, so Mr. North must feel the desperation keenly to even consider this step. "The newspapers would love this story, don't you think?" Her lips become a thin line. "'Fish baron's daughter in cahoots with the devil. Barricades herself with local priest.'"

I cannot help but chuckle. I never knew that Evelyn had such a biting sense of humor. "You should consider a career in journalism," I tell her. "I think you would be quite good at it."

"No," Evelyn says. "I am to be a wife—or so I thought before all this happened. James might not even want me if the press finds out about this."

I want to console her, but I know it is the truth. The Norths might never recover.

"How is your mother?" I ask instead. Mrs. North has been scarce since her "accident."

"Quite healthy again, but not sound of mind." I am taken aback by Evelyn's candor. "She wants us to wash our hands of Charlotte, but of course we can do no such thing. We love her, Miss Russel—all her sisters do. Father, too. He wants nothing but to help her, but she doesn't want our aid."

"She doesn't want anyone's help but the reverend's," I agree. "Though I am doubtful of his methods. They don't seem to be working very well."

"No." Evelyn gives a brittle laugh. "I would say they have been a spectacular failure. She is more under the devil's sway now than she was when she left home."

"And dangerous," I say, looking Evelyn in the eyes. "Charlotte—and the knocker—pose a threat to anyone who goes near them."

"Yes." She looks utterly pained. "That has been clear for a while now, and poor Mrs. Hill . . . I don't want to think it . . . but I do, Miss Russel. I cannot help but think that the poor woman would have been alive if . . ." She trails off, unable to say the words. Despite my earlier misgivings, I place my hand on Evelyn's. Charlotte's disturbing behavior has not entirely obliterated my altruism, it seems.

"How did it come to this?" I ask. "Dr. Crown, the unfortunate psychiatrist, had a theory that it was Charlotte herself who created the phenomenon, but I am not convinced. I do believe there is a knocker out there that is quite separate from Charlotte, but—"

"How did it get ahold of her?" Evelyn finishes my sentence and shifts on the chair. "I think Charlotte always wanted more than life could give her, Miss Russel. She has always been willful, restless . . . *passionate*. Her daydreams were always vivid, her ambitions always grand, and if you showed her a fence, she wanted to jump it—but Margaret's Keep is *not* grand, and the lives we are born to are bound by rules. I know you understand, Miss Russel." Something knowing has come into her eyes, and I startle.

Surely she cannot know about my past?

If she does, she does not comment on it, but just continues talking. "My mother is not cruel, Miss Russel, although I suppose she might appear that way. My mother is merely afraid. She grew up with cautionary tales about her aunt, who fled the family home to take up with a clerk. Due to this scandal, the girls were kept under lock and key more often than not growing up, and had it not been for Father and his ideas about fresh air and exercise, I suppose we would have been locked up, too." Evelyn smiles to soften the words, but it does not reach her eyes. She lifts the spoon out of the sugar bowl and adds some more to her tea. I sense that she is not through with her tale, and patiently wait while she stirs the sweetener in.

"Mother does not know how to raise happy children, Miss Russel. No one ever taught her how to do it. Father sees that—and he tries to help—but how do you convince a woman that what she has believed all her life is wrong? When it came to Charlotte, however, Mother's righteousness met an obstacle she simply could not overcome. I suppose it's in my sister's nature to always have her way. She always hated to bend her head, and the sense of . . . powerlessness that we all share was grating on her in ways that it never did on me." She sighs and looks out the window, at the grazing sheep and windswept fields. "I always wanted Charlotte to marry early," she says. "I wanted her to escape Mother and the island, but she would not. She wanted the reverend, she said—and now she has him."

"At a terrible price," I note.

"We all pay a price, Miss Russel." She looks at me again with that knowing in her eyes, and now I am all but convinced that she knows. "The trouble with my sister's sacrifice is that it hurts so many others. I have no doubt, Miss Russel, that Charlotte has willingly chosen to let the knocker into her life. Had it been me—or Adelaide—the devil had descended upon first, none of this would have happened. We would have been terrified of it. We would have fought it with all our might."

"Not Charlotte, though," I note.

"Not Charlotte," she confirms. "Charlotte took its power and made it her own."

I think about this for a moment, and wonder what it means. "But would she really kill?" I ask at last. "Though I see how the temptation of such a . . . servant can be alluring, would your sister truly kill another human being just to have her way?"

Evelyn lets out a shivering breath. "It has changed her. Charlotte was never *cruel*—never violent—before. The knocker is no fit company for humans, Miss Russel. Charlotte said it had no empathy. Perhaps it's just not in its nature."

"No, but Charlotte does. She feels."

"Less now, I think." A tear comes slipping out of Evelyn's eye. She quickly finds a handkerchief to stop it. "The worst thing," she says while dabbing at her tears, "is that I cannot entirely blame her. For the violence, yes, but not for accepting the invitation. Knowing her—the way that she was, the constant squabbles with Mother . . . She longed for a sense of control. The knocker came like a fairy godmother, offering her everything she needed."

"There are other ways," I say.

"Like your way?" Now the knowing in her eyes is stark. To my own great surprise, it does not make my heart race or make my mouth go dry. There is only a slight discomfort in the pit of my stomach.

"How do you know?" I ask, not unkindly.

"Aunt Anne recognized you the last time she was here. She always kept up with the gossip. I haven't told anyone," she quickly assures me. "You changed your name?"

I nod. "When I started teaching. Russel was my mother's maiden name, and the principal was most understanding. No one likes a scandal. Though I gave up my inheritance of my own volition, that was not how it was perceived, you see. People could not comprehend that someone would do so just to avoid getting married. It is supposed to be our crowning achievement—any woman's goal. The gossip was rife. They imagined all kinds of atrocities. Some said that I was born unnatural, others remembered my mother's supposed madness. Those with little knowledge of the circumstances simply believed that I had been disinherited in my father's will, and then they wondered why."

"I admire you for it, Miss Russel, I do." Her voice sounds very convincing. "It takes tremendous courage to do what you did and just walk away from it all."

"At a price," I say.

"There always is," Evelyn agrees.

"Not you, though. You don't walk. You stay, and marry Mr. Eckhardt."

"I never was much of a fighter," she replies. "I appreciate the comfort of the orderly. I feel that I deserve it now, having raised my sisters in Mother's stead." She says it without any self-pity, relaying the fact quite calmly. "I will not entirely abandon them, of course. They will be more than welcome to stay with me on the mainland. I have come to believe that I can do more for them there than I can out here, providing shelter as well as opening doors. Although none of it will happen if someone in the city finds out about Charlotte."

"Do you think she could come back from this and be who she was before?" I ask. How does one return from a dance with the devil?

She blinks away fresh tears. "I don't know. I cannot even get to her to assess her state of mind. She cannot continue like this. She must be forced back under control before something else happens. Something worse."

I offer because I feel I must, but with the scene in the garden fresh in mind, it is without any enthusiasm and only from a vague sense of duty. "Do you want me to go there, Miss North? Do you want me to speak to the reverend on the family's behalf?"

To my surprise, she shakes her head. "No, Miss Russel, I would never ask that of you. It is simply too dangerous. If Charlotte—or the knocker—perceives you as a threat, you might be in real danger. No, I want to know what you *know,* Miss Russel. You have been at the clergy house, and you have been close to Charlotte. I dearly wish to hear your thoughts."

Because she has been so devastatingly open with me—and because I am relieved not to have to be their messenger—I relay it all: Dr. Crown's assessment, Benjamin's sighting in the ceiling, and his subsequent trip to the mainland, including what he learned about the tower. I even tell her about Reverend Hill's decline and our encounter with Charlotte in the garden.

When I am quite done, Evelyn sits silently for a while. I pour more tea and drip some rum into our cups. When I am seated again, Evelyn finally speaks.

"I applaud your efforts," she says. "I had no idea that you had gone to such lengths to help my sister—and us."

"We did it mostly for ourselves," I admit, "to overcome our fear."

"And did it work?"

"In some ways." I shrug. "In other ways, it only made it worse."

"It's clear from what you are saying that the answers are on the mainland, and not here." Evelyn's face has taken on a thoughtful expression. She looks an awfully lot like Charlotte just then, and I cannot help but shudder. "Do you think Mr. West would be willing to go back? Or, even better, the both of you together? You could speak to Dr. Crown again, or anyone else who could offer a solution. We would cover all expenses—anything you need—and pay you for your time, too. I would go myself but . . . you know I cannot."

I think of what Benjamin and I had said earlier, about opening a detective agency, and cannot help but give a rueful smile. "I will discuss it with Mr. West," I promise, recognizing how a trip off the island might, in fact, be good for my health.

"We would be forever in your debt," says Evelyn, "no matter what comes of it." In her eyes, I see something that was not there before. It takes me a moment to recognize it as hope.

After she is gone, and I am alone, I sit back down at the kitchen table and watch the wind play in the field while waiting for Benjamin to come home. *Not quite done yet,* I think to myself. I had believed that our meeting with Charlotte in the garden marked the end of our direct involvement, but clearly it was not so.

I wonder what *I* would have done, at the age of eighteen—while I was still living under my father's thumb—if a knocker had arrived and offered me the power to have it all: both fortune and independence.

Would I have rejected it, or would I have embraced it?

·48·

ruth

We travel already the next day. That the matter is urgent is apparent, but before Evelyn enlisted us, our quest had had an air of meddling that our mission now has dispersed. We can freely look into the matter—and its possible cures—without feeling as though we are treading on forbidden land, which is a great relief. It is good sometimes to be valued for ones' strengths; and if there is one thing Benjamin and I know well, it is to look for facts and knowledge.

Benjamin's mainland apartment is almost as humble as my own on the island. While he is out for groceries, I take the opportunity to explore. His home consists of only one room with a sturdy table at the center, scattered with pieces of paper filled with scribbled notes, half-burned candles in brass candlesticks, matchboxes, sweets wrappers, and a dusting of tea leaves. The room is lined with shelves crammed with books, more loose papers, and journals. A small writing desk by the double window carries more of the same homely clutter, including an ornate brass frame displaying a photograph of an elderly lady, which I believe to be his beloved grandmother.

The left end of the room is outfitted as a functional kitchen, with a proper range—albeit a small one—a counter holding several cupboards, a water tap, and a wooden icebox, currently void of ice. Shelves above the counter hold an assortment of cups, glasses, and plates. Enough to set the table for eight, at least.

Behind a brown damask curtain to the left of the desk is the bed, neatly made and waiting beneath a checkered spread. My cheeks grow warm when I see it. Though we have spent every night in each other's arms of late, our intimacy somehow feels more dangerous on the mainland, more real. We are out in the world now, on a cobbled street lined by busy stores. The air is filled with traffic noises: horse-drawn carriages and electric trams; the shouting and chatter of people. The hazy existence on Margaret's Keep suddenly feels unreal.

But it is not. In my coat pocket rests a leather wallet I received from Evelyn North, crammed with large, crisp bills. She did not lie when she said they would spare no expense. The money is meant to open doors and grease wheels.

Buy us a solution—if there is one to be purchased.

I make myself comfortable in the kitchen and start to make tea, surprised by how easy it is to feel at home in this strange place. Though perhaps it is because I know the man who lives here so well. I can smell his scent in the air, even when he is not here.

By the time Benjamin returns, I am sitting at the table with my tea, quite content. I am leafing through some of his notes on other cases involving "knocking spirits." I do not find much new. Benjamin has done a fine job with his research. The man himself seems to be in an excellent mood when he deposits the heavy paper bags on the counter and lifts out beef and carrots. Perhaps he is happy to be home, I think, as he comes toward me, holding out an orange, as round and bright as the sun.

"I remember how you said you liked them," he tells me, placing it before me on the table. "I figured we both deserved a treat."

"We haven't done anything yet," I protest, but take the fruit into my hands.

"Just accepting the task was a feat, don't you think? Who in their right mind would even consider going further down this path?"

"Someone intent on quelling their fears," I reply.

"But the more we discover, the more there is to fear. It is supposed to be the other way around—once you know enough about the thing in question, it usually loses any air of mystery. But in the case of the knocker, it only gets worse. I have gone from not believing in anything to considering the existence of malevolent creatures."

"It might not be malevolent," I say. "Only very different from us." I start peeling the orange, savoring the fragrant smell. "Years from now, science may well have learned what this thing really is, and it will not seem very strange at all. Perhaps there will be textbooks describing its anatomy."

"Do you really think so?"

"I must believe so. Most things on this earth have an explanation."

He smiles. "Perhaps you will be the one to write that textbook."

"First we have to untangle it from Charlotte," I say. "And that, for one, is *not* an easy feat."

Benjamin becomes serious again. "I sent a message to Dr. Crown asking for a conversation, but I think we should go there tomorrow even if he doesn't reply. Although he is likely misguided about the knocker, he has knowledge of the phenomenon and might be able to tell us where to look next."

"I agree," I say, biting into the first luscious segment. "Though I cannot say that I like the man—or even respect him—he could still know something of value. Besides, Evelyn wanted us to speak to him, and she *is* the one paying."

I sound far more optimistic than I feel. The seriousness of the situation is a weight I cannot allow myself to fully feel, or I would go mad with it. It is better to think of it as an adventure—a compelling mystery to solve.

Yet, whenever I close my eyes, I see her again: Antonia Hill, and her frozen grin.

• • •

It is different this time, being in the city. Though Dr. Crown lives on a street not unlike the one I grew up on, with stately homes and an abundance of oak trees, it does not pain me as it used to do. I feel no homesickness, or sour regret. It does not feel as though it should have belonged to me, and I do not feel foolish for giving it all up.

Perhaps I have changed since I was here last.

Perhaps it is due to the man by my side.

Perhaps it had been the right choice all along.

I feel a slight trepidation as we walk up the stairs of the slender brick building, where ornate railings stand sentinel, guarding a green-painted door. There is a brass sign there, letting us know in neat letters that this is the office of Dr. William Crown. Seeing his name makes me feel uneasy. My last meeting with the doctor had been unpleasant, to put it mildly, and for the Crowns, it had ended in disaster.

He might not be too thrilled to welcome visitors from the island.

Benjamin seems not to feel my apprehension, but grabs hold of the lion-faced door knocker without any sign of hesitation, giving the door a couple of sharp raps.

It reminds me of the knocker.

An efficient-looking maid in a gray uniform opens the door. She quickly looks us over before uttering a greeting.

"Are you the islanders?" she asks.

"We are," I say, even though it is not entirely accurate. "I am Miss Russel, and this is Mr. West."

"The doctor is expecting you," she says, which is certainly a relief, since we never received a reply to our message.

Benjamin and I step inside, and the maid shows us through a small but well-lit marble hall into a room that is bound to be

Dr. Crown's office. The room has a large bay window looking out on the street. Bookshelves lined with leather bound tomes fight for attention with framed pictures depicting the human brain in various shades and forms. The wallpaper is a soft blue, and the window frames solid black. The desk, too, is black, and completely free of clutter besides a skull-shaped crystal paperweight and a couple of pristine leather satchels.

Dr. Crown, it seems, is a tidy man.

The doctor himself is not here yet, but the maid tells us to wait. Benjamin and I exchange a glance before sinking down into the two deep, upholstered chairs placed before the desk. It somehow reminds me of Reverend Hill's office, which is not an association I welcome at this point. After a while, the maid is back with a small trolley, carrying a teapot and several cups and saucers, as well as an assortment of small tarts.

"The doctor has not yet resumed his practice after the accident," she informs us, while wedging the small trolley in between our chairs. "He does not see any patients at present, and therefore has an open schedule." She dearly wants us to know that her employer is normally a very busy man.

"How is he doing?" I ask. I *have* been concerned for his health since the wreck.

"It's not my place to tell," she replies, fussing with the tea and handing out china. "But better now," she adds. "Eager to return to Margaret's Keep." It is clear from her face that she cannot fathom why.

"Thank you, Vivian," Dr. Crown says from the open door. "I can take it from here." The doctor is a sorry sight as he wanders into the room. A steel contraption has been attached to his head and shoulders: a cage of screws and metal rods. His face, though, is unobscured by the construction. He walks very slowly, shuffling his feet. It is far worse than I had hoped, and I am barely able to quell a gasp.

When the maid—Vivian—has closed the door behind her, Benjamin introduces himself and the two of them shake hands, then the doctor turns his gaze on me.

"What an unexpected pleasure," he says. "I did not think I would see you again, Miss Russel." Might it be that he has sensed my misgivings? He is, after all, a psychiatrist. Perhaps it was my display of temper the last time we met that had made him so convinced that a reunion was unlikely.

I decide to be honest with him, since honesty is what we need in return. "I had not imagined to be here either, seeing as how our last meeting ended on such a heated note, but here we are."

"Here we are, indeed." The doctor lowers himself into his chair with some difficulty. Every movement is painful, it seems, and his movements are stiff and careful. I wonder what Benjamin is thinking. We have all fallen victim to the same foe, after all.

"We heard that you will make a full recovery," I say, when he is seated. "I do hope that is true."

"Indeed, Miss Russel," he says again. "My physicians are most hopeful. My nephew is already up and about, fit as a fiddle, and I hope to be able to join him soon." He gives us a rueful smile. "What can I do for you?" He changes trajectory in his usual abrupt way. "I suppose you aren't here just to ask after my health?"

"It concerns Charlotte North," says Benjamin.

"Of course it does." The doctor's smile returns. "I take it there hasn't been any improvement?"

"I'm afraid not," I admit. "Rather, it has gotten worse, and her family is quite distraught. We are here on their behalf."

"The family who fears *scandal,*" he scoffs. "How can I possibly be of assistance?"

This is, indeed, the question.

"We were wondering, doctor," Benjamin says, "if we could fill you in on the latest events on the island, and then ask you for a new assessment. Perhaps you already have thoughts of your own, having suffered such a terrible accident."

Dr. Crown laughs behind his black desk, though it does not sound very joyous. "You wonder if I still think Charlotte North is behind the events, now that I have suffered damage myself?"

"Yes," I say. "Just that."

The doctor leans back the best that he can, wearing a thoughtful expression. His fingers are splayed out on the gray fabric of his waistcoat. "I still believe Charlotte North is the root and the cause," he says at last. "Nothing has changed—though I admit to being surprised by the ferocity of the phenomenon. I have never heard of anything quite like it, which is why I have asked—nay, *begged*—for another examination, though the reverend has so far not replied. By all means"—his gaze turns back to Benjamin—"fill me in on what has transpired since I left."

I enjoy half a cup of tea and a strawberry tart while Benjamin tells the doctor about his own horrid experience, and the subsequent research. He also relays how Charlotte and the reverend both have changed character in the wake of Mrs. Hill's death. I can tell how the circumstances regarding the latter gives the doctor pause.

"I had not heard of Mrs. Hill's passing," he says when Benjamin is quite done. "That is certainly worrisome news. The cause of death is not determined?"

"Not yet," I say. "The reverend sent her body for an autopsy, but the results are not yet back. Though for those of us that have experience with the knocker . . . we *know*." I lock my gaze with his. "In the same way that you *know* what caused your wreck."

"Sudden winds"—he gives a wry smile—"dirt thrown up from the road . . . Horses running wild for no reason at all . . . Impossible things, yes, I *know*."

"Considering just how *impossible* it all is, how is it that you will not consider an outside agent as the cause?" I ask him. "It seems to me that a girl developing such . . . unconscious abilities is just as outlandish as the presence of a 'demonic' creature."

"A good point, Miss Russel." He juts a finger in the air. "But we live in modern times now, and we have only just begun to learn what the human mind is capable of. Demons and devils belong to the past, while the future belongs to the brain. The more we learn about our own capabilities, the more the old stories and superstitions will be put to rest."

"So, you think Charlotte alone ended Mrs. Hill?" Benjamin asks.

"Not as an act of will, as such—"

"Unconsciously then?" I cut in.

"I would say so, yes." He places his elbows on the surface of the desk and leans forward. "Charlotte North is a battleground of desire and hatred—a boiling kettle, if you will. Sometimes the pressure simply becomes too much and the lid blows off."

"But Mr. West *saw* it. He saw its face and it looked nothing like Charlotte."

"If she can conjure a storm, why not a demon?" Dr. Crown looks between us, wearing an amused expression.

"I was inclined to believe it before," I admit. "It made sense to me in Reverend Hill's office, that the girl was the source of it all. But I have doubts now, doctor. It simply seems too much for a person—and she is changing as well, rapidly. Her family believes that she works in tandem with the creature, that she has taken it on as a servant."

Dr. Crown shakes his head. "Nothing but superstition. Long gone are the days of the witch pyres."

"But what can be *done*?" Benjamin asks. "If you are right, what can be done to cure Charlotte and restore her to her family?"

This wipes the smugness off the doctor's face at last. "She must be examined, of course—quite thoroughly," he says at last, and the bluster is gone from his voice. "A 'cure,' as such, is uncharted territory, but the leading theory is that if we can help Charlotte through her issues—or, locate her *wound*—the phenomenon will cease."

"She will not let that happen," I say.

"And we cannot wait that long," adds Benjamin.

"Surely there must be *something,*" I persist. "Something to give her family hope and ensure that no one else gets hurt." I give the contraption around his neck a pointed look.

To his credit, Dr. Crown does not immediately dismiss the idea, but seems to think it over. "There is a man," he says after a minute or so. "A priest called Alexander Jacob that I sometimes use if I have a patient with strong religious beliefs. I have found having a man of the cloth sitting in during their sessions can be of help in putting their minds at ease. He is a charlatan, though." His gaze darts between us. "Reverend Jacob will do anything for money, such as repel demons and placate ghosts . . . In my opinion, the man has no scruples—but he does have his faith, and it *is* strong. I also have come to respect his honest desire to help, even if his methods are anathema to me. He has also, on several occasions, sent patients here, realizing that their afflictions were of the mind rather than the soul . . . So perhaps he would be willing to help, even if his administrations would be nothing but a bandage on a festering wound."

"Anything," I say. "We will try *anything.*"

Dr. Crown sighs. "I believe you will." He takes another moment before continuing. "*If* you choose to enlist Jacob, the price for my referral will be his honest assessment of Charlotte North. I would, in fact," he adds slightly ominously, "very much like to know what he makes of her."

I nod my agreement. "But there will be no study," I say. "Not unless the Norths agree to it."

Another silent moment, and then the doctor gives a nod of his own. "I believe Jacob will enjoy this," he says. "The man will undoubtedly see it as a challenge."

I feel deeply relieved. I do not know this Reverend Jacob—I do not know if he will be useful or not—but we need fresh minds and new ideas, and Reverend Hill, especially, *does* need another priest.

"Your referral would be much appreciated," I say. "The island of Margaret's Keep is in your debt."

·49·

ruth

He looks like something out of the Bible—like a warrior angel ready to strike—standing there at the bow of the vessel with the salty wind ruffling his reddish-blond hair and his black coat billowing behind him. When he lifts his face to the sky, his Roman nose and the angular set of his jaw stands out against the blue. I am led to think of the Archangel Michael, or David before Goliath. Though, I know, of course, that he is just a man, and perhaps not able to help us at all.

It is just that I have never before met someone quite like Alexander Jacob.

He is in every way unique.

"Should I be jealous?" Benjamin has followed my gaze, and perhaps even noted my awe. He is sitting beside me on a large wooden crate loaded with goods for the grocery store. The three of us are on board the *Seagull*—the large vessel that makes the trip between Margaret's Keep and the mainland every day. It is captained by Tommy Boden—Mary Boden's brother and Noreen's nephew: a weather-worn man of few words, with a large beard and kind eyes. He, too, seemed quite struck by Reverend Jacob when we brought him on board, and keeps looking at him from the corners of his eyes, while puffing on his pipe and working the rudder. Perhaps it is the reverend's tall, thin silhouette that does it, crowned by that shiny halo of hair that no scissors could ever entirely tame.

"Don't be absurd," I tell Benjamin and swat at his arm. He is wearing the lovely red coat today, and I feel quite the chicken next to a peacock in my usual brown tweed. Reverend Jacob, though, is an eagle, carried forth on mighty brass wings. "He is a curious person, that is all."

"He is ferocious in his faith, that is for sure." Benjamin is still in shock, I think, from our first meeting with the reverend the night before. The three of us had eaten together at a homely pub—plates of stew and dark, foamy beer. It had all happened so very fast; the passion in our new savior had been so extremely sudden. We had barely had time to think, before we were on the *Seagull* again—a mere three days since we left—bound for Margaret's Keep. Hopefully bringing a solution in the form of this righteous man.

He, at least, seems confident that he knows what to do.

Leaving the mainland feels strangely melancholic. I feel as though our stay was way too short—and I do understand now what Benjamin meant when he said that it was good to take a break from the island. The world is more real on the mainland; reason shines brighter there. As the vessel moves steadily closer to Margaret's Keep, I wonder if we are fools to return, to reenter the gloom and the horror. We could have been on well-lit city streets. But, then, there is my promise to Evelyn and the hope that perhaps we can do something *good*—prevent another devastating attack, or even save lives. I feel as though I owe it to the islanders to try, and whenever my resolve wavers, I think of Adelaide and Sophie—my students—who are suffering innocents in all of this.

I am not prone to praying, but I do hope that Reverend Jacob is our answer.

The man seems to be done staring ahead and comes sauntering

back toward us. He looks slightly menacing as he drifts across the deck, sidestepping barrels and crates, with his robe flapping like wings around his body. His long face is covered in a sheen of sea spray—and as is mine, I suppose. When I speak, the taste of salt slips into my mouth.

"Reverend Hill is not expecting you," I tell him when he comes closer. I must speak very loudly to be heard over the motor. "You are not to be concerned, though. Should our attempt to install you in the clergy house fail, I am sure the Norths will be happy to have you. They are the ones who have enlisted your help after all."

"Oh, we will not be met with closed doors, I assure you, Miss Russel," Jacob answers in his confident way. "We come to do the Lord's work, and he will ensure that the gates are open."

I think of Reverend Hill and Charlotte, the way they huddle together behind the clergy house walls. "They have become quite reclusive," I say.

"It is the demon," he replies, using the word as if it was nothing at all. "It wants to separate them from others so it can work in peace. It will not stand for interruption." He nods sagely, underlining the words.

"It could be the grief," Benjamin notes, not quite as willing as I to play along with Reverend Jacob. "The man just lost his wife—"

"And he is living with a demon." Jacob arches a finely drawn eyebrow. "The grief makes him susceptible to it. Weak." He spits the word. "It crawls in him like maggots now, just as it has devoured the girl."

"Not entirely, I hope," I say, feeling queasy from the imagery.

"That is indeed the hope." Jacob towers over us, deftly moving with the boat. He must have spent some time traveling to gain those sea legs. "As long as we get to the demon before she lets it inside her body, the process can be reversed."

"And we are absolutely sure that entering her body is what the knocker wants?" Benjamin removes his spectacles to clean them with a piece of cloth.

"Oh yes." Reverend Jacob seems *very* sure. "They are *parasites,* the lot of them. Their ultimate goal is always to find a human host."

"But why?" I ask, still confused.

"To *live,* Miss Russel." He gives me a kind, if slightly overbearing, look. "They want to eat and drink and fornicate. They want to experience the pleasures of a human existence, but in order to do so, they must break down the will. Only when the defense is in tatters is the host willing to let it inside."

"How does it break down the will?" Benjamin is still cleaning his spectacles, rubbing stubborn flecks of seawater.

"It does what it can to cause an oppression and make the victim feel as though it is under attack, even from friends and family. Then it offers comforts and gifts—solutions to the problem. It is quite the deceiver, Mr. West. Quite the master manipulator."

"I saw it once," I realize with a shudder that has nothing to do with the cold wind. "It wore Charlotte's likeness. I saw it through the window, out in the clergy house yard."

Reverend Jacob gives a rueful laugh. "It was trying her on for size, I reckon—much like a dress rehearsal. It was practicing *being* her."

The idea of it is sickening. "What will happen to her, if it gets inside?"

"It depends on the will of the girl," he replies. "How strong she is—and how compatible with the will of the demon. Sometimes it can go quite dormant; other times it will completely take over. If that happens, the victim is unlikely to live long." He shrugs. "They deteriorate quite quickly, unable to keep their minds intact. If the girl is as strong as you say, though, she might well coexist with it—which is the worse outcome by far. People like that, harboring demons, can grow to great power. They learn how to harness the demon's might and use it to fulfill their ambitions. Priests and kings, generals and bankers." He ticks them off his fingers. "There are still demons walking this earth, Miss Russel, wearing all kinds of magnificent guises.

What you know them by is their cruelty—their utter contempt for others."

"You don't have to harbor a demon to be cruel," Benjamin protests. "History is rife with people who were cruel because they could be, or because it was in their nature."

"*Or* because they had a demon." Reverend Jacob smiles at him, still with that overbearing air about him, but I do not mind. As long as he can help, I can stand a little arrogance.

"*Demons,* though." Benjamin shakes his head. "It does sound outlandish." I absolutely agree with him, but then the knocker was always outlandish. And yet . . .

"Do you really believe it is the same creature as the demons in the Bible?" I ask him, and to my surprise, he shrugs.

"Does it truly matter, Miss Russel? For the record, I *do* believe it is the same creature, but do I think they were once angels, dwelling in the heavens above?" He cocks his head. "I don't know. They always seemed a little too earthly to me—like something that has never touched God's graces."

"Why Charlotte, though?" Benjamin asks. "Why this girl among all the others?"

Reverend Jacob stares out at the sea for a moment. "I cannot say why this particular woman was chosen above the rest, but there is usually already a flaw in their defenses. Victims may be prone to visions, or they are deeply unhappy. Perhaps there is an affinity—something for the demon to latch on to."

"We don't know for sure, though," I say, feeling that the conversation has brought us too far from the shores of reason. "It might not try to . . . *possess* her."

Reverend Jacob gives me the look of a mildly concerned father. "My dear Miss Russel, how do you think it came to your island? How did they manage to imprison a powerful creature that could raise storms and kill at will in a tower?" He pauses while watching us mull it over. To my own great embarrassment, I had not even thought of it. "Because it was *inside* Margaret," he says. "The demon could be captured because it lived inside her flesh, and *that* flesh could be drugged and controlled, transported and imprisoned. *That* is how it ended up in the tower."

It makes too much sense to be a falsehood; the puzzle pieces slot into place. "But why didn't it leave?" I ask. "Why didn't *it*—and Margaret—break free of the tower?"

"That, my friends, is something we have yet to discover," Reverend Jacob replies, sounding unconcerned. Rather, I see curiosity lighting up his pale blue eyes. "*Something* must have happened when the tower fell to let it loose. If we figure out what that was, perhaps the prison can be restored before the woman is overtaken."

"We went to the tower, but we saw nothing that could explain how it was kept in there," Benjamin notes.

"Then we must look closer," says Reverend Jacob.

Above us in the sky, seagulls are circling. To our right, I can see the tall, slender lighthouse. We are coming closer to shore—to Margaret's Keep—and my stomach ties up in a knot.

• • •

As we walk from the harbor to the clergy house, my apprehension intensifies with every step. Despite my carte blanche from Evelyn North, I know I am overstepping. Charlotte and Reverend Hill never asked for my involvement, and now I am about to take it one step further and introduce them to this peculiar stranger.

Perhaps she might set the knocker loose on me in return.

I take heart in what Benjamin had said to Charlotte during our last unhappy encounter: the knocker is *everyone's* problem now. And we have sworn to be bold, to endure fear's discomfort.

A sudden flash in my memory of Antonia Hill's death grin only cements my resolve.

Benjamin and Reverend Jacob come up behind me, carrying the

latter's trunk between them. We left our own suitcases at the grocery store and will pick them up once the reverend is installed. Reverend Jacob seems thrilled to be here, looking around him with excitement. His gaze often seeks out the jagged remains of the tower, and something else comes into his expression then: a hunger, like a wolf's.

I note with satisfaction that the knocker might just be about to finally meet a worthy opponent. Never mind if he is arrogant and overbearing. The knocker is that as well in its way. They will be well matched.

As we come closer to the clergy house, its white walls giving nothing away about what is happening within its shell, I begin steeling myself. So focused am I on this task that I barely even consider that we are about to step into the knocker's lair. This is my moment now. If we are to successfully insert Reverend Jacob into the house, it all depends on me.

Luckily, I know just where to turn to rustle up some confidence and authority.

By the time we ascend the stairs to the house and pause before the brown doors, I am back in the schoolroom, lifting a piece of chalk. I am Miss Russel through and through, and I will have no disarray in my class.

I lift my hand and knock in a most assertive way. When Noreen—blank eyed and tired looking—comes to answer, I demand to speak to Reverend Hill at once. The woman gives me a curious look, then looks again when she notices the stranger hovering behind me, but she asks no questions; just opens the door to let us in before going in search of the reverend.

The house feels stifling, dark. A scent of cooked meat hangs in the air. Benjamin and Reverend Jacob place the trunk on the floor while I start pacing the small hall, feeling tense and uncomfortable yet determined to see this through.

When the reverend arrives from the sitting room, looking quite disheveled, it is with a scent of brandy trailing in his wake. Charlotte comes, too, which unsettles me slightly. I was not prepared to see her today. She looks radiant, though—like a flower in bloom. She wears Mrs. Hill's blue shawl over her mourning attire. I dare a glance at Reverend Jacob, who is devouring the girl with his eyes—not with lust, though. No. It is an entirely different hunger that drives him.

"Reverend Hill," I say in greeting. "Charlotte. This is Reverend Jacob." I gesture with my hand, using my best classroom voice—the one that will brook no questions. "He is here to help, and I have promised him your hospitality." I give Reverend Hill a stern look.

Charlotte and Reverend Hill look to each other, their befuddlement apparent. "He is certainly most welcome," Reverend Hill says, though he sounds unsure and his gaze keeps darting back to Charlotte. "What kind of help, if I may ask?" Now his gaze is on Reverend Jacob, seemingly concerned.

Reverend Jacob takes a step forth. "I have ample experience with the type of issues that are plaguing this household," he states proudly. "I have, in the past, successfully helped on many such occasions, and would be happy to be of service here as well. I do, of course, have letters of recommendation." He motions to his trunk.

"You need *help,* Reverend," I say to Reverend Hill. "You cannot handle this alone." I notice how Charlotte has taken a few steps back, looking pale all of a sudden.

"I have it all well in hand—" he starts, but I interrupt him.

"Surely two priests are better than one? The knocker is still here, isn't it? Charlotte isn't freed from it yet. Surely, it must be a relief to have someone else to share the burden—someone with a different set of skills and experience with this type of phenomenon. Honestly, Reverend Hill, you ought to be thrilled." I dare him to make another excuse, then deliver the final blow. "The Norths want him here, as well. Evelyn enlisted us to seek out a cure." I look at Charlotte, but she does not look at me. She looks at Reverend Hill, with a warning in her eyes.

"Oh well, in that case." Reverend Hill gives a thin smile, and I cannot say if I truly feel pity for the man, or if I have come to loathe his weakness. "I am, of course, grateful for all the help I can get, but this is a house of mourning—"

"Yet it *is* where the knocker is. Where better to observe it than here? If Reverend Jacob truly is to be of help, this is where he must stay."

"This is not a condemnation of your efforts, Reverend," Benjamin says quietly from behind me. "It is merely reinforcement, to take some of the burden off your shoulders. You are, as you say, in mourning."

Reverend Jacob takes another step forward. "I will, of course, be most considerate of your circumstances," he says to his fellow reverend. "Perhaps I can even be of help in that regard. Sometimes, a priest needs a priest," he adds, with uncharacteristic warmth.

"You have not held a service since your wife's passing." I force some softness into my own voice as well. "This is not good, Reverend. Do your superiors know?"

Reverend Hill, looking like a half-drowned pup, shakes his head miserably. I can see that he swallows hard. "I am grateful," he utters at last, "of course."

"Good." I give him my best schoolroom smile—the one reserved for good behavior. "Then I trust Reverend Jacob is in the best of hands, and that the two of you will work together to rid us all of the menace."

Noreen has come drifting back into the hall, and speaks to Reverend Jacob in a voice dripping with relief. "You are very welcome here, Reverend." The look of gratitude she sends me is deeply touching. She must have had a very hard time of late.

"I am beyond happy to be of service," Reverend Jacob answers with some of his usual swagger, and even takes a bow before the flustered Noreen.

The only one who has said nothing during this encounter—who barely has done anything but to try to blend with the shadows—is Charlotte.

·50·

jasper

"Once, in Athens, I met a man whose whole family were beset by demons: his wife, his daughter, even his infirm father. It was a lost cause, of course, but we managed to save the man himself and the infant son." Reverend Jacob will not stop talking—*boasting*—about his incredible feats.

"Then I moved on to Vienna, where an elderly lady had put down her silk thread and needle and suddenly become a late-blooming belle of the ball, throwing all sorts of lavish parties, aided by a 'whisperer in the night.'" He butters a piece of toast, then starts peeling an egg. His long fingers work with exact precision, his gaze always watchful. Is this what a soldier of Christ looks like? I see nothing of myself in him. "The thing is, Reverend Hill"—the sharp gaze lands on me—"just because people do not want to believe they exist, such creatures are very much a reality, as you now well know."

"Yes," I say, voice hoarse. "I have had reason to adjust my beliefs of late." I have not managed to stomach more than a piece of apple and some coffee. Yesterday's liquor has left my head and stomach in turmoil, but today I cannot remedy the damage with another tipple, as

I usually do. It just will not do to appear drunk at nine o'clock in the morning with another reverend in the house. I curse Miss Russel for bringing him here. Mr. West had said it was no condemnation, but of course it is.

Reverend Jacob's presence is stark proof of my own incompetence.

On a better day, I might have appreciated the help—clung to fresh hope like a pup to a teat—but this is not that day, and the problems I face can certainly not be solved with holy water and prayer. We are far beyond that point, and Charlotte's clock keeps ticking, ticking . . . Eight days now, and counting. In two days, we leave, and I have still not done a thing to put my affairs in order. Shame is my constant companion these days.

Shame, and a deep sense of dread.

And now this insufferable man is intruding on my house and my mind, bringing with him a whirlwind of energy—which certainly yanks me back to reality—but that is not a good thing. It would have been better if I had remained in a state of melancholy and drink. Better for *me*, anyway. The world has nothing to offer me now but guilt and endless hardships, and I much prefer to avoid it. Let Charlotte take the reins. But I cannot do that now, with this chattering man at my table. He will not let me be. He wants to go out in a boat, he says, and he wants me to come with him.

"Miss Russel and Mr. West must come, too, of course, but perhaps not your delightful houseguest," he notes, even if Charlotte has made herself scarce this morning, just like she did last night at dinner, and he has no way of knowing just how delightful—or not—she is.

I feel betrayed that she leaves me to handle Reverend Jacob alone. He is here on *her* account, after all, commissioned by the Norths. Is she *protecting* the knocker now? Is she shielding it from him? Does the knocker *fear* Reverend Jacob? It certainly never feared me.

How did it all go so wrong?

"You shouldn't feel poorly for being unable to handle it, Reverend

Hill. Demons are tricky creatures, and it takes some experience and skill to get rid of them. But fear not." He waves the butter knife in the air. "As long as it hasn't moved into the girl, the battle is not lost." Last night, he had told me all about his theory that the knocker covets Charlotte's flesh. In this, I suppose, the creature and I are the same, though I certainly would not *possess* it.

"It has been quiet of late," I say, because it is the truth. "I haven't heard it at all for days. Perhaps it is already gone."

"Oh no, Reverend." My colleague shakes his head with a sad expression. "It is still here—I can smell it, you see. You would, too, if you didn't live with it. And I can feel it, as well, like an oppression in the air. You certainly still have a houseguest that isn't quite as delightful as Charlotte." He laughs. Why does he keep mentioning how "delightful" Charlotte is? Does he know about our shameful union? Can he smell that, too?

"It *could* be gone, though. Don't they ever disappear on their own?" I hate asking his opinion—acknowledge his expertise—but clearly I know nothing, so I must.

"They can." Reverend Jacob takes a hearty swig of his coffee and measures me with his unnerving gaze. "If the resistance is too strong, or if it finds greener pastures. Normally, my work consists of making the demon's task of overcoming the victim so bothersome and hard that it gives up. There are, however, rumors of ancient practices by which the foul thing can be trapped, and that is what I believe happened to this specimen before, when it first arrived on the island with Margaret. I am giddy as a schoolboy, to tell you the truth. I hope to find my *grail* here, Reverend—a demon trap, at last."

"We don't *know* for sure that it is the same one," I point out.

"Oh, please." He gives me an overbearing look. "Despite what some clergy say, they are *rare,* Reverend Hill, and the odds of more than one demon finding its way to this godforsaken island are close to nil." He chews his bread with satisfaction.

"We don't *know* for sure what happened to Margaret either." I am still grasping for straws—for some way to make this irritating person slightly less sure of himself. His confidence makes my own shortcomings loom large, and I am unsure if I can stomach another bout of self-loathing—especially not without liquor to soften the blow.

Reverend Jacob gives me a curious look. "*Of course* we know, Reverend. Mr. West's research laid out Margaret's origins quite plainly," he says, and I realize how I must not have paid attention. What research is he speaking of? What origins? When did this laying out occur? While I was sitting in my office sipping brandy? While I wept over my dead wife? I will not bring more shame upon myself by admitting that I do not know, so instead, I just nod and smile.

"So, we must go by low tide," the painfully energetic man continues, speaking of the boating trip again. "I already examined the ruins at daybreak, and there are a few things I hope to have confirmed by looking at the rubble beneath the cliff."

"We can hire a boat," I say, "and an oarsman."

"Wonderful." He beams at me. "It should not take long, once we get to the debris."

At least, with this outing, he will be kept away from Charlotte, and his keen eyes will not see the invisible trails of my hands on her flesh, or what possibly grows in her belly.

He will not know that the knocker is not Charlotte's only foe.

• • •

I had forgotten what fresh air feels like, the sting of salt on my skin. The sea today is playful. The waves leap and dance around the large rowboat, teased by the relentless wind. The sky is dirty gray above us, filtering the light, and a light drizzle mists our hats and coats. At the oars is the elder Mr. Newell, a fisherman by trade, but long since retired. The bearded man asks no questions, but just peers at us with narrow blue eyes under a brown, knitted cap. He is taking us from the harbor across the blue, rippling field of the sea with sure strokes. If he wonders why we want to look at the remains of Margaret's

Tower, he does not say, but he required a steep price for his services, so it is clear that he is apprehensive.

Perhaps the presence of two priests put his mind somewhat at ease. Enough, at least, to take on the job. I like to believe so, even if I have not felt very worthy of my collar of late.

To our left, Margaret's Keep's steep cliffs trickle by, topped with tufts of green grass. Miss Russel looks even smaller than usual in her nest of tweed, wool, and felt. Mr. West wears a worried look on his face. The man is dressed as if about to climb a mountain, with sturdy boots, a thick yellow coat, and leather gloves and hat. I suppose his profession has prepared him for all kinds of weather. Due to Newell's presence, none of us speak much before we get there—not even Jacob, which is a blessing. The reverend has found himself a place at the bow and stares ahead like a vengeful figurehead, letting the salt water spray his face. Perhaps he dreams of what he will do if he finds his holy grail—what quests he will go on, what feats he will accomplish. Mayhap he will be the first in the history of men to capture and study a demon.

It does not take long before we are at our destination and the jagged ruin appears above us. There are seagulls there, too, circling as if the structure were still in place. Newell maneuvers the boat to as close as he can get in the shallow water, and we busy ourselves with vacating the vessel, stepping down on the soft sand revealed by the low tide.

Under the cliff, among rocks of a more common variety, are several which I can tell, even from a distance, must have been cut and shaped by men: Margaret's Tower, in shambles. The sand is puddled and wet in places, sucking at the soles of my shoes. I admit that I enjoy being outside: the air, most of all, and my use of muscles long ignored. Even the ghost of yesterday's liquor recedes, leaving behind only a slight queasiness and a trembling in my hands. I never feared Margaret's Tower before, and neither, I realize, do I now. But then, if my companions are to be believed, the thing to fear is no longer here but drifts through the rooms of my own home.

For my inner eyes, I see Antonia at the window, looking at the tower that is not there, speaking about seagulls and hungry things.

I come back to reality with a start when Reverend Jacob finds his voice again. "I will need to enlist your expertise, Mr. West, to determine what is natural and what is man-made."

"Surely," Mr. West replies, effortlessly grabbing hold of Miss Russel to ferry her over a puddle. To my great surprise, Miss Russel does not seem to mind, and for the first time it strikes me that something might be blossoming between them. I had never thought Miss Russel one for romance, but clearly, I have been wrong.

When she is back on her feet, she turns her head and smiles at him, and the look in her eyes—the glittering warmth—reminds me so greatly of Antonia in the first days of our courtship that it cuts at my heart and leaves me breathless.

"You did not inspect the site before?" Reverend Jacob asks Mr. West, who shakes his head.

"It was of no concern to me then," he replies. "I only inspected the cliff wall."

"Did you get a chance to speak to Charlotte, Reverend Jacob?" Miss Russel asks as he strides before her, full of purpose.

"Charlotte was indisposed," I say quickly. "She has a headache."

Reverend Jacob gives a booming laugh. "You mustn't let yourself be duped, Reverend Hill. She is clearly being prevented by her *leech*." He looks back over his shoulder. Though he is wearing a wide-brimmed hat, the wind has taken hold of a few tresses of hair and whips them around his angular face. "I am sure I'll speak to the young lady in time," he tells Miss Russel. "For now, I am more concerned with the cure than the disease."

Miss Russel gives me a concerned look, likely sensing how my new houseguest rubs me the wrong way. "Are you all right, Reverend?"

I give a curt nod. I have nothing to say.

"Did you ever get a result from the autopsy?" she continues, and now all eyes—even Reverend Jacob's—are on me.

"I did," I admit in a hoarse voice. "They could not say." I look away from them all. "The cause remains undetermined."

Silence descends on our little group. I know what they are all thinking, because I have been thinking it, too. But we do not *know* for sure. No one *knows* for sure—besides the knocker.

Reverend Jacob has reached the first few rocks from the tower. They are gray and dull in the filtered daylight. With no concern for his clothes, he squats down to inspect them, and is soon joined by West, who squats down as well. Even Miss Russel comes to observe and watches eagerly as the men trace the surface of rock after rock with their hands. I look at the rocks, too, but all I can see that is out of the ordinary is a series of grooves, running in all directions.

"These two fit," Miss Russel says with triumph, looking down at a couple of rocks at her feet. Reverend Jacob and Mr. West are there at once, like bloodhounds having found their scent. They inspect the stones keenly, prod at them, and exchange excited looks.

Might it be they found the grail?

Mr. West rises to his feet and stretches. "I saw similar markings in the ruin that still stands, but I must admit I didn't even consider them anything other than normal wear. The possibility that they were made by men simply eluded me." He looks slightly abashed, and I feel for him. I, too, have been a disgrace to my profession of late.

"You weren't looking for it," Miss Russel instantly says.

"Miss Russel is right," Reverend Jacob echoes. "They are not as clear in the ruins. It seems they have been etched deeper higher up in the tower."

"I suppose they were better protected there as well," Miss Russel says.

I feel utterly confused, and step closer to try to make sense of their words. Reverend Jacob stands in the middle of the rubble; large slabs of stone are half-buried in the sand before his feet. "It is a maze," he exclaims with gusto. "A wonderfully large and intricate maze!"

Miss Russel laughs with delight, and Mr. West, too, is nothing but smiles.

"How utterly amazing," the teacher exclaims. "Who would have thought that the old tower held such a secret?"

"This is how they kept it contained." Reverend Jacob is bursting with victory. "It is a well-known trick, according to various folklore, to divert the attention of demons and ghouls by emptying out a bowl of peas, or a box of matches, to force the fiend to count them all. It is simply in their nature," he lectures. "I suppose this is something like it—only bigger. Surround the demon with a maze, and it has no choice but to travel it infinitely!"

I think of what Mrs. North had told me about Charlotte's childhood obsession with labyrinths and feel cold. Certainly, there can be no correlation?

"So, what do we do now?" Miss Russel is full of admiration for Reverend Jacob. "Build another tower?"

"Oh, Miss Russel, I do not believe that will be necessary. The tower was large because the vessel was a woman, but I think a smaller version will do just as well when the demon is in its natural state."

"Like a cage." Mr. West, too, sounds mightily impressed.

"Just that." Reverend Jacob purrs like a cat with a fish. "One that can be easily hidden and moved around."

"Perhaps you will be able to write that textbook after all, Ruth." Mr. West beams at his paramour, who laughs in reply.

"This certainly casts the mysterious mazes of the past in a different light," Reverend Jacob muses. "Might it be that they were all about the capture and containment of demons?"

They are like children, I think. Children with new and magnificent toys.

"What do you think, Reverend Hill?" Miss Russel's eyes seek mine; her cheeks are ruddy with excitement. "Isn't this marvelous?

Now we actually have a very real opportunity to get rid of the knocker once and for all."

"Yes, marvelous." I smile, but I do not truly feel it.

Then, as we move back toward Mr. Newell and the boat—my companions still both giddy and excited—I am suddenly struck by a mind-shattering thought: *What if he is right?*

What if this blustering, grating newcomer truly is *right,* and the knocker aims to possess Charlotte's flesh? What would it do to her? What would it do to a *child*? What if we end up leaving the island with a *demon* in tow? I have been so preoccupied with my own guilt and the weight of my sins that I had not truly considered it before. The idea instantly makes me feel sick, and I have to look away to hide my discomfort from the others.

No more liquor, I swear silently to myself as we reenter the boat. I need my wits about me if this is going to end in anything but disaster. The haze has finally lifted, and my eyes can clearly see. For the first time I realize how I, too, am captured and imprisoned, caught in a tower of my own making.

Left to the whims of my mistress.

·51·

charlotte

Had I known that he was coming, I would never have let him in, but things are different now. With the knocker living inside me, it can no longer watch the road, and so I was utterly taken aback when the other reverend suddenly stood in the hall, promising to take my knocker away.

We do not like him at all.

At first, Jasper seemed to agree with me. I could tell from the way that he spoke—the way that he moved—that he, too, found the newcomer a most unwelcome interruption. But then there was Miss Russel, all smug and fresh-faced, speaking with my father's authority, so what else could he do but obey? I cannot believe that Evelyn would do this to me, and enlist Miss Russel without even consulting me. I do not want help. I do not *need* help. My escape is just a few days away, and for the first time in my life, I am in control.

We are in control.

I managed to avoid Reverend Jacob all through the first day, and the morning after, too. Jasper said he understood that I needed peace and calm and not another upheaval like the one we had with

Dr. Crown, but something must have happened on their boating trip, because now he has suddenly changed his mind.

"You *must* speak to him," he says, standing in the attic room. Behind him, through the window, I can see the sun has traveled far. It will soon be night. "I'm afraid I have to insist, Charlotte. We *cannot* leave Margaret's Keep with the knocker in tow. This issue just cannot remain unresolved. It is dangerous, Charlotte."

I measure the gaunt-looking man before me, remembering how handsome he used to be, before. "It hasn't harmed me yet," I say.

"It doesn't mean it won't," he implores me with bloodshot eyes. "Think of Antonia, Charlotte—and Dr. Crown. Think of Miss Russel and Mr. West. Reverend Jacob says that it wants *you,* Charlotte. That it has been its aim all along—"

"Well, it can't have me," I say, with a fresh bout of annoyance brewing in my belly. "And surely our prayers have helped. You can keep the knocker at bay—"

"No, Charlotte, I cannot," he says, looking utterly miserable as he sinks down on my bed and hides his face in his hands. "I have failed you, Charlotte, in more ways than one, and the knocker has won. Nothing I do can banish it now."

"But if we marry," I say, "it would obliterate our sin, and surely you would be strong enough then—" I will not stay on Margaret's Keep. I will *not*.

"Why won't you speak to him, Charlotte? *Surely* you must be eager to rid yourself of the knocker—"

"I am," I interrupt, more furious by the second. "But I don't trust this man. He is a stranger, and recommended by the cruel Dr. Crown—"

"And commissioned by your father, Charlotte, whom we both owe our loyalty and repentance. No, we cannot leave this island before this matter is settled. You should *welcome* Reverend Jacob. He might well be our salvation. The problem of the knocker cannot be ignored any longer." He raises his voice when he says the last part, as if to challenge the knocker, believing it able to still flit among the rafters of the house rather than standing right in front of him. "I lost myself for a while, and perhaps it took a man of his confidence to rouse me from my sleep, but I am here now, Charlotte. I am, and I will not let you down again."

"I don't trust him," I complain once more, as I cannot think of a better reply. This is in every way inconvenient, and not what we wanted at all. "Think of the unborn child, Jasper," I try as a last resort.

"And yet"—he sounds both tired and defeated—"I cannot leave Margaret's Keep with you unless we find a cure. It is for the child's sake, too. I cannot risk anything happening to it. Think of what happened to Antonia," he says again.

"We cannot know for sure that it had anything to do with the knocker," I remind him.

"No." But his gaze is suddenly both stern and unwavering. "We cannot know for sure, Charlotte, and that is just why you must speak to Reverend Jacob."

I cannot do anything but clench my jaw and bite back the words that threaten to rush out of me. Now more than ever, it is crucial that Jasper not know the extent of my relationship with the spirit—that it is *me* now, and that I am it. It would only scare him and turn him away from me, and I do not want to abduct him by force, like some barbarian out of Evelyn's novels. He will know soon enough, when we are gone from here and it is safe.

When he has nowhere else to go.

"I will speak to him," I agree, "if only to put your mind at ease." Surely, the newcomer, too, can be duped. I have gained some experience in being the victim, and one last performance cannot hurt, I hope.

"I am happy to hear it, Charlotte." Jasper is up from the bed, embracing me. "The knocker must be dealt with before we can go, and I do believe Reverend Jacob can help with that, whatever else I might think of the man."

The statement leaves me rattled, long after the embrace has ended.

I do not *want* to get rid of the knocker—and I no longer think I can. I can feel it like a warmth in me, writhing and breathing whenever I breathe. It is in every part of my body, traveling in my bloodstream. It floods my mind with images: past, present, and even the future; laying out the possibilities. It tells me that I am strong, and cleverer than most.

It tells me I can fool this new priest that so rudely slipped through the door.

It tells me that our power is immense.

• • •

He is waiting for me in Jasper's office, wearing the same smug look on his face as when I saw him the day before. There is something about him that I cannot abide—something that *the knocker* cannot abide. We sense him in the same way that a mouse senses a cat, but at the same time, we *are* the cat, seeing in him nothing but a mouse.

"Charlotte North, at last." Reverend Jacob gives a slick smile and pulls out a chair for me, acting as if he owns the place although he is merely a guest. "I have been looking forward to our meeting," he says. "I believe I have some good news."

"Oh, that would certainly be welcome," I say, smoothing my stiff black skirt before taking my place on the straight-backed chair. "It has been nothing but misery here of late, with the passing of Mrs. Hill."

"Yes, a terrible business," he says, but does not offer condolences. Instead, he leans against the desk behind him and measures me with his pale gaze. "I have not met your demon yet, but I am sure I will in time. I can smell it, though. It lies heavy in the air. Do you smell it, Charlotte? The scent of meat roasting?"

"I do," I confirm, suddenly uneasy that he would smell it on me as well.

"But it is quiet now, isn't it? Did something happen to placate it?"

"I don't know," I say, moving restlessly on the chair. This scene reminds me too much of Dr. Crown and his rude interrogation. I will not let myself be treated like that again. "Perhaps it has grown weaker," I say. "Perhaps Reverend Hill's prayers have worked."

Reverend Jacob nods. "They aren't normally bothered by prayers, though—nor holy water. I once saw a possessed boy gobble up a whole tray of communion wafers."

"Oh." I feign surprise. "What *are* they bothered by, then?" It would surely be convenient to know.

The reverend shrugs. "Boredom," he says. "Too much resistance. They grow tired of their pursuits very quickly if the task proves too bothersome. *Your* demon, though—your 'knocker'—has been imprisoned for a very long time, doing whatever it could to break free—lighting faux candles in the window, I've heard, in an attempt to mimic its dead vessel's actions and coax a boat to shore." He looks at me expectantly, waiting for a response, but I do not quite grasp his meaning.

"Vessel?" I ask. "Is it Margaret you are speaking of?"

He just smiles, and I feel something shift, grow tense, inside me.

The knocker is alert now.

"Just that," Reverend Jacob says, smiling. "He came here with her, you see, embedded in her flesh. They built the tower with a maze for it to get lost in, doomed to forever travel along its walls, long after Margaret was gone." He shifts his gaze to the floor. "When the tower fell, it found you." When he looks up again, the smile is gone. "Now it is *your* flesh it wants as its nest."

"You cannot know that for sure," I say, though the news about the maze has left me feeling weak.

"I have evidence." The reverend speaks calmly. "I have seen the designs painstakingly carved into the inside of the tower walls."

"Margaret could have made them," I suggest, "driven to madness by despair."

He chuckles—which annoys me. "No, I think it was deliberately made to hold the demon—"

"I don't like that word, Reverend. We do not know what it is."

"But it's your friend, though." His eyes have narrowed. "Yes, I think it is. Has it brought you many gifts? Promised to be with you always? Did it help you escape your home?"

"I never asked for any of it." The knocker squirms in my belly now, feeding me with rage. I do my best to bite it back, to keep my composure and answer the man. It is harder, I find, to lie with conviction when you harbor the fiery apple of discord.

"I am sure you did not. But you *must* know the danger you are in. There is a price for its services: it *will* try to possess you." His gaze is imploring when he looks at me, wanting me to feel the graveness of the situation. "Has it asked you yet to be allowed inside?"

I shake my head. The silence in the house is nearly complete. There are no seagulls, no bleating sheep, not even a crackling from the fireplaces.

Only the sea is there—moving, always.

"I said, *Has it asked you yet?*" His fingers suddenly cup my chin, force me to look up at him. The pale eyes are blazing now, and I see a fire there to rival my own—though his is cold while mine is sizzling. This is not good—not good at all.

I use all my might to suppress the fury that comes rolling up from my belly. "No!" I shout the word, and yet it only comes out with some difficulty. Reverend Jacob stares at me—stares into my eyes—and then he lets me go.

"So soon?" He fishes a handkerchief out of his pocket to clean his hand. The one that he touched me with, I note. "How did it get to you so soon?"

"I don't— I don't understand, Reverend," I say in a hoarse voice. My heart beats rapidly; the knocker screams with fury.

"Yes, you do." The only light in the room comes in through the windows, painting his face in shadows. "How did it get to you? What did it promise you?"

In my mind, the knocker fires bullets of its own—moments in time seen from eyes not mine. There is the tower looming. There is the door. I see the inside of the walls, and the grooves running through them, forming a dizzying picture. I feel Margaret's despair as she looks up at the stairs, thinking of the days ahead alone. Her head is pounding and her mind fights a haze. She knows she has been poisoned. Tricked. The knocker inside her thrashes and writhes, but is helplessly drawn to the shapes on the walls.

There is no other way. A man's voice sounds from outside the door, heavy with regret, shivering with fear. *The priests all say it must be done.*

Then I am suddenly in the shed, staring out on the old, dusty room: the laden shelves and work clothing; the pictures I once drew with coal. I look out between the boards toward the derelict tower, see the tall, crumbling structure. I remember how I imagined—*felt*—that someone was looking back.

Someone who was just like me.

I remember using coal to draw mazes on the floor, then trying to find a way through. I remember how important it felt to accomplish. I *see* now—I understand—that the knocker was with me already then, begging a fellow prisoner for help. *Of course* it would come to me when it got loose. It would help me like I had tried to help it.

Next, I see an image more disturbing than the rest of them combined: it is a new tower, standing just where Margaret's did. This one is built of similar rocks, but there is a red door, and a shingled roof. I know that it is meant for me—to lock us both inside.

It is my warning from the knocker, my cue to let it loose.

I feel my own childhood pain blossoming anew, as I silently scream that *no one* shall ever lock me up again! Not Mother, no, never, and certainly not this *priest*!

It feels like no more than a second passes from the moment I let go until the time he is dead. I am up from my chair, that much I know, but how he flies across the room—how his head splits open—I cannot say. Neither can I quite recall how Jasper's letter opener ends up in his chest, protruding from his heart—a tiny sword. I think it was no more than a flick of the wrist, an act of will.

Because we wanted it so.

The righteous has fallen. His body is spent. The empty blue eyes stare up at the ceiling. I sink down to the floor, whimpering softly, while the knocker withdraws inside me, becoming a content, dull glow. I look at my hands. They are clean, and yet . . .

This time, there will be no doubt. No autopsy. No explanations. It is glaringly obvious to anyone with eyes that Reverend Jacob has been murdered, and the only thing left for me to do now is run.

·52·

charlotte

There is no wind when we leave Margaret's Keep. I know the stillness of the air will make the island women nervous, and compel them to craft wreaths of spare dough to offer to unseen forces in order to protect their loved ones out at sea. Quiet is a bad omen in a place whipped by relentless wind. The stillness is said to herald an oncoming storm—not just in the sky, but in hearts as well.

We boarded the *Seagull* shortly before it left the island, loaded to the brim with fish barrels for the mainland. If any of the fishermen were puzzled by our sudden appearance, our rushed and disheveled looks, or the volume of our luggage, they did not show it. They have been instructed to always find space for the Norths, and clearly Father has not yet excluded me from the arrangement. Jasper and I stand on the small deck as we glide away from Margaret's Keep. The broken tower looms above us like a mouth with ruined teeth; a crumbling crown.

A prison no more.

Somewhere behind the tower sits the clergy house, and in Jasper's office, Reverend Jacob lies dead. He will not be found before Noreen starts looking for us all. I feel sorry for the old woman who is so easily rattled, but it simply cannot be helped. The risk is too great if we stay.

When I turn my head to the right, I can see my childhood home with my sisters in it. They are sitting together, perhaps, having their breakfast. I wonder if they miss me—if they talk of me at all. I want to believe that they do in this moment, but I know that their perception of me will be very much changed by nightfall.

I wonder if the death of Reverend Jacob will hurt them, but likely it is Jasper, and not I, who will take the blame. Father will doubtlessly look for me, and worry if I have been kidnapped at knifepoint. I am sorry for the pain it will cause him, but it simply cannot be helped. There is no natural explanation for the letter opener in the reverend's heart, and there are no vagrants on Margaret's Keep on which to pin the blame. I considered saying the knocker did it all, but Miss Russel and Mr. West are already suspicious, and even my family has doubts. The mainland police cannot ignore such a blatant crime, and the law does not believe in spirits. I could show them, of course, but why waste a secret like mine? The weapon I carry is best wielded in secret. It told me so itself, when I asked.

There will always be towers, it said in its wordless way, slipping the knowledge into my mind. There will always be men who want to capture and control, and others who want to dissect for knowledge. The knocker belongs to me alone, and I belong to it.

Together there is no limit to what we can accomplish.

As my former home grows smaller behind me, I hope that Evelyn will have her wedding, that Adelaide and Sophie will lead happy lives, and that what I have done will not harm them. My heart aches when I think of my sisters, so I will think of them no longer.

Jasper stands beside me, black clad and haggard looking. I detect some relief in his eyes as he watches the island grow farther away. The gray sheep are just pinpricks now, the church spire just a shard of light, reflecting the golden sun. His hands shake badly before he grabs the railing, and the smell of stale liquor surrounds him like a cloak. I will remedy this inconvenient flaw when we are married. I did not go through all of this to become the wife of a drunkard. Needles in the wineglass will do the trick, or ashes in every bottle he picks.

His mind, though, might take a while to heal.

"This is not right, Charlotte. None of it is," he mutters, wetting his lips nervously.

"There was no other way," I answer in a voice so quiet that the crew cannot overhear us. "*We* know that the knocker did it, but the police will never believe it. You cannot try a spirit in a court of law. Not even my father's good name would be enough to save us."

"But they will look for us," he argues. "We won't get far."

"Have faith," I say, thinking that if push comes to shove, the knocker and I will handle it.

"Your parents will be terrified for you," he says next, letting out a shuddering breath.

"That may be so, but perhaps they will understand. They know about the knocker, after all, and may be able to puzzle together what happened."

"What are we to do, Charlotte?" None of my calm words reach him; the terror in his eyes is stark.

"Rome," I say. "We will go to Rome. I hear they have some experience with demons there. We will get rid of the knocker, Jasper." I pat his hand gently.

"Good." He lets out another shuddering breath. "I won't have that *thing* anywhere *near* the child."

I give his hand a little squeeze, telling him by gesture that it will be all right. His handsome face looks ashen, but it is nothing that rest cannot remedy. When the time is right and we are wed, I will tell him that there is no child—that the only thing living inside me is a different creature altogether. That we do not go to Rome to seek a cure, but because we must go *somewhere* and I have always wanted to see it.

My belly rumbles with hunger, as it often does since the knocker slipped inside. Everything tastes more—smells more—and the love-making, too, is different. The knocker is hungry for everything a body can provide, and rejoices in being flesh and blood again.

It has been waiting for a very long time, and satisfaction is no longer an issue.

The sea surrounds the *Seagull* like a sheet of wrinkled silk, glittering and content below the bright summer sun. The sky is blue and peaceful; hardly a cloud can be seen. Margaret's Keep is just a shadow now—a cursed fairy island disappearing in the mist.

Rise, waves, I think, and the silk rips apart to let sudden, tall waves come crashing against the vessel's sturdy side.

Blow, wind, I think, and the sudden gust is strong enough to whisk Jasper's hat off his head. He barely catches it before it can disappear out to sea, and the sight of the chase makes me smile.

Under my feet, there is a knocking inside the wooden boards, a merry little melody that Mary used to sing, about love and riches and everything good.

"Knock, knock," I whisper to the wind.

·53·

ruth

Fear, disappointment, and fury. I cycle through the emotions as if on a merry-go-round as Benjamin and I sit on the church steps, looking over at the clergy house, where two dark-clad mainland police officers have just stepped inside. The house is empty now. Reverend Jacob's body has been removed and shipped to the mainland, traveling in a crate filled with ice, just like Antonia Hill's.

Noreen has promptly retired, and is still reeling with the shock of finding the dead reverend on the office floor. Benjamin and I visited her in the small cottage she shares with her husband, where she has barricaded herself ever since. We brought her a box of sweets, but looking at her drawn face, I quickly realized that no amount of sugar was going to make her feel any better. For a talkative woman, she was very quiet, and I cannot help but feel guilty about Noreen as well. I should have taken better care of her—should have urged her to resign as soon as it became apparent that the knocker was not about to leave Charlotte's side.

Now she is quite broken—and so, quite frankly, am I.

Benjamin and I are on duty for the Norths again, meeting law enforcement officers at the harbor and guiding them to the clergy house. Sometimes we run errands around the island, asking people to come to the grocery store for questioning. The police have set up headquarters there, in Mr. North's cramped office. We are using one of the Norths' carriages as well, while carrying out our missions. The family is obviously very concerned for Charlotte, who is possibly in a murderer's care—or at least that is the pretense we all keep up. The two officers who just went inside the clergy house are looking for clues to the reverend's whereabouts.

My hunch tells me they will find nothing.

"We should never have brought him here," I lament to Benjamin, not for the first—and likely not the last—time.

"No, it was the right thing to do," he replies, also not for the first time. "Reverend Jacob knew the risks. He was an experienced man, and we did nothing but what common sense dictated: If you need to have the ground assessed, you call in a geologist. If you need tutoring for your children, you hire a teacher—"

"And if you need a *demon* taken care of, you call in an expert for that as well. Yes, I know."

"He simply underestimated the danger," Benjamin notes. The sky above us is crystal clear. No wind blows on Margaret's Keep. No wind has swept the island since that night. Today, it is sunny and warm enough that we left our coats and our hats in the carriage before sitting down on the stone steps. I even forgot my umbrella this morning—something that has rarely happened before. I somehow trust the sky not to shower me in rain, even if it always did before.

"We underestimated it, too," I reply. "Or we overestimated Reverend Jacob. He had a way about him that made you believe he could do anything."

"I think he believed that about himself as well." Benjamin gives a sad laugh. Today, he is wearing a white shirt and a mustard-colored waistcoat. It is very fetching. I see why the Norths think him a worthy ambassador to deal with the mainland police.

"I wonder what happened in that house that night," I say, noticing from the corner of my eye how my hair has come undone. Somehow, I cannot seem to care. It is good to let one's hair down, once in a while. I reach up and remove the few remaining pins still poking my scalp, then shake it out.

"We will likely never know exactly what happened," Benjamin replies, "but we can surmise."

"The knocker felt threatened and lashed out," I say. "Or Charlotte felt threatened and used the knocker." It is the only thing that makes sense—not that we would ever breathe a word of it to the police. What little they had gleaned of rumors by talking to the locals had already made them lift their eyebrows and shake their heads, muttering about foolish island superstitions. We knew they would never believe a word about spirits—and the Norths, of course, were adamant that no one outside of Margaret's Keep was to know about any of it, thinking it bad enough that the press had a field day writing about their possibly abducted daughter.

So far, though, Evelyn's engagement has held.

"Do you think the knocker will overtake her?" Benjamin asks, combing through my hair with his fingers.

"Perhaps it already has," I say, thinking of Reverend Jacob again. "If so, his plan wouldn't have worked, would it?"

"The little maze? The trap? No."

"He would have had to lock Charlotte up to capture it, and she certainly wouldn't have liked that idea." For my inner eyes, I see the tower—and then I see the brick building where my mother lived out her days. "Do you think the little maze would have worked, if he had been able to try it?"

"The idea seemed sound at the time," Benjamin replies. "Though how he had planned on getting it in there is a mystery."

"Yes, isn't it just?" My mind starts churning, working—pondering if it is possible.

"I wonder where they are now?" Benjamin looks out at the sea, at the waves washing to shore. The seagulls are content today; they do not scream at all. "Where would they go, with the police on their heels and the knocker in tow?"

"The latter is bound to be overjoyed," I say tersely. "It has escaped the island at last, and found itself a new vessel."

"But will she get rid of it? Will she even try?"

"The reverend might try," I say, without much conviction.

"If we could make the maze ourselves—create some kind of contraption . . ." His voice trails off; he still looks at the sea.

I stifle a smile. "You want to go after them." It is not a question.

"We ought to try, don't you think?" He looks at me, and I am happy to note some fiery determination in his eyes, something that has been sorely lacking in us both since Reverend Jacob's murder.

"And if we cannot find them?"

"Then we will find another demon," he replies. "We owe it to Reverend Jacob, don't you think? We ought to see if his plan would have worked."

"We would have to make the contraption first," I remind him. "It would have to be clever—and safe."

He nods. "And we'd need to figure out a way to get the demon inside."

"Perhaps we could try it on a weaker one first," I suggest. "One not so lovingly embraced by its victim."

"From what I read while doing my research, these attacks are rare, but occur often enough that we might be able to find another one. Perhaps Dr. Crown can be of help."

"Contraption first," I remind him, but I, too, feel the fire ignite. "It would be *just*," I say. "It would be the right thing to do. We know too much now about how to help that we cannot just walk away from it all—and even Reverend Jacob as good as admitted that religious convictions were optional in this type of work. I am fairly certain that doubters like us can handle it just as well as a priest."

"Maybe better," he agrees. "We would have a more scientific approach—write textbooks." He gives me a smile, the first joyous one I have seen in days.

"We would be 'demon detectives.'" I capture his hand and give it a squeeze.

"The best of their kind," he says with a chuckle. "You would have to leave the island, though, if we are to hunt for demons. Would it bother you very much?"

"No, not at all. Not after all of this." I nod in the direction of the clergy house. "I feel a certain responsibility for my students, that is true, but there are other teachers—and other reverends, too. I hear a new one is already on the way. It will be good for the islanders to resume hearing Sunday sermons. I hope the newcomer is strong and capable—able to help them heal."

"And the North girls?"

I shrug. "I can only do so much—and I would be doing this for them, too. Even for Charlotte, though she doesn't want my help."

"If we can make the trap work—"

"I know . . . Maybe we can help her then. And we will learn, too, Benjamin. We will read and study everything there is to know about demons, or whatever they are called. Perhaps we can find other cures—or other ways of dealing with them."

"You are not afraid anymore?"

"I think the fury has burned the rest of the fear out of me," I say honestly. "So in that respect, you were right. It *did* help to face the fear, to stand the unease and overcome. What about you? Are you still afraid?"

"No, I feel the same way, and now I want to conquer the fiend as well as I did the fear. It's malevolent and destructive, and ought not to be allowed to walk freely on this earth." His expression is serious, and I know he means every word.

"We have traps in place for wolves and bears," I muse. "So why not traps for demons? They are, by all accounts, even more dangerous."

Benjamin nods. "Now that we have seen how horrible these situations can become, it would be unethical to look the other way."

"And even if we cannot save Charlotte, maybe some other girl." I squeeze his hand again. "It would make me feel better, I think."

"Me, too." He smiles at me. "I could still take assignments to raise funds—and perhaps you could find short-term engagements, too." His mind is already looking to the future, carving out possibilities.

"We should probably get married," I say, with my heart suddenly thumping hard in my chest. "For simplicity's sake, if we are to travel together."

The stunned expression on his face is priceless. "It would certainly be . . . simpler," he stutters. "But wouldn't it go against your convictions?"

"I suppose marriage is better if chosen freely," I admit. "Though I retain the right to leave you at any time and without any undue bother—and you are never to lock me in an asylum—unless I am, in fact, insane." I give him my sternest look. "I will need this in writing and notarized," I add, meaning every word.

"Of course." A smile tugs at his lips. "It would certainly be my privilege—and an honor." His voice is thick and his grip of my hand tightens. He leans in and presses his lips against mine. A flutter of butterflies erupts in my belly, as if I were a dewy debutante about to embark on her first dance.

"Then, when we are married, we will go out in the world and catch demons," I say, quite satisfied.

"That we certainly will," says he, sounding quite satisfied, too.

In front of us the sea rolls out like a carpet; a road of salt to destinations unknown. I am no longer the woman I was when I first came here, hounded by shame and desperate. Margaret's Keep has been my rock and my healing—it has been my fate—but it is time to leave it behind now, along with the woman who was so afraid. I squeeze Benjamin's hand in mine, just as a sudden breeze comes in from the sea, and a draft of cold air hits my skin. I think I can hear words in it; a faint voice whispering in my ear.

Knock, knock, it says, like a spell.

acknowledgments

The Temptation of Charlotte North is a love letter to gothic storytelling, salty waves, and strong-willed girls with nowhere to go. I made it up, but had lots of help in shaping it and turning it into what it is now.

A huge thank-you to my editor, Anne Groell, and the team at Del Rey, who took this story from good to great, and gave it a pretty skin to live in. Thank you for taking such good care of Margaret's Keep and its peculiar inhabitants.

My agent, Brianne Johnson, provided some valuable feedback on an early draft that made the story ten times better. Thank you so much for your keen eye, good advice, and sense of narrative flow. I'm also immensely grateful to the rest of the team at HG Literary. I would be utterly lost without you.

There are many girls and women whose puzzling stories inspired this one. No matter what wreaked havoc in their lives, I'm sure their hardships were very real. I would like to mention: Virginia Campbell, Eleonore Zugun, Shirley Hitchings, Betsey Bell, Esther Cox, Janet Hodgson, Alma Fielding, Maria Jose Ferreira, Mary Ellen MacDonald, and Voirrey Irving. Furthermore, I want to highlight a particularly helpful book: *The Secret History of Poltergeists and Haunted Houses: From Pagan Folklore to Modern Manifestations* by Claude Lecouteux.

I also—very reluctantly—have to thank whatever scratched and knocked in *my* bedroom walls when I was a girl, and taught me all about what it feels like to be afraid in the night. I will never be grateful for that lesson, but this book wouldn't have existed without it, so—whatever it was—here's your due.

To Liv Lingborn and Øygunn Skaret: Thank you for keeping me company while figuring out this story. It's amazing what revelations you can stumble upon during a late-night phone call. To the seagulls—my summer scourge—and the Trondheim Fjord: forever infusing the air with salt, and providing endless inspiration.

As always, a big thank-you to my son, Jonah, and my hairy housemate, Tussa, for keeping me grounded throughout it all. There is no spell that can't be broken by a noisy fridge or cat barf.

ABOUT THE TYPE

This book was set in Perpetua, a typeface designed by the English artist Eric Gill (1882–1940), and cut by the Monotype Corporation between 1928 and 1930. Perpetua is a contemporary face of original design, without any direct historical antecedents. The shapes of the roman letters are derived from the techniques of stonecutting. The larger display sizes are extremely elegant and form a most distinguished series of inscriptional letters.

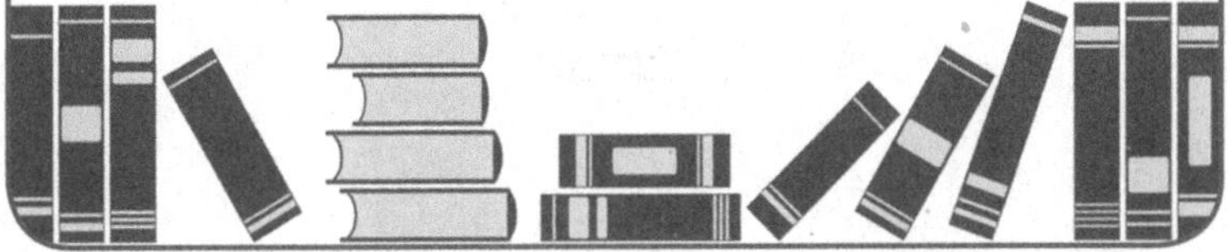

© LENE J. LØKKHAUG

CAMILLA BRUCE was born in central Norway and grew up in an old forest, next to an Iron Age burial mound. She holds a master's degree in comparative literature and has co-run a small press that published dark fairy tales. Camilla currently lives in Trondheim with her son and cat.

camillabruce.com

Instagram: @camillabruce_writing

X: @millacream